GHOSTDRIFT

GHOSTDRIFT

Book Four of the Finder Chronicles

Suzanne Palmer

DAW BOOKS
New York

Jacket illustration by Kekai Kotaki

Jacket design by Adam Auerbach

Edited by Katie Hoffman

DAW Book Collectors No. 1962

DAW Books
An imprint of Astra Publishing House
dawbooks.com
DAW Books and its logo are registered trademarks of Astra Publishing House

Printed in the United States of America

Library of Congress Cataloging-in-Publication Data

Names: Palmer, Suzanne (Science fiction writer), author.
Title: Ghostdrift / Suzanne Palmer.
Description: First edition. | New York : DAW Books, 2024. |
Series: The Finder Chronicles ; book 4
Identifiers: LCCN 2023058325 (print) | LCCN 2023058326 (ebook) |
ISBN 9780756418878 (hardcover) | ISBN 9780756418885 (ebook)
Subjects: LCGFT: Science fiction. | Novels.
Classification: LCC PS3616.A346 G46 2024 (print) |
LCC PS3616.A346 (ebook) | DDC 813/.6—dc23/eng/20240112
LC record available at https://lccn.loc.gov/2023058325
LC ebook record available at https://lccn.loc.gov/2023058326

First edition: May 2024
10 9 8 7 6 5 4 3 2 1

To my father
There will never be enough words.
Miss you.

Chapter 1

The afternoon breeze had come in right on time with the tide, rustling its ghostly fingers through the loose-woven, blue-green grasses of his hut. It sent the thin twist of smoke above his small, ornamental brazier into a disorganized panic, picked up the heat and cloying smell of the smoldering herbs, and left as a gift in their place the cool, clean scent of salt, sea, and sand. The Tea Master sat sideways in the doorway, a scraggly black cat with one white ear asleep in his lap, his back against the thin frame, and closed his eyes to the sun and turquoise waters as the breeze caressed his sweaty, tanned face, as if to say: *I know you.*

He could taste the distant rain with his indrawn breath, feel the lightning in it, and knew the storm would pass quickly when it finally came sometime overnight. For now, though, the crowds were thick and loud and happy, and he opened his eyes again to watch the mesmerizing dance of people—human, alt-human, not human—all with a love of the beach in common. Except one, who moved among them, peering at faces, searching.

A small, chirpy flock of ehrlets hunted at tide's edge, unconcerned by the people. Halfway between dragonfly and lemming, he could almost believe they were fat seagulls if he squinted enough, and then the sea, too, almost looked like home. There was nothing to be done about the two crescent moons hanging unevenly high in the sky above, although there had been plenty of nights on Earth he'd had enough to drink to believe he was seeing a dozen.

Though, truth was, he hadn't had a drink since the night he

arrived. *Arrived* suggested something more casual and less disorienting than how his time there had begun—one moment standing in an alien spaceship and the next being ankle-deep in surf with a cat attempting to claw its way inside his exosuit—but it had been the clean restart he'd needed. Someplace else, someone else, all in a subjective instant. He wondered if he would change again, now that he could see his endless, peaceful, perfect summer was, in fact, coming to as abrupt an end as it had begun.

The sky had shifted into the striated purples and reds of the Corallan sunset, framing the not-quite-human silhouette of the seeker against the half-dome of sun just now slipping below the horizon. They strode now with purpose, determined and relentless as the tide, unerringly toward his hut.

Three standard years, four months, and twenty-two days to find me, he thought. *Am I more upset or relieved?*

He wasn't sure; of all the people he expected to finally track him down, this one had never even crossed his mind as a possibility.

She stopped and stood in front of him, hands fidgeting together in front of her, extending and then retracting one claw at a time in a gesture he'd long ago learned was one of extreme stress. "Fergus Ferguson?" she said, at last. "You've changed color. Nanites?"

"The sun."

"I didn't know humans could do that."

"It's called a tan."

"It suits you. You look much less like a pale, dead cave-thing."

"Thanks, I think," he said. "Sit, Qai?"

She did, folding her white-gray fur-covered legs under her with all the grace of a panther, her long tail curled tightly against her thigh, and watched warily as he made her a cup of tea. His cat came out, took one look at the alien, and ghosted back into the safety of the hut.

He set the tea in front of her on a hand-carved wooden tray. Taking it, her hand shaking, she sipped, and then curled her lips back in a grimace, showing sharp teeth. "It's bitter," she said.

"It's meant to be," he said. "The tea is a metaphor for life."

She set the cup down. "I have no need for any more bitterness, then," she said. "I fear you will not forgive me adding some to yours."

"If you're here, you must need me."

"I do."

He tossed the remaining tea on the sand, turned the cup upside down on the tray, and stood. "So, where are we going?"

"Space," she said.

"Of course."

He went back into the hut, pulled a clean shirt on, and picked up his exosuit and his pack from where they had sat, unobtrusive and undisturbed, since he'd taken over the hut. Shaking out the accumulated sand and one squealing sandweebie, he slung his pack over one shoulder, not needing to check to know it was ready. It was a quick task to stuff cat food, his remaining supplies of tea, and his favorite cup—a small, bright-blue chipped thing easily a century old—in a bag, and then hand it and the small suitcase that was a portable litterbox to Qai, who took them without complaint or snark, which only deepened his worry.

"Come on, Mister Feefs," he said, coaxing his cat into his carrier. "The universe caught up to us at last."

The fire was already low, burning down for the night, all cups washed and waiting to be put away. Someone else would come along, as he had, and take his place. "You have a ship?"

"In orbit. I took a private shuttle down."

"Is Maha up there?" Fergus asked. Qai and Maha were two of the most inseparable people he knew. Partners, best friends, and probably more, though he never had felt any need to pry. The alt-human and the Dzenni were never far from each other.

"No," Qai said. "If she were, I wouldn't be here at all. You weren't easy to find, you know."

"I'd hoped to be impossible to find," he said. "Last I knew, there was a bounty out on me."

"Four separate bounties, and one is the largest I've ever heard of," she said. "If you're wondering if that's what brought me, understand it cost me more than three times the combined price on your head to find you."

"I'm flattered," he said. He was.

He began walking up the beach toward the low lights of town, gait uneven in the fickle, shifting sand. Qai walked beside him, her long stride easily matching his own. She'd trimmed her fur short again since last he'd seen her. "I'm not sure anyone else could have found you," she said after a while. "You don't look anything like you. No beard, you've changed your hair color, you're not pasty and thin. You even move differently. Even I wasn't sure you *were* you until I stepped up to your little grass house."

"How did you know, then?"

"Smell," she said, and at his pained expression, laughed. "I do have an advantage over the average hunter. I wouldn't worry unless another Dzenni you've known personally is hunting you. And your burning herbs were a good mask."

The beach was becoming quiet and empty, people drifting toward shelter in advance of the rain. Further down the strand, there was a boardwalk extending out into the churning surf, bright torches lit along its length, casting overlapping circles of orange on the undersides of the wide umbrellas and canopies overhead. Faint traces of a loud, happy crowd and louder music barely reached them over the low roar of the ocean he loved and was leaving behind.

"What if I didn't want to come?" he asked.

"Then I'd have stunned you, thrown you over my shoulder

like a sack of meat, and brought you along anyway," she said. She grinned, showing her fangs again. "Isn't it nicer this way?"

"I suppose," he answered. They reached the upper boardwalk, and he could not help but stop and look back. The last remnants of sunset had faded into a line of mauve-gray at the horizon. His hut was a dark shape crouching forlornly in the fading light, the last few beachwalkers out on the sands heading toward parties like moths to a campfire.

Qai waited patiently beside him; whatever she made of the beach, the waves, the world, she did not say. She looked tired, wrung out, full of a long-simmering rage.

"A storm is coming," he said at last.

"You don't know the half of it. Are you ready to go?"

"I suppose I must be," he said, and forced himself to turn his back to the ocean and start walking again. This far up on the beach, there were a few low, white-stone buildings, mostly ice cream stands, rent-a-rooms, a comm station, and a tiny landing pad for shuttles from the larger islands. It was only stepping up onto the ridged alloy decking of the ramp into Qai's shuttle that he realized with shock that he was still barefoot. When was the last time he'd worn shoes at all, much less his space boots? And where *were* his boots? He couldn't even guess, but he didn't think he'd seen them in at least a season.

You've gotten lazy and comfortable and findable, he told himself. *You're just stupidly lucky it was a friend who walked up that beach.*

. . . A friend he hadn't seen in years, who was clearly in trouble, and who wasn't being forthcoming with information. Not that it mattered; he was already aboard. He tucked Mister Feefs' carrier into one of the cargo nets at the back, then took the seat next to Qai in the cockpit, shrugged into the safety harness, and put his sand-encrusted feet up on the dash. Wiggling his toes, he watched dried sand sprinkle down around him. Qai either didn't notice or didn't feel the need to comment as she ran through system checks and powered up the engine.

Whoever was manning the port tower sounded like they'd been woken from a sound sleep. After some indeterminate mumbling, the clearance was granted, and Qai took the shuttle up with practiced ease.

"Now can you tell me what we're doing?" Fergus asked.

"We're going to go get Maha back," she said.

"Who has her?"

"Pirates."

Qai and Maha ran their smuggling and gray-market procurement op out of Crossroads Station out along the Bounds, and as far as he knew, they and the area pirates kept out of each other's way when not actively seeking out the other's business. It was a dangerous move—and one that could destabilize the entire local economy—to upset that delicate balance of professional criminal courtesy. He could see a clueless, overconfident newbie bumbling fatally into that kind of trouble, but if it was an amateur, Qai would have resolved it quickly and permanently, and without need of him. And she'd have had fully three-quarters of the Crossroads riffraff at her back.

Well, she did say it was complicated, he thought. "Have they asked for ransom yet?"

"Yes," she said. She pulled back sharply on the helm controls, and moments later they were rocketing through the wisps of noctilucent clouds in Coralla's upper atmosphere. Looking down, he could see the lower, thicker clouds building off the shore, see the muted flashes of lightning building within. It felt odd and uncomfortable not to be able to feel it.

"How much?" he asked, when she remained silent. "I don't have a lot of cred left I can access, but whatever I've got is yours."

"It's complicated," she said. "Now be quiet while I fly."

"Okay," he said. He might have been sitting on a beach for

over three years, but he hadn't lost his wits enough to bug a pilot when she didn't want to be bugged.

She remained grimly silent the remainder of the trip to orbit.

Qai's ship in orbit was shaped like nothing so much as a gigantic purple egg, unlike anything he had ever seen, but before he had a chance to ask about it, she pressed him—politely but urgently—ahead of her up the docking arm from the shuttle into the ship's oversized airlock. There were signs posted inside, half a meter above his head, in an unfamiliar alphabet where the letters were raised, sunken, or tilted to different degrees and angles, in a wide variant of hues of gray. He'd seen Dzenni text once—a mix of circles, curves, and dots—and this was not it.

"Whose ship?" he asked. Had Maha been kidnapped by alien pirates? *That could be interesting.*

Qai sealed the door behind them, then indicated he should walk ahead of her into the ship's curvy corridor. Just as he was sure she wasn't going to answer, she said, "A friend who owed me a favor. Ok'mah'a'roon."

"That's a name?"

"That's a place," she said. "Or, more accurately, it's a very shortened and simplistically expressed human-capable nickname for a place."

"What's it when not dumbed down for us, then?"

"Not something I can pronounce either, although out of sheer luck of physiology I can get slightly closer than you."

"I'm sorry you went through all this trouble to find me," he said. Qai growled low in frustration. "I'm sorry that I'm sorry?" he added quickly.

"As much as it makes things easier that you came along willingly, you are useless to me if you don't *fight*," she said. "You'll understand."

Fergus laughed. "Now that you found me, it was only a matter of time before someone else did, and probably not a friend. You told me Maha is in danger. I'm not going to refuse to help you, or abandon her. That's not what friends do."

"Amiable but at most occasional business associates, I'd call us."

"I say friends," he answered. "You know we are."

She snorted. "I think you drank too much of your own tea," she said, as the inner door rumbled open. "Either that or you baked your little monkey skull way too long in the sun. Say hello to George."

Fergus stepped into the airlock doorway and stopped in his tracks. He had seen many aliens in his life, but George was something new. They were about three meters tall, bright red, and rather like a cross between an enormous caterpillar, a sea slug, and a porcupine in the middle of a fireworks explosion. They stood in an upright, tapering S curve at what Fergus could recognize was the helm, though he figured his odds of being able to fly this ship in an emergency were probably not much better than if he jumped naked out into space and tried to push it. Long, faintly bioluminescent ripples stood out along the length of the alien's body on either side, undulating gently, their back a spiny profusion of long whip-hairs whose ends glowed like fiberoptics. Their front held two rows of fuzzy tentacle-feet, and as they faced them, eyes began to appear and disappear at the ends of tentacles.

"Hey, George," Qai said.

Colors shifted through the spectrum along the stiff hairs, and a voice in a thick Bounds accent translated from somewhere along the ridged ceiling. "Wah hey, took you smalltimes."

"He cooperated," Qai said. "This is MacInnis."

Now that's interesting, Fergus thought. Qai wasn't using his real name, and the choice of that alias in particular couldn't be coincidence.

"Helloes an' greetings, MacInnis," George said. "I am easiest being called George by you, with th' ey-em-eir words. Is this okay?"

"That's fine. I'm with the he-him-his words," Fergus said.

"Ahahaha yes so, humanguy," George said. Ey paused, then more tentacles opened up eyes, and some extended toward him, blinking. "'Tis a kitty? Kitty kitty?"

"Uh . . ." Fergus said, and looked down at the carrier still in his hand from when he'd come aboard. "Yes?"

"Kitty kitty yes!" George said. "As th' humans tell, it is looking like you, Qai."

"I don't look at all like that thing," Qai said, pointing at Mister Feefs.

"But you do, though," Fergus said. Qai bared her fangs at him. "Sorry, I didn't mean to offend you. You want me to skritch you behind your ears to make it up to you?"

"You want to spend the rest of this trip stuffed in a locker, slowly bleeding out?" Qai replied. She flexed her hands, extending all her claws one by one. "No? Then shut up."

"I'll shut up if you tell me what's going on and where we're going," Fergus said.

"I would think you'd have guessed that already," she said.

"Back to Crossroads?" Fergus asked.

"No. If anyone was stupid enough to keep Maha that close to my usual orbit, I'd have her back and a sack full of trophy heads to boot, and you'd still be sitting on your beach, wasting all your natural talents on *tourists*," Qai said.

And my unnatural talents, Fergus thought, but that was something Qai didn't know, and didn't need to know. "Sfazili Barrens, then?" he asked. It was the next-most-obvious guess where Qai's pirates might be.

"Yes," Qai answered. "Let me show you your cabin."

He followed her deeper into the ship.

The Sfazili Barrens was a stretch of empty space between the planet Guratahan Sfazil and the thin band of outer systems that were the nominal outskirts of human-familiar space, known as the

Bounds. Crossroads Station, where Qai and Maha usually kept shop, was in one of those systems. Beyond the Bounds was the Gap, which separated them from the next galactic spiral arm out; comparatively, the Barrens were a mere tide pool to the Gap's vast, desolate ocean of emptiness.

The Barrens' few star systems were meager and mostly uninhabited or uninhabitable, which usually meant the same thing. Because of the low density of star systems, there was also a distinct lack of the strange little divots in the fabric of space where one could easily and quickly jump from one to another like interdimensional connect-the-dots. If you didn't want to travel along the dotted lines, passive jump could get you from just about any point you wanted to any other, but it was orders of magnitude slower, barely a few times faster than lightspeed. Fergus had often explained the difference between passive and active jump as the difference between skipping a stone quickly across the surface of a pond versus folding the pond so that the two shores touched with your stone held between them.

Once you'd entered an active-jump conduit, you could drop out into normal space nearly anywhere along it, but you couldn't get back in except at one of the end points. That meant that if you got stuck in the Barrens, you were stuck there for a long while taking the slow way out. All of which made the area just inaccessible enough to be attractive to all the wrong sorts of people, from those looking for an opportunity to pursue independence, such as mini cults and dictatorships, to all kinds of wanton criming that was hard for any authority to track, much less to crack down on.

Some of the more-permanent settlements were Enclaves—self-sufficient floating space habitats in orbit around a star near a source of valuable ore or ice, or on exoplanets just viable for a small crew with nothing worth the effort of fighting over. And for anyone without material resources of their own, there were salvage and piracy. The line between those two was often blurrier than most people would be comfortable with, and many of the tales of swashbuckling pirates strained credibility at least as much as they entertained.

"Lot of pirates in the Barrens, but not too many that could get the advantage of you," he said, breaking the silence.

"Not many," Qai said, and pointed toward a tall, narrow door. "That's yours."

The door opened into a small room with mottled gray walls and a circular bed of sorts in the center that looked both awkward to get into and possibly even harder to get out of. He was suddenly bone-tired in a way he hadn't been since before he was deposited abruptly on Coralla with nothing more than his cat, his pack, and the echo of the sounds of crickets in his ears.

"Maybe even only one pirate," Fergus mused aloud.

"Maybe only one," Qai agreed.

There *was* only one pirate he could think of who operated both within the Barrens and out along the Bounds near Crossroads, and who would dare to kidnap Maha and be able to get away with it without fear of reprisals for upsetting the local power balance: Bas Belos of the Lekos Brotherhood, captain of the infamous ship *Sidewinder*. If he had taken Maha, though, Fergus couldn't begin to imagine *why*.

Qai popped a cylinder into a socket in the wall. "Ok'mah'a'roon respiratory mixture is off from what humans need. It's why you're so tired. This'll fix the atmo in here, and we won't be aboard long enough for you to spend much time elsewhere on the ship, anyway."

"Thanks," he said, set Mister Feefs on the bed, and crawled over beside him. It took his cat mere moments to hop up onto his chest and start turning him into a pincushion. "So, you going to tell me what the ransom is, at least? I am a professional finder, you know, and I assume you need me to help you *find* something."

Qai met his gaze for a moment, her face some mixture of

apprehension and guilt. "I don't need to find it," she said. "I know right where it is."

"Well, what is it?"

She shook her head and turned off the room lights. Moments later, he heard the door close and the click of a lock engaging. There were an annoying tickle in the back of his throat and belated recognition of a faint, sickly-sweet smell he knew.

Shit, he thought, and tried to get up, go unplug that cylinder, but the sedative already had enough of a hold on him that he couldn't muster the will to do anything more than continue to lie there, feeling very confused and very cross, and fight the losing fight to stay awake.

"You," Qai said, softly but audible, through the closed door. "The ransom is you."

Chapter 2

He awoke, muscles stiff and brain still wrapped by fog, with no sense of how long he'd been out other than the evidence presented by his body that it had been longer than just overnight. The door, when he managed to get himself upright and steady enough to check it, was still locked.

Not that he couldn't deal with the lock—and easily—but what would that get him? He couldn't just leap out an airlock into a jumpspace conduit in his bare feet and T-shirt, and even if he was willing to take down both George and Qai, he had no hope whatsoever of piloting this very-alien ship anywhere other than to their collective certain doom.

The routines of more than three years were not so easily disrupted, and while he thought about his lack of options, he found himself already starting his morning stretches. *Well, why not?* he thought. Though he would rather have had warm sand under his feet and morning sun on his back, he completed his usual set as best he could in the confines of his room. Coralla was about 70% Earth gravity, but George's eggship—he spent some time bouncing up and down on his toes, getting a feel for it—seemed closer to 40%. Some of the mujūryokudo kata were possible there that hadn't been on Coralla, and others were simply impossible to do with any gravity at all, or without crashing into the close walls trying anyhow.

Qai showed up after one particularly loud collision. Her fur was untidy, as if she had just been awakened. "Fergus," she said, and glared at him.

"Qai," he said, as pleasantly as he could. "Is it time for breakfast?"

"It's the middle of the night," she said. "My night, anyway, and mine is the one that matters."

"Sorry. I'm hungry," he said. "I think it's a rule you have to feed prisoners, at least between bouts of drugging them unconscious against their will."

"The only rules are my rules," Qai said. "I am regretting all the many times I've been nice to you."

"Like that time you stuffed me in a crate of frozen, biologically contaminated cow fetuses?" Fergus asked. "Or the time you manipulated my trust of you to abduct me and hand me over to murderous space pirates? Oh, wait, that's *this* time. I wonder if they'll still accept me as ransom if you've let me die of starvation on the way."

She put one hand over her eyes and forehead, and drew several deep, growly breaths before she was willing to look at him again. Twice she tried to speak, then finally she just reached out, grabbed his shirt collar, and yanked him out of his room and down the hall.

"Don't try anything," she warned. "Also, George doesn't know the full situation, so keep your flappy human lips shut. It won't help you any to tell em, and it sure as hell would make the rest of the trip more awkward for all of us. Especially you."

The new room she shoved him into was larger, though much of it was taken up by George, who was sitting on a large, purple, ottoman-like cushion. Several of eir tentacle-hands—including some that Fergus would swear had been eyes the day before—had morphed into fingerlike appendages, and others had grown mouths. Ey were watching a screen that, from the fleeting glimpses, appeared to be running at least partly off the human visible spectrum. Ey were also, two or three at a time, plucking pretzels out of a large bowl with some hands and feeding them to others, efficiently demolishing the contents of the bowl.

Ey paused as ey noticed Fergus, and held the bowl out in of-fering. "Share some, MacInnis?" ey said.

"Thank you, George," Fergus said, and took a small handful of pretzels in his cupped palms.

Duncan MacInnis had been the fake identity he'd used on Enceladus; Maha and Qai had gotten him a job there driving cargo haulers up and down through the ice bores, so they'd known that particular alias. It was also the name he was being hunted under by the Alliance, first for disrupting their rogue mil-itary operation under Enceladus's ice, then later for busting into their secure research facility on Earth and stealing a bunch of powerful alien artifacts that they were definitely attached to. Didn't matter that he'd saved the solar system, because they didn't know that and wouldn't believe him if he told them.

Neither would Qai. There were a lot of things Qai didn't know, which was very much for the better for them both, espe-cially if he now had to regard her as an enemy.

I should have picked a smaller, more-remote island to hide away on, he thought, and sat down on another big squishy pillow beside George. "What are you watching?" he asked.

"'Tis a food show," George said. "This contestor"—ey waved one tentacle at the screen, where Fergus couldn't make out any definitive shape—"is making a three-top cake using only ingre-dients found in th' Nennischekcho'oku system, while th' other contestor can only use its own secretions to make th' cake. Both will be terrible, ah! Who will lose?"

"The judge?" Fergus answered.

"Haaaaaaaaaaahhaooa," George said. "You are right."

"George, how much longer?" Qai asked.

"One more jump afore I road you into th' Barrens," George said.

"I owe you one," Qai replied.

"George owes you, you owe George, it is always one then th' other," George said.

"I'll owe you one too if you have something more to eat aboard," Fergus said. The pretzel bowl was empty. "Maybe not cake, though."

"Haa-aah," George said, and reached out with one tentacle-hand and popped open a wall cubby. "More prezzels!"

"Just as so many of my own people find humans culturally fascinating—and I can't count the number of dinners ruined arguing with my father and sister-sib about this as a kitling—the Ok'mah'a'roon-set are in love with your snack foods," Qai said.

"We like th' crunch," George said, and got up from eir seat and set the bowl down on the floor. "I must go prep for th' jump. Four more of your hours, Qai. Faster than you, but can't go faster than myself."

"As long as we don't go slower, either, that's fine," Qai said, and the alien gave a whole-body nod before moving more gracefully and quietly than Fergus had expected through the door and back toward the bridge.

"How long did you knock me out for?" Fergus asked.

"Long enough I had to go in and feed your animal," Qai said. She held up a furred hand. "It bit me."

"I can't imagine why," Fergus said.

"You're being deliberately annoying because you're angry at me, and it's what you always do when you are worried and need to buy time while you come up with a plan," Qai said. "I know you well enough, Fergus. There is no plan that will work between here and the handoff. After that . . . I wish you luck."

"Why me?"

"I have no idea," Qai said. "But they didn't want you dead. That would have been cheaper. And easier for us both, if this is about vengeance."

Fergus's stomach rumbled. "Ugh, I'm so hungry I'm dizzy," he said. "You got anything more than pretzels?"

She picked up a carton from the counter and tossed it to him. "Dried noodles," she said. "George is a room-temperature-foodavore. No cold storage, no cooking. And don't make a face at me; it's all I've got. And I wasn't lying about the air mix, earlier, even if I did spike it."

He sighed and opened the carton. The noodles were a greenish mass of tangles that broke apart when he poked them with his finger. Picking up a piece, he sucked on it tentatively. Dry, fairly bland, but not utterly without flavor.

"You could add water, I suppose," Qai said.

"Any chance of forks on board?"

She laughed, and he took that as the expected no.

"You spent much time in the Barrens?" Fergus asked as he broke the noodles up into smaller pieces and ate.

"I've crossed them in jump, for as much as that counts," Qai said. "The one time I had to go in to deal with an Enclave, I resolved to always delegate such trips going forward. You?"

"Same thing, pretty much," Fergus said. "I've been to both Hades Station and Cherish Enclave, but neither for long, and that with a fast ship not far from more-reasonable travel options. I've avoided jobs there ever since."

"Well, like it or not, we're going there," Qai said. She pulled open what looked like a small locker, and took out a pair of boots, which she set in front of him. "I've outfitted you enough times by now that I know your stats, and had them sent up with our resupply order; we stopped at Tanduou while you were sleeping."

"Drugged unconscious, more like," he said.

"Right, and still no apologies for that. You're a sneaky fucker I can't trust right now for obvious reasons. I couldn't afford to chase you down all over again, and Tanduou might have seemed like an opportunity to you. I wanted in and out with no fuss."

"Fuss, okay, but what about attention? Isn't George's ship just a bit conspicuous?" Fergus asked.

"Very conspicuous," Qai said. "Couldn't be helped; I needed the speed. We'll lose any entirely hypothetical tails when we jump into the Barrens."

"Someone could send a tracer after us in the jump conduit," he said.

"Not this ship. The Ok'mah'a'roon use a completely different drive technology than we do. Most of the peoples in this part of the galaxy got their jump tech from the Bomo'ri, but not them. Similar results, completely different method, so not traceable unless someone is familiar with Ok'mah'a'roon tech, and I would sooner bet on you suddenly squeezing a rogue asteroid out your ass than that."

"To be fair, we humans stole the tech from the Bomo'ri," Fergus said.

"Yes, and don't think they're not still *very* irked with you," she said. "But no tracer. Observation only, and we made a bunch of extra stops before Coralla, too, for extra cover. Not that you'd be stupid enough to go back there."

"You think I'll have that opportunity?" he asked.

"I know you well enough to know that the odds are good, whatever the pirates want with you, you'll figure out how to give them the slip eventually. As long as it happens on their watch, not mine."

She sat down on the couch next to him, an easy target if he wanted to knock her out, but there wasn't much point. And she looked tired, unhappier the closer they got to the handover. Not second thoughts—not with Maha's safety on the line—but something else.

Because she can say otherwise all she needs to, but she knows we are *friends.*

He picked up the magboots, checked them out. Top quality and new, not used. Qai didn't cheap out on them, for whatever that was worth. "So, you don't know what they want with me?" he asked.

"Not a clue," she said. It sounded honest. "You?"

"Me neither," he said. He sighed.

"You, uh, want me to take care of your cat?" Qai said.

"I promised him I'd never leave him behind again," Fergus said. "And anyway, anyone who messes with my cat is going to deeply regret it; I don't care who they are. Not even if you're handing me over to Bas Belos himself."

She didn't flinch or give any outward sign he'd hit his mark, but he didn't need confirmation, anyway. "If you're sure," she said.

"Yeah," he said. "Thanks, though."

"You understand Maha is more than just my partner—she's my life. I could no more function in this universe without her than I could without my own arms and legs and teeth and claws," Qai said. "If you find your own way out, after the exchange, we can have a drink to your survival back on Crossroads and I'll buy 'til you're too drunk to hold a glass. But Maha comes first. She *has* to. You understand that?"

"I do," he said. "The tide comes in, the tide goes out, and arguing with it gets you nothing but wet socks."

She shook her head and bit another pretzel in half. "For your sake, I hope your time on Coralla hasn't softened your brain as much as you act it."

"I guess we'll know when we know," he said, and dumped a handful of noodle shards into his mouth. The ship around them gave the smallest of shudders as it jumped.

Qai grimaced, fangs showing. She also relaxed, just slightly. *This is the last jump, after all,* he thought. When they dropped back into normal space, they'd be there, wherever they were meeting the pirates, and his chances to escape were all but gone.

"Have you ever played Venusian Monkeypoker?" she asked.

"What?" he asked, surprised by the non sequitur. "Yeah."

"You, Fergus, are like a human version of the Midnight Bar Brawl card. It doesn't matter whose hand you're in, once you've been played. I've never met anyone who could take a simple, unpleasant circumstance, with no variables and no options, and manage to turn it into the biggest fucking chaotic, unpredictable mess possible, and still walk out the far side," she said. "Or limp, at least; I saw that scar on your leg at the beach. Whatever is going on, it smells wrong, and I don't know how or why, but I know if I have to throw you down on the table, you'll figure it out. I only wish I crated you so I could make the trade without having to look you in the eye as I do it."

"And yet."

"And yet. The only comfort I can find in this whole mess is knowing that you're going to give them so much hell, and be so utterly and persistently annoying, that they will come to regard this exchange as the worst of all possible bargains," Qai said. She stood. "Next stop, we part ways. And may all the stars shine their good luck upon you, and forgive me for my part."

———

George's eggship dropped out of the middle of a jump conduit about a light-year into the Barrens, and a few hours later pulled up beside a derelict wreck of an old freighter hanging dead in space. Big chunks of its hull plating were missing, and others scored with weapons fire or torn inward where something had hit and punctured it repeatedly. From a tiny window near the airlock, Fergus saw the faded lettering of its name: *Slow Dreamer*.

Too slow, for a deadly place like this.

"We're here," Qai said. "Suit up. We're going for a walk."

If he hadn't been about to be handed over to one of the most infamous pirates of the age, Fergus would have been more excited to finally have the answer to the long-burning if unimportant question of how Qai managed to fit her rather long tail into an exosuit; he was disappointed that it didn't have its own sleeve, and instead she curled it up tight against her back and fit the suit over it. He knew better than to comment aloud that this way made her butt look gigantic, because everything else aside, she did have fangs.

Once they were outside the eggship's airlock, Qai shot a mag-clamp dart across the gulf. After testing that it was connected securely, she sent him ahead first along its cable. When they were both across, she released the cable, reeled it in, and unclamped the dart. "If it all goes bad, I don't want George dragging this whole wreck into jumpspace with em," Qai explained, as she hooked the dart onto a loop on her pack.

That made sense. There were many more ways this could go wrong than right, but still, *right* involved only one of them getting to leave at all. Qai shoved him ahead along the exterior of the ship, their magboots thunking along soundlessly until they hit a hole in the hull they could get through without risking tears to their suits. Again, Qai had him go in first. Fergus tried not to resent that; logically, the pirates would be less likely to shoot him than her, after all the effort and expense they'd gone through to get their hands on him alive.

The interior space—what little was left—had clearly been visited by salvagers, judging by the accreted junk and stripped-down hulks of systems floating within. A sharply bent bulkhead door on the far side of the room was gaping wide, and Qai gestured him ahead. "How do we know where to go?" he asked.

"There are UV markings, outside normal human vision range," she said. "I don't like it."

"Me either," he said, but switched his goggles to widen their spectrum detection. His blandly nondescript exosuit was a top-of-the-line military model, at least as of about four years ago, and either Qai didn't know that or didn't care. *Almost certainly the latter,* Fergus thought glumly. It was hard enough to have hidden advantages over your enemies, but over friends?

At least now he could make out the arrows neatly stenciled onto the walls, though he still let Qai direct him whenever they encountered a turn, more to be difficult than out of any hope she didn't already know he could see them. That the marks weren't hasty scrawls suggested this was a regular meeting spot, and he wished he'd had any sense of exactly where in the Barrens they were. If he got out of this alive, it would be good to know which way to go.

Next arrow sent them up and through a blasted-away section of the ship that had a desiccated corpse still strapped into a jump seat. Someone had attached a sign—with nails, but he decided it was best to refuse to notice that detail, even if surely the corpse had been long dead before that particular disrespect—to its chest that read POOR YORICK. Fergus couldn't keep himself from chuckling at that.

"Did you know him?" Qai asked over their suit comms.

"Alas, no," he said. Yorick's uniform was that of Haudie South's civilian cargo service and at least forty years out of date. So either the freighter was that old, or Yorick was the final recipient of vintage hand-me-downs.

The idea that someone had been through there with, if not a tasteful sense of humor, some knowledge of literature made him feel just ever so slightly better about his own chances of survival. *Just avoid the guy with the nail gun,* he thought.

They arrived at a bulkhead door that was out of place in the wreckage, not least because it was whole, lit, and clearly transplanted over from a Sfazili military ship. Qai motioned Fergus to stand to one side and, with her eye carefully on him and a hand on the energy pistol at her hip, banged loudly on it. A few moments later, it ground open, revealing another door about three meters in. An airlock, then. Qai crooked one claw at Fergus and then pointed that he should go first once again.

The bulkhead door closed behind them. "If they were going to kill us, this would be a great spot for it," Fergus said conversationally.

"Thanks for pointing out the obvious," Qai said. "If they try to gas us, I hope you don't mind if I take your air tanks."

"Oh, sure, no, what's a little air between friends?" he replied. "Help yourself."

He could feel the vague sensation of light pressure that meant the chamber was being filled with atmosphere. His suit's display in the corner of his vision concurred and let him know it was a pretty Earth-standard gas mix, nothing unusual or nefarious or incapacitating. Moments after they reached pressure, the inner door opened.

I was wrong, Fergus thought. They hadn't stolen an airlock off a Sfazili light cruiser; they had parked an entire, mostly intact, cruiser inside the remains of the freighter.

"Nice. It's like spaceship turducken," he said, as his eyes roamed around the well-kept interior of what must have once been a deployment staging dock, and finally alighted on the reception waiting for them.

Maha stood at the back of the room. An alt-human, she had modified her physical phenotype long before Fergus had ever met her to run glowing lines, like cracks in a lava field, all over her ebony skin. Last time they'd met the lines were green, but now they were silver, her hair a matching sweep that would have been a spectacular mohawk before several months of neglect. She looked otherwise healthy, if thinner, though the thick, explosive cuff wrapped around her upper arm spoke of immediate and lethal jeopardy.

A pale, rail-thin, short man in a long black duster stood next to her, casually leaning his weight on one foot, while in the center of the room, in a chair, sat another man, with a short black beard shaved down one cheek to show off the ritual markings of the Lekos Brotherhood. The seated man was handsome in that very rare and particular way that was both intrinsic to and indistinguishable from the danger he posed. Bas Belos.

Whatever pride he might have felt in correctly guessing who

was behind his abduction was lost in the rush of any hope he had for escape abandoning him.

"Maha," Qai said, breaking the silence.

"Qai," Maha answered; her eyes shifted to Fergus, and he saw the same conflict in them that Qai had tried to hide.

"Mr. MacInnis, I presume?" Belos asked. The pirate leaned forward, crossing his arms across his black brocade vest, and fixed his sharp, chestnut eyes on him.

"I am he," Fergus said.

"Len?" Belos asked.

The pirate beside Maha held up a small device and pointed it at Fergus, waited a few moments, then lowered it. "What we've got fer a biosig matches," he said.

"What was the name of your hauler on Enceladus?" Belos asked Fergus.

"*Hexanchus*," Fergus said.

"Show me the scar on your leg," Belos said. "Please."

Fergus shrugged out of his exosuit and stood there in his Marsball T-shirt and shorts, pointing to the misshapen, star-shaped scar where he'd once—and once was more than enough—been shot with a harpoon gun.

Belos nodded. "Here is how this is going to work," he said, addressing Qai. "You don't trust me; I don't trust you. I could kill you and your partner right here, right now to wrap up loose ends, but Maha and I have had some decent, if unfriendly, conversations, and it would be a poor capstone to my extended hospitality. It would also likely hinder Mr. MacInnis's full cooperation with me. And if I let you go, since I know absolutely nothing about the capabilities of that very unique ship you arrived in, presumably you could blow me and this freighter into dust the moment you're off it. And yes, that assumes you're willing to also kill your friend here, but if he wasn't at least somewhat expendable to you, we wouldn't be here right now, would we?"

Qai's scowl deepened, and Fergus could see her claws show-ing, but she said nothing. *Because even if she hates it, Belos isn't wrong,* Fergus thought.

"I think we both know each other's reputations well enough to not want to part ways with any more of a grudge than neces-sary," Belos continued. "And your slippery friend here, with such an impressive reputation, has no reason to trust either of us—certainly not me, and not, now, *you.* All of which leaves us, at this moment, with uncomfortable uncertainty."

"Agreed," Qai said. "You have a suggestion?"

Belos smiled, all amusement but no warmth. "If your friend MacInnis came with me willingly, would you consider that suffi-cient to set aside at least immediate hostilities? Once I am done with him and have what I want, you do what you feel you need to. No one can hide in the Barrens forever—you want a reckon-ing, you'll get your chance."

"Why the hell would he go along with you?" Qai asked. "And what if he says no?"

"He won't," Belos said. He tilted his head and settled his un-nerving gaze back on Fergus. "Mr. MacInnis, I am going to make you an offer you can't refuse."

———

There was a small armory off the staging dock, and after Len thoroughly and expertly patted him down for weapons, he fol-lowed Belos there. All his trepidation was now snuggled like a piece of fragile glass in a fine gold cushion of unbearable curios-ity. Belos's relaxed stroll, unconcerned about any danger from Fergus behind him, only made Fergus feel all the more out of his depth and on perilously uncertain ground. Even if it was all a head game, it was working.

Whatever weapons had been in the room when it was a functioning warship were gone. There was a small stockpile of long-shelf-life food and first aid supplies, and sitting on a stool was a cube-shaped metal box. Belos ran his hand across the top of it, lifted his palm to look for dust, then glanced over at Fergus, waiting.

"What's inside?" Fergus asked, unable to help himself.

Belos smiled again. "Something so rare, it is practically mythical," he said. "Something I know you will recognize, and grasp its worth." He picked up the cube, ran his hands over it again in odd gestures—movement that might have been captured by dust, had it not been swept off—and then the lid opened.

Fergus didn't step forward, though it was almost excruciating not to. "You kidnapped the second-most-dangerous person within three star systems of Crossroads, antagonizing her partner who is the first most dangerous, so you could get them to drag me here and show me a *box*?" he asked.

"You'll understand," Belos said.

"But why?" Fergus said. "Whether or not you believe whatever's in there will convince me to stay here of my own free will, what could possibly be worth that trouble to you?"

Belos perched on the stool, still-open box tucked under one arm. "Not to be egotistical about it, but I assume you've heard of me."

"Yes," Fergus said.

"And what do you know about me?" Belos prompted.

"Well, you're famous," Fergus said, "though of course your hagiography could only be written by people absolutely full of their own hubris for surviving their encounters with you. But, aside from your current reputation as one of the most persistent, dangerous, and unpredictable pirates anywhere between the Barrens and the Gap itself, it's said you came from Earth. Southwest Territories."

"What used to be New Mexico, yes," Belos said. "You ever been there?"

"As it happens, yes," Fergus said.

"We grew up near a river," Belos said. "Not a big one, but water is water, and with half the world turning to desert, it's your single most important asset. And it's also the thing most likely to draw negative attention, people who want your water and don't care how many families and kids and old people they gotta kill to get their buckets into it. Where we were, if it wasn't the remnants of the Arizonan White Army trying to sneak in and murder us, it was the Texas Republic hunting them and happy to use us as their personal resupply and recreation stop. I learned a lot from the two groups, none of them things that would be considered respectable job skills."

"I imagine not," Fergus said.

"So, after one raid too many, we got out—me and my sister. We were fifteen. I wouldn't have gotten out without her. She was always the smarter, braver, bolder of the two of us. You've heard of her, too?"

"Yes. Bel Belos," Fergus said. "You and her, the famous pirate twins, in the ships *Sidewinder* and *Rattler*, terrorizing the Barrens together and striking fear in the heart of any Alliance ship hapless enough to be sent after you. It's quite the tale, though I don't know how much of it is real."

"Some, but not all, of course," Belos said. "Go on."

"After hunting you both for years, and looking extremely in-competent for not catching you, the Alliance finally got lucky and took out *Rattler*, a decade or so ago," Fergus said. "Word is they've been running scared of your vengeance ever since, won't even come near the Barrens unless in heavily armed groups, and as long as you stay put in here and only prey on the largely lawless locals—or the poor, which is too often its own disqualification for justice—they're happy to not be forced to confront you."

Belos scratched at the underside of his chin, where the tattoos met the edge of his beard. "All right," he said. "Let me tell you what I know about you. MacInnis isn't your real name, of course, though I haven't yet found your real one. I'm not sure I care, now that I have you in front of me. But you find things. You find things that are impossible to find, that no one else can, and you plow through anyone and everyone who gets in your way. I'd met with Arum Gilger and his henchman Graf, many times; we were, in our own ways, working slightly different angles of the same business."

"Oh," Fergus said. "I'm sorry for your loss?"

Belos laughed, and there wasn't one atom of anxiety anywhere in the sound. "That you took him out? We toasted your anonymous health for the achievement. I know about the Shipmakers, and that they'd hired you, and then when the Shipyard was attacked and they disappeared, you found them in turn, under ten *kilometers* of ice, and destroyed an entire rogue Alliance faction to get them out. I am not easily impressed, MacInnis, but you have impressed me. Or at least your reputation, and we know what a mix of fact and fiction those can be. You are here because I want you to find something for me, something more precious to me than any wealth in the galaxy. Something worth making an enemy out of your very dangerous smuggler friends out there. This, here, right now"—he gestured loosely around him, at the room and the ship and the ship around that—"this is a job offer."

"If you want me to find the Alliance crew that took out *Rattler*, I don't think I can," Fergus said. "Just being honest with you on that. The Alliance and I have a lovely game of mutual hatred going, and I can't get within light-years of them without bringing a truly extraordinary amount of shit down on myself and everyone around me."

"No, you misunderstand me," Belos said. His expression had darkened, his gaze hardened. "The Alliance *lied*. They didn't kill *Rattler*; she disappeared, twelve years ago. When they figured out she was gone and no one knew anything about what happened, they took credit for the kill to make themselves look less ineffectual. We both had sworn to our parents that we would never leave each other behind, never leave each other unavenged. They were killed by raiders less than a month after we left. Ever since *Rattler* disappeared, I've been trying to find out what happened to my sister, the how and the where and the *who*. And I can't."

"You want *me* to find out what happened to her," Fergus said.

"Yes. I'm getting older, and someday a lot of overdue karma is going to catch up with me, and I don't doubt I won't see it coming. I know there is no rational hope Bel is still alive, but I need to *know*, one way or the other, before my own luck runs out. You will join my ship as a new crewmember, and together we will search. And when we finally get my answers, and know at whose hands her end came, you can go free. With my eternal gratitude and the contents of this box."

"You want me to become a pirate?"

"Yes."

"I'm not a killer," Fergus protested.

"Your eyes don't entirely agree with that."

"What if I say no?"

Belos tapped his long fingers along the side of the box. "I have no plan for that," he said, "because I sincerely do not believe you can refuse." He stood, and held out the box again.

"I'm flattered," Fergus said, though more he was just scared and angry, "but I don't think there's anything you can offer that would—"

He stopped speaking, as Belos tipped the box forward and he caught a glimpse of the thing inside: a dull sphere about the size of a melon, with a single, small letter, *H*, etched on the side. Not an H, he knew, but the Greek letter *eta*.

Fergus felt all the air in his lungs slowly escape as he deflated, shoulders slumping, mind whirling in a chaotic free fall. He felt rooted to the floor, rooted to the cruiser and the corpse of the ship around it, as his last lingering expectation that he might get back to his beach, his hut, his sunshine and solitude, dissolved into nothing.

It was one of the pallai: sentient, self-aware AIs that, according to even the best mindsystem engineers, shouldn't exist. Didn't exist, to almost everybody's knowledge. Those few who knew better made the phrase "willing to kill for it" seem woefully inadequate to the carnage that followed in their wake.

"Who knows you have this?" he asked.

"Me. Len. My first mate. And now you," Belos said. "That's all."

"The person you got it from?"

"Is not in a condition to talk, short of a séance."

"What happens if I still say no?" he asked, even though he already knew he wasn't going to.

"To you? You can leave with your friends," Belos said.

"Not to me. To it," Fergus clarified.

"I'm sure I can sell it for enough cred for my entire crew to retire in luxury, and hire a hundred others to attempt the task I want you for," Belos said. "Who knows? One of them could get lucky."

As soon as the palla hit the market, word of it would reach the wrong ears, and they would track down every step it could have taken, everyone even tangentially associated with it, and anyone associated with them, to make sure knowledge of it *died*. No one would be safe, not Belos, not Fergus, not Qai and Maha or his family or any of his friends or acquaintances, anywhere. There would be no hiding.

"I'll need to get the rest of my stuff," he said, as Belos smiled and closed the lid.

Chapter 3

Qai returned to the eggship to get Fergus's bags and Mister Feefs, and when she brought them back, she took Fergus aside. He'd put his exosuit back on, and they used their private comms, but she didn't want anyone reading their lips or running a vibration scan off their faceplates. "He doesn't have something over you?" Qai asked. "You're really staying of your own free will?"

"Yeah," he said, "I am. Not that it really makes a difference."

"It does," she said. "What the hell did he offer you?"

"I can't tell you," Fergus said. "Get Maha out of here and home safe, okay? And don't worry about me. Or at least not any more than you would anyway."

Qai shook her head and grimaced, running a tongue over one of her fangs as she studied him. "Maha and I would have found a way to find you and get you back," she said. "It might have taken a while, but we wouldn't have completely abandoned you."

"I know," he said, which was a lie.

"Tell me you're not still sun-addled from snorting beach sand," she said. "Tell me you can handle whatever this is."

He laughed. "I am not still, nor was I ever, *sun-addled*. Relaxed, yes. Happy, yes. *Bored*, yes, gloriously so. I don't know if I can handle this, but I guess I'm going to find out. The only thing I ask is that if I don't ever make it back, please let my sister know—without too much detail, please—what happened to me. She should have had a better brother than me, but she deserves to know."

"You have a *sister*?" Qai exclaimed.

"Yep. You found me; you can find her without trouble. Just don't fucking come after me or, worse, get her involved in a rescue mission. I am *choosing* this. Got it?"

"Got it. I don't get it, but I got it." Qai handed him his cat, then a bag of potato chips as a parting gift from George. "Good luck. Or, as we say on Dzen Prime, may easy hunting carry you to the feast."

Fergus nodded, picked up his last duffle, and walked toward the back of the room.

"Len," Belos said.

The pirate standing silently beside Maha reached over and undid the explosive cuff on Maha's arm, and Maha rubbed at her skin. Len picked up a bundle on the floor and handed it to her. "Yer suit, miss," he said.

Maha took it and pulled it on over her tunic and pants. Before snapping down her face shield, she walked over to Fergus. "Thank you," she said. "We won't forget."

And then she ran to Qai and they wrapped their arms around each other, gave one last, long, unhappy, dissatisfied look at Fergus, and cycled themselves back out of the lock.

"Just so you can verify that I am a man of my word," Belos said, and snapped his fingers.

Len touched a wall, and a screen lit up with a mosaic of views from both inside the freighter and the exterior where George's ship still waited. Maha and Qai moved from one view to the next, in little asynchronous jumps, until they were outside and Qai was firing her clamp dart back over to the eggship.

They crossed and went in.

"Fergus?" Qai asked over their suit comm connection, still just in range.

"Yeah," he said. "You safe?"

"We're safe."

"Please thank George for the ride. And the crisps," Fergus said. "And then get the hell out of here."

The eggship pulled away, banked to turn, and then accelerated until there was the telltale flash it had jumped, and was gone. He was alone in the Barrens in the company and care of murderers and thieves.

From the carrier in his hand, Mister Feefs let out a single loud, mournful yowl.

"Tell me that's not a fucking *cat*?" Belos asked, in the surprised silence that followed.

———

They left the embedded cruiser by another airlock and followed different tunnels through the freighter wreck to a small shuttle bay concealed inside the remains of the forward cargo hold. The shuttle was nondescript but solid, looked nonthreatening, and surely was very far from that. "In," Len said, opening the airlock and half-shoving Fergus inside. He followed, and then Belos behind.

Len took the pilot's seat, and Belos sat across from Fergus as they both strapped themselves in.

"You need a name," Belos said. "You can't go around being MacInnis, with all those bounties on you."

"How about—" Fergus started to say.

Belos raised one jet-black eyebrow in obvious disapproval, and Fergus fell quiet. "I get to pick," Belos said. "Something funny, like Bugshit? No, because I don't need the rest of my crew picking on you more than they already will."

Belos stared at him a while, thinking, as Len slid the shuttle out of the hidden dock, through a narrow channel torn through the structure of the old freighter, and out into space. George's ship was long gone, and the stars visible ahead were faint, far between, and woefully unfamiliar.

As they turned, heading farther into the Bounds, the freighter behind them was a sad, broken, forgotten speck, and his last, brief connection to anything and everything he knew.

Something thumped against the inside of the carrier at his feet, startling him, and he smiled. *Not quite everything,* he thought.

"Vetch," Belos said. "You look like a Vetch. So Vetch it is."

It wasn't a name he would have picked himself, but maybe that was a good thing. "I can live with that," Fergus said.

"You better hope so," Belos said. "Here's the story. We bartered for you back with a hostage exchange, and you came off the crew of the ship *Bonepicket.*"

"Wasn't that destroyed in a skirmish near Aurora Enclave about three years back?" Fergus asked.

Belos nodded. "You've heard of it?"

"I try to keep up on things," Fergus said. News was very slow on Coralla's smaller islands, and what attention he paid to the ambient gossip was mostly just looking for any signs of trouble heading his way. But his memory was as reluctant to let go of every tiny crumb of information as ever, no matter how useless it seemed at the time.

"You're an old friend's cousin and I owe him an honor debt, so I traded for you. You've been held in indenture on Aurora, and now you're with us. An Enclave would explain your paleness."

"Hey," Fergus protested. "I am *tan*. This is the most tan I've ever been in my whole life."

Belos shook his head. "I am genuinely sad for you," he said, sounding not at all so. "As it happens, I lost a member of my crew about a half year ago—"

"Cudder tripped o'er 'is own flapping lips and fell out an airlock," Len interrupted from up front. "A trag'dy."

"Just so," Belos said. "A bit of advice for you, Vetch: never let yourself get so comfortable that you start thinking loyalty to me or my ship is negotiable or can be anything less than absolute. But, as you can see, I'm down one crewmember, and conveniently, here you are to fill it. You think you're good enough with weapons and can get up to speed fast enough on the ship's armaments, to not be a liability in battle?"

"Yeah," Fergus said. "I'm not much of a one for guns; I tend to opt for the indirect approach to get what I want, whenever possible. But I am willing and able to defend myself, and if the ship's weapons are fairly standard, I should be able to handle them."

Len snickered from up front. "You'll be loving the cannon-balls, then," he said.

Fergus laughed. "Sure," he said. "Space cannonballs, easy."

Belos looked amused, but whatever the joke was, neither was sharing. "Len, here, has as his primary responsibility—and do not underestimate it—making people suddenly very dead. He's paranoid, sneaky as shadow, and he pays a lot more attention than he ever looks like he does. I trust him, he trusts me, and that circle is closed—if he decides to stick a knife in you, I might ask him why, but I'm not going to second-guess him. He knows everything about how and why you are here."

"And the rest of your crew?"

Belos gave a half-shrug. "Some more than others. You are a man used to aliases and roles; play your part well and you'll never need to care about who knows what. If you find yourself stuck, ask me or Len. It would be much less complicated for everyone if no one gets any surprises. You understand this?"

"I got it," Fergus said.

"You'll meet the rest when we get back to *Sidewinder* in about six and half hours, so you have plenty of time to figure out how to make a good first impression."

Fergus chuckled. "I've never made a good first impression on anyone in my life," he said. "Probably not second impression, either."

"During her stay with us, Maha seemed determined to convince me you were more trouble than you were worth," Belos said. "Please understand: I know finding out what happened to my sister is a long shot. *You* are a long shot. I am trusting that you're a man of your word, because that's what all the stories and fragments of information about you tell me. But if you think you can play me, or you put my ship or my crew in danger, I will not hesitate to cut you up or cut you down. I can tell from here that one of your ears is a regrow. Accident? Torture?"

"Torture," Fergus said. "Enceladus."

Belos nodded. "Then you and I understand each other perfectly. Yes?"

"Yes," Fergus said.

"I only have one more question for you right now," Belos said. "Why a *cat*?"

"I saved him," Fergus said. "And he saved me. And anyway, if I leave him behind, he angry-pees on everything. So, here we are; we're a package deal. You want my cooperation and my loyalty, fine, and I know this isn't going to be a smooth ride. I won't hurt innocents, and I think you already knew that. I'll do my absolute best to find out what happened to *Rattler* and her crew if I can, and I will defend myself and this ship and the rest of the crew to whatever extent is necessary, but if you ever threaten my cat, I *will* kill you."

Len guffawed. "Hooo hooo!" he said. "Maybe some meat an' teeth ter this cudder aff all. Gonna be fun times when it all goes belly-up raw."

"And it always does, eventually," Belos said.

"Aye, my captain, it always do," Len said. "Hang on, going ter passey jump. Shuttle ain't pretty but it'll get us home, shakin' an' screamin' the whole way."

Sidewinder was not an attractive ship, nor was it ever meant to be. It was small, mean, and fully committed to its business of being a predator of larger, nicer, richer vessels. It was compact and matte-black, nothing to break up its blocky outline except for a pair of enormous, solid arms that projected out from the front like straightened mandibles, or the horns of a devil's purse: ramming arms.

Fergus wondered how often they got used; people probably become very cooperative when the other option was having holes poked in the only thing keeping their air in. People with a reasonable, objective sense of their own mortality, anyway—some of the punched-in holes on *Slow Dreamer* made horrible sense now.

The pirate ship bristled with armor-plated maneuvering jets, and low-profile weaponry sprouted from the top and hung from the bottom like tumors of war. There were telltale signs of a half-dozen round doors along each side that made him think, as surely Len had intended him to with his earlier jest, of the gunports and cannons of old Earth sailing vessels.

Everything on the exterior of the ship was there by necessity alone, nothing that could get ripped off, damaged, grabbed, or otherwise give away an advantage; this ship was designed in anticipation of the kind of collision that any sane ship, sane captain, would avoid. If it was as agile as it also looked, he understood why Belos had the lethal reputation he did.

What the bloody hell am I doing here? he asked himself. *I'm not one of these people.*

Which raised the question of who *did* he belong with? While he was sure there were people in his life who'd welcome him back—and, equally, no lack of people who wouldn't—he'd never quite convinced himself he fit anywhere even when he knew who he was and what he was doing. It had been years since he'd had any real purpose, unless you counted making tea, feeding a cat, and trying to keep sand out of his shorts.

Even if this wasn't the kind of job he'd have chosen, maybe it wasn't entirely a bad thing it had come along.

He reminded himself he was there because Maha needed to be rescued, and because someone eventually would have tracked him down to Coralla who didn't need him for his skills. Depending on which of the many people he'd pissed off found him, the best he could hope for would be a swift execution. At least then he'd be dead before someone discovered his apparently bland, normal Earth-Scots body had unknown alien squidware tucked into it and threw him on a dissection table. He didn't like the idea of not dying on his own terms.

And, as always, there was the thing Belos had dangled in front of him: one of the pallai, not a what, but a *who*.

The other time he'd encountered one, deep in the ice-covered ocean of Enceladus, it had been described as the holy grail. No one knew where they came from or how many there were—though being marked with Greek letters, it suggested both an Earth connection and a limited number—but if you were unconcerned with morality, the uses such could be put to were legion; the palla on Enceladus had been in the hands of a rogue Alliance military group hoping to build an army of untraceable, perfect weapons.

Getting it out of there cost him an ear; getting his friends out of there too meant convincing everyone still alive who knew about it that the palla had been crushed in the catastrophic implosion of Ballard Substation.

In actual fact, he had left the palla Tau under the ice, happily embedded in the entire subsurface ocean's many systems. Probably by now it had taken over most of the surface and orbital ones, too, with no one any the wiser. It was one of the few secrets he had entirely to his own keeping, and he meant to keep it that way.

The palla Eta, Belos's expertly chosen bribe, hadn't looked active, but then, neither had Tau when Fergus hauled it out of the impending wreckage of the substation. Maybe it was broken, dead, but maybe not. And maybe what little survival instinct he had left after too many close calls, too many choices he shouldn't have survived, left him sentimental about others lost and alone in the void.

Or I'm greedy, he thought, though that wasn't it, or at least not in a monetary or possessive way. Greedy for the company of others who wouldn't care that he wasn't really human anymore but not anything else either, and who didn't have anything to fear from him.

As their shuttle settled into the small bay at the back of *Sidewinder* directly below two large, heavily shielded jump engines, he considered that the company of pirates also met that second criterion, and it wasn't at all an optimistic feeling.

The inside of *Sidewinder* was narrow and utilitarian, and there was an interior bulkhead every five meters—not paranoid, if you made a habit of ramming your ship into other people's—but it was decently lit and clean. Fergus had been in worse places and much more obvious peril, and he wished this ship made more effort to remind him he was not safe there, and certainly not free.

As they came forward from the docks, the rest of the crew of *Sidewinder* stood lining, or leaning against, the corridor wall, waiting.

The first was a large, heavily muscled, dark-skinned man with no hair and a cybernetic implant running across his left temple. "This is Fendayre, our ship's engineer," Belos said. "He half-built both *Sidewinder* and *Rattler.*"

"And whatever I didn't has been shot off and replaced by me," Fendayre said. "Call me Fendi."

Beside him was another man who barely came up to his shoulder but was just as bald, though he sported a grayish goatee. The man looked him over, down at Mister Feefs' carrier, and raised his eyebrows in surprise. "I'm Rabbit," the man said, and held out a hand. Fergus shook it.

"Rabbit here is our weapons specialist," Belos said, and then indicated the next man down. "This is Mr. Kaybe Shale. He's my first mate." Shale was almost as pale as pre-tan Fergus, wearing the crisp, perfectly tailored jacket of an officer in Sfazili Security Services over a white shirt and black pants, as if about to attend a formal reception.

Past him were two very imposing people, about evenly matched in scariness. The woman had the short, stocky build of a Sfazili groundsider, all muscle and immovable object, and while the man beside her didn't have any of her obvious markers of high-grav genetic adaptation, he had clearly found other ways of compensating. They were leaning shoulder to massive shoulder, playing some sort of variant on rock-paper-scissors. "Deciding who gets to pick a fight with you first," the woman said, as the man grinned and declared he'd won.

"Trinket and Yolo," Belos introduced them. "They menace the reluctant, and when that fails, shoot and hit things."

Last, but not least, was a short woman of medium build, medium age, and medium tone, wearing similarly average gray clothes. The one side of her head that was shaved also showed an implant port, smaller and sleeker than Fendayre's, and her expression of total neutrality made him instantly peel off the mental *most dangerous* label from the first mate and assign it to her instead. "And this is Marche. Intelligence," Belos said, and that sure sounded like a euphemism for something much less savory and much more hands-on. As they nodded to one another, his eyes took in her clothes, and the lines and folds of it, and found at least four places where there was likely some sort of blade stowed before he let his gaze move on.

"Everyone, this here is Vetch," Belos announced. "You remember I had a blood debt to settle, and here he is. He will be serving as a provisional member of our crew while we see what use he has, and in an advisory role based on his time aboard the *Bonepicket*. They were an extremely successful crew until the end, and I'm hoping he brings some of that luck with him. He understands his place in the crew is bottom-of-the-well, and will listen to whatever orders any of you give, but if I find any of you hazing or abusing him in an undue fashion, we will have words. Understood?"

"Of course, Captain," Marche said smoothly, her voice soft and disarming and terrifying, her eyes still entirely on Fergus.

The others added their own assent before the first mate snapped his fingers. "All right, you lot," Shale said. "Time to be away. Vetch, what's your clock?"

Time was meaningless in space. There were common standards based on Earth time that sometimes poorly fit the local reality, planets whose physical days and orbital years differed vastly from humanity's original world, but on ships that roamed between the stars, even that was impossible to synchronize in any useful way with anyone or anything else. What mattered was each ship's arbitrary consensus, and the body's internal time. Fergus's body was telling him that it was late into the night, and he said as much.

"We're midday here, so you'll need to catch up," Shale said. "Fendi, grab him an instameal and then show him his cabin."

"Right," Fendayre said, as the others dissipated back into the rest of the ship.

Somewhere up the corridor he heard someone exclaim, "Did I hear a *cat*?"

"Vetch?" Shale said, before Fendi could drag him off. "It's going to be a busy day tomorrow. My advice is to sleep as well as you can, as long as you can. And welcome aboard *Sidewinder.* This is your home now. We may be a bunch of violent sociopaths, misfits, and criminals, but we're family."

Maybe I'll fit in after all, Fergus thought glumly, and followed Fendayre's impatient, beckoning wave down the narrow corridor into the depths of the ship. At least there was no danger of thinking he was among friends.

————

Despite Shale's entirely sound advice to sleep in, Fergus found himself awake at what was still early morning ship's time. Fendayre had shown him the galley during a quick tour of the parts of the ship not currently off-limits to him as provisional crew, and had told him he was fine to make use of it as he pleased as long as he cleaned up after himself and didn't consume an unfair portion of anything with limited quantities. After being assured that coffee was plentiful, he decided anything else that might not be was a bearable burden.

Though he was not in a mood for coffee, not yet. He had woken up thinking himself still on the beach, reaching for a nonexistent canvas flap to let in a sea breeze that was now hundreds of light-years behind them. He used the small air shower in his equally tiny cabin, dressed in a comfortable pair of shorts and his favorite beach shirt, put on sandals, and took his lone teacup, whisk, and loose tea to the galley with him.

He set the foodmaker on a thirty-minute timer to start the coffee, drew a decent amount of near-boiling water, and then sat cross-legged on the floor of the small combo dining area / conference room attached to it and made his tea, not rushing the preparation, taking each step as a deliberate action. When the tea was finished, he closed his eyes and sipped, pondering the meaning of where he had now found himself. Thoughts of Qai and Maha and George, who would not be out of the Barrens for quite some time yet. Thoughts about the semi-feral beach kids who often showed up at his hut, knowing he was safe and he'd feed them. And he thought about his sister Isla, who had not seen him since the Asiig took him away, though he'd managed to send a few short messages through such circuitous routes, he remained certain no one had traced them. The inability to get any kind of word back, any contact in return, had never felt more painful than it was also necessary, though it had felt an awful lot of both.

The tea was still bitter.

Mister Feefs had followed him down to the galley, and after Fergus had washed out his teacup, pot, and instruments, he set a small plate of cat kibble down for him. Then he stood in the open area of the room—not very large, but unlike his cabin, he could stand with his arms out and not touch both walls—and closed his eyes, took off his sandals, and began to work his way through his mujūryokudo stretches, letting himself settle into the artificial gravity (about 65% Earth, he estimated) and the touch of space on his bare arms, aware of what a meager slice of an infinite reality he, in three dimensions, could feel. And there was a comfort in that, too, having once deliberately collapsed a multidimensional tunnel on himself in what should have been certain and instantaneous death. That he was still alive to drink tea and listen to his cat's faint *grep-grep-grep* as he demolished the kibble, was still, three and a half years later, astonishingly incomprehensible. He had found peace on Coralla, but gratitude remained out of reach.

As he worked through the physical stretches, from the simple into the complicated, into the forms and movements that could be combat, could be dance, he also stretched the electricity that now lived in his gut, stuck there by the Asiig pretty much just to fuck with him and see what happened, and which he had finally come to accept was *his*. Was *him*.

Fergus could feel the faint trills of the current up and down his arms and legs, just under the surface of his skin, racing through his bones and nerves. He could bring it right to the edge and keep it there, in perfect balance, not a single spark escaping. *Two martial arts in one,* he thought. External and internal, the visible and the secret. And the knowledge that there really was no difference except in his head. He could feel the electricity of the ship's systems in his mind, the pathways and bright spots and low ones, and he thought that the contact he had with the ship, just through his bare feet, was probably sufficient to short out the entire thing if he wanted to.

If he wanted to die there, of course. Not that that would be fair to his cat.

Fergus smiled as he finished his set, then opened his eyes to see Marche and Yolo had entered and were sitting on a couch, watching him, most of the pot of coffee he'd started already gone.

"Was that some kinda dirtsider dance?" Yolo asked. "All that slow-motion wigglin' about? D'ya want us to sing for you next time?"

Marche looked less amused, more interested. "What's the form?" she asked.

"Mujūryokudo," he said. "Primarily for zero gravity, but it's very adaptable."

She was still studying him, and he wondered if she ever blinked. To break away, he rolled his shoulders, grabbed a clean mug, and poured himself the remainder of the coffee.

Marche and Yolo exchanged looks. "Guess it's time for yer 'naugural beatin'," Yolo said.

"For what? Finishing the coffee? I started the pot," Fergus said. "I can start another."

"Because we need to see how you can handle yourself," Marche said, all sweetness and reason. "We can't just sit around waiting until we're all in a fight together to discover you can't tell your ass from your fist."

"None of that dancin' looked like fighting moves," Yolo said.

"Not to disrespect you, Yolo, but subtlety isn't one of your styles," Marche said.

"Hey, my style is fine," Yolo said, "an' I'm not the one here dressed like an idiot."

"Better to look like an idiot than be one," Fergus said, sipping at his coffee.

"What?" Yolo said. "Newbie, you starting something with me?"

Fergus shrugged. "*You* were starting something with *me*. I'm just going along for the ride."

Yolo stood up, cracked his knuckles, and took the few short steps to cross the room to where Fergus stood. Even though the man was shorter than Fergus, he was twice his width and oozed violence, like someone who fought like other people breathed.

Fergus took another sip of his coffee.

When Yolo got close enough, the pirate swung, almost lazily, and tried to slap the coffee mug out of his hands. Fergus easily dodged, saved his coffee, and took another slow, unconcerned sip.

Yolo doubled over, laughing.

"I did say he didn't look like the flinching type," Marche observed.

"Guess not," Yolo said, straightening up, his smile still broad and entertained. This time, when the strike came, it was fast and sudden, almost no physical broadcast, and to save his coffee, Fergus had to throw up his arm and block. As the blow landed, he stuck out his own bare foot and swept Yolo's legs out from under him.

Yolo fell, and Fergus kept hold of his mug, but it slopped hot coffee all over his hand and shirt. "Damn it," he said. "I just washed this."

"There's an autowash in the back," Marche said. "Bas says you were on the *Bonepicket*? That was a legendary crew."

"Nothing compared to *Sidewinder*, though," Fergus said. "You just do what you do, right? And you do it well or you die. Sometimes both, sometimes neither."

"Ain't that the truth," Yolo said, sitting up on the floor and not looking at all offended at having been summarily dumped there. "Welcome 'board, Vetch. Bring us some of that *Bonepicket* luck, eh? I ain't got my savings to retire yet."

Marche got up off the sofa and held out a hand to Yolo to help him up. "I've seen how you spend your cred, Yolo. Better hope you still got a couple of centuries before you retire."

"Aw, who am I kidding?" Yolo said. "My retirement'll be findin' myself on the wrong end of an airlock or a gun, and then I won't need no cred at all, anyway. What about you, Vetch? What brings you out to this short life of hurt and murder?"

"I was bored," Fergus said.

"I bet you were," Marche said.

Shale walked in, took in the arrangement of people, and glanced over at Marche. "He flinch?" the first mate asked.

"Nope," Marche said. "Yolo owes me fifty."

Yolo let out a groan. "Yeah, yeah, an' you another thirty, Shale. I know. But who fights barefoot in fuckin' space?"

"A man who doesn't flinch, obviously," Shale answered. He tilted his head to regard Fergus. "We have ship rotations. I'm just coming off helm, and the captain is taking over for a while. As provisional crew, you aren't allowed on the bridge until we get to know you a lot better, and Fendi will need to check you out with engineering stuff before you touch anything down there. So, until the captain or I say otherwise, you are working with Rabbit on his shifts, and he's going to check you out on your weaponry skills. He should be up for breakfast shortly, and I suggest not talking to him until he's got at least one cup of coffee into him. You have any questions?"

"None yet," Fergus said.

"Good. I leave you under Rabbit's tender management for your first day."

"Yay-oh," Rabbit said, coming in the door. "I miss the fight?"

"Yep. You're too late, as always," Yolo said.

"You ever disassembled and cleaned a plasma rifle, Vetch?" Rabbit asked. "'Cause those things junk up awful fast, and the life of a pirate is only as fun as your weapons working when you need 'em. No, don't answer me yet—why the *fuck* is the coffee pot empty?"

"As Yolo just said, I'm afraid you're too early," Marche said, and hit the button to start the next brew with the side of her fist on her way back out of the room. "Welcome to your new life of high piracy, low violence, and petty complaints, Vetch. Don't get too comfortable."

Chapter 4

Rabbit was an exacting, borderline obsessive taskmaster when it came to the care, handling, and maintenance of his weaponry. The small shop across from the locked room that Fergus assumed was the armory had every tool imaginable, all clean and orderly and put in their proper place. A screen hung on a moveable arm with documentation, some official, some clearly written by others in the field who found those manuals less than satisfactory under duress, and Rabbit's exhaustive notes on all of them. There was also a small but high-end fab unit there, which Rabbit explained with only a small amount of irritation that he shared with Fendi when the other man needed parts in Engineering.

Rabbit's idea of a necessary lesson seemed only partially focused on assessing Fergus's competence with assorted tasks and more on making sure Fergus knew exactly how Rabbit felt about all the shortcuts and sloppy doings that bugged him the absolute most, and the specific types of interpersonal violence he forbore applying as long-term solutions to lazy people despite obvious justification.

When asked about the scar on his leg, and then having to provide lots of details on the harpoon gun that had been used to shoot him—not his most cherished memories, given the circumstances—that seemed to edge him into slightly favorable territory. And once Rabbit realized Fergus wasn't hopeless and wasn't argumentative about process, he dug in with enthusiastic energy, showing Fergus how everything worked and, more importantly, the very fine details of all the ways in which things could suddenly fail on you and what to do if any of that happened, if you survived long enough to have the chance.

"Worst-case scenario, throw yer weapon atcher target an' run like hell," Rabbit concluded. "Probs won't get you far, but at least it has the element of surprise." He checked the time on the screen and started cleaning up the things he'd taken out to show Fergus. "Lunchtime. You hungry?"

Fergus hadn't noticed he was starving until right that moment, but he suddenly was, almost unbearably so. "Yeah," he said. "I haven't really eaten well in a long time."

Rabbit guffawed and slapped him on the arm with his free hand as he continued tucking things into drawers. "You won't here, either, unless you cook for yourself. Save your appetite for when we hit Ijikijolo Station."

"Where?" Fergus asked.

"Nowhere, Vetch. The absolute middle of nowhere." Rabbit ushered him out the door and locked up the workshop. Fergus made a mental note to see what the kitchen had that he could feed Mister Feefs, because his supply of kibble wouldn't last more than a few weeks at best; it was outside usual contingency planning to be prepared for your own sudden kidnapping. He wondered if he should have taken Qai up on her offer to take him.

Doesn't matter now, he thought. *We're in this together.*

He trailed behind Rabbit back to the galley, where Bas Belos was already sitting down with a sphere of soup and more coffee. "How'd he do?" Belos asked, using his thumb to wipe a droplet of soup from the edge of his beard.

"Pretty much a beginner, but he's got a sharp eye for detail an' you don't have to tell him things twice," Rabbit said.

"Did you anyway?" Belos asked.

Rabbit grinned. "Ahcourse I did. Maybe even three or four times, 'cause that's what *I* do."

Fergus didn't bother to confirm that. He had a near-perfect memory, sometimes as much of a curse as a blessing, but he didn't trust anyone else who claimed to have the same. Not when his life might depend on it.

Rabbit showed him where the instameals were stored, and he took a curried pea one, twisted it to start it heating, then stood there, not sure what to do with himself. Belos took another sip of his soup, then leaned back in his chair. "Rabbit, when you're done sorting through every single pack in that cupboard and finally settle on the high-protein parmesan like you always do, I need some time to have a discussion with Provisional Mr. Vetch here."

"Rightee, boss," Rabbit said, and held out a pack. "Linguini. Look, *not* the parmesan, Captain Thinks-He-Knows-Everything." He waved the foodpack triumphantly, got three steps toward the galley door, then turned around, swearing prodigiously under his breath, and swapped it for another mealpack, which he hid under his shirt as he scurried out.

"Sit, Vetch," Belos said, and pointed at the chair opposite. Fergus obligingly sat and set the now-broilingly hot instameal pack down on the table in front of him, venting it to let it cool. "So. Let's talk."

Fergus peeled back the lid and stirred the contents. He was pretty sure he wasn't already in trouble, though he was never, ever one hundred percent certain about that. "About the search for *Rattler*, I assume?" he asked hopefully.

"About anything," Belos said. "You are now my crew, and regardless of how you got here, we're all responsible for each other. You have questions? Concerns?"

"I'm going to need a few things, if that's possible," Fergus said. Not just cat food; he'd been clean-shaven since he arrived on Coralla, and he wasn't sure if he was ready to let the aggressively colonizing new stubble on his chin go full beard. His natural red would return, too, without hair nanites to change it, but who out there would recognize him? Oddly, finding himself voluntarily (by a *very* thin technicality) dragooned onto a pirate ship might be the safest he'd been in a long while. He wasn't sure which scared him more: that he might find it impossible to be his old self again, or far too easy.

Either way it went, he didn't figure he'd have much choice in the matter, anyway.

"We'll be making a brief supply stop shortly," Belos said. "What else?"

"Tell me more about *Sidewinder*," Fergus said. "I've been to the shuttle bay, my cabin, Rabbit's workshop, and here. The interior layout feels very different from most ships."

"Both *Rattler* and *Sidewinder* were designed specifically to maximize survival from catastrophic damage, particularly high-speed collisions. The more critical a piece of infrastructure, the further in toward the center it is," Belos said. He pointed over Fergus's head toward the back wall. "The bridge is just a bit forward of the halfway mark, behind the med bay, ahead of Engineering and the armory."

"No windows I could find," Fergus said. "Weak points?"

"Exactly," Belos said. "And in a fight, they can be distracting. No one can resist looking out to see certain doom heading toward them. We have screens instead. View is better, anyway."

"Of certain doom?"

"Of everything," Belos said. "When I lay my eyes at last on my doom, I'll regret not having a window just to be able to say I saw it with my own eyes, in whatever afterlife or next universe I find myself in. Until then, screens it is. Bunks are above us, with all sorts of stuff between my people and the outside hull, only some of which I'll tell you about if you genuinely need to know. Right now, you don't. Cargo is below us beside the shuttle bay. If you want privacy, your bunk's all you got, and the walls aren't that thick between. If you want company, there's the galley. If you want entertainment, you have your brain and whatever imagination you brought on board with you. For reasons I am sure you appreciate, we are very rarely connected to any networks outside the ship. The only exception to that was the dedicated channel between us and *Rattler*, and that's been silent now for too long."

"Speaking of *Rattler*, I'll need all the data you've got on her disappearance, no matter how small the detail," Fergus said.

"Of course," Belos said. "I can send it to your handpad."

"Uh. I don't own one, at the moment. That's one of the things I need to pick up," Fergus said. "As you yourself just said, it's best to stay off the nets if you don't want to be found."

"It worked quite well for you," Belos said. "I'd been looking for you for a while and never found a trace that wasn't already years stale."

"So, you kidnapped a friend to betray me," Fergus said.

"Yes," Belos said. He leaned back in his chair, crossing his legs, and regarded Fergus for a long moment, as if waiting to see if Fergus would demand an apology. When Fergus didn't, he smiled. "An excellent plan, as it turned out."

"Remains to be seen," Fergus said, returning his smile.

Belos laughed. "So it does," he said. "Thank you for the timely reminder not to underestimate you. In the meantime, we'll be at Ijikijolo Station in a day and a half, to recharge the ship and do some trading; it's one of our safe havens out here. We can pick you up a handpad then, along with anything else you might need."

"I've never heard of Ijikijolo," Fergus said.

Belos moved his soup bowl over to the table next to them, and indicated Fergus should do the same. When their table was clear, Belos snapped his fingers. "Eyes," he said. "Holo map, please. Circumference set to the Barrens, indicate us."

A holographic map sprung up over the table. "Eyes is the Ship's mindsystem?" Fergus asked.

"Short for *Snake-eyes*. My sister named my ship's computer, and I named hers. For luck." He sighed. "We were so incredibly young. I named hers Fang. It all feels like a joke now. I mean, it was then, too, but back then we thought it was *funny*."

Funny was not something Fergus had thought to associate with notorious space pirates, but assuming that *Rattler* hadn't just been blown into tiny fragments, understanding who Bel Belos was might be crucial for finding out what happened to her. And surviving. And getting home again, or at least somewhere new he could call home for a while.

The map of the Bounds was familiar along its edges, and he recognized a number of the Enclaves and asteroid-mining camps just inside that thinning perimeter of stars. Aurora Enclave was dangerous enough that he'd always managed to avoid it, unlike the friendlier Hades Station nearby. A handful of other places were just names he'd heard in passing: Traprock Mine, Stinkhole, Innich Station. If he had to, he could have navigated his way home from any of them, and knew enough not to run afoul of anyone while passing through, but the tiny red dot that he figured had to be *Sidewinder* was well past them all, and the few places with labels were places he knew absolutely nothing about.

Ijikijolo was the nearest object, and it put them about a quarter of the way into the Barrens. Knowing how far they could have traveled since the rendezvous and handover meant he could very roughly estimate the location of the *Slow Dreamer*, which was not on the map. Even if it was faster than any human-engineered ships, George's egg was going to have at least ten days' journey before they reached any kind of civilization or possibility of an active jump point again. *Hard for anyone to trace, if you were being followed,* he thought. *Also much harder for anyone to find and rescue you.*

"So, where was the last place you saw *Rattler*?" Fergus asked.

"Ijikijolo, as it happens," Belos said. "We often split up, to make it harder for anyone to track us down, and only got together for rare special occasions or when a target was big enough to need us both. That stop was for our birthday."

"And communication after that?"

"About two weeks later, routine check-in," Belos said. "*Rattler*'s position was here." He stuck his index finger into the hologram to indicate a small, white dot.

Fergus leaned forward and used finger motions to expand that section of the hologram. The dot was a binary brown dwarf system labeled THE KEETS, with a trio of malnourished, lifeless planets morosely orbiting around them. "Where was *Rattler* going?" Fergus asked.

"Toward Beserai," Belos said. "We'd heard rumor of a freighter moving some ice through. Easy picking, for a great payoff: water is extremely valuable, but unless you wanna live on top of it, it's not worth shit until someone cuts it up into portable chunks. I'd just gotten a fair haul of parts from an abandoned freighter salvage and still had more than half my cargo space full of unmoved goods, so we agreed Bel would take it. We never heard from *Rattler* again, and she never made it anywhere near Beserai. I've spent years crisscrossing the space in between, and there are enough other ships out there that, if they aren't friends, would still jump at the reward I've offered for any information. Yet, nothing."

"Beserai is a long way from here," Fergus said. The irregular, roughly oblong shape of the Barrens made the path from the Keets to Beserai at least three months' travel by passive jump, and no active-jump entry points anywhere along the way. "Why not backtrack to Guratahan Sfazil and grab their jump point across to Haudernelle? That would have cut out ninety-five percent of your travel time, not to mention made it far more likely that your ice hauler would still have been there."

"The Barrens is not always what it seems, and it has more than a few tricks up its sleeves," Belos said. He snapped his fingers, and the map disappeared. "Nasty tricks, mostly, but not necessarily without their uses. You'll see after Ijikijolo. Right now, you have an appointment with Yolo and Trinket for some sparring practice down in Cargo. I trust you don't bruise too easy."

————

By the time they reached Ijikijolo, Fergus had quite a number of spectacular bruises in varying stages of deepening, and none of them, in his not-so-humble opinion, were gotten easily. He took some wry satisfaction that for all that both Yolo and Trinket had spent their entire lives scrapping with others for both fun and survival, and had a lot more weight behind their hits than his still-skinny ass, he was reasonably sure he had given as good as he'd gotten.

A lot of the bruises were from trial and error on his part, from which he had determined three things: one, neither of them fought fair in the slightest; two, neither of them wanted to hurt him badly; but three, both wanted to hurt him at least some.

However intense the sparring had become, it had never escalated to the point where his internal electric bees stirred up enough to cause problems, and that was a victory independent of whatever reciprocal damage he'd done; they thought it was two on one, but he was also fighting the battle on an unseen additional front. Even that had become second nature, letting himself be as mindful of how the Asiig alterations to his body were feeling much the same as of thirst, body aches, and all his other nature-given physical signals.

To be fair, he'd been beat on for sport as long as he could remember. *Wait until real danger, and then we'll see,* he thought, then added, *and if I'm in real danger, we'll see if I care.*

Ijikijolo Station was, at least outwardly, not all that different from other deep-space stations Fergus had been to—just a random hole in space where someone desperate had decided to set up camp, and which had managed to accrete space junk until it could hold its own air and heat, and attract others. Someone, some-where along the way, had dragged an icy asteroid over to it, or vice versa, which was riddled with ice-mining rigs and the rhythmic pockmarks of its own automated consumption. The two objects circled another brown dwarf—there seemed to be a lot of them around, almost as plentiful as more-youthful stars were scarce—that was named, at least according to his new crewmates, the Bean.

What did stand out was how compact the station was, compared to other, more sprawling structures Fergus had seen, and how many obvious gun stations bristled across every available chunk of exterior that had line of sight on any angle of approach.

It was also brightly lit, beckoning enough to promise sanctuary, garishly colored enough to promise more unsavory things if that was what you were seeking. There were half a dozen ships docked either at or near the station, and none of them looked the part of do-gooders. *We aren't, either,* Fergus reminded himself, watching from the galley screen as Shale pulled them up to one of the empty airlock extensions and locked them on.

"We'll be here about a day," Belos told him, as the crew gathered near the airlock. "Station runs on a twenty-five-hour clock. Given your newbie status both among us and to this station, I'm assigning Trinket as your chaperone. She'll help you pick up whatever things you need, keep an eye on you while you check out the station—within reason—but I want you back on board by ship's midnight. Don't try to ditch her. My apologies if that cuts into any notions you may have for some short-lived romance or chemical vacations, but this is a place where safer is better than sorry. Got it?"

"Got it," Fergus said. He didn't have those particular entertainments in mind, but he did want some time to roam and take things in on his own. *If you were Belos, you wouldn't trust you, either,* he told himself. It was too soon to test Belos's forbearance for disobedience, especially for no tangible gain except satisfying curiosity.

He and Trinket followed Belos and Fendi out, as Len grumbled unhappily at the airlock about catching up to them later.

The station was relatively clean, relatively unsmelly, and just as claustrophobically tight and structurally dubious as Fergus had expected. They rounded a tight corner, passing two people in asteroid-miner overalls, who gave them as wide a berth as they could, and Fergus reciprocated in like avoidance, bumping the wall with his shoulder. Somewhere above him, a loose ventilation grill rattled in response, a high-pitched, high-frequency sound, and he found himself involuntarily throwing himself back across the corridor to the far side in panic.

"Whoa there, Vetch! Twitchy much?" Trinket asked, reaching out to pull him back to their side and out of the way of the next trio of people coming toward them. Her expression was half mocking, half concerned.

"Sorry. The sound reminded me of something unpleasant," Fergus said. Something unpleasant like being eaten alive by millions of tiny metallic scavengers in a collapsing interdimensional tunnel, the sound they made that still haunted his dreams. "I'm good now."

If Trinket's expression said she didn't quite believe him, she let it drop anyway. "Main market is ahead. You know what you need?"

"A new handpad. Maybe a few more shirts and some socks, and a couple other personal items. Also, I need to visit a synth and get some nutrition cubes made."

"The food's not bad onboard," Trinket said. "Especially when Shale gets in a mood and decides to cook."

"It's for my cat," Fergus said.

"Oh, right, your animal. You got the formula on a datastick or something? No way that's in the common library."

"Nah," Fergus said. "I remember it."

One thick eyebrow went up. "Those are some damned long codes, even for simple shit."

Fergus shrugged. "I've ordered it a lot," he said.

The market was spread out in the belly of what must have once been a very large freighter. Lighting was poor from above, but most vendors had individual spotlights on their own wares; Fergus could hear the faint but familiar sound of someone winding one up. "Foodstuffs and water is in the cage," Trinket said, and pointed to where a large blast hatch had been retrofitted with heavy bars. "Keeps desperate people from makin' trouble."

"Then they aren't really desperate," Fergus said.

Trinket nodded. "Right," she said. "But here, everyone looks out fer each the other, and when you're here, we all one big fam, 'cause we need to be for this place to stay workin'. Oasis rules. Cost of going up against the station is yer life."

"And no one tests that?"

"Sure they do, once a while," Trinket said, sucking in air between her teeth. "The ugly shit that come down don't fade from yer memory for a long while. Hando?"

It took a second for Fergus to put together that the subject had changed, and Trinket meant *handpad*. She was pointing to a raised platform, up above a person selling colorful bolts of plastiweave cloth, where there was a row of various electronics on display in a cage. "That's Jia. She's level fair, even with noobs, and she won't let you buy shit-shit 'nless you piss her off. You got cred?"

"Some," he said.

"Okay, go up and get yerself yer hando. I'm gonna order me a new blanket fabbed, and if you're done first, you wait right here. You got that, Vetch?"

"I got that," Fergus answered.

"Great," Trinket said, and slapped him on the shoulder hard

enough, he almost lost his balance. "Then we'll get yer other stuff and go have a drink."

He watched her disappear into the fabric shop, feeling more than a little pissy about being constantly told the same thing. Really, where did they think he was gonna *go*, anyway?

Although, as he climbed the steep metal stairs up to the electronics shop, he found himself scoping out escape routes, hiding places, looking at the movement and flow of people around him. People wore an eclectic mix of rockcrapper gear and obsolete, mismatched bits of uniforms from various military services. How many of those were secondhand, stolen off a corpse, or still proudly worn by someone who had jumped service for a freer life? It was impossible to tell, which was maybe the point. He missed his open sky, his wide stretch of beach empty at dawn, no sound except the surf and the faint trills of the sandweebies tumbling back and forth along the tide's receding line. More than any of it, he missed being able to see trouble heading toward him long before it reached him. Not that that had done him much good, that last time.

He went up the corrugated metal steps to Jia's. There were two other people up there, and he half-listened to their conversation—some spacer pidgin he didn't know, though the occasional word veered into sight of familiarity—as he mulled over the handpad choices on display. The prices were painfully high compared to just about any shop he could walk into on Haudernelle, but he didn't begrudge the merchant the markup; Haudernelle was a long, long way away, and new stock was hard to come by and harder still to transport between the edge of the Barrens and there.

He avoided the repurposed ones, being far too paranoid to trust one even if he did intend to wipe and reset every bit in the entire thing. The manufacturer-sealed ones were a lot more, but though he'd still wipe it, he'd lose less sleep over it.

"Can I help you?" a voice asked, and he turned to find one of the women at his elbow. She was wearing a close-fit, black spacer hijab covered with tiny, twinkling stars, and a thick pair of high-tech scanning goggles perched up on her forehead. "Lookin' for a new handpad?"

"Yes, please," he said.

"What's your main need? Full-body experiential journaling? Nav calculations? Holoporn? Alien holoporn?" she asked.

"I'm not much for entertainment," he said. "I'm looking for something with fast processing, a decent internal logic system, and heavy on the security. Still sealed."

"Haven't seen you here before," she said. "I'm Jia."

"I'm Vetch," he said. "Haven't been here before."

"Whose ship you ride in?"

He had been to enough places like this to know that there was little point trying to hide something the rumor mill must already be running with, especially with one new ship in dock and his escort still loudly haggling over a bolt of red fleece just over the rail. "*Sidewinder*," he said.

"Yeah? What you doing for them?"

He shrugged. "Damned if I know! Whatever they tell me. I'm sure they would never intentionally drag me into any kind of mischief or danger, right?"

She laughed. "You'll be wanting this one, then," she said, and used her palm to unlock the cage before pulling out a still-wrapped and -sealed non-descript black pad. "It's a Perreault A2600, got a 5C rating against fire, flood, impact damage including most small-caliber projectile bullets, and even has an EMP resistance buffer. It can operate down to 150 Kelvin, and survive extended periods at 15 Kelvin as long as you let it warm back up before turning it on. Try not to nuke it, throw it into a sun, or drop it into a Yuaknari acid toilet, and you'll probably be fine."

"Sounds perfect," he said. "What's the cost?"

She told him, and he tried very, very hard not to make a face or any awkward sounds as he dug out a handful of credit chits, poked through them for several moments, then dumped all but three in her hand.

"You won't regret it," she said, smiled, and handed him the pad.

"Thank you," he said, and glanced over the rail to see how Trinket's bartering was going. She was nowhere in sight. "Lost my babysitter," he said. "I better go."

"Good luck, Vetch, and welcome to Ijikijolo," she said, locked back up the cage, and then turned back to the trader, and they resumed their conversation.

Fergus went down the stairs again and poked his head among the tall stacks of fabrics until he was certain Trinket was nowhere to be seen. It was, he thought, likely his best—and possibly only—chance to make a run for it. And far too convenient to attempt, even if he had a plan and a way off the station, which he didn't. So, he went to look for Trinket elsewhere in the market instead.

He was careful to stay close enough to the fabric seller and Jia's to be easily spotted if Trinket returned, and for it to be clear he wasn't trying to escape or hide, but he also took his time; regardless of the fact that he'd decided running now was a poor choice in terms of his immediate survival, it didn't mean there wasn't information there to be taken in, impressions to be made, possibilities and potential plans to be safely tucked away for another day. And besides, the lure of the palla and solving a mystery with the magnitude and challenge of *Rattler*'s disappearance appealed to a hunger that had been building for years.

Okay, he admitted, *I might have been a bit* too *bored on the beach.*

Everyone he could see on the station was human, which was unusual this far out from Earth, though there was a high percentage of alt-humans—humans who had modified their physical appearance, either for adaptability to inhospitable environments or for aesthetics, like Maha—among the crowds. There was a certain snobbery about alts, not apparent there, that often went hand-in-hand with anti-alien bias, especially among hate groups like Humans First. None of that, though, had the fervor of paranoia about aliens mucking around in secret and nefarious ways with human biology.

Most aliens thought this was hilariously silly, because really, why would they bother? But then there were the Asiig, and Fergus was none too eager to find himself having to explain that particular exception. It was generally in his best interests if people continued to believe that whatever the Asiig did to people didn't involve letting them live to roam back into an unsuspecting, *pure* population.

As he mused about that, he bought a hair-care kit, found a formulary, got a several-month supply of food for Mister Feefs, and then wandered back toward the fabric seller. Trinket was still nowhere to be seen, but over the noise of several dozen traders and their customers locked in fiscal combat and the unsteady whine of the air systems, he heard the distinct sounds of trouble coming from between and behind a rotor shop and a motion-tattoo booth. He was reasonably sure one of the voices belonged to Belos.

If the captain got himself killed, he didn't imagine the Provisional Mr. Vetch would have long to wait for a knife to the throat or a one-way trip out a convenient airlock, depending on how hands-on someone was feeling.

Cautiously, he followed the sound of the voices and found himself outside a small, automated cargo depot that moved stuff to and from the docks. If there was any useful avenue of escape there, he would have to be extremely desperate to try it; after once escaping through cargo tunnels on Cernee where he survived only because he had a local guide who knew every centimeter of the tunnels and had the timing between crates down, he was keenly disinterested in trying his luck again. And anyway, there was a heavy security gate in front of the tunnel loader, and in front of that were four heavily armed, heavily sized men pointing guns at Belos and Len. Neither of the latter seemed especially concerned, although both had their hands out from their sides. No Trinket, but he'd worry about her later.

From his hiding place he listened for a few minutes. Two of the armed men were named—*nicknamed*, Fergus assumed—Fin-fin and Assface, and they seemed to be certain that Belos had pinched some of their cargo the last time *Sidewinder* had been there. "You know none of my crew would break oasis rules," Belos said to them. "But if you have proof, you can be sure I'll take care of it."

"An' I'll care fer the body," Len added.

"It's too late for that," Fin-fin said. "Pay up. Times ten for the insult and makin' us chase you."

Len laughed, a short, sharp bark that made Fergus shiver involuntarily. "Hain't been no insult," he said, "'cept to say yer a liar. You wanna better jab, ye gonna pay *me* for it."

"Pay yeh a nickel-token if yeh swear not ter bleed out on my boots," Assface said. "Just had 'em cleaned."

Fergus didn't even see Len's hand move, but suddenly there was a knife in it. Anyone else, he'd think it a poor choice against a gun, but the effortless speed at which it appeared suggested it might be a fairer fight than it should be. And Belos still didn't look worried. But maybe that was more about his image than the circumstance.

Well, shit, Fergus thought. *Distraction time.* He pulled a small, specially modified ball bearing from one of his pockets and gripped it in his hand, letting electricity sing up from his gut, through his arm and fingers, and fill it.

Lacking his slingshot, he crouched at the corner, peered around again, and then rolled it hard across the floor to hit the gate.

Sparks flew up, and everyone jumped in surprise. That gave him time to run forward and sweep Fin-fin's legs out from under him and grab the gun out of his hand as he fell. Assface roared and ran at Belos, while the third attacker made for Fergus.

Fergus was ready and waiting for just such a move, and kicked the attacker sharply in the face; when it was clear the man wasn't getting back up immediately, he tossed the gun he'd stolen out of the room, then put up his fists, ready for the next attack.

"Why did you throw away the gun, Vetch?" Belos called out, exasperated, as he and Assface dodged and punched at each other and Len was standing over the two men Fergus had downed.

"I don't like them," Fergus answered.

"Yeah, but Fin's gonna want it back," Len said.

Assface started guffawing, took one more swing at Belos before Belos spun him around and kicked him, sending him stumbling across the room, trying and failing to regain his balance. Fergus stepped out of the way of the man, who was caught, a split second before hitting the floor, by Trinket, who had come up behind him without making the slightest sound.

"Thanks, Trinks," Assface wheezed out between laughs. "Yer lovely beautiful."

She dropped him the rest of the way to the floor.

"So, this was a setup?" Fergus asked. "Testing me?"

"Yep," Len said. "Plus-A fer not running, maybe a D on the smarts because o' tossin' the gun."

"What if I'd kept it and shot these guys?" Fergus asked, as Len—knife vanished again—helped Fin-fin to his feet, then checked on the third man down.

"That's why I was here, watching from behind," Trinket said. "Woulda stopped you. Probably."

The third man was up on his feet, wiping blood from his nose. "Shit, but I need a drink. You're payin', Bas."

"First couple of rounds, anyway," Belos said. "After that, I know how much you all can drink, and I'm not that rich. C'mon, Vetch. Time to meet the locals."

There was a bar that took up most of an entire old cargo ship that had been added, like a blister, to the underside of Ijikijolo Station. An old-fashioned neon sign over the blast doors in the entry declared it to be THE RATTESKILLER. The ceiling was awash in holographic strobing colors in time to music that seemed to emanate from every single solid object within, providing most of the meager light. There were a couple dozen people inside, just as much a mix as he'd seen in the station corridors, and they all watched with varying interest as Belos's crew and their three attackers came in and took a wide table near the bar itself.

The three were introduced as Assface, Fin-Fin, and Gunny, all cargo haulers between gigs who had holed up at the station until a new job came their way that, as Fin-fin put it, didn't *suck like a slow-motion vacuum implosion*. Apparently, staging an ambush for Fergus's benefit was just the right balance of short and fun, for some cred and free drinks, to alleviate their boredom.

"You all already know this is my new crewie, Vetch," Belos introduced him in turn. "He's still learning the ropes."

"Got some bad instincts," Len said. "Throwin' a gun away."

"That flash was good, though," Assface said. "Didn't see that comin'."

"And he's got hisself a solid punch," Gunny said. His nose had stopped bleeding, but there was still a crusty mess under one nostril above his pale blond moustache. "Not a bad brawler. Now pay up."

Belos climbed up onto one of the barstools, his long black coat flapping around him like raven wings, and clapped once. The bar fell quiet, and the music faded to a low murmur. "Friends," he said, "this is Vetch. He's one of mine. Do with that information what you will. A round on me, for your kind consideration."

"S'traddy, when someaw new comes aboard," Len explained to Fergus.

The bartender appeared, a short, stout woman with a purple buzz cut and a mishmash of implants along her skull and neck, and snapped her fingers. It took less than two minutes for her staff to hand out small glasses of a sapphire-blue drink to everyone there.

"To Vetch!" Belos called out, and raised his glass from his makeshift pedestal.

"To Vetch!" the rest of the bar roared back, and everyone chugged down their drinks.

Fergus followed suit, and it was all he could do not to splutter and choke at the vile sourness of whatever had been poured for him. It was worse, even, than Corallan tea, and that he was smart enough to *sip*. No one else seemed to be having difficulty, which made him all the more determined not to show any of the distress now trying very hard to take control of his face and lungs and upper digestive tract.

"For Vetch! For the galaxy!" Belos called out the moment his glass was empty, and jumped off his stool and slammed the glass down on the table with a loud *thunk*.

"For Vetch! Die with honor!" everyone called back to the staccato beat of dozens of glasses, then everything snapped back to normal conversation, the music churned itself back up to near-deafening, and no one paid them any more attention at all.

The bartender slapped him on the back on her way past, right on the same bruised shoulder blade that Trinket kept aiming for. "What's your habit, Newman Vetch?" she asked. "Carried out in a coffin, on a stretcher, by your crew, or take it light and easy?"

"I'd prefer light and easy," he said, "unless there's some dumb macho thing that's gonna make trouble for me later on if I don't keep up."

"I gotcha," she said. "I'm Ratte."

"Vetch," he said, though surely she knew that. "I get the bar name now. I thought it was just a bad spelling of *rathskeller*."

"Ooooh, Bas got hisself a brainy one! Maybe he'll finally let me have Yolo back," she said. "But no, neither the *Ratte* nor the *killer* are accidental. Mind you don't cause too much trouble in my bar or give my staff any hasslin'."

"I wouldn't dream of it," he said.

She slipped him a glass of water with a wink and moved on.

Chapter 5

◆—◆—◆

Fergus had about four seconds of warning that someone was coming before the station doors into *Sidewinder*'s docking bay ground open with a squeal, and Marche, wearing a very small, very silver dress and boots he was sure qualified as lethal weapons on at least a dozen civilized worlds, strode in to find him leaning against the docking console, looking as innocent as possible, projecting a holographic mouse around the bay while his cat jumped and raced after it.

"What are you doing?" she asked.

"Playing with Mister Feefs," Fergus said. "He was bored."

"Out here? At four in the morning?"

"My sleep schedule is still off, and I needed some air."

"Yeah? So you picked a place that smells this much like beer puke?" she asked. "No, seriously, what are you doing, Vetch?"

"Playing with—"

"No," she interrupted. "Why are you leaning up against the docking-bay console, in particular?"

"It's warm?" he tried.

From her expression, he was fairly sure he could guess exactly which orifice of his she was considering cramming one of her boots up, and likely how far; when she pointed at him, then off to one side, he sheepishly stepped away from the console with his confuddler still dangling from the cracked-open panel, jacked into his brand-new handpad.

She stepped up and inspected the setup without touching.

"You trying to hack the station mindsystem?" she asked. "I can already tell you it's been tried before, and more than a few of the ambitious are now out decorating space with their bodies."

"One, no, I'm not hacking the main station systems, though if I absolutely had to, I think I could," Fergus said. "Two, no one wants me for a decoration. I mean, have you looked at me? I'm so pale, I probably reflect light like a fucking moon, and the glare would keep everyone awake all night long. Three, I'm only talking to the cargo system's maintenance logs, which are low-security, low-priority, and no one knows I'm there or would likely care."

"Why?" Marche asked.

"Just curious about comings and goings," he said. "There are date-stamped counters for numbers and weights of items transported in and out, because you're supposed to do routine maintenance when they hit a certain threshold. Also, cargo stops when there's refueling happening, and those intervals are also logged."

"How far back you looking?" she asked, one eyebrow up in interest.

"I dunno, last few days or weeks, whatever it's got," he lied. He'd been happy to discover no one had ever purged the logs, going back well before the last rendezvous of *Rattler* and *Sidewinder*, twelve years earlier.

"Why, though?"

"Curiosity. Boredom. Paranoia," he says. "Lot you can learn, reading between the lines. For example, there's a small mining rig in one of the spinward bays whose refueling interval is way too long for your typical local passive-jump craft. Also, they haven't offloaded anything."

"Maybe they're just here to relax," she said.

"Rockcrappers? They relax in ways that make a lot of noise and usually involve extensive property damage. You see anything like that going on?"

"I had business of my own last night, and wasn't in the Ratteskiller," Marche said. "You, on the other hand: I would have expected them to have to carry you back to the ship unconscious, that being the goal of the exercise. Don't tell me you drank Yolo and Trinket under the table?"

"Depends on whether cheating counts," he said.

"That depends on if you get caught," she answered.

Mister Feefs came over and rubbed up against his leg before tentatively sticking a claw into his ankle. "Yes, yes, cat, I stopped playing with you," Fergus said, "I'm sorry."

"Is that thing some kind of penance?" Marche asked, pointing at the cat, who was now far across the bay, scrabbling up the wall, trying to reach the newly reappeared mouse.

Fergus thought about it. "Maybe," he said, at last. "You ever have a pet?"

She shook her head. "No. It's not really a common thing, except among dirtsiders. Which you don't really seem like."

"I've been a lot of things, none of them long enough to stick," Fergus said. "But, back to the subject, I'm willing to bet that mining ship isn't a mining ship."

"What do you think it is?" she asked.

"Maybe the Alliance in disguise, or one of the more militant local Enclaves trying to mingle anonymously."

"How much you betting?" Marche asked.

Fergus laughed. "You want a cat? I don't have much else."

"No, and anyway, I wouldn't take the bet," Marche said. "It's a modified-exterior Alliance Koi-class light cruiser."

"That matches the fuel intake, yeah," Fergus said. "That or a Goby. You knew?"

"I'm Bas's intelligence," she said. "If I didn't know, I wouldn't deserve my job."

"How long you been on *Sidewinder*, anyway?" Fergus asked.

"Fishing, Vetch? Four years," she said. "Or thereabouts. How long were you on the *Bonepicket*?"

"Not quite a year before Aurora got us," Fergus said. "Bad timing on my part, I guess. But the Alliance ship . . . shouldn't we be worried about it?"

"Not right now, no. They wouldn't do shit near Ijikijolo, and once we leave here, they won't have much luck following us. They never do, but it doesn't stop them from trying now and then," she said. "We know they're here, and they know we know, but we all *pretend*. It's like a game of cat and mou— Oh, I get that saying now."

"I should tell you that I'm definitely not the first person who's looked at these logs, though I'm not leaving any trace of my own. So, someone knows at least something about *Sidewinder*'s architecture and capabilities."

"Or they don't know as much as they think," Marche said.

"Because you have at least one reserve tank off a common feed port, with an inline cutover, to mask your fuel capacity?" Fergus asked, and noted with satisfaction that she suddenly stood up straighter, though her expression stayed very, very carefully neutral. "There's a tiny lag in the flow when the cutover is active."

Whatever she was going to say—confirm, deny, or evade— was lost when, behind Fergus, his confuddler beeped. He turned off the holomouse, unjacked the confuddler, and carefully closed up the console panel again before tucking everything back away in his bag. Fergus scooped his cat up under his arm and then nodded with his chin toward the airlock into *Sidewinder*. "After you?" he asked.

"Oh, no, you go first," she said. "You are a surprisingly interesting person, Vetch, and I don't trust interesting people. I wasn't sure what Bas was thinking when he said you'd be useful, but clearly, he wasn't wrong. Do let me know what other conclusions you pull from that data."

She followed him through the dock airlock onto *Sidewinder*, and damned if it didn't feel like she was critically appraising every molecule of his being from behind. Over his shoulder, Mister Feefs did him the favor of returning the stare he didn't dare himself.

———

Yolo roused him by pounding on his door so hard, the metal creaked; Fergus's internal clock was still trending toward Coralla time and expecting a slow start to the day over the rising murmur of the tide, but grudgingly he had to acknowledge that by ship time, it was nearly noon. He did not, however, feel Yolo deserved any credit for that fact, as the man looked like 120 kilos of abject misery and hatred of every one of his own five senses.

Well, he *had* drunk the man under the table. If Yolo had been determined to win that battle, he maybe should have checked more often how many of Fergus's refills were more than a top-off, and how many of them were water, anyway.

"Fight practice," Yolo grunted. "Now."

Fergus obeyed.

It became quickly clear, as they circled each other down in the empty part of the cargo hold, that Yolo was both badly wanting to work out his hangover with his fists but also assuming his adversary was in a similar condition to his own. It wasn't too much effort to stay just enough ahead of Yolo to make it appear like he was getting close to a strike, without getting far enough ahead to make it clear he was playing with him. After forty minutes of awkward lunges, obvious feints, and gigantic, room-sweeping swings he could see coming with his eyes closed, he must have dodged just nimbly enough, by accident, to give the game away, and Yolo stepped back, breathing heavily, and pulled a knife.

Fergus put both hands, palm out, down by his sides, ready to move however necessary. His control was such that not a single hair on his arms stirred or sparked. His internal bees were wide awake, ready, and completely under control. He smiled at Yolo, saw the shift from suspicion to fury, and was braced and ready when a single voice cut across the cargo floor.

"Yolo," Bas snapped.

The blade vanished, not quite fast enough to hide how Yolo slipped it up a hidden slit in his sleeve. That little bit of knowledge, Fergus thought, was worth the sweat and exhaustion.

Yolo shrugged, as if nothing had happened. "We're done," he said, and stalked off toward the ladder tube.

"Pretty impressive for all you drank last night," Belos said. "Or did you?"

"I drank as much as you," Fergus answered. He wasn't the only one getting watered-down drinks on the sly from the obliging bar owner.

"Yolo is always looking for a fight after a night of too much fun," Belos said. "Usually, he and Trinket slug it out, but our newbie is an obvious target. Or so he thought."

Fergus stretched, rolling his shoulders, feeling his electricity go back to sleep deep within. "I didn't want to make him feel bad," he said. "But I also didn't want to get hit."

"Better than being stabbed," Belos said.

"I wasn't worried about him stabbing me. I was more worried about having to actually hurt him to stop him," Fergus said. "I mean, us being on the same team and all."

"Yolo *is* on your team, and he'll come through for you if you need it. Just avoid him when he's really hung over and let Trinket deal, from now on, if you can," Belos said. He sounded in equal measures frustrated and amused. "That assumes, of course, that she's not refusing to leave her cabin because of some new blanket she says is so warm and comfortable, she's never getting up again.

"While we're still at the station, we have water exchange, so if you want to take a real shower, you can. Five minutes," Belos added. "Crew meeting in the galley in twenty. Be there."

———

Five minutes was hardly a drop in an ocean versus the joy of living on a beach, and the water was acrid with various decontaminants and chlorine—or at least, that's what he hoped the smell was—but he enjoyed every second of it, leaning his forehead against the cool wall as steam billowed around him.

When time was up, Fergus reluctantly let the water go back to wherever it came from and whatever new chemicals awaited it, and rubbed his very stubbly chin. He'd stayed clean-shaven his entire time on Coralla, as one measure of protection under a wide-open sky—having kept a beard for most of his life meant that his original facial contours were nothing anyone had seen or any surveillance system recorded. Now, though . . . was he genuinely still worried about the Alliance spotting him, much less coming after him, there? Or that Digital Midendian, assuming they still wanted revenge for his theft of their precious alien artifact pieces, could reach this far?

Regardless of the circumstances under which he had ended up aboard *Sidewinder*, he doubted Belos would let him be taken without one hell of a fight. And other than his cat, no one he loved could get hurt if someone tried.

"Okay, beard," he said out loud to the mirror. "You can grow again."

He got dressed, putting on his brand-new T-shirt with the logo of the Ratteskiller on it, and, feeling oddly and comfortingly himself in a way he hadn't in a long time, headed toward the galley and crew meeting, and found himself hoping there would be breakfast.

———

Belos stood at the head of the table, as Kaybe and Marche took the seats to either side of him. Len and Rabbit were arguing over something in the foodmaker, and Fendi had taken the chair at the other end and was sitting there, giant arms folded across his chest and head tilted down onto one shoulder as if sound asleep. Fergus stood for a moment, not quite wanting to accidentally take anyone else's usual place, when Fendi—without appearing to move at all—kicked a chair out and nearly over. "Sit," he growled, without looking up. "You're making me tired."

Fergus sat. Rabbit finally took the seat between him and Kaybe, muttering something under his breath. Len set a large bowl down on the table with a thud. "Groats," he declared.

"They're green," Fendi said. "Greenish-blue."

"Groats an' lichen," Len said. "'S'nutritional."

"Groats an' lichen *and* . . . ?" Rabbit asked, pointedly.

"Rum," Len said. "'S'a traddy breakfast a'home. Ya not banging down on my culture, Rabbit, I'd ask?"

Rabbit put his hand to his face and pinched together his eyebrows, lips pressed tightly together as he shook his head.

Len looked around the table. "How many bowls, then?" he asked brightly.

Everyone looked at everyone else.

Once, while Fergus had been in Cernee, chasing down a stolen spaceship, he'd had occasion to try lichen—a staple in deep-space habs, genetically modified for hardiness and nutrition, not taste—and thought the inclusion of rum was not an unreasonable decision. "I'll try it," he said, knowing he would probably regret it.

"Aw, Vetch!" Len declared, smiling, as he ladled viscous slop into a bowl and pushed it his way.

Len sat, and watched intently as Fergus took a spoonful and ate some of his rummy green groats. When Fergus didn't make a face or spit them out, he seemed genuinely happy.

"Suck-up," Rabbit muttered.

"Hey, I've eaten worse," Fergus said. "You ever tried Veirakan Fooge-burm?"

This time, everyone at the table groaned, and Fendi made the sign of the star over his heart.

"Might as well pass it 'round," Belos said.

"Are we waiting for Trinket and Yolo?" Fergus asked.

"Neither of them particularly care where we go next," Kaybe said, "as long as there's a possibility of profit and a likelihood of committing violence."

"Marche, what's our security situation?" Belos asked.

"We got Alliance moles on-station again," she said. "As usual, disguised as miners, hanging out in Ratte's and other public areas, trying to pick up intel. New crew, not any better at blending in than previous ones. Seems likely the ship is the ESS *Stiletto* out of Haudernelle."

"How long has it been here?" Belos asked.

"Couple of days," Marche said. "Couldn't get a specific arrival time out of anyone. Vetch, you know?"

"Why would—" Fendi started to say.

Fergus coughed. "Four standard days before us. They seem to be preparing to leave soon," he said. The rest of the table was quiet. "Uh, I did some poking around on my own. You think they're planning on following us?"

Marche and Belos exchanged a look, then Belos said, "Possibly. They've tried before, but usually they're after someone else, someone more manageable. They've been coming in once or twice a standard year for five years or so now; the Alliance can't get away with openly entering the Barrens unless they travel in pairs, and then everyone knows they're coming. Most of us caught on to the fake mining ships right off. The wannabes, and those who just aren't paying attention . . . well. Having a self-renewing supply of low-hanging fruit serves the rest of us, I guess."

"Five years?" Fergus said. "How did you determine that?"

"It's an approximate guess, based on when they were first identified by a trusted source," Belos said. "Why? Did your 'poking around' suggest something else?"

"They first visited Ijikijolo twelve and a half years ago," Fergus said. "Or at least, that's the earliest trace I could find."

The change in Belos's posture was subtle enough that if he hadn't been looking for it, he wouldn't have seen the transformation from casual to intent listener, from relaxed to tense. Everyone else at the table seemed to have gone rigid in place. Len, beside Belos, stared down the table at Fergus. The man's gaze was as sharp as the knives he carried, and Fergus barely managed not to flinch under its points.

"Interesting," Belos said, as if it was anything but, breaking the moment of intense silence. "Any other security concerns?"

"A fair bit of speculation about our new guy Vetch, here," Marche said. "Not usually the case in our line of work that absolutely no one has heard of someone, but if anyone has intel or dirt on Vetch, they weren't telling or selling."

"I told you I know what I need to know," Belos said.

"Yeah, but you haven't told me what *I* need to know," Marche said.

"Do you trust me?" Belos said. "Because we haven't left station yet."

"I trust you," she said. "I don't trust him, and until I know enough to be satisfied I can, I don't trust myself to do my job."

"We can discuss this later," Belos said.

"But—"

"*Later*," Belos snapped. "Other security concerns?"

"None that I know of," Marche said, pointedly. She glanced again at Fergus. "But, Fendi, we might want to look into a small redesign around our fuel failover switch, when we have time. Nothing critical, just leaning in to some extra paranoia."

"No such thing as extra paranoia," Fendi said. "I'll add it to my maintenance list."

"On to financial prospects," Belos said. "What do we have?"

"Ice convoy from Glaszerstrom to Aurora Enclave, already en route. Aurora is riding shotgun," Kaybe said. "Your former friends, Vetch, if you want to drop in on them and kneecap a few, for old times' sake."

"As much as I'm sure that appeals, I'm not nearly desperate enough and not nearly dumb enough to hit anything involving Aurora without a lot of time to plan and even more time to come to my senses," Belos said. Everyone nodded in agreement, including Fergus. "What else?"

"Small, unmarked ship trying to sneak through unnoticed, entered the Barrens spinward from Beserai, keeping their path erratic," Fendi said. "Spotter wants ten percent."

"Who?"

"Pebbles, station Engineering," Fendi said. "She'll put in on it, recognizes it could come up empty."

"Unmarked, you said," Kaybe asked. "Any idea whose it is?"

"Not a clue," Fendi said, "but you don't strip a ship down to generic and go scurrying slo-mo across the Bounds if you're on legit business."

"Did the spotter pass along any data on its path so far?" Fergus asked.

"Yeah, hang on," Fendi said. He pulled out his own handpad, swiped across it a few times, then the table lit up with a holographic map and a light blue zigzag across one corner.

"Basellan," Belos, Fergus, and Marche all said simultaneously. Arum Gilger, who'd tried to take over the settlement Cernee by killing anyone in his way, including several attempts on Fergus's life just for being in the wrong place at the wrong time, had been an exiled son of Basellan aristocracy looking to make his own empire. That had made him only slightly less unbearable than the glory-of-death-by-combat cult he'd rallied around him.

"Basellan sketchy shit ain't always profitable sketchy shit," Rabbit said. The man got up, got a squeeze-tube of ketchup out of the cupboards, and under Len's stabby glare emptied half the tube onto his bowl of groats, stirred it, then ate with a look of intense dissatisfaction.

"Pass that?" Fendi asked, pointing to the remainder of the tube.

"What else we got?" Belos asked, before the conversation could lapse into murder. "Focus, people."

"Food convoy from Moritau passing through," Marche said. "Easy mark, but not much pay for the work of stealing food out of starving miners' mouths. Looks like there's a new skunk runner trying to set up operation between Cherish and Stinkhole, but no regular pattern yet; might be a stretch before they settle in and get careless."

"Spotter?"

"Tip came straight from Ratte," Marche said. "Doesn't want a cut, long as whatever we do, we shut them down permanently."

"Competition?" Fergus asked, which earned him a dirty look from both Fendi and Rabbit.

"Common sense," Marche said. "The Barrens is an ecosystem. It's a harsh one, but it's not without rules. Like the oasis rule, some things are necessary to keep the balance."

"So, you are fine with killing people but draw the line at drugs?" Fergus asked.

"People want drugs, there are local suppliers, part of the communities who have to live in and answer to those communities, and they watch out for anyone getting over their heads," Marche said. "Outside drug runners make problems that make bodies."

"Think global, pop yer pills local," Len quipped. "So, who we goin' at? I say Basellans, then swing back 'round ter Ratte's runner on the flip."

"Agreed," Kaybe said.

"I think we should go hang off near Haudernelle, see if we can catch something interesting sneaking in or out outside the usual channels," Fendi said.

Rabbit looked at Fendi, then heaved a sigh. "Either that or Basellans. I don't care."

"And you, Vetch?" Marche asked. "You looking for some payback against Aurora? Ice sound tempting? It brings a good profit."

"I don't want to go anywhere near Aurora or have anything to do with them anytime soon," Fergus said, which was no lie.

More, he didn't particularly want to go get involved in *any* piratical aggression, but until he solved Belos's mystery, the odds were going to keep increasing that he'd be part of something he wasn't going to ever feel okay about. "I say the Basellans," he finished. Intercepting that ship took them closest to the path *Rattler* had taken when it left Ijikijolo, twelve years earlier. Also, in his experience, most Basellans were assholes doing terrible things—inevitable, he supposed, when you let a colony fester, unchallenged, in its own genetic-superiority bullshit for too long.

Belos slapped his hands down on the table. "Basellans it is, then," he said. "Marche and Kaybe, set a departure time, run the usual checks, and let Trinket and Yolo know we're going. Space is calling."

———

At Belos's direction, Marche reluctantly dragged Fergus to the bridge with her to watch her run her security checks as *Sidewinder* pulled away from Ijikijolo. He'd passed their test on-station, but he didn't expect he was going to be allowed here unsupervised for a long time, if ever. He didn't mind; he wasn't particularly interested in sabotaging the ship or making trouble, at least not yet.

Sidewinder moved outward in a slow, lazy, uneven spiral. "Keeps anyone from knowing exactly which way we're going," Marche explained. "First thing, we let Eyes do a signal sweep in our vicinity while I send a small botswarm out to do a visual scan."

She pointed to a screen where a 3-D model of the ship was assembling itself via small, expanding circles until they overlapped, and then moved on. "That's that, there. They'll flag anything new or anomalous, and Eyes keeps a running analysis going, but I like to keep half an eye on it, anyway."

"Okay," Fergus said. "Then what?"

"Once the bots are back in, and if no one is following us, we'll speed up until we're out of the range of anyone at the station and there's nothing on our sensors," Marche said. "Then we pick our heading and jump. How did you do it on the *Bonepicket*?"

"I wasn't on the bridge very much," Fergus said.

"What did you say you did aboard, then?" Marche asked.

"Sock washer," Fergus said. There was a faint snicker from Kaybe, at the helm.

Marche leaned back in her seat, folding her arms across her chest, glared at him, then turned to Kaybe. "Okay, so, what gives? You know I *really* don't like having secrets kept from me, and right now I feel like I'm the only one not in on the joke."

"Which is what makes it so fun," Kaybe countered. "Vetch is along for a special project. More than that, you've got to get it from the captain directly."

"So, I'm just supposed to trust him?" she asked, with great indignation.

"Oh, no, I didn't say *that*," Kaybe said. "But I don't think he's the murder-us-all-in-our-sleep type."

"No," she agreed, eyeing Fergus. "Which makes a preemptive strike unreasonable on my part, I suppose."

"Signal check and exterior scan are clear," an unfamiliar feminine voice said. "No one has departed station since we undocked."

"Thanks, Eyes," Marche said. "Pull the bots in and let's get out of here."

The screen in front of the helm lit up with an overlay of fast-scrolling numbers and lines as Kaybe selected and set in a course. Then he tapped his earpiece. "Captain, we're clear. Heading out."

Whatever Belos responded, Kaybe made one last final, tiny adjustment to his display, then pulled down the handle to engage the passive jump engines. *Sidewinder* growled underfoot, half vibration and half power surge, and Fergus glanced toward the front screen, half-expecting it to be the familiar sight of the stars fading into black, but there was no window there, only Kaybe's maps and movement data, lines condensing down to a point as they hit full jump.

Something else on the ship started singing, a burst of electrical signal from over their heads and forward. Fergus looked around, but whatever it was, neither Marche nor Kaybe seemed to notice or be concerned. *Because only you can sense electricity, you idiot,* he told himself.

"The captain said the med bay is forward?" Fergus asked.

"Why, you got sudden motion sickness?" Marche asked.

"Just a nervous stomach," he said. "If you don't mind, I think I'll go get myself something for it. Be right back."

Marche rolled her eyes but waved him away.

Fergus unclipped his safety tether and left the bridge. The med bay door opened at his touch, and he stepped in and slid a stool roughly into the center of the room and reset its magnetic foot-pads to hold it in place.

He was just tall enough, standing on top of the stool, to place his palms against the ceiling of the med bay. Closing his eyes, he let his seventh sense feel around the signal-maker. It was definitely directly above now, although still separated by some distance. *On the outside of the ship?* he wondered.

A bug planted on a ship was very much Alliance style.

"The pill dispensary is over there," a voice said, and he opened his eyes to see Marche standing, leaning in the open door, and pointing toward the very large, very obvious autoformulary in the corner of the room.

"Oh," he said. "I must have missed it. Whose quarters are directly above us?"

"Rabbit's," Marche said. "Why?"

"No reason," Fergus said, and climbed down off the stool. "That reminds me, I wanted to ask Rabbit a question about pistol voltage environmental variable compensators. No time like the present."

"He probably went back to sleep," Marche said. "He's alternate shift."

"He loves gun questions, though," Fergus said, and carefully avoided brushing against Marche—mindful of the preemptive strike comment earlier—as he slipped past her and to the ladder tube.

She followed him up to the crew deck. "You're an odd person, Vetch," she said, as she climbed out of the tube behind him and followed him to Rabbit's door.

Fergus knocked, gently.

"WHAT?" Rabbit bellowed from inside. "Fucking go 'WAY!"

"Vetch has a gun question," Marche said. "Apparently, it's pressing."

The door slid open, and Rabbit stood there glowering, wearing only a pair of blue polka-dot shorts. The number of scars on the man's body easily rivaled Fergus's own, at least up until his most recent "repair" by the Asiig that had left him covered in millions of tiny lines, as if he had been glued back together from tiny splinters.

"What?" Rabbit growled again, not as loudly but no less hostile. "You know I'm not a morning person, Marche."

"You would think, in a place where there is no actual difference between night and day, that there wouldn't be people who aren't 'morning people,' but here you are," Marche said. "I just came along to observe, in case there's any regrettable stabbing of the newbie."

"Uh," Fergus said, and sidestepped Rabbit into his room, then climbed up onto the man's small desk and put one index finger against his ceiling. "What's up here?"

"Not a gun," Rabbit said.

"The hull?" Marche said. "This is a stupid guessing game."

"No, something with active signal. Part of the comm system?" Fergus asked.

"There's nothing out there," Marche said. "Nothing making signal. We *checked*. We always check. You watched."

"It turned on the moment we hit jump," Fergus said.

"What did?"

"Whatever's out there."

"Nothing's out there!" Marche exclaimed. "And even if there was, how would you know?"

"I have exceptionally keen hearing," Fergus said.

"Can you get out of my room?" Rabbit asked. "Afore I cut you?"

Fergus climbed down off the desk. "The bot scans . . . do you keep those?" he asked.

"Of course," Marche said.

"Great, then back to the bridge," Fergus said.

"Oh, no, we're not bothering Kaybe with this bullshit," Marche said. "I can pull it up for you on the table display in the galley. Besides, I need a drink."

"Bye," Rabbit snarled, and slammed the door shut in their faces.

Fergus followed Marche back down to the tube to the galley, where she took her time making some sort of nutrition shake before turning on the table display. "Eyes, give us the scans taken as we departed Ijikijolo. Full read permissions to Vetch."

"Thanks, Eyes," Fergus said as the holographic model popped up over the table. "Can you give me all the data you have on this spot, here?" He poked his finger at the model. "Zoom in, two-meter radius, please?"

The ship's mindsystem obeyed, and Fergus stared at the crisp, smooth image of the hull's exterior. "See?" Marche said, looking over his shoulder. "Nothing."

"Cycle through the full spectrum," Fergus asked, and only a very faint shimmer to the image indicated it was changing.

Marche slurped at her drink in clear nonverbal condescension.

"Wait, pause," he said. There had been a just slightly longer shimmer. "Go back, one-twentieth speed."

Marche set her drink down and leaned over his shoulder, staring intently at the screen. *She saw something too,* he thought, then there it 'was, like a faint shadow on the image, gone again just as fast.

"Pause again," Fergus said. "Forward one dataframe at a time."

"There," Marche said, and pointed to the barest hint of a circle.

"What is it?" Fergus asked.

"I don't know," Marche said. "Eyes, what is this line?"

"It is a visual glitch caused by noise in the data at that frequency, which falls within the normal margin of error," the ship said. "Conclusion: there is nothing there."

"That's a hell of a coincidence, if so," Fergus said.

"Well, we can't go out and look mid-jump," Marche said. She frowned, tugging at her lip in thought. "Eyes, check this against all previous scans in memory. Is the glitch just in this scan? Or does it appear in others, in the same or other places?"

"I will need a few minutes to fully reintegrate the error logs from previous scans," Eyes said.

Marche took her empty drink bulb over to the autowash, and Fergus got up and made himself coffee and rehydrated a pack of breakfast biscuits. After Len's rummy groats, they were nicely dull. Marche muttered something and, at Fergus's inquiring look, repeated herself louder. "I don't like coincidences," she said.

"Me neither," Fergus agreed.

"I have determined that similar patterns of data irregularity only occur in that one specific location," Eyes announced.

"For how long?" Marche asked.

"The most recent fully clean scan I have on record is from four years ago. I can be more specific if you'd like."

"Shit," Marche said, and glared at Fergus as if he had somehow caused this. "Tell Kaybe to drop to normal space at his earliest convenience, and let the captain know we may have a problem."

"Done," Eyes said, and a few moments later, the background rumble of the engines changed pitch, and there was the telltale prickling of the inertial dampers kicking in just as they dropped back to sub-lightspeed.

The signal cut out immediately.

"It stopped," Fergus said, cocking one ear upward as if it really was something he'd heard.

"That makes no sense," Marche said. "No one can pick up signal when you're jumping; it loses all coherence and just leaks away. Why?"

"If active jump is folding space between two compatible points to remove the distance in between, passive jump is more like folding the space in between a whole lot of little times, like a paper fan," Fergus said. "If you closed a paper fan and drew a line on it with ink, then opened the fan, you'd have a dotted line."

"Not a coherent signal," Marche said. "You couldn't send any information that way."

"No, but what if the signal *is* the message? If you have sufficiently distributed detection—which wouldn't have to be big at all—then you can pick up bits of that dotted line and roughly know which way someone went, and where from and to," Fergus said. "If you aren't trying to actually catch up to someone, you can learn a lot just observing from multiple points. Someone's been tracking *Sidewinder* for four years."

"Marche," Belos said, striding into the galley. He was shirtless, his hair loose and unkempt, and—completely at odds with his ruthless, universally feared space pirate look—he was in fuzzy purple socks. "What the fuck is going on?"

Kaybe was a half-step behind him. "We're out in normal space," he said. "Just sitting here, going nowhere, doing nothing. You got an explanation for why?" he asked.

Marche groaned. "Eyes, you explain," she said, then grabbed a fistful of Fergus's shirt and yanked, pulling him after her. "Newbie and I are going for a little spacewalk."

Chapter 6

Fendi came back into the galley, where everyone was clustered around the table, waiting with different levels of impatience. Yolo and Trinket had spent the last half hour trying to slap each other, while Rabbit had fallen asleep in his chair, head on his arms, lightly snoring. The engineer set the object down in the center of the table. It was a small cylindrical unit that had bored itself into the surface of the ship's hull, with a fifth of a millimeter-thick disk, like a hat, to lie virtually flush against the plating and give it camouflage.

"Vetch was right," Fendi said. "Pretty simple logics, set to scream its head off any time it's out of normal space. There's so much random noise out there in jump, we'd have had trouble finding it even if we knew it was there." He eyed Fergus suspiciously.

"I have exceptionally keen—" Fergus started to say.

"—Hearing, yes, so you said," Marche finished for him.

"It's a redhead thing," Fergus added, defensively.

"Look, if you've got augments and just don't want to say, don't trust us yet, we get it. Not everyone is okay with alts, even way out here," Belos said. "So, Marche, four years we've had this bug on us without it being noticed?"

"It's possible it's been here a lot longer," Marche said. "One of the first things I did after coming on board was revamp your scan and security protocols. My predecessor wasn't as thorough, nor did he archive any of the data."

"Is it Alliance?" Belos asked.

"Looks like," Fendi said. "Hard to be sure, and of course who made it doesn't gotta be the same as who deployed it."

"If it was Alliance, you'd think they'd have used it to go after us, long before now," Rabbit said, without lifting his head.

"But if it was one of our competitors, the same would be true," Kaybe said. "Maybe even more true. So, why track us this long without acting? Unless the signal leak into normal space is just not as useful as they hoped."

"We can't assume that," Marche said.

"I know, but nothing else makes sense," Kaybe said.

"Put word out to the *Sisuile* and the *Phiala*. Friendly ships, much as there is such a thing out here," Belos said, glancing at Fergus as he added that brief explanation. "Have them check their own hulls, but keep it quiet. Not sure I trust anyone else, but we need to know if it's just us."

"Will do," Kaybe said, and left for the bridge.

Belos picked up the object and turned it over in his hands, brow furrowed.

"Trying to decide if you should put it back?" Fergus asked.

Belos looked up in surprise. "Yes," he said. "I don't have enough information to know if I want to tip my hand that we found it. We've got a while to decide, if it only activates while we're on the move, but eventually, they'll notice they've stopped getting signal."

"If it were me . . ." Fergus started, then wondered if he was about to overstep, and fell silent.

"Continue," Belos ordered.

"If it were me, and I'd put that on your ship all these years ago without doing anything about it, it'd be because I didn't have what I wanted yet," Fergus said. "I don't know your patterns enough to know how predictable you are, but if this is the Alliance and they've got their people listening to the same rumors and tips you all are hearing, they could make a really good guess where you're going every time you leave the station. So, whatever they want, it's not you. Or not only you."

"And if it was you instead of me, just finding that thing on your ship, what would you do?" Belos asked. "Play captain for a moment."

"I don't like not knowing things," Fergus said. "Also, I'd be seriously pissed off that I hadn't spotted it before now."

"Sure," Belos said, "but what do you *do*?"

"Put it back, as if we never found it," Fergus said. If the Alliance was hunting them, he had good reason to want to slip out of their reach as soon as possible. "Then I'd head somewhere unexpected, somewhere I wouldn't normally go, maybe a place I'd never been before. Hang out there just long enough for it to look like I must've been up to something, then leave someone or something behind so I see who shows up there after I've left."

"And how do we do that?" Kaybe said. "We don't keep that kind of surveillance tech on board; our concerns are almost always both immediate and local."

"I say we just smash it up and get on go," Len said. "If they ain't made a move by now, they're jes' scaredy cowards an' not fer us fearin'."

"I agree with Len," Rabbit said. "Not our vibe t' worry what's ahind us, only ahead."

"I don't like not knowing who it is," Marche said.

"Me either," Kaybe added. "We've survived this long by being more dangerous than anyone else but also by being *smart* about it."

"Fendi?" Belos asked.

"I'm not disagreeing with Rabbit or Len for the practicality, but I'm offended that someone stuck this shit on *my* ship, as if they can just do as they please without my say-so, and that makes me very much want to arrange the opportunity to shoot them in the fucking face," Fendi said.

Rabbit leaned back in his chair and folded his arms across his chest. "I can respect that," he said.

Kaybe checked his handpad. "Word back from the *Sisuile*; they don't have one but appreciate the heads-up."

"Okay," Belos said. "For now, we put ours back, and we're going to continue heading as if we're making for the Basellan ship. That's far enough that it buys us some time. I want extra attention paid to the very edges of our scanner range, in case someone is shadowing us after all. I need to think about where and how we want to set our trap, but as soon as I do, whoever's playing games with us, it's our turn."

Trinket wandered in and grabbed a drink from the dispenser. "Someone say games?" she asked. "Will it involve hitting people?"

"Oh, almost definitely," Belos said.

———

The cat was already snoring, frozen mid-knead with one claw stuck, almost absent-mindedly, into Fergus's left leg, when Marche banged on his cabin door. The cat took a good chunk of Fergus's skin with him when he leapt up, yowled like a demon possessed, bounced face-first off the cabin wall, and disappeared behind Fergus's pack where it was loosely tethered in the corner.

"Am I interrupting something?" Marche asked. Not waiting for an answer, she added, "You're wanted on the bridge. Now."

He got up, sighed at the new hole joining many others of the same size and source in his pants, and followed her out.

Kaybe and Belos were both back on the bridge, and as Fergus sat back in his earlier seat, Marche settled in at Len's station and studiously ignored both Kaybe and Belos's raised eyebrows. "I'm staying," she said.

"Fine, stay, but be quiet," Belos said. "Vetch, you ever heard of the Stank Palace?"

"No," Fergus said. "Sounds delightful, though."

"It was a briefly inhabited, hollowed-out bit of space rock that someone once fancied could be a city, down now to just a handful of desperate miners, none of whom stay long," Belos said. "I've never been there, so that's where we're going. And if anyone asks, I'm telling them it's your fault."

"Wonderful," Fergus said. "Where is it?"

Kaybe switched on a holographic map over the navigation station, smaller than the one in the galley but with much crisper resolution. "This is us," he said, and pointed to a red dot crawling slowly away from a tiny white circle labeled Ijikijolo. "We're in passive jump, heading over to this dot here which represents pretty much a hole in space, then from there we're taking a shortcut to the Keets."

"Shortcut?" Fergus asked. "How? There's no active jump points anywhere around either here or there. There can't be—no stars or planets big or complex enough to spin them off their gravity wells." The one other type of shortcut he did know about—alien interdimensional tunnels that nearly killed him—were a secret he was, he'd been told repeatedly, the only human in on. For reasons much bigger than himself, it needed to stay that way.

"I know you told me you haven't spent much time in the Barrens," Belos said, studiously ignoring Marche's sudden stare at that, "so think about it for a moment. There is a low—almost nonexistent—density of star systems here. What stars we have are small, dim, and unimpressive. Why?"

"I just assumed it was natural," Fergus said. "Star density is bound to vary."

"I expect you've traveled far more extensively than I have," Belos said. "Found any other dead zones like the Barrens?"

"The Gap," Fergus said, "but—"

"But that's what we'd expect, between galactic arms. How about right in the middle of one?"

"No," Fergus said.

"You know what the Barrens does have a lot of?"

"Pirates," Fergus answered.

"Rocks. Debris. Exoplanets with no stars. Crappy little brown dwarfs, at about the same distribution as everywhere else, except all by their lonesome selves," Belos said. "How would you explain that?"

"I wouldn't," Fergus laughed. "I'm no scientist. I leave that up to—" He almost said *my sister*, but that was info he was unwilling to divulge and unwilling to think too much about. All compelling reasons aside, he *had* abandoned her for the second time and, this time, had done so knowing he was doing exactly that. "Others," he finished.

"So, it could happen, yeah?" Kaybe asked.

"I guess," Fergus said. "I mean, here we are."

"Here's a fact you are unaware of," Belos said. "I don't hold it against you, because only a very few of us know. The Barrens is full of active jump points."

"It can't be," Fergus said. "Everything we know—"

"—Says you need big, complicated gravity sources to cause them," Belos said. "And yet, as you said, here we are. The jump points are unstable as hell, and even the sounder ones are unbelievably dangerous. A few have collapsed or become untethered in real space at one end. Almost as if . . ."

Kaybe and Belos watched as Fergus added it up.

"Almost as if there were once bigger stars here, and now there aren't," Fergus said. He leaned back in his chair, rubbed his stubbly beginnings of a beard. "That's . . . I don't know. Stars come and go, but there are no gas clouds here, no star nurseries, no red giants, nothing. If you're right, a hell of a lot of stars disappeared at once and left no trace."

"Yes," Belos said. "The logical conclusion is that something very bad, very beyond our comprehension, once happened here."

"And left shortcuts for the daring and those with nothing left to live for," Kaybe said, and grinned. "The Ghostdrift."

"It's real?" Marche spoke up, incredulous. "I've been hearing those stories for years—everyone has—but I always thought they were just drunken old spacer yarns meant to frighten."

"And mostly, they are just that. The stories are ridiculous, over-the-top superstitious, and laughably implausible. I've even heard a persistent one that when you come out the other end, you'll have been turned into a turtle," Belos said. "But at the heart of all the weird stories, underneath the embellishments and outright fabrications, there's a core piece of truth hiding: the jump points *do* exist. They range from just barely passable to a guaranteed death, pulled apart by the Drift when the jump conduit fails around you."

"Wonderful," Marche said. "And this one, we're going to take?"

"Bumpy," Kaybe said. "Definitely bumpy. But no worse than that, probably because it's short."

"Once we're at the Keets, we'll passive-jump again to the Stank Palace," Belos said. "And then we set a trap."

"With punching, if possible, for Yolo and Trinket," Kaybe added.

"Whatever gets us answers," Belos said. "Assuming Mr. Vetch's theory is correct and someone is tailing us around."

"I had a thought on that," Fergus said, and meaningfully glanced at Marche, who rolled her eyes back at him and gave him the middle finger.

"You may speak plainly," Belos said.

"Well, as I said, whoever bugged *Sidewinder* must not have gotten what it wanted out of it yet," Fergus said. "Meanwhile, you are also running around, looking for something you haven't found either. What if you're both looking for the same thing, and they're just hedging their bets in case you get there first?"

Belos stood up, rather suddenly, and tightened his fists. "Why, though? Why would anyone other than *me* care about the fate of my twin?"

"I care," Kaybe said, softly. "We were friends too. I'd have signed on with her instead of you, but you make better coffee."

"Ahhhhh," Marche said, quietly, as if some long-standing mystery had been solved. "Of course. *Rattler.* I never could quite believe that the Alliance could have bested her."

"They didn't," Belos said. "I want to know who did and how."

"And that's why he's here?" Marche asked, jacking one thumb over toward Fergus.

"Mr. Vetch has a particular talent for the impossible," Belos said.

"You could have asked me," Marche said. "I'm not too stupid either."

"There is no one, as far as I know, better at what he does than Vetch is," Belos said. "That said, no, you are not at all stupid, Marche, and more than that, I trust *you* completely. The same is not entirely true of Mr. Vetch—sorry, Vetch, you and I both know circumstances will always dictate wariness of one another—and I need your focus on *that*, not chasing down my ghosts."

"What's his real name, then?" Marche demanded. "Give me that, to start."

Belos shrugged. "I don't know. I expect if I did, it would only add to Mr. Vetch's distrust of me."

"Fine," Marche said, and rounded on Vetch. "If you don't trust *us*, why are you here?"

"The challenge, as presented, was deeply compelling," Fergus said. "And I was bored."

"Not to interrupt the party, but we're about to drop out near the Keets," Kaybe said.

"Great," Belos said. He pointed at Vetch, then at Marche. "You two. Work together, and work out a plan. Give me a list of what you need, and if we can pick it up at the Keets, we will. You have one hour."

———

"This is all going to go horribly wrong," Marche said.

"Oh, probably," Fergus said. They were about three levels and a half-dozen airlocks—all but one working—deep into the Stank Palace, and he had been leaving a very obvious trail of food wrappers and, with apologies to Marche, was now emptying the liquid waste reservoir of his suit in a corner of one of the tunnels. In his defense, it added nothing that wasn't already there, just freshened it up by a decade or two. He was also periodically tapping the rock overhead with the end of an old pool cue he'd borrowed off Trinket and affixed a narrow canister of nanochips to; each time he pressed it against the rock, it stuck one tiny chip up in the shadows against the dark rock.

Every system on the Stank Palace was unstable and near failing; the intermittent electronic splutter made good cover for the minute flash of signal each chip would make when something breached its proximity sensors. If one was looking closely, in just the right spot, one could potentially get lucky enough to spot one, but the odds were against it even then, and as Fergus assured Marche, *no one ever remembers to look up.* Especially when there was stuff on the floor already catching your attention, or at least making you mind where you stepped.

And anyway, if everything went as planned, anyone coming up behind them would be in a hurry, and their focus would be on what lay ahead, not above.

Over the decades since the Palace was abandoned, asteroid miners had dug in on the far side of the rock, but according to Marche's information, those few who stayed in residence longer than a week or two at a time tended to avoid the original Palace tunnels and any possible encounters with pirates or scavengers passing through. Tended, maybe, but from the evidence, it wasn't an absolute. That also worked for them.

Trash and worse aside, someone, somewhere long ago, must have loved this place. Enough to get the rock spinning so there was some vague imitation of gravity, to put a hand-painted welcome sign inside the first airlock, even if subsequent visitors had defaced it with a dozen different languages and alphabets' worth of crudity and aggressive pessimism. The tunnels throughout the rock had remnants of drawings done in luminescent paint, deeply amateurish but recognizable, to include buildings with crenellated walls giving way to columns and arches, all of it exactly like what someone who had never been inside a palace might imagine one looked like.

A few sections of wall had stone blocks lovingly drawn in, with an attempt at shading to give them depth; some were also clearly drawn while more drunk, or more bored, than others. One or two seemed to have been done by another hand entirely in a different ink, and Fergus liked the idea that the mysterious original artist of the Palace had had a coconspirator or friend, though of course there was no way of knowing if they ever physically overlapped. He wondered what the Shielders of Cernee, who covered their walls with intricate histories that were regarded as both living records and a means of manifesting reality itself, would make of these. Not much, probably. He also wondered if the Shielders—who he had left deeply annoyed with him—were still drawing pictures of him staying away from Cernee. Baseless superstition or not, so far, it had worked.

He nudged their motorized cart to the left, and it trundled along between the two of them with its cargo of mostly junk-filled boxes and crates. If he were their hypothetical pursuer, he'd scan the shit out of every millimeter of the boxes before opening anything, anticipating the possibility of a trap. Which is why the stuff wasn't the trap, only the lure.

"Ahead," Marche said. The tunnel had steadily widened as other side tunnels connected in, and they walked through a pair of large blast doors with the faded and peeling remnants of a truly ornate paint job into what Fergus immediately dubbed the Throne Room, mostly because of the throne at the far end.

It was carved of stone, and chunks lay littered around it on the floor where it had been blasted with an indeterminate number of tools and weapons, though there were also signs of attempts to patch it back together. Behind the throne, on the wall, a giant crown had been painted, and scrawled across it in red paint—at least, Fergus hoped it was paint—were the words FUCK YOUR IMPERIALIST NOSTALGIA. He felt a lot of empathy with the unknown Palace designer, but the later commenter had a valid point.

Fergus parked the cart and unloaded the crates, setting aside the three with their own supplies inside. Then he stacked the remainder in front of the throne carefully, as if he cared what was inside, so as to not leave any subtle cues that something was off. *You're overthinking this, Fergus,* he told himself.

As he worked, Marche set up a portable power supply and transmitter, just strong enough to reach anyone within shuttle distance of the Palace, but on the old, obsolete frequency that Bas and his twin used to use between themselves. When she was done, she set a fabbed engine part that Fendi had assured them was particular to *Rattler* and *Sidewinder* atop the crates, and placed a small, handwritten note that just said: MISS YOU -BB

"There," Marche said. "That looks convincing."

"As much as possible on short notice, anyway," Fergus said. "Should we check in?"

"On it," she said. She pulled out her handheld. "*Sidewinder*, we're set down here. What's your status?"

"Fendi and Rabbit just finished rigging the bug," Belos said. "Last chance before we leave you to your fates."

"We're good," Marche said.

"Awright," Len said, over the channel. "I'm takin' th' shuttle up back so's ter give you lovebugs some privatsy. Jes' don't forget ter mute yer mics, for the sake of my tender earholes."

Marche glared at Fergus, as if this was all somehow his fault. "Don't look at me," Fergus said. "I'm not much of a smoocher."

Len cackled, then cut his comms. Back on the surface, he'd be pulling the shuttle out of the Stank Palace's decrepit landing hangar to head back to *Sidewinder*.

Ten minutes later, Belos called down. "We're out," he said. "Should be in jump for about two hours, then we'll wait for your signal. If we don't hear from you, we'll be back in ten days and we'll come in shooting. *Sidewinder* out."

When the connection ended, Marche let out a long, grumbly breath. "I'll go secure a campsite for us. You finish chipping the passageways," she said. "I don't want any surprises."

Fergus couldn't argue with that. Carrying his cue stick, he made his way back through the tunnels toward where they came in.

By now they had a good map of the main corridor down to the throne room. Fergus returned to the airlock that led out to the surface dock, and worked his way back toward Marche, checking each branching side passage on the way. He found only empty rooms, one collapsed corridor, and an internal airlock that looked like it hadn't been operational in decades. Some tunnels twisted around to join others that then looped back to the main, but ultimately, there wasn't any way someone coming in the front door could reach the throne room without traversing a significant portion of the main hall. The passages from the back of the throne room eventually had to join up with the miner tunnels and their entrance on the far side of the rock, but they'd have other warnings if trouble came from that direction; asteroid miners— *rockcrappers*, out there—were very much simple fight-or-flight folk and did neither quietly.

Marche was waiting in the throne room for him, sitting atop

one of the staged crates. "Sometimes, I get frustrated with the lack of subtlety the rest of the crew seems to default to," she said, "but I'm grateful to you for demonstrating that too much subtlety is also extremely tedious."

"You're welcome, I think," he said. "We have a camp?"

"Yes," she said. She stood up and he followed her through one of the side entrances and a few forks down until they hit another small storeroom. All their kit was set up there, mostly obscured by leftover mining equipment and debris. She had also unpacked and set up their tent, with its own power and air supply. Short of the entire rock disintegrating around them, it would keep them safe through most minor catastrophes.

Keep one of us safe, anyway, Fergus mused. It would have been a tight fit for two, and Marche had made it clear that she wasn't interested in sharing. And to be fair, he wasn't keen on being asleep in her company, either, since he had even fewer reasons to trust her than vice versa. "I'll take first watch," he volunteered, and she didn't argue.

He was tired but not ready to sleep. And anyway, he missed his cat, for all that the beast had done his best not to let him have a full night's peaceful sleep since the day he'd lured the stray back to his quarters in the ocean substation under Enceladus's ice.

For the first few hours, he checked and rechecked all his detection equipment, including the portable holo-map that displayed a 3-D model of tiny green dots, each one corresponding to a chip tacked to the tunnel roof. He also spent a long time sitting still, eyes closed, listening intently to the sounds—and currents—of the rock around them. He could feel the unevenly spaced, receding line of chips only faintly and for a short distance, more like spots in his vision than any concrete image. The electrical murmur of the rockcrapper encampment was likewise only just on the threshold of his awareness. He wondered how much the bright blaze of their camp behind him washed out other signals, and it was tempting to shut everything down, just for a few moments, to see if his perception outward improved, but not only would that piss off Marche, he was pretty sure when he refused to explain why he did it, she'd gut him and dump him down a hole to see if she could yo-yo him with his own intestines. She had, after all, threatened as much.

Ten days could be a very long time, if no one ever showed up. Not that he'd be eager to have to tell Belos he'd guessed wrong. *But I bet I haven't,* he thought. The question was who would show up, and how quickly; a lot of information would come from just those two answers.

After exhausting all his mulling skills on information he just didn't have yet, instead he thought about all the ways he could escape from *Sidewinder,* if he had to, with a minimum of killing-or-being-killed, and while also getting his cat out safely. There, at least, every single day, he had more of an understanding of the ship and its crew, more opportunities and vulnerabilities and clear dangers. *Mostly the latter,* he thought glumly. Marche, for example, he was learning could move virtually silently, as she was now sneaking up on him, knife in hand but not in a strike position. No doubt she was testing to see if she could get the upper hand on him, which she likely would have if not for the fact that he didn't need eyes or ears to feel the electricity of her body.

He picked up a pebble from the camp floor, tossed it idly in his hand a few times to get a feel for the shape and how their meager spin-grav pulled on it as she crept up slowly behind him, then threw it so it bounced off one their crates and flew over his shoulder. He heard the faint *thup* of it hitting her exosuit.

She swore under her breath, and Fergus smiled before turning. "All's clear," he said.

"Good aim," she said. "What gave me away?"

He felt no need at all to answer that. "My turn to sleep?" he asked instead.

"Yes," she said. "Get it while you can. Six hours."

Fergus ducked into the tent, sealed it, and curled up on the foam pad that was not much, but infinitely more comfortable than rock. He'd barely closed his eyes, thinking about his grass hut on Coralla and missing the night breezes that always stole in through the gaps in the reeds, when Marche was suddenly there, prodding him sharply with her boot.

"I lied," she said. "You got forty-five minutes. Company's arrived."

Chapter 7

They came in cautiously, judging by the slow shift of dots from green to red on the holo-map as they passed into the range of one chip, then on to the next. Fergus had set the chips far enough apart that a single person should only be detected by one at a time, but there were stretches where four dots stayed red. "We're definitely outnumbered," Fergus said.

Beside him, Marche was checking an energy rifle with cold efficiency. "It's not the starting numbers that matter. Count when we're done, if you still care about it then," she said, then frowned at him. "You want to arm up, Vetch? Any day now."

"I don't do guns," Fergus said.

She snorted. "Great. They left me down here with deadweight for backup," she said. "Don't expect any of us to collect your body from here when it's all over."

"You just hold up your end, and I'll take care of mine," Fergus said. He gestured at the holo-map. "Pattern of approach is standard Alliance protocol; they're doing it by the book. You get around behind them and cut off their retreat, and I'll neutralize them when they enter the throne room. Channel six-four-six."

"Oh sure, you'll neutralize them. How, by leaping out and shouting 'Boo!' at them?" she scoffed. "I'll do that, and you can go watch the exit to make sure no reinforcements are coming."

"I'd rather—"

"It wasn't a suggestion, Vetch," she said. "Channel six-four-six, fine. Get moving."

Fergus sighed, and slipped into the tunnels, hoping she didn't get herself killed. *Maybe a little harmlessly humiliated, though,* he thought.

His exosuit was top-of-the-line military-grade, and he had to admit there was a nostalgic thrill at putting it into stealth mode and turning on his night-vision goggles, like old times again. Heading up his loop, he reached the intersection with the main tunnel and paused, listening intently. He couldn't hear the party ahead of him, which spoke to the care they were taking, nor could he hear anyone closer to the airlock entrance beyond the reach of their closest bug, but he didn't need to; he could feel someone hovering just this side of the airlock. It wasn't signal leaking from their suit that gave them away—whatever it was, it was as good as his own, and he could barely feel it—but their very electrically noisy gun. What he wanted was for them to move closer into the tunnel, but they were maintaining their position with annoying diligence.

"They're in the throne room." Marche's voice came over the comms. "Checking out all the gifts we brought. They seem pretty excited."

The guard at the airlock disappeared back inside, and about five minutes later, two more people came out and headed off down the tunnels as the guard took up his station again. "Two more coming your way," Fergus told Marche, though they'd show up on her display soon enough. "That's gotta be a good portion of the crew. Will check it out and let you know."

"Sure, you do that," Marche answered.

Fergus unsealed the palm of one of his suit gloves and fished another ball bearing out of his pockets, charging it up inside his fist. Crouching down, he leaned on the tunnel wall and forward until he could throw the bearing at full force. It struck the man in the knee, and Fergus could just hear the heavily muffled curse from the man as his suit shorted out. Fergus was already back on his feet and running; if it was anything like his own suit, he had four seconds until it rebooted and the guard could call for help.

The man was distracted enough not to see him coming in the dark until the last moment, and before he could bring his weapon fully up, Fergus tackled him hard to the floor and zapped him again.

As his own suit rebooted too, he yanked open the seals on the man's hood and ripped free the comms module from inside, then picked up the gun and shorted it.

He'd knocked the wind out of the guard, and the man was gasping to get air back in his lungs, his eyes wide in surprise and fear. "You'll be fine. Sorry," he told the guy, then put his palm on the man's forehead and zapped him unconscious.

His own display, when it came back on, showed the two new crew still heading down the tunnel toward Marche, none the wiser. *So far, so good*, he thought.

The guard was about his own height and not much heavier, and his exosuit close enough to his own—generic matte-black was the past, present, and likely future fashion—that in a pinch they were probably not too distinguishable, except for a patch on the man's sleeve with a logo of overlapping white-lined cubes.

Kneeling next to him, Fergus pulled out his knife, flipped it open, and carefully excised the patch from the man's suit without damaging it. Done, he dug the remains of the roll of adhesive he'd used to prime the ceiling sensors out of his other pocket and activated two glue dots before sticking the patch on his own sleeve. Once he was satisfied it wouldn't fall off, he plugged the stolen comm module in beside his own. The module was in audio-encryption mode, which was good news; encryption always added a bit of distortion and buzz, which on top of signal issues inside the rock would help disguise his unfamiliar voice.

As gently as he could, he dragged the still-unconscious-but-breathing-much-better-now guard around the corner out of sight into the side tunnel. He considered following after the other two, then decided Marche could run her own show. Instead, he took a deep breath, another, and then cycled himself through the airlock into the docking bay.

A shorter man, his suit hood down, thickly built and with a neck like a tree trunk, was leaning against the hull of a large shuttle that barely fit in the bay. He turned as Fergus came through the second lock. "Bower?" he asked. "Why the hell aren't you at your watch post?"

Fergus tried to imitate the man's accent; Earth, certainly, probably Pacifica. "My bladder hose came loose and it's leaking all inside my suit," he said.

Treeneck scowled. "You know that could wait."

Fergus pitched his voice higher, as if panicking, and did an odd little hopping jig, pulling at the crotch of his suit. "But it burns!" he squeaked, moving closer.

"You stupid—" Treeneck started to say, and must have just realized he wasn't Bower at the same moment as Fergus got close enough to strike. The man twisted, dodging, then grabbed hold of Fergus's forearm with both hands to throw him.

Fergus tumbled and rolled, coming up facing back toward Treeneck, ready to zap again if the jolt he'd given through the man's grip on his arm had been too short to take the man down, but Treeneck's momentum from the throw had turned into a sideways slump, and he hit the ground, hard, and didn't move.

He took Treeneck's comms unit and gun, too, then climbed into the shuttle. Finding it empty, he locked the door.

Despite the nondescript exterior, the interior was a wholly unmodified, standard Alliance craft. He felt a twinge of anxiety and shoved it down hard; he had known, deep down, that was who their followers were going to end up being. At least right now, he was in control.

Fergus rummaged through the cabinets until he found a

drinking-water dispenser, and filled and drank several bottles before he felt the parchedness of using his Asiig gift finally recede
back to tolerable levels. Then he slipped into the helm seat, plugged
in his confuddler, and sat back, sipping his remaining water more
leisurely as it went to work cracking and infiltrating the shuttle's
systems.

The shuttle belonged to the Alliance cruiser ESS *Paradigm*, on
long-term covert assignment in the Barrens. The details of the
mission weren't in the shuttle's general memory, but Fergus was
fairly certain he already knew the answer and, as long as Marche
didn't go overboard homicidal, knew they'd have people who
could confirm.

Crew manifest was ten. So, Marche had six, he'd taken out
two, which left two aboard *Paradigm* itself, parked just above the
Stank Palace.

Now what? he asked himself.

His suit comms lit up again. "You dead yet, Vetch?" Marche
asked.

"Not yet," he answered. "You?"

"Not yet," she said. "I've got these four secured, and I'm just
waiting on the next party to join us. What's your status?"

"Two down, two left," he said. "You need me to come back
there?"

"*No,*" she snapped, and cut the connection.

Fine, he thought.

One thing he knew all too well about the Alliance—and he
had to assume he'd dealt with them more directly and in person
than Belos's crew had—was that if you wanted information, and
it wasn't possible to sneak or hack it out of them, you needed the
biggest leverage you could get your hands on.

He went back out into the docking bay, grabbed Treeneck—
Lester the pilot, if he had understood the crew manifest correctly—
under the armpits and hauled him on board the shuttle. He

dumped the pilot in the back, found the typical assortment of police-soldier paraphernalia in a locker, and used two pairs of hand-binders to cuff the man by wrist and ankle to the seat supports.

Fergus returned to the helm, powered up the shuttle, and as soon as the bay doors opened, exited the Palace for space.

"Shuttle, report," a stern, baritone voice immediately blared out of the shuttle console.

"Bower here, Captain. I've got a medical emergency and I'm returning to ship," Fergus replied. "Lester's hurt."

"What?" the voice said. "He was supposed to stay on the shuttle until the team reported back."

"He came out to empty his suit bladder and fell in a hole," Fergus said. "The scream—"

"When did you learn to fly?"

"I've done some reading up," Fergus said. *This was a really bad idea,* he thought. *Would the Alliance captain shoot at his own shuttle?* "Lester is giving me instructions. It's tricky, though, so I'm going to disconnect until I can land."

"You—" the voice started to say, but Fergus closed the connection.

A rusty-looking freighter with a suspiciously cruiser-like profile was directly ahead, and a bright rectangle of light was the shuttle bay opening.

"Here goes the worst idea I've had in three and a half years," he said, and eased the shuttle in.

One armed crewperson was waiting inside, suited up. Fergus set the shuttle down as if nothing was amiss, and locked it down as the bay doors closed again behind him. As soon as the bay was pressurized, the shuttle door opened from the outside, and the crewperson stood just far enough to be out of reach, gun trained directly at the door. "Sorry, Bower, just being careful," she said. "Come on out."

Fergus climbed out, hands up. Lucky him that the manifest

he'd hacked had only listed one woman on the crew. "What the hell, Cardenas?" he asked.

She gestured him to move aside and kept her gun still pointing at the empty door. "Anyone else on board?"

"Just Lester," Fergus said. "He needs help."

"Stay here," she said, and went aboard. Fergus waited until she was through the doorway then followed. "Hey! Why is—" she started to shout, as Fergus slapped a hand on her back and took her down, too, adding her to the chain of restraints already on Lester.

He closed and sealed the shuttle door, then used his confuddler to override and change all the access codes. Just in time, as he saw the attempt to remotely shut down oxygen on board come in, hit the modified system, and get rejected.

"Nice play," the captain's voice came over the shuttle speaker. "Clearly, you're not some uppity rockcrapper, so you must be Belos himself."

Fergus laughed. "Not a bad guess, but no. An interested third party, only. That said, I have all your crew, Captain Todd."

"If you've hurt any—"

"I haven't, no," Fergus said. "Nor do I particularly want to, unless I'm forced to defend myself. My current associates may be another matter, being more enthusiastic about violence than I am."

"What do you want?"

"I'd very much like to have a very frank and open Q&A session with you about everything you know about the Belos twins," Fergus said. "I mean, it does seem to be a topic you're interested in, so why not share?"

"I would consider answering a few questions, for guarantees about my crew," the captain said.

"Consider away," Fergus said. "I'll call you back in ten. And I just assume I don't need to actually waste both our time with ultimatums or unsubtle speculation about what would happen if I fired off the shuttle's main guns inside your bay, so just consider whatever most effective deterrent to trying something I wouldn't approve of hereby threatened. Okay?"

"Got it," the captain snarled, and disconnected.

Fergus tapped back on his comm with Marche. "Hey," he said, "you got your end of things under control?"

"Of course," Marche replied. "I'm sitting on my six, waiting to hear from your sorry ass. *Sidewinder* is on its way back, about an hour and a half now."

"Good," Fergus said.

"Do you have things handled on your end? You've still got the door secured? None of these"—there was a muffled grunt of pain, as if Marche had just kicked someone—"are giving me info yet, even though I've asked nicely, and I want to catch my breath before I start cutting on any of them."

"They're from the Alliance ship *Paradigm*, currently right outside the Palace and disguised as an old cargo ship. Ten crew total," Fergus said.

"Then I've got more than half of them already. You're slacking," Marche said. "How many more are left?"

"Just the captain," Fergus said. "We've been having a discussion about the situation, and he's thinking."

"Figuring out how to turn the advantage, more likely," Marche said. "It would have been better to keep the element of surprise; he still has a whole-ass cruiser he can use to mess with us. And where are you? Your signal is weak."

"Sitting in the belly of that whole-ass cruiser, with their own shuttle guns pointed right at all the tender bits," Fergus said.

Marche gave a short, surprised laugh. "Okay, I retract my earlier statement: you're clearly not completely slacking," she said. "Don't get too comfortable, though. These assholes have been banging around the Barrens for long enough that they won't be too timid about fighting back, even if it means breaking their own rules."

"Their rules are really only meant for everyone else, anyway," Fergus said, more bitterly than he intended. "Call me back if anything changes."

Now I just have to find a way to kill an hour and a half, he thought, and cracked his knuckles in anticipation.

———

He caught and disabled two maintenance drones trying to interfere with the shuttle, had one more noncommittal but definitely hostile conversation with *Paradigm*'s captain, before *Sidewinder* appeared in the distance and closed quickly, poised directly in front of *Paradigm*'s bridge, armed and dangerous and inescapable.

After getting assurances from both Fergus and Belos that his crew was mostly unharmed—one had a good concussion and another had been shot in the knee—Captain Todd agreed to be escorted down to the surface for a conversation and return of prisoners.

Todd boarded Fergus's captured shuttle and sat opposite him, out of reach, hands up. Fergus hadn't found any weapons on him and was confident that he hadn't missed any unless they were very small and completely powered down.

"Thank you for your cooperation, Captain," Fergus said. He backed the shuttle out of the bay and headed back down the short distance to the Palace.

"It's awkward talking to a blank face shield," Todd said. "My hood is down; I won't try anything with the atmo. You can lower your own."

"I'm shockingly ugly," Fergus said. "Born that way, I'm afraid."

The captain shrugged as best he could without lowering his hands. He didn't seem particularly surprised that ploy hadn't worked, and later, when he got his shuttle back, he'd probably be equally unsurprised to find Fergus had wiped any and all biometric data and interior recordings made since the shuttle first landed down below.

As a show of good faith, Fergus had let him drag Lester and Cardenas out into *Paradigm*'s bay before they'd left, though Fergus had insisted they remain zip-tied together and to a post, to limit any trouble they could make. He hoped that was enough to keep the captain—and thus the other captain, who was now waiting impatiently for them in the throne room—on their own best behavior.

Len met them on the far side of the airlock and escorted them in. Todd looked around a bit too much for Fergus's liking, as if memorizing every resource or potential opportunity for later. He'd have done the same thing in the man's place, which was precisely why he hated it. From the way Len walked a few paces behind them, hands fidgeting as if curling around an invisible knife, Len disapproved of the attention too.

Whatever *Paradigm*'s captain had hoped to find, they reached the throne room without incident. Bas was sitting on the throne, all in black, his brocade vest open, showing a muscled chest covered in scars; with his beard and long hair and sharp, dark eyes, he lacked only a crown—or horns—to look the part of some evil demon king. Belos's near-mythical reputation was, it seemed, as cleverly crafted an impression as everything else the man did.

Marche stood beside him, and the two Alliance crew who'd been hurt during capture were on the floor at their feet. One was sitting cross-legged, hands bound behind him, knee wrapped tightly with a rough cloth bandage already soaked in blood. The other was slumped back against the throne itself, his eyes focusing and unfocusing, hand against his head.

"Where's the rest of my crew?" Todd demanded.

"Safe, elsewhere in the tunnels," Belos said. "Don't want to tempt you toward misfortune by keeping all my eggs in one basket right in front of you."

Todd gritted his teeth. "How do I know they're okay?"

"These two can verify we left them only about ten minutes ago, alive and well if unhappy," Belos said. "Since then? You have only my word."

"And what's that worth?" Todd asked.

"How long have you been tailing me, dogging my every movement, talking to anyone who'd talk back to you? If you don't already know the answer to that question, I don't know what to say," Belos said.

Todd's scowl deepened, but he didn't push the point. "What do you want?"

"I want to know everything," Belos said. "First, though, I want to know why you've been following me."

"You're a dangerous outlaw, a longtime threat to peace and order in the Barrens. Of course the Alliance would send someone after you to apprehend you," Todd said.

Belos gave the slightest gesture, and the injured crewmember with the shot knee suddenly cried out. Fergus had hardly seen Len move, but the fidgety fingers were already putting away a blade. "I don't like lies, Captain," Belos said. "Assume I already know enough to catch any others."

"We've been following you for a while," Todd said, carefully.

"Yes. And yet, you've never seemed to catch up to me. Why's that?"

"Because our orders were just to watch," Todd said.

"Why?"

When Todd didn't immediately answer, Len coughed meaningfully behind him. "We were hoping you'd lead us to something else," Todd answered, grudgingly.

"And that is?" Belos asked.

"Your sister, of course, and whatever happened to her," Todd said. "I'd have thought you were bright enough to have figured that out on your own."

Len grabbed the much-larger man by the neck and drove him to the ground, his blade against his cheek, right below his eye. "Care, care, Earth man," Len said. "T'aint too bright yerself, t' be flappin' yer lips that way at us."

Bas leaned forward, his expression one more of entertainment than offense. "It's interesting, isn't it," he said, "that your oh-so-upright and trustworthy Alliance told everyone that you'd killed her. Are you saying that's untrue?"

"It was a *strategic announcement*," Todd said, grimacing in distaste. "Or so our Public Relations Office informed us."

"I'm not clear on why, though," Belos said. "Not why the Alliance would take credit for something it didn't in fact achieve, to stop looking like incompetent buffoons, mind you, but why all these years you're still chasing her ghost, when I've been right here, an active threat, and you know you've got the jump on me. It makes me think there's something you know that I don't. Understand me, I will soak this entire rock in the blood of your crew, one by one, until I am satisfied that you've enlightened me."

"Jes' say so when, an' I'll get a start," Len murmured, not taking his eyes off Todd.

"It's not your sister we wanted," Todd said. "It's what she took with her. Can you get the fuck off me now, please?"

Len *tsk*ed and stood up, though he kept the knife out.

"*Rattler*'s holds were virtually empty when we last parted, and she never made it to the ice freighter she'd been planning to go after, because of your people," Belos said. He stood up, looming over the room from the throne dais. "What could you possibly think she *had*?"

"Three Alliance ships were in pursuit. They disappeared after her. *With* her. And as much as you want to know what happened to your sister, we want to know what happened to them. Three crews, eighty-two people. *Good* people, just gone, as completely without a trace as *Rattler*," Todd said. "We've been searching all this time, and if there were even so much as a single rivet left of any of our ships floating in the Barrens, we'd have found it by now. We aren't out here for vengeance; we're out here looking to bury our dead."

Belos stepped down and gestured to Marche. "We need to talk," he said, and the two of them left the throne room.

Len made a big show of pretending to yawn. "Talkin' again, an' still no stabbin'," he lamented. He pointed at Todd with his knife. "You can go sit with yer crewies, dokey?"

Todd did so and, keeping his voice low, checked in on their condition. Fergus did his best not to eavesdrop and instead stood there and listened to the room, to the rock, to the little bright pockets and faint lines of electricity all around them, unchanged. It was comforting to let his weird new sense take it all in, assimilate it into all the feedback coming from his other senses. He could feel Belos and Marche returning before he heard them approach.

"Here's what I offer and what I want," Belos said, without preamble. "I want all the data you have on your own search, for *Rattler* or for your ships, everywhere you've gone, every clue you've found, every bit of detail there is. And in return, if I find any trace of your ships, I will get that information back to you. Are we agreed?"

Todd stood. "You're going to let us go, as you swore?"

"Our resourceful Mr. Vetch here is going to go back to your ship with you and get a download of the data I require. I assure you he won't take anything unrelated to the matter at hand, but also, if you are contemplating a double cross, know that I ultimately don't need him or any of your crew alive to get what I want."

Todd shot Fergus a look, as if appraising his loyalty in the face of that admission.

"It's true, I'm expendable," Fergus said, and shrugged. "Doesn't mean I won't fight back if you try to mess with me, and so far, I've only been *playing*."

Belos gave a half-smile. "As he said. You don't want to see him angry. When he has the data, he'll bring the shuttle back here and your crew can go back to your ship, and we will leave you be. But if you cross me, try to follow us, or you get in my way again, I will make certain no one finds so much as a single molecule of *Paradigm* to spill tears over."

Todd nodded. "If you keep your word, agreed. But I'll tell you honestly we haven't found any new leads in a long time; when you see there's no recent data, it's not because I held back; it's because there *is* none."

"Thank you for your candor," Belos said, and clasped his hands behind his back. "Vetch, go get me that data."

———

Belos, Marche, Len, and Fergus took their own shuttle back up to *Sidewinder* as soon as Fergus had returned with a copy of *Paradigm*'s records. The archived search data came from four previous ships assigned to Project Gemini, the rather fitting, if overly officious, name of the operation to tail one Belos twin in hopes of being led to the other.

Once onboard, Kaybe wasted no time getting them underway, and the Stank Palace and *Paradigm* faded to pale dots behind them before falling out of sight entirely. "How long do you need to look at that data?" Belos asked Fergus.

"A few hours, at least to get a sense of what's there," Fergus said. "More after that, to understand the details, but I won't know until I get into it."

"Take a break first, sleep, whatever you need, but make it as short as you are able. I want you to work with Marche," Belos said. "I don't know how long it'll take Captain Todd to call in backup and get back on our tail."

"Oh, I think we'll have a decent lead before that happens," Fergus said.

"What did you do?" Marche asked, from the shuttle-bay vestibule where she was hanging up and checking over her exosuit.

"I left a virus in the shuttle's computer," Fergus said. "Soon as they dock and connect it up to *Paradigm*'s systems, they're going to be occupied for a while."

"What did you do?" Belos was the one to ask, this time. "I did give my word."

"Nothing harmful," Fergus said. "I left them a friendly puzzle."

Marche gave a groan of exasperation. "I'm tired, and I feel grubby, and I'd very much like a shower. Don't make me hurt you to speed this conversation up. What puzzle?"

"Name ten monsters from mid-twentieth-century Earth Japanese cinema," Fergus said. "Seven right answers, they get comms back. Eight, engines, and at ten they get navigation back and the puzzle deletes itself. They can guess wrong as many times as it takes."

Belos blinked, and laughed. "I can see why you're a man with a lot of very committed enemies. Well done, Vetch."

". . . Chupacabra?" Marche asked.

"Nope," Fergus answered.

"Capybara?"

"Definitely no."

Marche glared. "It's a stupid puzzle, anyway. I'll see you in the conference room in three hours, and you damned well better have fresh coffee waiting. Chinchilla?"

"No."

She stomped out, one arm and the rude gesture of her hand the last to pass out of sight.

Chapter 8

Fergus cleaned up, caught five and a half hours of much-needed sleep, then took his handpad and *Paradigm*'s data down to the small lounge and lay on the couch, pad propped up on his stomach and connected to the holo-map of the Barrens currently rotating slowly over the conference table. Mister Feefs, having given up the third time he tried and failed to successfully establish a beachhead between Fergus and screen, was sulking between his knees, kneading his pant leg, and occasionally testing for attention by sticking a few sharp claws through into Fergus's skin.

Marche came in and sat on the edge of the table, watching the map as it spun and Fergus slowly uploaded more points of data to it. "Without a weapon, and you still took on that cruiser," she said. "How?"

"Element of surprise, mostly," Fergus said. "When that failed, I annoyed them into submission. It's my special gift." He glanced past the screen quickly and caught just a hint of a smile from Marche.

"What have we got?" she asked, waving at the map.

"Todd didn't lie, though he wasn't a hundred percent forthcoming," Fergus said. "There were four Alliance ships in pursuit of *Rattler* at the time she vanished: two small cruisers, *Silver Mist* and *Fire Island*, who picked her up and fell in behind her as she left the Keets, and the larger ship, *Stiletto*, which was the command ship of the trio and was waiting past there. Fourth was *Tango*, which was disguised as the ice freighter out of Beserai that she was after."

"It was a trap from the get-go," Marche said. "Someone at the Keets set her up?"

"Yep to the first, and nope to the second," Fergus answered, "The tip about the ice freighter was passed on at Ijikijolo by an unnamed informant there who was getting a bounty for anyone the Alliance captured or killed, and who they'd been feeding targets to for years."

"None of the regulars at Ijikijolo would sell any of the rest of us out, not to the Alliance," Marche said.

"But someone did, at least up until the trap for *Rattler* went so horribly wrong," Fergus said. "The Alliance didn't know if their contact had been compromised, and couldn't risk continuing the association."

"Is there a name for this informant?" Belos asked from the doorway.

"No," Fergus said. "Nor any identifying information. It wasn't something Todd and crew needed to know. You don't have any idea where the tip came from?"

"No. It was someone on Bel's crew who got it, not me. I didn't ask, because she was just as capable of vetting a source as I was."

"But it had to have been someone who came into regular contact with crews coming in, and been trusted. A vendor, maybe? What shops were there, twelve years ago?"

Belos rubbed the bearded side of his chin. "I'd have to think about that," he said. "It was a long time ago. Jia, of course, and a couple of others I'm sure about. When we're out of jump, I can drop a line to Ratte and ask her. The Ratteskiller's been there for at least two standard decades, and she knows everyone."

"Are you certain it wasn't her?" Fergus asked.

Belos's face darkened. "I trust her," he said.

"And so would have your sister," Fergus pointed out. "I'm not saying it's her, but . . . can you be sure? Everyone goes to the bar, eventually."

"Keep digging for more info on the source," Belos said. "I won't entertain that line of thinking until every other one has been exhausted. What else do we have?"

"I collated the signal data from *Silver Mist* and *Fire Island*, which were the first two Alliance ships on *Rattler*'s tail," Fergus said. He tapped his screen, and the map lit up with two red dots. "This is where they were, prior to *Rattler*'s arrival. Notice they're positioned in the umbra of the Keets, where anyone coming from the direction of Ijikijolo wouldn't see them. They got into this position less than an hour before *Rattler* dropped out of passive jump."

"So, they knew someone was coming," Belos said.

"Yes. They stayed out of sight until *Rattler* left again, about six hours later. She left in your usual evasive pattern, and you can see them react, trying to keep the rock between them." He played that through on high speed: the arrival, in the form of a blue dot, and its departure and the movement of the red. When the blue dot vanished, they moved after it. Those dots then also vanished, as expected; there was no useful navigation locality data that could be determined in jump.

"Wait a second," Marche said. "If this is the data from the Alliance ships, and they were behind the Keets to hide from *Rattler*'s sensors, wouldn't they equally have been blocked?"

"Yes," Fergus said. "They must have had a spotter somewhere on the surface feeding this data to them, or more likely a backdoor into the Keets shipping-traffic management system. Since *Rattler* would not have been in range of any of them when she jumped, and they were too far away to send a tracer after her, they must already have known which way she would go to catch up with her later."

Fergus tapped again, and two more red dots appeared on the far edge of the map. "This is the disguised ice freighter and the heavy cruiser *Stiletto*, waiting for *Rattler* to arrive. But she never did. Here, the light cruisers *Fire Island* and *Silver Mist* arrive, and all three jump back along the path to the Keets, trying to find where *Rattler* went," he said. "Watch them pop in and out, on separate tracks, back and forth along the path. This info was aggregated by *Tango*, which was still hanging out near the edge, and receiving reports from all three cruisers. The lag, though, is about forty-one minutes.

"Here, we see the red dot that represents *Fire Island* pop out and stop. The beginning of a message comes through from them but is cut off almost immediately. When *Silver Mist* appears over here, they pick up the message fragment and immediately jump again, to *Fire Island*'s last known position, as does *Stiletto*. Position data is still coming back to *Tango*, but no more messages come through."

"So, *Rattler* spotted *Fire Island* and jammed their signal, just as they started to send for backup," Belos said. "And probably they blocked *Rattler* in turn so she couldn't call for help either."

"Seems likely," Fergus said. "*Fire Island* and *Silver Mist* take off together in this direction, and when *Stiletto* arrives in that sector, she does the same." A third red dot appeared where the other two had been on the map and headed after them, closing the distance, and then suddenly all three dots vanished.

"What happened? They all jumped again?" Marche asked.

"That was when *Tango* stopped receiving any data at all," Fergus said. "Something happened, anywhere up to forty-one minutes earlier. *Tango* sends out a call for help and heads to that area, but they're slow. They're designed to be bait, not for pursuit. By the time *Tango* gets there, there is no sign of any of the three Alliance ships, nor *Rattler* herself. There is no debris, nothing indicative of combat, and no trace whatsoever. And there's nothing in that area. No planets, no stars, nothing. If any of the ships had taken a passive jump, they would have had to come out somewhere, but none of them were ever seen again. Rather like the

Bermuda Triangle back on Earth, except I think I know the solution to this puzzle."

Belos nods, slowly, thoughtfully. *He got it too,* Fergus thought.

"What?" Marche asked.

"Is there one?" Fergus asked.

"Yes," Belos said.

"One *what*?" Marche asked again, glaring.

"Active jump point," Fergus said.

"Another active jump point?" Marche asked. "I'm starting to think the Barrens were poorly named, after all. And how dangerous is this one?"

"I'd have put it firmly in the category of certain death," Belos said. "Unstable as all hell, and even just trying to open it is almost impossible. The one ship I know of that survived an attempt to take it had its jump stabilizers ripped off during massive fluctuations within seconds of jumping, and just barely managed to drop out into realspace. Half the crew died, the ship was so damaged it never flew again, and the captain retired to Tanduou and swore to never set foot off a solid surface again. You'd have to be truly desperate—"

"Like if you have two Alliance cruisers on your tail and a third coming in, and there's no other way out?" Fergus interjected. "I mean, the official policy was to bring prisoners in alive, but you and your sister had made a mockery of the Alliance more than a few times over the years."

"Yes. Then maybe, just maybe, you'd try your luck. Even if you die, at least they didn't get you," Belos said. "You could fly right through that point in space a hundred times and never think to look for a jump point there, where it should be impossible. But if they saw *Rattler* jump and went after her, then either they ended up somewhere they can't get back from, or the Drift tore them all up into fine particles and scattered them across this half of the galaxy. That would explain why we've never found a trace."

"What do we do now?" Marche asked.

"Call a meeting. All crew," Belos said. "And plot a course for Vetch's triangle."

———

"We're going *where*?! I'm out," Yolo said.

"The fuck you mean, you're out?" Trinket asked, leaning away from him and staring as if he'd just unexpectedly morphed into something slimy and larval.

"I mean, I don't want to die, not for nothing," Yolo said. "One thing to die in a fight, but get grinded-up in the Ghostdrift like nothin' more than a bit of gristle? No thanks."

"We're partners. I'd go back for you, if you were lost," Trinket said. "Wouldn't you do the same for me?"

"Not for such a long shot, when it was for sure you were already dead anyway," Yolo said. "Sorry."

Rabbit sighed, gripping the table edge as if bracing himself. "Yolo ain't whole wrong," he said. "Been a long, long time, and no sign of nothin' of the *Rattler*. I'd say, if I were clear-eyeing it, it's a bad deal."

"So, you're out, too?" Kaybe asked.

"Not sayin' that," Rabbit said. "Said if I was clear-eyed, but I'd also have to be froze-hearted. Wouldn't walk from my ship an' my captain, even if you pointed us right at hell. Couldn't stand not to know how it ends, 'f nothing else."

"What he said," Fendi added.

"Same," Marche said, "not least because I think the Alliance is gonna be hot for us for a long while, and this gets us out of their reach for a while. Or longer."

Belos turned to Kaybe, who hadn't spoken yet. "What?" Kaybe asked, looking offended. "Don't even, Bas. You know where I stand."

Len had been sitting there, one bony-fingered hand splayed

out on the tabletop, and rhythmically stabbing his knife back and forth between his fingers. "An' me, in to the end."

"Ain't you gonna ask Mr. Vetch, here?" Yolo asked. "He just got rescued, and he don't really know us. Might be attached to livin' a bit longer."

"I like adventures," Fergus said. "And I sat around doing very little of it for too long." That was true, whether one meant his real beach on Coralla or his fictional captivity at the hands of Aurora Enclave.

"Just you, then, Yolo," Belos said.

"Come on, bro," Trinket said. "Don't abandon me."

"Come with me, then," Yolo said. "And you, Vetch. Lots of other adventures out there better'n throwing your life away on this bullshit. You're scrawny and weird but good in a fight. Could be the three of us, a team."

"I could do ya matchin' team scars," Len said, flipping his knife around before resuming his pattern.

"No," Belos said. "Everyone decides on their own this time. This is not about loyalty. This is about family." He stood up, and cracked his knuckles. "Kaybe, let me know when we're in reach of the Keets, and everyone can decide for sure what they want then. In the meantime, I need some quiet."

He left the conference room. Everyone exchanged uneasy glances, except Trinket, who was staring at Yolo, and Yolo, who was staring at the table. Fergus stood up next. "I didn't get a lot of sleep," he said. "Wouldn't want to throw my life away while not awake enough to enjoy it."

Belos was waiting for him in his cabin, sitting on the end of his bunk, Mr. Feefs accepting, tentatively, scratches on his head. "I'm serious about 'everyone decides,'" Belos said. "That includes you. You've gotten me closer to finding out what happened to my sister in a handful of days than I did in years. I took a gamble on you, one last long shot, and I already got far more back than I expected—no offense, but I thought when you couldn't do it, with your reputation, maybe I'd finally be able to accept that it was impossible and let it go."

Fergus turned the lights up to full and held out one of his hands, palm up. "Ever look closely at me?" he asked. "In good light?"

Belos took his hand, peered at it, then turned it over, and examined his arm. "What are all those tiny lines everywhere?" he asked.

Suddenly self-conscious, Fergus pulled his hand away. "Scars. That's the universe's mark on me, reminding me it owns me," he said. "Don't ask how it happened, but know that I've survived more impossible things than I ever should have, and a few I didn't really want to."

"Those scars . . ."

"My whole body. Even my tongue." He stuck it out for a moment. "Once—and I was very drunk, before you ask—I cut my arm, and they were inside, too. It took me a long time to get over that."

"So, you want out? You've earned it," Belos said.

"No, that's the thing. I'm terrified, all the time, of what comes next, and that it'll catch me unaware," Fergus said. "When Qai dragged me off as ransom to you, it felt like I'd been waiting for that moment every hour, every day, no matter how much I tried to be at peace. It was almost a relief. I mean, definitely also a huge fucking annoyance, but at least I knew then what was next? And that I was walking toward it, rather than it sneaking up behind me. And here's the next-next thing: attempting to jump through an unstable, deadly dangerous wormhole in search, once again, of the impossible. I'd much rather die doing that than sit around on a barstool, watching Yolo try to fistfight his own face."

"Yolo is not the brightest. What he wants is to have a chance to shoot at, kick, or hit something, and for prizes to come out."

"Pirating as substitute piñata?" Fergus asked.

Belos gave a short bark of laughter. "I haven't thought about piñatas since we were kids, before everything in our town went to shit," he said. He stared off into space for a moment, remembering. "Our uncle made us one, out of old paper and ribbon, for our tenth birthday. Of course, you couldn't get candy then, either, so our aunt baked muffins instead, and they ended up smashed all over the ground. Didn't stop us from eating what pieces we could find, and never mind the dirt. Funny to think how poor we were, and yet I've never felt richer. I guess you're coming with us, then?"

"Yeah, might as well," Fergus said. "I got nothing better to do, anyway."

"Fine." Belos displaced the cat gently and stood up. "I'll let Yolo know he's on his own. Maybe he'll go back to Ijikijolo and beg Ratte for his old bouncer job back. If he's smart, anyway. Oh, and Vetch?"

"Yeah?" Fergus asked.

"Thanks for understanding, and seeing it through. You didn't have to."

"No worries, Captain. Now get out," Fergus said. "I need my beauty sleep."

———

They dropped out of passive jump a fair distance from the Keets; having just deeply inconvenienced an Alliance cruiser, Belos wanted to play it safer than usual, and Marche agreed that shaking up their old habits was probably going to be a necessity for their survival in the future.

Assuming they survived the present.

As soon as they were in normal space, Kaybe hit the alarm. "Two Alliance ships," he announced over the ship comms, and everyone scrambled for their stations, except Fergus, who still didn't really have one, so he headed to the bridge.

"Minute and a half until I'm in position to jump out again,"

Kaybe said from the helm. "Assuming no one gets in our way, which they certainly seem to be trying to do. They were waiting for us. We need everyone on guns who can be and safety tethers locked. Captain, I need to know where we're going."

"To *Rattler*'s last known location," Belos said. "If the Alliance knew we were heading here, we have to assume they know where we're going next. If we don't get there first, we'll never get our chance."

"You said you'd drop me off," Yolo said from the doorway.

Belos glared over his shoulder. "The situation has changed," he said. "As perhaps you can see for yourself."

"I need people on *guns*," Kaybe growled.

Bas glanced at Fergus. "Len is on starboard guns with Fendi, Rabbit and Trinks on port. Get in Len's station there on forward weapons and buckle the fuck up."

Fergus did as he was told. He powered up the display on Len's weaponry console and quickly ran through the specs and available options. The amount of firepower on *Sidewinder*, for its size, was egregious overkill, and in the moment, he was grateful for all of it. The only tricky part would be using the forward guns in such a way that he didn't kill anyone but didn't give them the chance to kill or follow them, either.

"Bas . . ." Yolo started, and at Belos's glare, amended that hastily. "Captain. This is nuts. We're all going to die, for *nothing*, when we could just live like we have been. It's a good life. Jump somewhere else."

"Yolo, please leave my bridge," Kaybe said. "Jumping in twenty . . ."

"But—"

Belos stood up and punched Yolo so hard, the man bounced off the metal floor when he collided with it, just as the whole ship shook. "We're hit," Kaybe said. "I don't got time to look where it came from."

"I got it," Fergus said. One of the two Alliance cruisers was cutting across in front of them, firing madly in hopes of hitting again or at least forcing them to change course and abort their jump run. They were flying at an angle, trying to keep their engines out of direct line of fire, but Fergus wasn't after them. Once he had his shot locked in, he squeezed the handle of the firing stick and watched with satisfaction the brief glint of metal and ship parts spraying out from behind the ship.

"Target that wide and you barely graze it?" Kaybe asked.

"Hit exactly what I was aiming for," Fergus said. "Alliance ships have a sensor behind the dorsal fin tied into navigation but also tied into all their positioning thrusters as a safety precaution."

"They can't turn," Belos said. He had taken his seat again and clipped in, leaving Yolo lying out cold on the floor, slowly sliding sideways as Kaybe banked hard to clear the crippled ship.

"Or jump," Fergus said. "Safety isn't going to let them do anything other than brake, which they're gonna want to do before they crash into the Keets." He hoped they were smart enough to do that before it was too late, especially after he took the effort to disable instead of kill.

"Still, a hull puncture followed by a little exploding decompression would have been nice," Kaybe said. "Second ship is behind us. I can't jump until it's clear, 'cause I don't want to drag it with us."

In both active and passive jump, if two objects entered close enough to each other, strange things happened. With passive, that usually meant collision and heavy damage that would dump them both out into normal space again, which could be anything from a very bad bump to the entire universe swatting you like the tiny, tiny flea you were. Active jump, you'd be lucky if you got either of those two options, as opposed to the molecules of one ship trying to occupy the same space as the other and working things out in an atom-by-atom negotiation, or getting pitched out of the center of the jump conduit into the fractal chaos of the edges—the Drift—and being subatomically redistributed across thousands of light-years.

Yolo isn't wrong to be afraid of the Drift, Fergus thought. If you had to pick one thing to give you pause, that was an excellent choice.

The remaining Alliance cruiser was doing its best to stay out of Fergus's sights, though clearly operating on guesswork; it wobbled in and out of the zone where Fergus could take a shot at it, waiting for it to stay in shot long enough to get a lock and, hopefully, a nonlethal one. He was just about to consider he might not get that option when there was a bright flash.

"Rabbit one, the Space-Po none," Rabbit's voice came over the comms. On Fergus's display, the entire front end of the ship had been blown apart, and while he tried very hard not to look for them, he was pretty sure he saw a few bodies go flying off with the wreckage.

"Jumping now," Kaybe declared, and *Sidewinder* rattled and shook as it leapt past lightspeed.

Belos got up when the ship had steadied, and poked Yolo with his boot toe. The man groaned. "Vetch," he said. "Newbie rules. You're on trash duty. Get this man off my bridge and down to Medical."

———

"Vetch's Triangle," as the crew had taken to referring to it, was still half a day's travel away, and as stoic as Belos himself seemed about what lay ahead, the tension on the ship kept creeping upward. Fergus gave up trying to find calm in his cabin—he felt restless, half anticipation and half something else he didn't want to put a name to—and relocated to the lounge. There, he went through the ritual of brewing Corallan tea, breathing in the steam and finding his center. His core was still full of his electrical gift, more astir than it had been in a while, and there was comfort in wrapping his consciousness around it and lulling it back into a place of rest, wholly a part of his intentional being again.

With his eyes closed and senses extended, he could feel *Sidewinder* around him, and the strange energies of their movement. Within, Trinket visiting a concussed Yolo down in medical, Rabbit in the armory being a bit too diligent about inspecting and cleaning everything, Fendi and Kaybe asleep, Belos at the helm, and Marche making another attempt to sneak up on him without him noticing.

He drew out the packet of leaves—some of the last, as it happened. It was a shame to waste them, but sometimes, you had to bend to necessity. He balanced them there, on the end of his wooden spoon, as if still inhaling their essence, until with one fast flick of the wrist he managed to nail Marche with the sodden clump right in the forehead.

"You shit-whelped, crusty-ass bag of soggy old dicks, Vetch," she swore. "How the fuck did you hear me?"

"You whistle just a little bit when you breathe," Fergus lied.

"I do not!" she snapped.

Fergus shrugged and took a long sip of scalding tea. Still tasted terrible, but he didn't mind; arguably, it was why he drank it. Marche sat down on one of the couches, and he could hear her breathing carefully, quietly, listening, and he chuckled. "Fuck you," she said.

Marche didn't often swear, so he knew the anticipation was getting to her, too.

Trinket left Yolo where he was tethered to the med unit and came up to the lounge. She sat across from Marche. "Tea?" Fergus asked, and offered her the cup.

"Is it sweet?" she asked.

"Hell, no," Fergus said. "Sorta nasty, actually."

"Good," she said, and took the cup and downed it in a single gulp. She handed him the teacup back, grimacing. "Ooof, that's awful. That Corallan?"

"Yes," Fergus said, surprised, and wondering if he'd given some information away he may not have wanted to.

"Fadsji tea's better," Marche said.

"Everyone's tea is better," Fergus said. "That's not the point."

"Well, it's what I needed, I guess. Thanks," Trinket said.

"You're welcome," Fergus said.

"Where did you get Corallan tea on Aurora Enclave?" Marche asked, as if she didn't already know he was nowhere near there.

"Came in from a raid. No one else wanted it, obviously," Fergus said. "Are you whistling again?"

"Fuck you," Marche said again.

"So," Trinket said. "Yolo says we're all going to die. I trust the captain, but . . . I don't really understand where we're going, and I didn't want to say so in front of everybody."

"You understand the difference between active and passive jump?" Fergus asked.

"Active is a hell of a lot faster, but passive you can go anywhere to anywhere," Trinket said.

"Pretty much right in terms of effect," Fergus said. "But how they work is very different, most of which you don't need to know, and I'm not going to explain the math because I don't understand the math either. We got passive-jump tech from the Veirakans at first contact at Io, and that lets you go faster than light by making microfolds in space to make it shorter. Except you're not actually folding space but more manifesting yourself across space as if it were folded and . . . Yeah. That's how that works. You can go faster than light that way, any way you want, but only so much faster. Then there's active jump."

"Which we stole from the Bomo'ri," Marche said.

"Yep, and they're still pissy about it," Fergus said. "Not our fault they shot a jump-point probe within our curious little monkey-finger reach. Fortunately for us, they mostly stay over in their galactic spiral arm, and we stay in ours, and there's a nice big gap in between us. And no one wants to go over the Gap anyway, because the Asiig are also there."

"I don't think they're real," Marche said.

Fergus got up and washed out his cup, rinsing his spoon, then got a cloth and cleaned up the tea blot on the floor. "Maybe not," he said. "It is an effective deterrent, though."

"Yeah," Trinket said. "I've heard more than enough stories to keep me awake nights, when I was a kid, and still give me a few bad dreams, even now."

"Anyway, if you think about passive jump as making all sorts of little tiny folds in space to make the distance along the surface shorter, active jump is grabbing space by the ends and mashing it together and punching a hole right through from one side to the other," Fergus said. "Much faster, but you have to start at an existing hole, and those holes are made over time by big, complex gravity fields. So, that's supposedly why there are none in the Barrens, except that's not actually true."

"You're talking 'bout the Ghostdrift," she said. "We've all heard talk, but you know how spacers are. Full o' brave noise about real things that should scare 'em, and scared of 'maginary things that shouldn't."

"Yeah," Fergus said. "So, either jump points are impossible, or we don't really understand what conditions create them after all. But according to the captain, the ones here are less stable than normal ones, and even normal ones are less stable the longer they reach."

"And we're going to jump through one that's not normal and is super long," Trinket said.

"That's the plan," Fergus said.

Trinket let out a deep breath. "Okay," she said. "At least I get it now. I don't like not knowing, but maybe it's easier when you don't, if you're gonna die."

"I suppose by the time you have the answer to that, it's too late," Fergus said. "Like everything else."

"Could you two be any gloomier?" Marche asked. "Every day we're out here, we could die. Enemies, the Alliance, one bad hull rupture, you name it, it can kill us at any time. But if we pull this off, you know what kind of secret advantage we'll have? Especially if it means Bas can finally find peace over losing his sister and get his head fully back into the game."

"Sure," Trinket said, though she didn't sound happy. "I'm gonna go back and check on Yolo. He hit his head pretty hard."

After Trinket left, Marche studied Fergus silently for several minutes. "I wish I knew what motivated you," she said.

"Bored optimism, mostly," he said.

"That's not an answer."

"I suppose not," Fergus said. "Ask me again on the other side."

He packed up his tea supplies and headed back to his cabin. If nothing else, no matter the near-certain doom hanging over them, his cat would be expecting to be fed.

———

Sidewinder came out of jump far enough outside the triangle to not be within range of anyone inside it, just in case they weren't the first ones there. Kaybe fired off a microprobe and then they immediately relocated, in case someone spotted it and tried to trace it back.

"Four Alliance ships," he reported. "One is the *Paradigm*."

"Shit, really?" Fergus said. "I need better trivia questions."

"We have the advantage, still," Belos said. "First, they don't know where we are yet, so we have the element of surprise. Second, they don't know what they're looking for or where. Space is awfully big and empty, even when you know exactly what you want."

"Which raises a question," Fergus said.

Kaybe tapped a few buttons and uploaded an overlay onto the nav map. "The rogue jump points were mapped by a crazy old astrophysicist named Messier about thirty years ago who first came here to investigate why the Barrens were, well, barren," he said. "While he wouldn't out-and-out tell anyone what he was doing out here, and I guess his home institute cut him off for chasing an obsession, if you got him drunk enough, he'd spill it to anyone buying. He was before our time, but my mothers ran a smuggling op between Beenjai and Ijikijolo, and I dare say they became friends, of a sort. They didn't believe in his wild theories either, but just before he disappeared down one of his tunnels for good, he left all his collected data and analyses in their shop."

"Ah," Fergus said. "The map."

"Yeah. My mothers shared it with me and my siblings, and a few trusted others, and although some hint of his work has leaked, most of it is not credible without the backing data—perhaps not even then—and useless without the map."

"*Rattler* had the map, though," Fergus said.

"Both of us," Belos said. "Kaybe's moms kind of adopted my sister and me, when we first arrived here with almost no experience and some very unrealistic expectations of how setting ourselves up as pirates was gonna go. I don't think we'd have survived long enough to figure out what we were doing if they hadn't. We've used a few of the shorter, more stable points in a pinch but always treated them as a last-ditch move."

Kaybe narrowed the field of the nav map and eliminated all the extraneous details of the overlay except the jump point itself, a glowing yellow dot in the center of the screen. "I'll need four minutes between shutting down the passive-jump engines and getting the active-jump ones online," he said. "You have a plan for how to pass those four minutes that doesn't involve getting shot up by some angry government fuckers, Bas?"

"Can we make some kind of distraction?" Fergus asked.

"We could shoot Yolo out in a lifepod right into their faces," Belos said, "but Trinks would never forgive me. She's having a hard-enough time dealing with him losing his nerve and wanting to bail on us."

"Maybe he'd volunteer," Fergus said. "He's terrified."

"They'd execute him for sure," Kaybe said. "Oh, I know, the Alliance talks up the whole *ooh fair trial rehabilitation we promise*, but you just know it'd be a *he was resisting we had no choice* end. Same for any of us."

"So, let's not let them catch us," Belos said. "Send an empty lifepod? I hate to waste one, but all things considered, either we won't need it anyway, or we won't need it ever. Vetch, can you prep it?"

"On it," Fergus said. He left the bridge and made his way down to the back of the cargo bay where the lifepods were stored; there were only four, which with a crew of nine was very optimistic, very pessimistic, or both.

Lifepods were designed to be self-supporting for a significant duration but also to broadcast the shit out of its location and its origins, so that any potential rescuers could find it and then go look for more survivors. Fergus plugged into the system and easily inserted a routine that would scramble its launch-location data, giving false info several light-years off. As he checked the other routines, he found an organic-materials sensor, which would trigger to indicate a life form aboard even if actual life signals failed. He went back to his cabin, fetched Mister Feefs' litterbox, and dumped the contents from the reservoir into the cramped passenger bed. Hopefully, Belos wouldn't change his mind and want the lifepod back.

Done, he sealed up the pod again and exited the launch chamber. "Ready when you are," he called up to the bridge.

"Moving to position we want to release it from," Kaybe replied. "I need everyone on board who can to suit the fuck up and then get in their bunks and fully strap down. Trinket, get Yolo secured and then yourself; he doesn't need to bang his head again if we can help it. Assume this is going to be the roughest ride of your lives, if the Alliance doesn't shoot us down before we even get there."

Fergus went back to his cabin, started to put on his suit, then realized if the ship was breached, Mister Feefs had no protection. Did they even make exosuits for cats? he wondered. So, he checked his oxygen bottles and made sure his suit was ready, then got into his bunk without it, waiting for the cat to come curl up next to him, which he did.

Fergus buckled up and wrapped one protective arm around the cat. How weird was it, how much this one furry, obstinate, randomly destructive mammal meant enough to him that he was unwilling to let it die without him? He sighed, scratched the cat's head, closed his eyes, and waited.

He felt the vibration of the lifepod launching, even as he also felt the energy spike. Then *Sidewinder* was moving again, going to passive jump for a short few minutes before dropping out and the engines going dead. Seconds later, he felt the other engines, the ones he'd wondered why any ship in the Barrens would bother with the expense of, start to power up.

"All but one Alliance ship took the bait," Belos reported over the comms. "*Paradigm* is still lurking, but they're not near enough to our target point to be a danger quite yet. It's going to be close. No promises there will be any further updates."

Over the comms, Kaybe counted down from ten, and then the whole world turned itself inside out.

It was akin to being shaken like a pebble in a tin can, while the can was also being crushed and simultaneously pulled outward and apart, and everything around him—sound, ship, electricity—screamed.

Mister Feefs sank all his claws into Fergus's arm and clung there, and what was one more scream, after all?

It seemed to go on forever, until Fergus could no longer remember what stillness and quiet ever could have felt like. Hours, certainly. Days? He didn't think so, but it was hard to even think about time as anything meaningful anymore.

And then, miraculously, it subsided.

Alarms were blaring everywhere. He couldn't feel parts of the ship anymore, and hoped they were just without power rather than torn off somewhere behind them. His whole body hurt, and when he opened his eyes, it was dark in his cabin except for streaks of light that were his eyeballs slowly freaking out about whatever abuse the jump had subjected them to. Carefully, he disconnected Mister Feefs one claw at a time, while the cat glared at him as if he was solely and personally responsible for all ill in the universe, and then put his suit on. He was just wondering how to check if there was still air on the other side of his door when the lights spluttered back on.

"Hull breach in cargo; rest of ship remains airtight. We've taken heavy damage, a lot of systems are down, but we're still sailing," Belos's voice came. "Mr. Vetch, get up here to the bridge. You're going to want to see this."

Two of the corridor walls had buckled, jamming one of the interior bulkhead doors, and he had to pry it far enough apart to squeeze through, but he arrived on the bridge despite that in what felt like record time.

The front display screen, now visibly cracked, showed a vast panorama of space. What stars there were were distant, concentrated in a blurry line not unlike the view of the galaxy edge-on from Earth, though there—as in the Barrens—there were other stars to fill the sky around them. Here, there was almost nothing very far above or below that starry horizon.

"I think we're in the Gap," Fergus said. He had come close to the edges of their spiral arm before—Crossroads Station was on the outskirts of it—but had never dared quite leave his stars behind. They were deep out into the void.

One solitary star was much closer, enough that they were clearly within its gravitational system, maybe six or seven AUs away, though it was hard to be sure until they could scan it more thoroughly and get a better sense of its size and position. Despite its nearness, it was affected by the same blurriness as the distant line of other stars. *Possibly a malfunction of the screen?* he wondered. As he stared, the movement of the blurred areas suddenly resolved in his mind not as visual defects or negative space but as a field of dark objects in space ahead of them.

Kaybe must have come to the same conclusion around the same time, for just as Fergus was reaching for the controls, the first mate was already doing so, running a full-spectrum scan.

The objects were ships, or at least once had been. There must have been nearly a hundred of them, some of the shapes familiar and some inconceivably alien, and every one of them was torn and mangled and ruptured, floating in a sea of debris that occluded their view of the stars ahead.

"Hell," Kaybe swore under his breath.

They'd chased Belos's ghost all the way to a graveyard.

Chapter 9

"Everyone check in," Belos commanded. "If you're not dead, get to your area ASAP and check for damage. If you are dead, you can take a five-minute breather first. Assume we're in hostile territory until I give the all-clear. Fendi, go check the engines; if we need to get out of here fast, I want to have that option. Rabbit and Len, check the guns, same reason."

"I'm scanning for *Rattler*," Kaybe said. "It might take a while; there's a lot of shit out there."

"Any idea whose they are?" Belos asked.

"A couple of Alliance ships, at least one Sfazili freighter, some smaller homegrown one-off freighters. Most are hard to identify in their present condition. I'd say about three, four dozen of the obviously human ones."

"What else we got? Not human, I mean."

"Guessing from the scans, about ten, maybe fifteen alien ships. There's enough visible consistency among the bigger pieces to make me think maybe they're all from only one kind of alien, but I don't recognize the design at all," Kaybe said. "Eyes has several processors and a cooling stack down, so I'm using all her resources for the initial scans. I'll have a better analysis when she's back fully online."

"Can you pull up a visual of one that's relatively intact?" Fergus asked.

"Sure thing," Kaybe said, and tapped at his console. A three-dimensional rendering of a vessel appeared on the screen. It was chunkier than most human ships tended to be, except for maybe the most-utilitarian cargo freighters, but also tall and rounded along the top with vertical flanges running down the full length, and what looked like engine ports ringing the base. Fergus tried to rotate the ship image to a more sensible orientation, but nothing quite looked right. However, it did look just a little familiar; nothing he'd ever seen with his own eyes, but . . .

"Ah," he said, softly, when he remembered. It was in an old documentary news clip he'd seen just after he'd run away from Earth and was lounging around Mars, not yet having found himself any productive trouble to get into. The documentary wasn't on a ship but an opportunistically stolen probe; still, it was enough similar that he was confident of the identification. "We're definitely in the Gap. That's Bomo'ri."

"What?" Kaybe said. "Shit. You don't think the Alliance got in a fight with them? My opinion of their smarts isn't *that* low."

"No," Belos said. "The casualties would be wholly one-sided. And it wouldn't explain all the other ships—some of the wrecks out there are much older than others. This was something else, and I don't like not knowing what. Vetch, I want you and Rabbit to take the shuttle and go get a closer look while we work on ship repairs. Get as much data as you can on what happened to them, what kind of weapons were used, whether they fought each other or something else, *anything.* I also want an approximate age range of what's out there, especially what's most recent, so we have some idea if there may still be an active threat. If you have to go extravehicular, do it."

"Got it," Fergus said.

As he headed out of the bridge to go find Rabbit, Belos stopped him with one hand outstretched. "If *Rattler*'s in that debris field, it's in a lot of pieces."

"If there's a piece so big as a mouse turd, I'll find it," Fergus said. He had taken a good scan of *Sidewinder*'s composite materials signature when he'd first come aboard, and *Rattler* had been built at the same time, in the same yard. "Uh, it just might take a while."

"We're gonna be here awhile," Kaybe said from the helm. "Bas, you need to come look over the diagnostic reports coming in."

Fergus fetched his suit from his cabin, checked his air bottles multiple times, then headed toward Rabbit's work room. On his way past Yolo's cabin, he heard Trinket's voice, and before he could dodge, she came barreling out of Yolo's door and right into Fergus, who had to throw both hands out and catch the wall before he bounced head-first off it.

"Sorry," Trinket said. "Yolo's got his sour assvalve glued shut and it's backing shit up into his brain."

"I thought he was in Medical," Fergus said.

"Fendi and I moved him here soon as we made it outta jump," she said. "You'd think being alive would make him happy again, but no. Maybe I should hit him on the head again."

"Maybe," Fergus said. "Give him a bit of time to get over it."

"If you say so. 'Til then, he's locked in," Trinket said, scowling. She pounded on the door that had slid shut behind her. "And I'm not bringing you any food until you stop being an ass. You hear me, Yolo? Should I pound *louder*? Does it make your *head hurt*?"

"Fuck you, Trinks!" an anguished shout came from inside the cabin, and Trinket smiled.

"He'll figure himself out," she said, and headed down toward the kitchenette.

"Vetch, that you?" Yolo called from inside his cabin.

"Yeah," Fergus answered, somewhat reluctantly. He should have left when Trinket did.

"How bad is it? Where are we? Are we going to be able to get home?"

"We're pretty battered, but nothing we can't fix, I don't think," Fergus said. "We're somewhere in the Gap; more than that, it's hard to say."

"I can help with repairs, if you let me out," Yolo said. He sounded contrite, or maybe just embarrassed. "I mean, I'm much better at breakin' stuff than fixin' it, but I can carry things, hold tools, stuff like that. Anything to get us out of here."

"Not my decision to make," Fergus said. "When you get a chance to square things with the captain, I'm sure he'll find something for you to do. But you should probably rest while you can; concussions aren't something to mess around with."

". . . okay."

When Yolo said nothing else for a bit, Fergus took advantage of the silence and escaped any remaining chance of conversation. He wasn't sure if he felt irritation, sympathy, or pity for the man. If he was certain of anything, it was that it was never easy the first time your fears caught up to you, especially when you'd thought you'd outrun them long before.

———

Fergus picked a small Sfazili cargo ship that was more intact than most of the others. Rabbit had parked the shuttle just outside the debris field and was running scanners on everything else as Fergus used his exosuit jets to make a slow pass over and around the remains of the ship. He could just make out the ship's name, GSCS *Adenia*. A commercial ship registered on the Guratahan Sfazil planet itself, and not the more usual berth of its more legality-ambivalent moon, Tanduou. So, likely not a smuggler.

"They hit the engines first," Fergus said. The weapon scoring on the hull was heaviest there.

"Well, duh-oh," Rabbit said. "So would I. Don't want my prizes takin' theyselves away."

"Anything here look looted to you?" Fergus asked.

". . . No, least not ship parts," Rabbit said. "Maybe go peek inside?"

Fergus sighed, and when he found a hole in the hull big enough to float through, he did. The first interior blast door he reached was still closed, though the missing chunk of wall beside it had rendered it useless. He braced himself as best he could against the wall and cranked at the manual release until the doors ground open about a half-meter before they jammed hard, but not before a desiccated arm in a Sfazili exosuit dangled through the gap, like it was reaching for him.

"Shit," Fergus said, momentarily spooked. As disrespectful as it felt, he used his boot to kick it back in and away before he dared stick his head and upper body through to look. One more body farther in was dangling on the end of a safety tether, but there was plenty of room to go around, which he did with haste. "Matching crew uniforms," he said over the comm channel to Rabbit. "Not some fly-by-night operation, anyway. I'd guess from the insignias and suit style, this wreck is at least three decades old."

"I've got a partial out here going back almost half a century," Rabbit said. "Wouldn't've thought anyone was out here that far back."

"Old colony ships, mostly," Fergus said.

"That tracks. Maybe we don't wanna go in one a' those."

"No, probably not," Fergus agreed. He reached another door, got it open about the same distance as the last, and slipped through. He was on the bridge, along with several former crew loitering in and around the stations. He gently sent the one nearest the ship computer sailing toward the far wall, pulled himself under the console, and pried open the maintenance hatch. Inside were the emergency datalog and the ship's memory bank bristling with heat sinks now coated in hoarfrost. He pulled both out, stuck the datalog in his pocket and the memory bank under his arm, and turned around to kick off back out the way he'd come in. There was a gaping hole on the other wall of the bridge that had been in his peripheral vision coming in, but now he was looking straight out at the wreckage of a recent-model Alliance light cruiser.

Fergus left through the hole, activated his magboots so he could steady himself on the cargo ship's hull, and zoomed in with his goggles. He could just make out the first four letters of the ship's name, SILV. Whatever had obliterated the rest of the letters—and he thought he had a pretty good guess what they were—had also completely disintegrated the entire front third of the cruiser's nose. "Uh, I think I found *Silver Mist*," he told Rabbit. "Right vintage, anyway. Definitely no survivors."

He sent Rabbit his bearing and visuals. "I can't get in close w' the shuttle," Rabbit said. "Whole halo of crap 'round it. Need me to park and evac with you?"

"No," Fergus said. "If trouble comes along, I want us ready to get out."

"Thinkin' being ready dint help anyaw these cudders none," Rabbit said, and Fergus didn't like one bit how sharp that point was.

He used his suit jets to maneuver over to the remnant of the cruiser. It had the same external scoring as the Sfazili cargo ship, again concentrated near the engines, but also some more familiar blast patterns along what was left of the starboard side. There was too much damage, and too much time had elapsed, to know which had happened first, or how far apart in time. As much as he wasn't fond of the Alliance—after all, they *were* hunting him—he felt bad for them if they'd lost to two enemies at once.

It wasn't hard to get into the cruiser, with the gigantic gaping hole where a lot of the ship had once been, but unfortunately the missing part included the bridge. Any chance of pinching their logs was gone with it.

Explosive decompression made a mess with unsuited bodies that time had not made any better, and he avoided several such messes until he found a more-intact, suited-up body and could read the shoulder insignia. "Confirmed it," he said. "This was *Silver Mist*. About *Rattler*'s weapons, was there anything special . . ."

"No way she done that kinda hurt," Rabbit said. "Side damage, yeah, from chasin' or bechased, but naw the big bite outta it."

Fergus sighed. "I was afraid of that. Nothing here was looted, either, near as I can tell. Just destroyed and left to rot. What've you got?"

"Lotta same, I think," Rabbit said. "Ev'ry ship, same damage, an' not a pattern I've ever seen, neither."

"So, a third group took out everything here," Fergus said.

"Unless the Bomo'ri were shootin' up their own, yeah," Rabbit said. "You know what I hain't got? Any ships not either ours or theirs. I seen thousands a' diff'rent human-made ships over my life—civ and mil, amateur and pro—and even the weird ones you can tell someit about where it came from by the shape, or if it's broke up too small, the materials signature. Scanners're finding nothing new. This many wrecks, for this many years, and neither ah us ever took even *one* in return? I don't like that none at all."

"Or the enemy took their own wreckage away after the battle," Fergus said.

"Naw, not without leavin' at least some crumbs ahind the scans would catch," Rabbit said. "Out here, hain't a lot of other suspects, so I guess we know who done all this. The Asiig."

Fergus almost lost his grip on the chunk of hull he was crawling over. "Uh," he said. "I don't think so, though."

"Why not? They're just the other arm over, and stories all say they come in all-powerful in th' dark and take people away and you can't fight and no one ever comes back," Rabbit said. "Figgir I know I ain't ever seen one 'cause I'm still alive, and anyone sez they have are lying cause they got the breath to say it."

Not that Fergus had been about to admit to having any association—voluntary or otherwise—with the Asiig, anyway. Instead, he said, "Yeah, but the stories say they always take the people. I've got three corpses in my line of sight right now that says that didn't happen here."

"I dunno. Who else coulda done it and beat the Bomo'ri, too? Not us," Rabbit said. "Sayin' it again, I don't like any of this at *all*. Sooner we're out and back safe in the Barrens, the better. What you got next?"

"Heading over to one of the Bomo'ri wrecks," Fergus said. Had a human ever been inside one of their ships? He didn't think so, since the Bomo'ri regarded the whole of the human race as little better than vermin, and were still deeply aggrieved about humanity stealing their active-jump technology. Fortunately for humanity, their way of dealing with that anger involved sulking rather than genocidal retribution.

Close up, the amount of incidental pitting on the Bomo'ri ship from slow-motion collisions with debris was substantial, and he found himself wondering how long it had been out there. There was no easy way to judge, knowing virtually nothing about the evolution of Bomo'ri ships, nor what their exteriors were made of and how durable they were or weren't. But it felt old, in his gut.

He went in through one of the larger holes and paused to turn on every sensor-recording apparatus his suit and goggles had; it was unlikely he'd ever get a chance to explore one of these again once they left this place. *If we leave this place*, he thought. "Any word from *Sidewinder*?" he asked.

"Lotta words if you count Fendi swearing," Rabbit said. "They're all busy, and I'm not gonna bug 'em 'less we have to."

"Fair enough," Fergus said, and then turned a corner to find himself face-to-face with his first dead Bomo'ri. Until now, faces were all anyone had seen of them, yelling at them over a screen, but here was a whole one, and it was nothing like he'd expected. The dead Bomo'ri was physically big, and if it wasn't floating in zero gravity but standing, it would have towered over Fergus. It made him think of a centaur, if one drastically shortened the body between front and back legs, and thickened everything up like an elephant; the head was less a separate thing and more a forward-sloping, neckless mass as thick as the rest of it, with a pair of arms in the middle to either side, tipped with remarkably delicate digits. The front of the non-head held a row of five small eye sockets. Unable to help his curiosity, he drew closer and saw that indeed the formidable alien was covered, where it wasn't clothed, in very short, stiff fur, some of which had been painted or dyed in patterns. "Huh," he said. The more aliens he met, the less extraordinary it became every time the realization struck that they were just people too, no matter the differences.

Except maybe the Asiig. He wasn't there on them, maybe because he'd never had a moment yet where they didn't scare him shitless.

The Bomo'ri equivalent of a helm was a circular station with a narrow gap for getting inside. He didn't think more than one or two could fit in there at once, but the whole circle was covered with controls and screens. Did it rotate? Did the Bomo'ri just spin in circles? Other instruments appeared to be on drop links from the ceiling, though without gravity, they were now a tangled, smashed mess.

Nothing there was familiar enough to figure out how to get at any data, much less be able to read it later. He caught images of everything he could, including text that was mostly overlapping circles and arc segments, and then backed out. "Nothing obviously looted from the Bomo'ri, either," he said to Rabbit. "Bodies left behind. What've you got?"

"More a' the same-same," Rabbit said. "A few of these we might be able to scrape some good bits out of, if we need 'em, but what a waste a' everything."

"Yeah," Fergus said. Hard to disagree with that.

As much as he could explore this shipwreck for days, for his own curiosity and knowledge, there wasn't anything there to help them, nor any more easily read clues to what happened than they already had. Reluctantly, he pulled himself back out of the wreckage and stood atop it, surveying the field of debris around him.

The human ships had little in common that he could see—in age, in origin, in size or function—other than how they died. The Bomo'ri ships all appeared to be similar, though that could either mean they were contemporaneous to one another or just that the Bomo'ri didn't change their designs much. They were all also closer in toward the loose center of the field, which could either mean they were there first, or nothing of the sort. It was always possible that the physics of being in orbit was slowly sorting them, the same way big pebbles eventually rose to the top of the small ones in riverbeds.

The lack of answers, of basic information needed to sketch a timeline of events from, was as frustrating as the need for it felt unbearably pressing. All those ships, and he felt nothing at all, not even a spark, from any of them. The near-total lack of stars felt like a shroud over it all.

"It could take years to find any real answers here," Fergus said. "I don't know if I should be fascinated or creeped out."

"Me neither," Rabbit said. "Kaybe says they got a prelim scan of the rest a' the system, lotta rocks an' ice further out from us, and one good-size planet in the goldy zone that's got signs of atmosphere. Could be someit there worth checkin'."

"Maybe," Fergus said. "Not sure if—"

"Hang fer, ship's calling," Rabbit interrupted. The silence on the line was brief. "Says they got some strange reads comin' from ahind us, near where we dumped out into norm space. Captain wants us back aboard as fast as we can flap our wings back over."

Fergus had already started moving at the word *strange*. "On my way," he said. "Four minutes."

"Make it two, I'll make yer mornin' coffee fer a week," Rabbit said.

That was worth not passing up. Fergus figured he could re-charge his jets later, and put them on full burn toward the shuttle, parked now in the nearest clear space above the remains of *Silver Mist*. He'd never been out in space this close to a jump-conduit terminus, and though he couldn't feel much—they were multidimensional gravitational phenomena, not electromagnetic ones—there was something, tickling at the very edge of his senses, that was either new or he hadn't noticed before.

He was through the shuttle airlock at the two-minute, ten-second mark. "I'm in," he said, the moment the outer door closed, and the shuttle accelerated rapidly away. Either Rabbit had a clear path or a *lot* of motivation.

That earlier, ticklish sensation became points, like a dozen pebbles dropped in still water sending out ripples that grew wider, stronger. "I think we're about to find out who destroyed all these ships," he said, climbing up into the copilot's seat beside Rabbit.

Rabbit eyed him. "Don't be telling me that's your super hearing hearin' things even in space, 'cause t'aint no sound waves out here," he said.

Fergus shrugged. There was no easy way to explain it, certainly not right now. "I just have a feeling," he said.

Rabbit stared at him a moment longer, then hit the comms to *Sidewinder*. "Look alive. Vetch thinks we're about to have hostile company," he said. He didn't wait for a reply but transferred the helm over to Fergus.

"You drive while I suit up, jess in case," he said.

"Got it," Fergus said. He took over as Rabbit unclipped himself from his seat and went into the back.

Sidewinder had drifted several hundred kilometers from where they'd emerged from the jump conduit and was now well inside the orbital path of the ship graveyard, but the shuttle was fast when you cared more about speed than saving energy, and right now Fergus cared a *lot* more.

"*Sidewinder*, shuttle here. We're coming in hot. Advise on the situation."

"Vetch. Rabbit okay?"

"He's suiting up as a precaution," Fergus said. "Given how many big holes are in all the ships out here, not a bad idea for you all to do same."

"We're on it, except Fendi, who, predictably, says he'd rather die with the ship," Kaybe said.

Rabbit reappeared and leaned over the comm mic. "Tell Fendi to get his ass suited up or I'll see he dies afore the ship, and then who's gonna fix it for us? He want *me* getting my hands all over his engines?"

"Message passed on," Kaybe said a moment later. "Fendi says, and I quote, 'You ain't touching shit o' mine, you sleazy little Bounds gunweasel.'"

Rabbit smiled, took his seat, and looked over the helm control. "Fendi's square now," he said. "Trajectory's sweet-on; you're not a bad pilot. Better'n me, I think. You wanna stay drivin', case I hafta shoot at someit?"

"Since you're certainly better at shooting, sure," Fergus said. If they had to defend themselves, he very much preferred they hit. "We should be back aboard *Sidewinder* in six minutes."

Behind him, he felt those strange ripple-waves begin to collapse back in on themselves, and had a sinking feeling six minutes was going to be too late. "Hang on, Rabbit; I'm overriding safeties to get us more speed."

"You need special access—" Rabbit started to say, but Fergus already had his confuddler in and overriding the shuttle's security systems.

"Make that four minutes," Fergus said. "*Sidewinder*, what's behind us?"

"Nothing yet, but we got energy building near the conduit endpoint," Kaybe said. "We still aren't in a position to jump out;

Fendi says he needs at least another half-day on the active-jump engines to get them functional."

"What about passive?"

"Functional but failing a bunch of safety checks," Kaybe said. "If we're lucky—"

"Too late," Fergus interrupted. "They're here."

The shuttle's sensors lit up, only a half-second after his own perception of the energies caught the arrival of fourteen ships, each only a little bit larger than the shuttle but moving faster than anything he'd ever seen, and that included the Asiig. They felt odd in some way he couldn't quite put his finger on.

Rabbit was at the sensor controls, furiously running scans. "Hard to get a firin' lock on," he said. "Scans keep jitterin' all over. But they're coming in fast as shadow. Damn fuckies, but it's gonna be close."

Fergus didn't think it would be, and not in their favor.

"Belos here," the captain came over the comms. "Shuttle bay already has cracks, so if you can get aboard faster without being gentle about it, I won't take offense. We're going to try to get some distance with the passive-jump engines the second you're inside."

"Twenty seconds," Fergus said. Already the newcomers had closed almost half the distance between them. "Ten. Rabbit, brace yourself."

Rabbit was manually aligning the shuttle's gunsights with their pursuers and gave a half-wave to tell Fergus to shut up.

Fergus hit the reverse thrusters just seconds before they flew through the open dock doors, so that they hit the back wall with a resounding, bone-shaking crash rather than embedding the shuttle halfway through it. "We're in," he called.

"Oh, trust me, we felt it," Kaybe said. "Already beginning evasive maneuvers."

Fergus could feel the first blast of energy coming, and he unclipped his tether, grabbed Rabbit out of his seat, and threw him to the floor of the shuttle as everything exploded around them. He felt the searing energy across his back as every muscle in his body contracted at once, and he felt that energy light up all the tiny threads that had grown throughout his body from the core alien organ that the Asiig had planted deep in his gut. It was like burning from the inside out, and he screamed despite himself.

Sparks rained down from where the shuttle's console blew, and everything went dark and suddenly silent.

"Shit," he heard Rabbit's muffled voice. "I think we're dead in the water."

Fergus's whole body felt alive and on fire, hopelessly clenched up, but the idea that out there, in the vast emptiness between the galaxy's arms, a pirate that had no doubt lived his entire life in space would still use that phrase, as if they sailed in water instead of vacuum, struck him as so darkly hilarious that he laughed, even with tears still running down his face from the pain.

Or maybe the man just meant he'd peed his suit. *I shouldn't ask*, he thought. He couldn't feel the ship's energy anymore, so either his gift had been burnt out of him or overloaded so badly it shut down, or they were, in fact, dead in the proverbial or euphemistic water. His suit was trying to reboot, red lights flickering in his goggle's peripheral display.

Rabbit groaned and pushed Fergus gently off him. "Your suit's aw blinky," he said. "You okay?"

"I don't think so," Fergus said, though the full-body cramp that gripped him seemed to be easing, and he could breathe now without having to force it. "You?"

"Think you took the worst of it," Rabbit said. He pulled himself up to sitting on the shuttle floor. "Whoa, well, that scratched the paint some fair. Don't hear the engines no more."

"Me neither," Fergus said. "We should get out of here."

"Yeah," Rabbit said. He grabbed the seat back and hauled himself upright from the floor, swearing under his breath and moving stiffly. Then, without needing to ask, he bent down again and hauled Fergus up. "Can you walk?"

"Not gonna win any races, but I think so, as long as the walls and floor don't keep trying to take a swing at me," Fergus said.

They had just gotten out of the shuttle and to the double blast doors into *Sidewinder*'s interior when the next blast came in, and the shuttle engine exploded. Burning-hot debris pelted them as the artificial gravity gave out. Fergus managed to wrap one hand around the safety bar beside the door, and Rabbit, who'd kept an arm on him to steady him as they'd walked, was able to turn it into a grip on his shoulder. It was excruciating but brief, as Rabbit used that momentary leverage to get his other hand on the same bar.

There was no longer any power to open the door, but Fergus had done this before, too many times, and in the dark felt for the manual override and cranked it open.

They pushed through the door together, and Fergus shut and sealed it behind them. Rabbit already had the access panel to the manual release for the inner door open and began cranking on it the second the outer door sealed, and they got out into the corridor just as the third blast hit and the entire ship groaned and shuddered around them. Fergus's suit rebooted again. "EMP," he said, when his comms came back up. "Makes sense; disable all a ship's systems and defenses, then come in for an easy kill."

"Yer a cheery shit, Vetch," Rabbit said. "You get to the bridge fer yerself? I'm gonna check on Fendi and offer my hands."

"Yeah," Fergus said.

"And, Vetch?"

"Yeah?"

"Thanks," Rabbit said, and pushed his way down the corridor.

Fergus kicked off the wall toward the next bar and the ladder shaft up. As bad as the shutdown of ship's systems was, the lack of gravity was his friend, as his muscles, no longer in spasm, found grievance in every movement.

He got to the bridge and found Belos, Kaybe, Len, and Marche there. "Vetch," Belos said. "Find yourself a seat and strap down."

"Systems back online in five," Kaybe said. "Looks like you guessed right, Captain; closing in now for a better shot."

"Soon as we got power to the normspace engines, give me a broadside, Len," Belos said. "I want to take at least half of them with me before they finish us off."

"Cannonballs loaded and primed," Len said.

"Wait, cannonballs for real?!" Fergus exclaimed. "Of all the—"

"Be quiet, Vetch," Belos snapped, not taking his eyes off the screen in front of them, which flickered back into life, and Kaybe slammed the helm yoke to one side and they spun around.

"Locked on and firing," Len said, and the ship shook again as six large, fast-spinning spheres blasted out of *Sidewinder*'s port side.

Fergus could feel them singing with energy, sharpening as his Asiig-given sense woke up, and he let out an audible sigh of appreciation. With that spin, and their own electric field, they'd punch right through almost any kind of energy shield. Or the ones he knew about, anyway; the alien ships heading toward them were utterly unfamiliar and still felt insubstantial in his mind. As the cannonballs closed the distance, adjusting course to stay on target, the alien ships scattered and regrouped, then again as the cannonballs looped around and headed back in.

The alien ships reminded Fergus of glittery-dark maple seeds, though these were not spinning lazily in summer air but moving with elegant, predatory precision.

"I think they're bioships," Fergus said, thinking out loud, as one cannonball of the six finally connected with its target, and the alien ship shrugged the attack off. Three of them fired at once, energy blasts coming in from much closer, and hit their side.

Everything went dark again. "Fire on mid-deck," Kaybe announced. "No idea how bad; systems down again. I think we lost the norm engines and thrusters on that side. We might get another reboot out of our anti-EMP mods, but it's gonna be at least three minutes."

"They're already in range to hit us," Marche said. "Three minutes is five minutes too long."

"Ideas, anyone?" Belos said. "Now's the time for 'em, if you've got 'em. Otherwise, I just wanna say it's been a pleasure, pirating with you all, and if there's a bar in the next life, first round is on me."

Fergus had closed his eyes, trying to concentrate on sensing what was happening, but opened them suddenly. "They're turning away," he said. "Back toward the jump point."

"How do you know *that*?" Marche asked.

No killing shots came in, and when the screen and sensors finally flickered back on, it showed the aliens all converging back toward the jump point. Two cannonballs were still racing after them, until Len hit a button. "Recallin'," he said.

"What the hell, Vetch? What do you know?" Marche demanded.

Fergus ignored her. "Something else is coming through the jump," he said.

"Oh great, reinforcements," Kaybe said. "Why just kill when you can overkill?"

"No, it's . . ." Fergus said, waiting and trying to figure out what was next, when the new ship coalesced into space from the conduit, and the outline was no stranger at all. Two others appeared behind it seconds later.

"Well, hell, that looks an awful lot like the Alliance ship *Paradigm*," Belos said. "They followed us after all. And they brought their friends."

"They're not going to survive this either," Fergus said.

"No, I imagine not, but they've bought us a very, very small amount of time," Belos said. "Kaybe, what are our options?"

"We've only got one side of normal engines left, so unless we wanna spin donuts while we wait, they're not going to help us,"

Kaybe said. "But I can route their power to our passive-jump engines, which, if they don't explode the moment we power 'em up, might get us some small distance away. More than that, I've got nothing."

"The planet," Fergus said. "Can we get there?"

"Maybe," Kaybe said. "Not sure we got the control we need to land gracefully, though."

"Do it," Belos said, as behind them one of the Alliance ships disappeared in a halo of brief light.

"Aye, aye, Captain," Kaybe said. "Firing up passive jump. First round in the afterlife, you promised."

The sound the ship made as it leapt up to speed was like they'd scraped the entire surface of the universe like a chalkboard. Every surface vibrated, and the engines hiccoughed, each one like being slapped by an angry god, but they hit speed and everything blurred around them.

Sidewinder emerged just in time to go screaming into the atmosphere of the planet and through thick, angry clouds. When the ship emerged from the underside of their cover, the ground was near, and Kaybe fought the ship into a shallower descent over the green-brown land below.

Fergus leaned forward and just thought he'd spotted other wreckage below when Kaybe swore and signed a star over his heart.

"Power has failed to eighty percent of the braking system and inertial dampers," Kaybe announced. "Everyone brace yourselves. This is gonna hurt." He took them down, crashing through giant blue-green fern-like things, until *Sidewinder* hit the edge of a small body of water, cut across it, and came to a sudden, violent, final stop on the far shore.

Chapter 10

———◆———

He hurt all over, his mouth had the coppery taste of blood, and he couldn't remember who he'd lost a fight with, or why. "Lae me alone!" he said, and tried to swat at the hand shaking him. "Ah tauld ye ah didnae sneak any raisins on board, Ignatio, ye pest!"

This earned him an especially vigorous shake. "Vetch!" someone yelled in his ear. He cracked open one eye, wiped blood from it, and then as memory returned, he did his best to sit up, only to find his seat on the bridge had come loose in the crash and sent itself and him crashing into the front consoles. It was Marche who was shaking him, and she didn't look any better than he felt, with dark blood smeared across her forehead and soaking through a hole in her suit on one side of her abdomen.

"Shit," he said, and gingerly moved the chair off himself with one arm, as the other screamed at him. "I think I've dislocated my shoulder. You okay?"

"I'm alive," she said. "Nice accent there. Earth Irish, huh?"

"You caught me," he said, between gritted teeth. "Help me up?"

She gripped his free hand and hauled him upright, and he whimpered as his shoulder protested. Before he could find something to bash it against to set it, she grabbed him and yanked his arm forward, rotated and shook it, and it popped back into place. The screaming pain became a dull throb that would become annoying later but for now was an enormous relief.

Kaybe was watching him from his pilot's seat, which no longer seemed attached to the floor. His left leg was distinctly at the wrong angle from the knee down, and Fergus thought it likely he'd gone flying too. The man was pale and shaking, and although he was watching them, his focus did not seem entirely sharp. "M'okay," he murmured. "Just need to rest a bit an' I'll be fine."

"He's going into shock," Marche said. "Help me get him out of that chair?"

"Yeah," Fergus said, and despite feeble protests from Kaybe, together they managed to get him onto a cleared patch of floor.

"I'll see if I can find something to raise his feet. Or one of them, anyway. Not sure I want to touch the other," Marche said. "The captain's gone forward to see what he can get from the med bay."

"And the others?" Fergus asked.

"Len is trying to get to Engineering. We haven't heard from Fendi or Rabbit yet, who were down there when we landed," she said. *Landed* was a very rosy way of putting it, but Fergus had no desire to quibble. "Ship comms are down, so it's just our suits—channel four-two-two."

He switched his comms over. "—forward bulkhead jammed," Belos was saying. "Need extra hands if anyone's got 'em."

"I can go, if you don't need me to stay," Fergus told Marche.

"Go," Marche said.

He left the bridge, careful not to trip over any of the stuff that had come loose in the crash. Mostly, it was all little stuff, except for the two chairs that had broken free; given the force of the impact, it was lucky they weren't all dead. If they'd been in anything less armored and designed for collision than *Sidewinder*, likely they would have been.

Belos was in the corridor outside the med bay, still wrestling with the off-kilter blast door one-handed. His suit was rolled down to his waist and he'd taken his shirt off, which he'd turned into a makeshift sling. He nodded to Fergus as he approached. "Fractured clavicle, if past experience holds true," he said. "How'd you fare?"

"Dislocated shoulder, probably only partial. Marche reset it for me," Fergus said. He reached in with his good arm, and together they managed to get the door open another half-meter, which was enough to slip through.

The med bay was in more disarray than the bridge, but the autoformulary and the cabinetry had survived intact. "Grab an autosplint. Lower cabinet, on the left," Belos said, running quickly through the menus on the autoformulary and selecting the meds he wanted. As the machine chugged away producing them, he pulled open a drawer and threw a partial roll of pain patches at Fergus. "We have more. Don't be afraid to use one. Dislocated shoulders hurt like hell."

"Wouldn't be my first," Fergus said, and found the leg splints. "What about you?"

"I want to stay clear-eyed for now," Belos said. "Did you see it as we were coming in?"

"The wreckage? Yeah," Fergus said. "It was partially over-grown, so it's been here a while. Maybe six, seven kilometers on the other side of the lake, though I could be off by half that again in either direction."

Belos grunted. "I was thinking seven or eight, but not with any more certainty. We're going to need parts, I think. Fendi checked in yet?"

"Not yet," Fergus said.

The autoformulary beeped and a half-dozen fab capsules slid out of the bottom into the waiting tray with a *thunk*. Belos picked up a couple and began tucking them into his sling. Fergus took the rest and followed the captain back to the bridge. Marche and Belos together worked on getting the smart splint onto Kaybe's leg, slapped a bunch of med patches on him, then Belos tucked his coat up under his legs to raise them and help with the shock. "That'll do for now," Belos said. He stood up stiffly. "Len checked in yet?"

"Just before you came in. Still trying to get into Engineering.

Damage is bad astern, but no fire, and other than the shuttle bay, our air seals are holding," Marche said.

"I'm going down there," Belos said. "Vetch, check on Trinks. Yolo too, but if he gets belligerent with you, you think you can handle him?"

"If I have to, I can," Fergus said.

"Good man," Belos said. "Take some tranq patches with you just in case, though; Yolo is not one for being smart enough to stay down when he should."

Fergus had to force another door to get up to the quarters level. His shoulder was aching and he realized he was starting to think with satisfaction about the possibility of Yolo picking a fight with him, so he stopped quickly in his own quarters long enough to check on Mister Feefs. It looked as if the crash had pulled his bunk partially free, dumping cat, mattress, and blankets in one go; furiously pitiful meowing came from underneath it all.

He freed the cat and checked him over to find him not seriously hurt, though he was keeping one front paw tucked against his chest protectively. He shoved the bunk back upright and set the cat down in a nest of blankets, scratching him gently on the head as he told him things were okay, before closing his door again and heading to Trink's.

He knocked. "Trinket, it's Vetch. You okay?"

"What the fuck hit us?" she called from inside.

"A planet," he said.

There was a snort. "Yeah, sure felt like that, too," she said. He heard the snap of her unlocking her safety straps, and then she opened the door. Her eyes were red and puffy, but otherwise she looked healthy. "What about the aliens? Why didn't they finish us off?"

"We were just about to get our asses kicked into the next life when the Alliance showed up and made a handy distraction," Fergus said. "We ran while we could."

"Nice o' them to help us," she said. "We're on the ground? Everyone's okay?"

"Yes, and no," Fergus said. "We're still figuring out who's hurt and how badly. I came to check on you and Yolo."

"How is he?"

"I checked on you first," Fergus said. "Want to come with me?"

"Yeah," she said. She went ahead of him and pounded hard on Yolo's door. "Hey, ya dink, you alive in there?"

"Fuck off. Where are we? Did we go back?"

"Hahaha, no such luck," Trinket said. "But we're alive. You done being a mutinous bastard so I can let you out? Be real with me now, Yolo; you know I know when you're lying."

"I'm not going to make trouble," Yolo said.

Trinket glanced back at Fergus and shrugged. "Sounds like true," she said quietly.

"We're going to need all the help we can get," Fergus replied, keeping his voice low, too. "Might as well find out now if he's going to be a problem rather than later."

She unlocked the door and opened it. Yolo was sitting on his bunk, sporting a deep purple bruise on his jawline. His eyes darted to Fergus and narrowed, as if daring him to make a crack about it. *I'm not the only one half-hoping for a fight*, he thought, but this was not the time or place.

"Where are we, then?" Yolo asked.

"Planetside somewhere in the Gap," Fergus told him, instead. "Still trying to assess the situation, but we've got injuries. You offered to help earlier—the ship needs all hands if we're going to get out of here again."

"Are we? Going to get out of here, I mean," Yolo said. "Or is the captain just gonna keep finding other ways to kill us, chasing ghosts?"

"You'd have to take that up with the captain," Fergus said.

Trinket shook her head. "Better fuckin' *not*," she said emphatically. "You tempted, you rethink that hard."

"I don't wanna think about *anything*," Yolo said. "Just give me something to *do*."

"I'm heading back to the bridge," Fergus said. "The captain and Len are on their way to Engineering, but a lot of the interior bulkheads are jammed and probably need to be forced. Check in with them?"

Sending Yolo in the direction of Belos right now was a good way to end up permanently down a man, and he wasn't figuring it'd be the one with the broken collarbone to lose that fight, but there really wasn't much choice he could see.

"We got it," Trinket said. She caught his eye and gave him a slight nod. She could handle Yolo. "What channel we on?"

"Four-two-two," Fergus told her. "Shout if you need anything."

"Right," she said, and steered Yolo ahead of her down the corridor to the rear drop tube, and after watching them go, Fergus headed back to the bridge.

Kaybe's color was improved, and Marche was sitting between him and the main console, her attention divided between them. When Fergus came in, she leaned back, her face drained and exhausted, dried blood still caking her shirt. "He's doing better," she said.

"Glad to hear it," he said. "What else you figured out?"

"We have a few sensors still working. Outside atmosphere is breathable but not the healthiest. High humidity with a low pH, and a lot of organic particulate matter floating around," she said.

"So, alien pollen soup?" Fergus asked.

"Not inaccurate," she said. "We're going to have to do some sampling and culture the shit out of it to have any idea how safe it is in the long term, but we're not really set up for that. Fendi could rig something, I expect, given time and a lot of boredom; we have equipment for doing chemical analysis of things we've acquired on our travels, but it's not really intended for biological stuff."

"You think we're going to be here awhile," Fergus said, though he had no doubts about it himself.

"I think we're going to be here for the rest of our lives," Marche said, "but that doesn't mean I *accept* that. I—"

She was interrupted by both their suit comms lighting up. "We're in," Belos's voice came. "Fendi was trapped under a collapsed shelving unit, but the four of us were able to lift it and get him out, and he's going to be okay."

"Rabbit?" Marche asked.

"Rabbit wasn't tethered when we hit," Belos said.

"Shit. Is he—?"

"I don't think we can do much for him," Belos said. "There's a lot of wreckage between us and the med bay, and I don't think we can move him without killing him anyway. His neck might be broken."

"No portable med-chambers?" Fergus asked.

"Two down here, but they have no power. Fendi could maybe reroute something, eventually, but he's not going to be functional for a while. There's no time."

"I'm coming down," Fergus said.

He ran, not caring about the sharp ache in his shoulder with the jolt of each step. Gravity felt about three-fifths Earth, though he was too tired and anxious and full of adrenaline to be entirely sure.

Doors had been wedged open ahead, but some of the gaps were narrow enough that Fergus had to turn sideways to fit through. As it was, they were never going to be able to carry anyone out. When he made it through the last set of doors into Engineering, Fendi was curled up on the floor, breathing in short, painful gasps, and in between each trying to argue with Belos and Len to help him up.

Fergus stopped and stood in the doorway, and felt for the power that should be all around them, a fine network in the walls calling out to him, but there was nothing. "Vetch . . ." Belos started to say, but Fergus held up one finger in a gesture to wait, and then closed his eyes to listen more intently.

There was something, faint and self-contained. "What's in there?" he asked, pointing to a door.

"Just my old junk," Fendi wheezed.

"Something with its own power supply?"

"What? No," Fendi said. "Just *junk.*"

"Vetch, we don't have time for nonsense," Belos said, eyes narrowed. "If you don't have any *real* ideas—"

"Wait, shit, no," Fendi said, between breaths. "My old portable fab unit. It has its own power block."

"How the *fuck* you know that?!" Yolo demanded, whirling on Fergus.

Fergus ignored him and tried the door, but it was locked, and there was no power to the controls. Unlike bulkheads, a closet didn't merit a manual override.

"What do we have that could cut the door?" Belos asked.

"Nothing that don't need power," Len said.

"Check the workbench?" Fergus suggested, and in the brief instant that everyone had glanced over to the other end of the room to see if there was anything promising there, he put his hand against the lock and gave it just enough of a zap to activate the unlock button, which he hit. ". . . Never mind. Maybe it was just jammed," he said, and pressed on the door with his hands and pushed, sliding it open.

He moved a few crates and relocated a couple of piles of stuff, and hauled out the portable fab unit. Flipping it over and holding it against his chest with one arm, he pried open the base and un-slotted the power block. When he turned around, block raised in triumph, everyone was watching him.

"What?" he asked, peeved. "Can we *save* Rabbit now, or are we going to play kiss-and-tell first?"

Belos took the block out of his hand. "Priorities, people," he said. It took him and Fergus only a few minutes to figure out how to connect it up to the auxiliary power cable, and then the chamber came online. Fergus had always thought med-chambers looked like someone had crossed a refrigerator with a coffin, and he found himself very much trying to see it right now only as the first.

"I'm not sure how long that block will last," he said. "It's old."

"It buys us time," Belos said.

Yolo, Trinket, and Belos picked up Rabbit carefully, as Fergus kept his head steady; his neck was at a bad angle, but Rabbit was still breathing, and that wasn't anything they wanted to make worse. Fortunately for them all, Rabbit was a slight man, and they got him into the chamber and the lid closed without any mishaps. Once closed, the chamber ran scans, and lit up a lot of red and orange lights even as it got to work, inserting needles and adding monitors as the glass lid turned translucent, then opaque.

That, Fergus knew, meant the chamber had assessed a reasonable chance of not being able to save its patient and was trying to spare any onlooker from either that event or the likely messy and traumatic measures it would have to take to head it off.

"Len, stay here with Rabbit," Belos said. "Yolo and Trinks, you think you can help get Fendi up to the med bay? There's power there."

"I can get up," Fendi protested, though he made absolutely no move to do so.

"Sure," Len said. "An' maybe that flat lung yer wheezin' through will leak out yer ass an' fly off like a wee sad balloon when you do."

Fendi mustered enough to give Len the middle finger, and Trinket used the opportunity to grab his arm and, with Yolo, haul him up to his feet, where he immediately turned pale and started to tremble violently. "We gotcha," Trinket said, and they moved him carefully but also rapidly out.

"Vetch, conference room," Belos said, and Fergus followed him from Engineering.

He expected the captain to grill him about the closet door and knowing the portable fab unit was there, but Belos sat down at the head of the table and put his boots up on the table, and studied him for several uncomfortable minutes before speaking. "You seem to have a lot of skills," Belos said.

"Being able to pick up new things comes in handy," Fergus said.

"If Rabbit survives at all, he's going to be down and out for a long time. With Fendi hurt, I've lost my two main engineers. You seem to have enough knowledge that you can do most of the footwork of assessing the physical status of *Sidewinder*, and communicate with Fendi to come up with a critical fix list and recommendations."

"To get out of here?" Fergus asked.

"To survive," Belos said. "That first, then we'll see. It may be two or three days before Fendi is much help, so other than identifying anything that's likely to kill us sooner rather than later, we also need to find out more about where we are and what resources and dangers are outside the ship. We're all going to have to double up on jobs for a while. Or triple up. You have any issues with that you want to bring up now?"

"No," Fergus said, "but I want to get a drone or two out and go see what that wreckage is, and get a feel for the land around us at first chance."

"We'll take turns exploring, once we know the ship isn't going to suddenly explode and kill us all," Belos said. "Immediate safety first. Good work finding the power block."

"I'm very good at finding things," Fergus said.

"So I've seen. The real magic will be if we can find a way off this planet." Belos slapped his one good hand on the table and heaved a deep breath. "In the short term, I'd settle for not losing any of my crew, but I think we've done all we can do for them right now. You hurt?"

"Battered, but nothing I haven't been before," Fergus said.

"And your cat?"

Fergus raised one eyebrow. "Same," he said. "Thank you for asking."

"After all, we might have to eat it," Belos said, and at Fergus's sudden start, he laughed, then stood up. "Go get what rest you can, while I check in with Marche and Kaybe. You can be sure we won't let you oversleep."

———

Five hours of sleep felt luxuriously irresponsible, and he dragged himself out of bed and his cabin to see what he'd missed, and what there was that needed doing that he could do.

So far, the power block on Rabbit's med-chamber was holding, but Fergus could feel it struggling. He could also feel where the breaks were in the power conduits to the stern of the ship, deep in the walls, and set about ripping open wall panels and fixing them, one by one.

When he got the main fab unit reconnected, he had it spit out a long cable, and he switched the med-chamber over to ship's power. Whatever the chamber was doing with Rabbit, it still wasn't willing to let them see, but it hadn't given up or lost the fight yet, so neither was Fergus.

That done, he set the fab unit to print a dozen solar-cell blankets and more long cables. Kaybe and Marche were mostly busy trying to repair the damage to Eyes, the ship's mindsystem, but Marche came down just as he was putting on his exosuit to carry the first of the blankets out and set them up atop the ship, and silently put her own suit on, grabbed the next one just rolling out of the unit, and followed him.

It was night out; according to the scans they'd taken before the attack and the crash, the planet had just over a thirty-two-hour day, and they were still several hours out from dawn. It was easier to spread the blankets out and clip them down with two people, so the work went fast, and then Fergus sat on the top of the hull and looked out over their new home and tried to take in as much sensory information as he could.

Even with his goggles' night vision, it was dark. They'd crashed into the edges of a forest of fern-like structures, which waved gently in the low breeze coming in off the lake they'd skipped across like an ill-thrown stone. They were more like grass than trees, for all their height, and that had been their good fortune when they'd hit; oak trees, or their like, would have begrudged their passing much more aggressively.

There were also night sounds, not the insect buzzes and chirps of Earth but *clicks* and *snaps*, and many hidden somethings were calling out in deep bass hums in short bursts, repeated irregularly and echoing in competition back and forth across the water.

He thought about opening his hood, trying to imitate one of the calls and see what happened, but although eventually they would have to either get off this planet or give up and let the planet's biome claim them, for now he was in no hurry to be ahead of precautionary testing for what was floating around in the dense, moisture-saturated air. So, he watched and listened and tried to imagine what else might be out there, might be watching them back in curiosity and wonder. Or—always a possibility—in hunger.

Marche sat next to him, not touching but not far, and did the same as he was. Or, at least, she was observing; she didn't share her thoughts, pessimistic or otherwise.

Being marooned was, Fergus thought, not really much different from his four years of exile on Coralla, with the exception of the latter being mostly voluntary. Here was, ironically, a much safer haven from the enemies he knew were always seeking him out, but it remained to be seen what he'd traded the main local danger of bad sunburns and sand in all your food for.

Also, Coralla's night sky had had stars.

Here, the band of the galactic arm was a murky line of light cutting in an arc across the sky. There was nothing distinct to navigate by, wish upon, or build fanciful, comforting tales around. He had opened his mouth to break the silence and remark on what an unexpected loss that was, when a slow-moving shooting star caught his eye. It was followed by several more.

Marche had seen it too. "Debris?" she asked, uncertainly.

"No," he said, and stood up. "Lifepods."

————

Fendi was not able to do anything physical but insisted on being helped over to sit at the galley table as Fergus and Marche sent drones out over the frond-forest at dawn. Kaybe and Belos were there, running through the latest status reports from Eyes and from Yolo and Trinket, who were suited up and sending back visual data and commentary from the exterior. Together they prioritized the extensive and growing list of broken stuff they'd found.

Len was going through the armory inventory and kept glancing over at Rabbit's empty seat.

Little by little, holographic map pixels were filling in on the table display from the drones. "The lifepods seem to have gone down somewhere not far from the old wreckage on the far side of the lake," Marche said. "If that was an old Alliance ship, maybe there was still an active beacon they homed in on."

"Seems more plausible than just coincidence, with a whole planet to crash on," Fergus said. "How soon do we think we'll have the long-range scanners and comms gear working?"

"Another day. I suppose half-day here," Fendi said. "Just need a patient and willing set of hands to do the grunt work for me."

"Coming up on the far side of the lake," Marche said. She had the VR drone rig visor down, though he could just make out her face through the greenish flicker. He pulled his own down and took his drone off autopilot. Marche's drone was to his right—west, they'd decided, based on which direction the sun had risen that morning—and about two hundred meters away. He dove into the fern-forest, wanting a better feel for the environment itself, as she kept to the higher vantage point of the open skies and, with it, better speed.

The frond structures of his "ferns" were limited to the upper reaches of each stalk, making for a volatile equivalent of a canopy about a dozen meters above the forest floor. Below, where the sunlight was more dappled and inconsistent as the wind tossed the frond cover above, there was other plant-like life, including tall clusters of purplish, feather-like structures and low, tangled vines covered with blue fruiting bodies. If they finished their survey without incident, he'd try to pick one on his way back. At some point, they were going to have to find something edible, or at least sufficiently non-toxic they could blend it with their existing foodstuffs to extend their supply.

Some bluish critter, not much bigger than a gerbil, ran out from under one of the feather-shrubs, hopping on two long, spindly legs, and changed color to blend with the brown plant litter surrounding the base of the frond-trees. If it weren't for the drone's infrared layer, it would have virtually disappeared.

Camouflage means predators, Fergus thought. Hopefully, whatever else was out there was not much bigger than the hopper.

He found the first piece of wreckage before Marche did, a section of a wing flap that was half-buried in mud and frond-litter. "Looks like Alliance to me," he heard Kaybe say, back in the room he'd almost forgotten he was really in.

"I see the bulk of it ahead," Marche said. "The vegetation around it shows signs of having been cut back, though not in a while. Without knowing how fast this stuff grows, hard to say how long."

"So, there were survivors," Belos said.

"They must've seen us come in," Kaybe said. "We went screaming right over their heads. So, why haven't they come knocking?"

"Travelin' at night maybe is a bad go," Len said.

"And by daybreak, the lifepods had come in, and a lot closer to them. Maybe they don't have the resources to split up, or they wanted to go for their own first," Kaybe said.

"Or they're all dead and the clearing was done a long time ago," Marche added. "We don't know how long this ship's been here."

"Actually, we do," Fergus said, as his drone broke out from cover and got a clear shot of the faded but still legible registration on the side of the ship. "It's *Fire Island*, the other cruiser that was chasing *Rattler*."

"Look for survivors," Belos said, his voice steady but intense. "I have questions I am very eager to get some answers to."

"I see another clearing," Marche said. "Going ahead to check that out."

Fergus flew his drone along the circumference of the wreck. It was in better condition than its sister ship in orbit, but not by a whole lot. The hull was covered in the same burn scars as the drifting wrecks had been—and that *Sidewinder* now sported—though now they were tempered by a splotchy coating of green growing up on it. There were signs of catastrophic hull damage that had newer plates welded over the worst of it, and as he passed around the back to check out the engines, he found a makeshift scaffolding up against the tail of the ship made of thick bundles of interwoven frond stalks. He rose vertically, up the scaffolding toward where the cruiser's top-mounted active-jump engines were, and found his view filled with a pair of dirty, very worn boots.

Fergus flew higher, as the owner of the boots crouched and met him eye to drone-eye. She was older than him, maybe by a decade, muscular and not too tall, wearing some sort of woven purple-green outfit and the very tattered remains of an Alliance uniform jacket tied by its sleeves around her waist, jammed with a variety of tools. More spilled out of a bag beside her.

"Well, that's not an Alliance drone," she said. "I mean, I haven't seen one in a long time, and maybe they've changed a lot, but one thing I know won't have changed is the Corps's need to plaster their logo all over everything."

There wasn't an external speaker on the drone, but he waggled the rotor arms and hoped she'd take it as agreement.

She seemed to. She set down the large, makeshift tool she was holding on the scaffolding surface, and then sat, her legs dangling over the edge. "I'm Riji, Chief Engineer. Only engineer," she said. "Thanks for stopping by, Sir or Madam or Mx. Drone, but I gotta say, after all this time, you absolutely ran out the betting pool on when you'd get here. I had good cred riding on pirates within six months."

There was no way she could see him stare at that, but she laughed anyway. "You can't think we wouldn't recognize that chonky ship's silhouette instantly, going right over our heads," she explained.

She slipped a water bottle out of her tool bag and took a long pull from it, then gestured around her at the forest. "Welcome to Solo," she said, "your brand-new, home sweet ass-end-of-nowhere, dead-end home."

Chapter 11

Two hours and a hastily called meeting later, Belos declared that they needed to send a delegation to meet their neighbors face-to-face. "I don't want a fight if we can avoid it, but neither are we surrendering or otherwise giving them any authority over us," Belos told Fergus and Marche on their way out. "We need information, and since you two joined *Sidewinder*'s crew after *Rattler* vanished and *Fire Island* ended up on this planet, that may buy you two some small, initial benefit of the doubt that the rest of us won't have."

"Then why send Len, too?" Marche asked.

"Because I also want them to know that, if it suits me, I will not hesitate to kill every last one of them to get what I need," Belos said. "Len is my *stick*."

"Har har, tha' means yer the carrot, Vetch," Len said.

Fergus was sure he could still hear the man snickering as they sealed up their suits and headed out.

The ground for some distance around the lake was muddy and covered ankle-deep with old, decaying stalks and a rich tangle of interwoven growing things that seemed unnaturally good at snagging your foot as you walked and sending you falling on your face. There was also a proliferation of thorn-covered balls, some as much as half a meter wide, that made tripping even more of a hazard. After one mishap too many with them, Len let out a string of swears and kicked one as hard as he could, and they discovered they were not in any way connected to the ground and thus easily punted out of their path.

Of the three of them that had been sent over to negotiate with the *Fire Island* survivors, only Fergus had any real experience with traversing thickly overgrown terrain, and whenever he noticed Marche getting as frustrated as Len, he'd find an excuse to halt for a break until impatience won out over irritation.

There were a number of mobile creatures living in and under the brush, but other than quick, chipmunk-sized flashes of blues and purples, none of them were able to get any good look at what they were. They also startled several flocks of yellow flying things with two long, flappy wings on each side, one above the other, so that they looked like they were clapping as they flew.

At least so far, the wildlife was more afraid of the humans than vice versa, which suited Fergus just fine. While he didn't have any great optimism of ever finding a planet where absolutely nothing that lived there wanted to bite, sting, pinch, or chew on you, if there was one, it would be nice for it to be the planet he was probably going to be stuck on for the rest of his life.

As the shoreline rose and the ground dried out, they found themselves moving through frond-trees with long, flute-like structures growing like corncobs around their stalks. They were bright red, and when Fergus knocked into one with his shoulder after getting his boot caught in one of the tumbleweeds, warm, sticky, yellow-green liquid spilled all down the arm and back of his suit. Len laughed at that and dubbed it "booger sap."

On the far side of the lake, they intersected a trail cut through the forest that led them directly to the clearing around the wreck of *Fire Island*.

Before they'd set out, Belos had made it clear that Len shouldn't stab anyone they might later need. Just to be sure, when they spotted the lone figure lounging in a woven hammock, Fergus made enough noise that sneaking up on them was no longer a possibility. Though with the whistling calls of the four-wing birds as they scattered ahead of them, it was probably never likely to start with.

The man sat up, lazily, which set the hammock into a gentle swing. He was a large-enough man he would have towered over Yolo, if the latter had been here, and not lost any advantage in bulk or muscle. He had long, gray-black hair and matching beard, all of it kept loosely under control with braids, and his right leg ended at the knee in a prosthetic leg made of the same woven grass as everything else. He regarded them as they stopped at the edge of the clearing, then coughed. "I'm Ajac," he said. "This a civilized visit?"

"We'd like it to be," Fergus said. "I'm Vetch."

"If you're still worrying about the air, don't be," Ajac said. "Nothing toxic, either chemical or biological, though until you get used to the mix, you're going to have to be careful not to overdo things or you'll pass out before you figure out you have to breathe more. Oh, and giant-pollen days are a suckful and a half."

Fergus opened his face plate and then shrugged back his hood. The humidity made him feel like he was instantly drowning, and it was full of scents that were a heady mix of pleasant and putrid. He must've made a face, because Ajac smiled. "You get used to it quick, and then mostly don't notice it anymore," he said. "Who're your friends?"

"This is Marche," Fergus said, indicating her, "and this is Len. We're—"

"Oh, now there's a familiar face," Ajac said, as Len took his hood down. "I definitely saw the files on you."

"Good readin'? Lotsa murderin' and mayhemin'?" Len asked.

"Definitely, yes," Ajac said. "I don't know you other two, though. Had some crew turnover?"

"A bit. It's an occupational hazard," Marche said. "So, where are the others? Vetch met your engineer named Riji, via drone, but that's all we know."

"Mostly out on an errand. As you can see, my days of vigorous hikes are behind me."

"Off checking out the lifepods?" Fergus guessed.

"Yes," Ajac said. "Guess you saw them coming in too. Once everyone's settled in and been introduced, I'm sure you both will have interesting stories to tell, if you don't try to kill each other first."

Marche spread out her hands. "We just want to survive long enough to get off this planet and get back to our business," she said. "Animosity isn't going to help any of us, and if you Alliance folks are willing to declare a truce, we'll uphold our end."

"Gotta ask the new Alliance folks," Ajac said. "I retired. Wrote out my resignation on a piece of paper, folded it up into an airplane, and threw it out into the forest, where someone may or may not ever find it. Just as reliable as the normal Corps bureaucracy, and when it's time to collect back pay on my pension, I got witnesses."

"Planet smells like someit nasty-puked flowers all over," Len said. "Ask fer double pay fer sufferin'."

Ajac pointed at Len in appreciative acknowledgment. "For a pirate, you are a smart and sensible man, sir."

"Fer an Alliance guy, yer not at all makin' me wanna stab you yet," Len replied.

"See, it's like we're best friends already," Fergus said.

Ajac swung a cane out in front of himself and stood up, then smoothed down his shirt. "I need to ask some questions, so bear with me, and please be honest," he said. "First, you three the only ones that headed over here, or are there others out hiding in the jungle?"

"Just us," Marche said. "We were the only ones that could be spared from working on our ship."

"How many of you, total?" Ajac asked.

"How many of you?" Marche asked in return.

"Fair enough; I'll give you this one. We're five. Six of us survived the attack and then the crash, but we lost a person about a year later."

"Sickness? Predators? Self-removal?" Marche asked.

"He drowned in the lake," Ajac said. "Your turn."

"Nine, but it's touch and go whether it'll be eight," Marche said.

"And Bas Belos himself?"

"Sends his personal regards," Marche said.

"Are you three armed?" Ajac asked.

"I'm not," Fergus said, at which both Len and Marche rolled their eyes. Neither of them answered.

Ajac did not miss the obvious meaning in that. "Okay, so, two of you. That's fine; that's better than expected. As it happens, I'm not, but that's because if you do anything to me, you're gonna not only have the rest of us coming for your heads, but you also are not going to be getting any useful information from us on how to survive here," he said. "And lemme tell you, when you get hungry enough, you're going to start experimenting, and there are a lot of things here that will make you vomit, give you chills, uncontrollable shaking, and stabbing cramps, leave you hallucinating and paranoid, and give you the runs so bad, you'll feel like your asshole is trying to suck you inside-out and shit out your entire body, and you'll be begging someone to put you out of your misery. Speaking of, you hungry?"

Fergus laughed. "Actually, yeah," he said. "Long walk."

Len smiled. "What he said."

Marche looked at them both skeptically. "Did either of you just hear the whole 'hallucinations and diarrhea' thing? Yes? Of course you did. What kind of opsec condition could that leave us in?"

"Weren't be near as funny to do tah us now he warned us," Len said.

"That's true," Ajac said.

Marche grimaced. "I suppose I've eaten Len's cooking; what could I possibly have left to be afraid of?"

"Hey!" Len protested. "You disrespectin' my groats?"

"I would never," Marche said.

"Well, I can't offer you anything as fancy as groats, but Riji should be back soon with a basket of food. We'd offer you dinner back in our camp, but we'll have other guests there tonight. Since they don't know about your lot yet, you could see how that could get awkward," Ajac said.

"I sure can," Fergus said.

"We've been on this planet long enough we aren't a part of any current grudges, and we aren't looking to pick sides or be forced to choose one. Our loyalty is to ourselves, and we aren't showing our whole hand to either of you, not until there's a lot more earned trust," Ajac said. "So, I want to be clear: either we all leave together, or we all need to learn to coexist. We've had peace for a long time, and no one—not you, not them—is going to wreck that."

Riji emerged from the jungle into the clearing and, as predicted, was carrying a large woven basket. "What Ajac said," she added. "There's only so many bodies that'll fit in the lake. Food?"

———

It felt like it should be late afternoon heading into evening when they started the trek back to *Sidewinder*, but the slow-moving sun was still beating down through the canopy, and the air was so humid, it felt like steam was rising out of the ground around them. Len opted to fully suit up again, but mindful of both the energy drain and the uncertain future of recharging later, Fergus carried his bundled up under one arm, and a small grass string-bag of baked chewy things in the other. His habitual shorts-and-T-shirt attire was serving him well, and though he wished he could swap his heavy boots for his sandals, that would have to wait until they cleared their own path around the lake to join up with the existing ones. He had no optimism that they'd escape there soon enough to make the effort unnecessary.

Marche had her suit peeled down to her waist and was sweating profusely.

"So, what do you think?" he asked her, at least as much for her opinion as to distract her from her misery.

"I think Ajac and Riji were telling the truth when they said they'd left the idea of the Alliance behind a long time ago," Marche said, "but I'm not convinced that spending time with their own, even after so long, won't re-up their loyalty quickly."

Riji and Ajac didn't give them a count of the other survivors, but Fergus had seen seven lifepods, which meant the number of new Alliance personnel they had to contend with was a number no greater than seven and possibly less. The aliens were practiced and efficient at killing ships, and that any of them had survived was remarkable. That *Sidewinder*'s crew had made it down there virtually intact was entirely due to the Alliance ships unwittingly distracting them at the moment of denouement, giving *Sidewinder* their chance to make a desperate run for it.

Fergus didn't figure the newbies would be magnanimous enough not to resent them for leaving them to bear the brunt of the attack, even if neither of them had known what they were getting into, and certainly no one aboard *Sidewinder* had asked or expected them to follow into the Ghostdrift.

"I suspect it depends a lot on how the lifepodders behave," Fergus said. "If they get right down to trying to order the Islanders around, they are not going to get very far, at least judging by those two."

"We don't know about the other three, though," she said.

That was true, though he felt he had a preliminary sense of what two of them were like from their conversation. Cole—their nominal leader, though that seemed merely a formality that hadn't needed to be exercised since the early days after their crash—and Safani, their medic, were off getting the lifepod survivors relocated back to their camp, which is why they hadn't been at the *Island* to meet them in person, but they did not seem like the types to make trouble without cause.

The absence of any chatter about their fifth person stood out.

What Fergus had gleaned consisted of his name—Earlan—and the impression that no one had seen him in quite some time, as well as that his reappearances in camp were irregular in occurrence and duration, and almost always a complete surprise.

Fergus didn't get the sense that the others worried about him, except for his physical and mental well-being, but he was not ready to accord the label *benign* to someone both unknown and unpredictable until at least one, if not both, of those things were no longer true. It was some consolation that the man would have a hard time skulking around *Sidewinder* without being sensed or spotted.

With luck, if Earlan did come wandering back, he'd be more interested in the podders than them anyway.

"The podders won't have much to offer, other than being more hands for labor. But they're also more mouths for the Islanders to feed," Marche said. "We have the stocks to be self-sufficient long enough to wait out any power plays from the podders, and the peoplepower to establish our own long-term food sources and shelter in the meantime."

"And we bring resources to the table that the podders don't," Fergus said. "*Fire Island* took significant damage both when it came out of jump and the aliens hit it, and then more when it crashlanded. It's a mishmash of parts, some of which must have come from older wrecks elsewhere on the surface, but ever getting it off the ground again is another story."

"Gettin' off the ground then gettin' past the gatekeepers is a nuther-nuther story," Len added.

"Yeah," Fergus said. "My point is, either the podders will see the wisdom in mutual cooperation, or they'll antagonize the Islanders, who'll need our help if any of us are to have a chance of escaping this planet. All we have to do is be seen as playing by Islander rules for a bit and not be the bigger assholes."

"Don' like rules," Len opined.

There hadn't actually been much in the way of demands from the Islanders; primarily, they wanted the *Sidewinder* crew to stay away from their camp unless or until invited, and if they could stay mostly over on their side of the lake, even better. That said, Marche had already given permission for Cole to come to them, tomorrow if it didn't rain, or the next sunny day if it did, to talk with Belos directly.

"Do you think we're going to be stuck here?" Marche asked. "For the rest of our lives?"

"I don't know," Fergus said. "There's a lot more of us now, so I would think that increases our chances of getting off the surface."

"And then what? As Len just said, even if we do get off the surface, what's to stop us getting shot full of holes again?" Marche said.

"Nothing is happening anytime soon," Fergus said. "We have time to compare notes, look at each other's data, and see if we can find a way. At least we're alive, right? This isn't so bad. The tree-things are lovely, the air is breathable, there's food, and we all have each other."

Marche grunted, and wiped the sweat from her forehead with her arm, just as a glob of booger sap dripped down from the canopy and landed on her cheek. "That's more than enough cheery, rah-rah optimism for now, Vetch," she said, and kicked a thornball out of her path as hard as she could. "I hate planets."

———

It rained for the next three days straight, and everyone aboard *Sidewinder* began to grate on each other's nerves. It didn't wholly make sense to Fergus, since after all, they'd spent months at a time together, for years or decades, within the confines of the ship, but there was something about not going anywhere, not having a clear purpose and the power and agency to pursue it, that made them all feel far more trapped. And really, they were.

As soon as the sun broke through the clouds on the fourth morning, Fergus went outside with a large machete from the armory and began chopping down and piling up stacks of wavetree fronds—Ajac had called them that, and he saw no reason not to follow their example, since they were there to name things first. Extending the open area around *Sidewinder* was a good distraction from sitting in his cabin, listening to Yolo and Trinket argue, and anyway, he very much liked the idea of having a wider perimeter to spot incoming guests.

When he got tired, he sat down on a rock in the middle of his newly created clearing, set a pot of water and booger sap to simmering over a small fire nearby, and set to work weaving together his wavetree stalks into thick ropes. He'd spent enough time repairing his tea hut that, although the material was strange under his fingers, the braiding work was familiar enough to be comfortably mindless.

Fendi was testing the environmental systems onboard and the airtightness of the damaged bulkheads, and hadn't been able to guarantee continued airflow to their cabins, so Mister Feefs was sitting nearby, surveying the new planet with deep suspicion and obvious dislike.

Marche and Kaybe came over and watched him for a bit. Kaybe had an opaque monocle over one eye and a control vambrace on his bare forearm, which meant he was currently on area drone-patrol duty. "What're you doing?" Kaybe asked after a while.

"Thought I'd build some shelter out here so that even if it's raining, we don't all have to be inside," Fergus said. "Also we can make scaffolding and shade for working on ship repairs."

"They're just ropes, though," Kaybe said.

"The Islanders got them to be rigid somehow," Marche said. "We should see if we can find out how."

"Already done. Riji told me while you were distracted, trying to trick Ajac into giving up more detail on the lifepodders," Fergus said. "It's the booger sap. Add some water, soak your woven piece, bend it to the shape you want, and when it dries, it sets up like steel."

"And what information did you give her in exchange for that valuable tidbit?" Marche asked.

"Marsball championship winners and scores for the last ten years," Fergus said. "She's an Olympian fan, sadly, but I'm doing my best not to hold that against her."

"I could not care less about sports, and don't take my knowledge of one fact to indicate otherwise, but isn't the Olympus team the all-time champs?"

"Yeah," Fergus said.

"Then why wouldn't that be everyone's favorite, including yours?" she asked.

"I'm a rooting-for-the-underdog kind of bloke," Fergus said.

"Yeah, well, this is the first time in a very long time I've felt like the underdog," Kaybe said. "I don't like it at all."

"Yes, but you have *Vetch* rooting for you," Marche said, not even trying to hide the sarcasm.

"Oh, that does make me feel better! Thanks, Marche!" Kaybe said brightly, and clapped her enthusiastically on the back. "Now look alive; we got visitors coming in."

Riji was the only familiar face of the three people who emerged from the waveforest into their clearing. Cole was skinny in a wiry, athletic way, and hadn't let his hair grow out like Ajac, but he walked with an easy, confident gait that, in Fergus's experience, suggested he'd either been a junior officer at best, or if he did hold a senior position, he'd earned it via combat rather than ass-kissing and pedantic rules-lawyering. He expected which one it was would make itself apparent quickly.

Safani was shorter than Cole, and had a thicker body type that was no less athletic. She had a bulky medical pack on, but moved as if she didn't; she was wearing a deep red tank top, and her bare shoulders and arms were a smooth, muscular deep brown. "You got a man down?" she asked as they entered the clearing. Her expression was all business, giving nothing away.

"Marche, you want to take her to Rabbit and let the boss know our guests have arrived?" Kaybe asked.

Marche nodded, and held out a hand, gesturing Safani toward the ship. "I'm Marche," she said. "Happy to meet you. If you—"

She was interrupted by a furry black bullet suddenly letting out a yowl, leaping across Fergus's lap, and disappearing through the open cargo doors into the ship ahead of them.

The medic stopped and stared. "Was that a *cat*?" she asked.

"Yes, and don't even ask, I don't know what in the hell—"

"I love cats," Safani interrupted, her neutral facade falling away as she broke into a huge grin. "Do you think I can pet it, maybe? What's its name?"

"Oh," Marche said, blinking for a moment. "I'm sure you can. His name is . . . uh. Floofs. Master Floofs. We all simply adore him."

"I think I'm going to like you people after all," Safani said.

Marche indicated she should go in first, then, after she had, turned and glared at Fergus from the top of the ramp.

"Floofs, huh?" he asked. "And you adore him?"

"You: shut it, or else," Marche said, drawing a line across her throat with her finger before heading in after Safani.

Cole was standing a respectful distance away, waiting patiently, as Riji moved in to get a closer look at the damage to *Sidewinder.* "After all these years, I can't wait to finally see the inside of one of these ships," she said. "Damn, but that's a mean-looking piece of work."

"Thanks, I think," Fendi said, emerging from the hold doors with Belos. "I'm Fendayre. Engineer. I designed and built both *Rattler* and *Sidewinder.*"

"Riji. Engineer," she said, and stuck out her hand for him to shake. "I've rebuilt about eighty percent of *Fire Island*, so far, but I'm almost out of decent materials."

"Marche said you've been using scrap from other shipwrecks?" Fendi asked.

"Yeah. Planet is littered with them. Not many other places to run to, so everyone who could, tried to get here. Most of them didn't survive the landing," she said.

"Did any?"

"Other than us? There are remnants of what looks like make-shift camps and some skeletons," she said. "Some aren't human. There were a bunch of alien ships up in the debris field that were all the same but didn't match our attackers. We didn't recognize either."

"The wrecks were Bomo'ri," Fergus spoke up. "Sorry. Didn't mean to interrupt."

"Not a worry," Riji said. "We thought maybe the Bomo'ri were the ones who attacked us, but I guess by process of elimination, that must've been the Asiig."

"Vetch doesn't think so," Fendi said.

"No? Why not? Who else would be out here?" she asked.

"I don't know yet," Fergus said. "But it's not the Asiig."

"How can you know that?"

"Because I've seen their ships," he said, and didn't add, *I've been inside, gotten the tour, and been taxied around the galaxy mostly against my will in one, too.*

"No one's seen their ships and lived to tell," Riji said.

"Not true. They fly by Cernee at least a couple of times a standard year, looking for people unwisely out and about, and scaring the shit out of the locals," Fergus said. "Cernee is outside the usual Alliance jurisdiction, though, and everyone is poor, so no one pays any attention to what's going on there."

"This guy for real?" Cole asked.

Belos nodded. "I trust his judgment," he said. "His insights are sometimes strange at first, but he hasn't been wrong yet."

"And how long has he been on your crew?"

"Six years," Belos lied. "But we digress. The question is: do you and the other *Fire Island*ers want off this planet as much as we do, and will the other new planetary residents cooperate?"

Cole sat on one of the other rocks and rubbed at his chin. "They're not there yet," he said at last. "I mean, they're elated to discover that a few of us survived, but they blame you and your sister for them being here, and that's not wholly untrue."

"We never asked them to follow us," Belos said. "I'd go so far as to say we made quite a lot of effort *not* to be followed."

"Devotion to duty is a lot more compelling when you're never away from it," Cole said. "I've made it clear to them that I expect a truce on the ground, and at least for now, while we're feeding and taking care of their injuries, they accept my authority. The same goes for your people. It's still a big if, whether we can get off this planet at all by pooling our resources, but even best-case, it's still going to take time. They'll come around after a while, if nothing else happens to create new conflicts."

"I've made it clear to my people that we are not going to start anything," Belos said.

"That's all I can ask," Cole said. He held up a small datachit. "As a gesture of good faith, I've brought all of *Fire Island*'s recordings from our encounter with the aliens, up until they permanently fried our ship mindsystem."

"How did you land, then?"

"Badly," Cole said. "Ajac manually piloted us down. Saved the few of us still alive, and I doubt many could've done better with a crushed leg. None of our med-chambers survived the crash, so Safani had to amputate it. Just another thing we couldn't save or fix."

"From what I saw, you've done a hell of a job on *Fire Island* so far," Fergus said. "You think it'll fly again?"

"No mindsystem," Cole said. "We spent years trying to get the ship back online, before we gave up. We've tried to connect what we can back up to the bridge to operate manually, but there's only five of us—or there were, until now—and it's too much. We'd have given up long ago except there's not much else to do around here. Also, Riji is stubborn."

"I am," Riji confirmed. "I have to be, since everything has to be improvised. Including tools, since we lost half of those in the crash, too. I'd give Ajac's other leg for a damned polarized relay coupling spanner."

"I have one," Fendi said. "And even if I didn't, we have a fab unit."

Riji's face lit up. "Aww, now," she said. "I think we've found a solid basis for trade."

Cole smiled. "I suspect your ship is still more spaceworthy than ours, but once the diplomatic niceties with the podders have been satisfied, we can pivot to working on whichever would give us the best chance of escape."

Fendi shook his head. "I don't know," he said. "At least you've got other Alliance wrecks to scavenge for compatible parts."

Riji frowned. "I mean, but you have your parts source too?"

she asked, puzzled. "We just need to figure out how to haul what you need—"

"Parts source?" Fendi asked.

"Well, yeah. The wreck of *Rattler*—" She broke off as Belos and Fendi stared at her. "Isn't that why you're here? It came down just up on the other side of the mountains."

Chapter 12

B elos took the data from Cole with distracted gratitude as Fendi fabbed a spanner for Riji. The only moment where he seemed to emerge fully from whatever thoughts were storming through his head was when Safani reported that the med-chamber seemed to be operating properly and had stabilized Rabbit, though it was too early to tell how well it would be able to repair all the damage. "If you hadn't gotten him into the chamber when you did, he wouldn't have made it," she said. "Honestly, I'm surprised he outlived sustaining the original injuries."

"He's as stubborn as they come," Belos said. "Thank you very much for checking on him."

"It's what I do," she said. "I'm willing to come over and check on him again in a few days, if you'd like."

"We would appreciate that," Belos said.

"If you need a guide on your hike up to *Rattler*—" Cole started to say, but Belos shook his head.

"You understand, I've been searching for answers on what happened to my sister's ship since the day she disappeared," Belos said. "This is . . . a difficult moment. I would like it to be a private one, for me and my crew."

"I understand," Cole said. "I had hoped to facilitate a conversation between you and Captain Todd, one of the survivors of the—"

"—*Paradigm*," Fergus interrupted. "I do believe we've already met. Not, I'm afraid, under ideal circumstances."

"The last conversation we had with your Captain Todd, he told me that what he wanted was to find and bury his dead. It has turned out that not all of you are quite so deceased," Belos said. "Do remind him of that conversation, and ask that he accord me the same respect and space to do the same for my own."

"Of course," Cole said. "As to my earlier offer of a guide, there aren't a lot of dangers on Solo, but there are still some. If you'd like me to brief one of your crew . . ."

"Vetch here will be glad to listen to whatever warnings you have, and pass them on as needed," Belos said. "If you'll excuse me, I have some things to attend to." Belos disappeared back into *Sidewinder* just as Fendi emerged, spanner in hand.

Fendi handed Riji the spanner, and she turned it over in her hand as if he'd handed her a bar of gold. "Thank you," she said. "You have no idea how helpful this will be."

"I broke one once and had to wait 'til we limped into port to buy the recipe so I could make a new one, so I get it," Fendi said. "I'm not going on the expedition up the mountains, so if you want to stop by and compare notes, let me know. I don't want to go too far from Rabbit, but I want to get out of here—get him out of here, to a real medical facility—just as badly as you all do. We still have to figure out how to get past the aliens at the jump point, but if we can't get off the ground, that won't matter."

"I don't know how much of use is on that data chit, but it's what we've got," Cole said. "It all happened very fast, and we were so busy just trying to survive, none of us saw much of what else was happening around us. Believe me, we've all replayed the attack in our heads, and in our nightmares, ever since. As much as I dare to hope we'll find a way home again, I can't say I'm not also terrified of facing those ships again."

"Same," Safani added.

"We have time," Fergus said. "Maybe with our shared data, along with whatever Todd's people managed to see and record, we'll have enough to come up with a plan."

"Speaking of plans, let me tell you about what Safani affectionately calls Surprise Face-Attack Stinging Shitbugs," Cole said. "Because once you get up into the cooler hills, they are going to be everywhere."

Riji shuddered. "They *swarm*," she said.

"Great," Fergus said.

"Oh, and Cole, don't forget about the Stomper-Crushers," Riji said.

"Or the Needle-Blaster Trigger Trees," Safani said.

"Or the Screaming Ankle-Chomping Night Horrors," Riji said.

"Or the—" Safani started to say.

Fergus held up a hand. "One monster at a time, please, and I really hope you're making all this up just to mess with us."

Riji smiled. "I guess you'll find out, won't you?"

———

It was a two-day hike up over the mountains, and that was local-planet days, not Earthhabit days. Fergus led, since he'd memorized the map and had gotten the full rundown of dangers and annoyances from the Islanders, and about a third of the way into trying to explain them to the others, mid-sentence on the Hella Constipation Berries, Belos had decided it would take longer to tell them the dangers than to just have him go first and shout "Look out!" or "Don't touch that!" if they encountered anything bad.

Belos and Kaybe came next; Kaybe had been adamant that there were no circumstances in which he'd be left behind short of his death. Bel Belos and the other *Rattler* crew had been as close to being family to him as they were to Bas.

Trinket brought up the rear. She was still angry with Yolo, and despite the latter claiming he wanted to repair things with his former best friend, she was not having any of it, at least not yet, and more than one of their arguments had turned into shoving matches.

Since the revelation about his sister's ship, Belos's temper had become a simmering thing, like an underground fire whose spread was only detectable by the occasional odd wisps of smoke. Yolo had also broken his trust and now seemed oblivious to the much greater danger that posed in the captain's current mood.

Separating them for a while was the obvious best thing for all, but especially for Yolo's longevity, even if he wasn't smart enough to realize it.

The wavetrees thinned out as they got higher up, and were slowly replaced by another form of local plant life, which were long turquoise sprays of what looked like serrated-edge grass blades sticking up from twisty, bump-covered trunks. "Try not to jostle those too hard," he warned the others, looking back over his shoulder to the rest of the group just in time to stumble into one himself and feel dozens of tiny needles blow right through his shirt and sink into his chest. "Aaugh!" he shouted, jumped back, bumped another and got more needles shot into his thigh.

"Thank you for the excellent demonstration, Vetch," Belos said. "Do you need to stop for a moment so you can recompose yourself?"

"Yeah," Fergus said. He moved very carefully away from the Trigger Trees into a clearing, peeled his shirt carefully away from his side, and plucked out the bright blue needles one by one, wiping blood off his fingers every few as his grip got too slippery. Then he looked down at his thigh. "Uh, I'm going to need some privacy," he said.

Kaybe stuck his monocle in and hefted a mini drone up into the air. A few minutes later, he brought it back in, shut it down to conserve its battery, and popped his monocle back in his bag.

"There's a clearing about four hundred meters ahead, and a pond. It'll make a good place to break for a bit. Meet us there?"

"Yeah," Fergus said.

The others filed past him, all carefully avoiding the Trigger Trees, and as Trinket went by last, she patted him on the shoulder and handed him a tube of skin sealant from her pack.

Once they were out of sight, he heaved one last indignant, put-upon-unfairly-by-the-universe sigh, dropped his shorts, and removed the second set of needles before smearing some of the sealant over the tiny pinpricks of blood they'd left behind. There was a rock nearby, and after putting his shorts back on, he sat gingerly on it and looked closely at one of the needles. It was not that far different from a porcupine quill, though made of fiber rather than keratinous hair. They both had the same nasty, barbed hook at the end.

It was a very efficient defense mechanism, and there was nothing particularly out of the ordinary about it as such, except that it made no sense for evolution to have provided for defense unless there was something out there on *offense.*

He closed his eyes and let his extra sense take in the world around him in a widening circle. It was easy to find the other three, already most of the way toward the clearing. Behind him, in the distance, he could feel both *Sidewinder* and *Fire Island.* The Islander camp was faint in his perceptions, and mostly only detectable because the lifepods had been hauled to the edge of it, and he could feel the energy of them.

Forgetting about people, he tried to sense what else was out there, and immediately found *Rattler,* still emanating low energy, ahead.

About a kilometer away, moving slowly in the direction of the wreck, was another strong source of electrical signal, definitely not natural but technological. The mysterious Earlan? Everyone else was accounted for, and Riji had told him that Earlan wandered far and wide, only returning to their camp for a few days at a time before taking off again.

Nearer, but much harder to pick out, a tight group of some sort of very large creature was moving away from them, deeper into the waveforest; he only felt them at all because there were so many, so close together. That they were going in the other direction was a relief. Whatever they were, maybe they were just as uninterested in the prospect of encountering him.

They camped at the clearing, restless by the time the long night finally faded into a grayish, overcast dawn. Fergus lay in the tent he was sharing with Trinket for a long time after he woke, taking in the world again.

The herd was farther away but not by much, perhaps waiting for them to pass and be gone from their favorite stomping grounds.

Stomper-Crushers, Riji had quipped, which he'd added to the list of fake-sounding things right alongside Needle-Blaster Trigger Trees. He moved that over into the *maybe not a lie* column and decided that, regardless, all of them needed better, less-ridiculous names.

Unlike them, Earlan—or whatever it was, with its artificial signal source—was still heading toward *Rattler*, and at his current pace, would get there a full half-day ahead of them.

Fergus decided he would worry about it when they got closer.

"You talk in your sleep, yanno," Trinket spoke up from deep within her sleeping bag. "Not that I could understand almost any of it."

"And what you could?"

"You kept asking someone named Venetia to come get you," she said. "A lover?"

"A friend," he answered. A friend who was a spaceship, as it happened, but he was a long way away from being willing to drop that kind of traceable information so casually, no matter how permanently marooned they might be.

"Yeah, well, if she comes and gets you, can I catch a lift?"

He laughed and sat up in his own bag, rubbing at his face. "If she does, absolutely," he said, "but I've been gone long enough that I don't expect anyone's even looking for me anymore. And if they were, they would not be looking anywhere near here."

"Yeah. Aurora Enclave," Trinket said, and he nodded, remembering that was his cover story. "Out of one prison right onto another. Rough luck."

"At least this one has sunlight," Fergus said. He got up, rolled up his bag, and set it to compact itself back down to a more-portable bundle.

He left the tent to give Trinket privacy, if she needed it, and saw that Kaybe had started a small fire and had a pot balanced on a rock in the middle of it. "Bas went ahead to scout," Kaybe said. "You want to go check on him and let him know coffee in ten?"

"Sure," Fergus said. He shook out his boots of the previous day's accumulated dirt and dead frond-bits, slipped them on, and headed up the hillside. It was easy enough to find Belos once he got out past the last few trees. Belos stood on a rock along a ridge ahead, looking out and down on the far side.

Fergus made sure to make enough noise not to startle the captain, and climbed up to stand near him.

Rattler lay below, half-obscured by overgrowth. One of its ramming arms was gone, and it lay at an angle on one side, with massive burn marks and scoring up and down its length. From this vantage point, they could see the twist in its body, the holes where the hull had been punctured, the plating torn away.

"I know there's no way she survived," Belos spoke up. "I accepted she was dead a long time ago and told myself I only wanted answers, but dammit, Vetch, turns out I wanted to have *hope*."

"I'm sorry," Fergus said.

Belos stood up straighter. "No apologies necessary. I gave you the impossible job of finding those answers, and here we are. In the end, it's still a lot more than I had."

"Kaybe has coffee almost ready," Fergus said.

"Good," Belos said, and together they headed back down toward their campsite. "Then we pack up and keep going. I want to get down there while we still have plenty of daylight left."

———

The other side of the mountain was more treacherous, as Cole had warned them. About halfway down to the valley floor, they found themselves on a large, flat ledge atypical of most of their descent, and unanimously decided on a much-needed break.

As Kaybe broke out snacks, Fergus sat with his legs dangling over the edge of the rock and went looking with his Asiig sense for Earlan's signal. It was moving around the circumference of *Rattler*, stopping at intervals for several minutes at a time before moving on, and after each stop, the signal from him got fainter, more diffuse.

Now that he was feeling for lighter electrical noise, he realized there was a source only a few dozen meters down from where they were. It seemed they were not the only ones who thought the ledge was too good a resting place to pass up.

Fergus had already ditched his pack with the others, but he went back to it and pulled out his water bottle, and took a long drink. Then he pulled out his suit goggles and toggled them to a manual feed, and looked for a roundabout way down that would not take him directly at the source of the nearby signal.

"Vetch, where are you going?" Kaybe called after him.

"Going to check something," he answered. "Be back shortly."

A few moments later, Belos was climbing down behind him. "No one goes alone," the pirate said.

He followed Fergus downslope through the thickening forest of wavetrees. They were far enough down that the wreck of *Rattler* would no longer visible to them, even if there weren't trees in the way, but none of the signal there had changed location or intensity. The source of the nearer signal was now at about the same height as they were and in a more direct line from the ledge than Fergus had taken.

He crept slowly sideways through the wavetrees, careful not to disturb any, until he was close enough to look ahead and up and see what was making the signal. He'd expected some sort of sensor, not yet activated, but as soon as he spotted it, he stopped in his tracks and put up a hand to warn Belos. "It's a detonator," he whispered, "attached to a thin woven bag."

"A trap," Belos said. "Can you see how it's triggered?"

"Not yet," Fergus said, and took another step closer, and then peered all around. A thin wire ran down the side of the wavetree away from the edge and, once on the ground, disappeared into the leaf debris built up below. The debris was recently disturbed, and Fergus knelt carefully and lifted fronds until he found it running past him and to another tree, crossing the clearest path through. "Trip wire, from here over to there," he said, and pointed along it.

"How in the stars did you— No, forget I asked," Belos said. "I know for an absolute certainty you didn't place this; otherwise, I'd be convinced the only way you could know this was here was that you'd done it yourself. And I know you're just going to tell me again about your exceptional hearing."

"That is not a lie," Fergus said. "What I have not been forthcoming about, and I'm only doing so now because I need to tell you other things that I have no apparent way of knowing, is that I can hear electricity."

"Like, a hum?" Belos asked, with clear skepticism.

"It's more complicated than that," Fergus said. "But I heard this device, and I can hear others."

"Where?" Belos asked.

"Down around *Rattler*. There's someone there. My guess is it's the missing Islander, Earlan."

"How do you know *that*?" Belos asked, voice rising.

Fergus shrugged. "I've already told you more than I want to. Either you trust me or you don't."

"Shit," Belos said. "That's hard to believe. Enhanced hearing is one thing, but augments for that? I've never even caught a hint of any tech like that, and there are a lot of unlicensed aug labs in the Barrens that shop for customers or experimental subjects at Ijikijolo. I— Oh, hell, *that's* how you found the bug on the outside of *Sidewinder*."

"Yeah," Fergus said. "It was loud."

Belos was silent for a long stretch, thinking.

"I'd rather you not tell anyone else," Fergus said, after a while.

"Only if I have to. The safety of my crew always comes before any such promises," Belos said. "The Islanders originally had a sixth person, who they said had drowned. Maybe that was a lie. Could there be two people down there?"

"I think it's just one, but I'm not near enough to tell for sure," Fergus said. "That said, Earlan was their intelligence officer, and he had some kind of breakdown and left the camp. This sneaky-spy bullshit fits with that. The dead guy was some kind of officer."

"Suggestions for what we do now?" Belos asked.

"We come down the way Earlan was expecting us to, and we just don't set off his tripwire. He won't know if we just missed it or it malfunctioned. Either of those is a more likely scenario than that we spotted it," Fergus said. "Wish I knew what was in the bag, though."

"Are there more ahead of us?" Belos asked.

"Likely around the perimeter of *Rattler* itself," Fergus said.

Belos ran his hand over his half-beard, then over the Lekos Brotherhood ink beside it. "Rain coming in, you think?" he asked.

Fergus looked up at the sky through the canopy, and it was definitely getting gray. "Another half-hour or so, I'd guess," he said.

"You don't strike me as the sort of man who'd be uncomfortable operating alone," Belos said.

Fergus gave a short laugh. "No, not so much."

"You think Earlan can see us when we're up on that ledge?"

"I expect he'll find a way to watch it, if he can. What are you thinking?"

"Pitch our tents as if we're planning to wait out the rain. It would be a reasonable choice. Then the rest of us go ahead, leaving the tents and you behind as decoys."

"So, either he comes to us and we catch him by surprise midway, or when you're nearly to *Rattler*, I take down the tents and then trip the explosive," Fergus said. "That way, I get to find out what's in the bag, and he thinks he knows where we are."

"Exactly," Belos said. "You would have made an excellent real pirate, you know, if only you were a little more inclined toward violence."

"Thanks," Fergus said.

"It's going to take a bit for me to wrap my head around this ability of yours enough to factor it into our plans," Belos said. "One hell of a party trick you've got. I'd love to know where you got it installed."

"Speaking of tricks," Fergus said, backpedaling away from *that* unwanted conversation, "don't forget Earlan's an intelligence guy. Good bet he'll be paranoid enough to have a fallback plan."

"I live for the pleasure of ruining people's plans and fallback plans," Belos said. "Time to go back and brief the team."

The rain came in just after they'd set up the tents, and the steam rising up from the forest made excellent cover for the other three to start their descent from the ledge.

Kaybe left him half a pot of coffee, so he sat just inside the tent flaps and watched with his goggles, listening to the other three's chatter on his earpiece. When they neared the tripwire, he talked them around it safely.

"How the hell did you know that was there? Or where we are right now?" Trinket demanded.

"I am a mighty, all-powerful wizard," Fergus said. "Even the trees are my eyes and ears, and the earth itself whispers to me of your passing."

"That is a creepy-ass answer," Trinket said. "What's worse is that I almost believe you."

As the ground leveled out closer to the wreck, the team fell silent. He could sense them spreading out, moving through the waveforest like they were born to it instead of completely out of their usual combat environments. When they had all taken up positions and stopped moving, Kaybe checked in. His voice had the distinctive low hum that meant it had been subvocalized on his end. "I see him. He's sitting atop the remaining ramming arm."

"You ready for me to make some noise?" Fergus asked.

"Do it," Belos said.

Fergus set the tents to compact and then dropped off the ledge into the waveforest. It didn't take him long to find the same spot, and he stepped carefully over the tripwire, got a solid footing on the wet leaves at sufficient distance that he wasn't too worried about the immediate fallout of setting off the detonator, then pulled his slingshot and a metal ball out of his pack.

It only took him a few seconds to charge up the ball. The flow of the electricity through his body felt good, like stretching a muscle starting to fall asleep.

He nailed it on the first try.

The trap activated, sending a bright red flare screaming up through the canopy into the gray sky. The explosion of the flare when it launched was just enough to break apart the top of the grass bag fastened directly below it. It fell heavily to the ground and split open, releasing a swarm of many angry somethings into the air.

Fergus was far enough away to not be in any immediate danger, and he took care to back farther away slowly and quietly. From Riji's early description, they were Surprise Face-Attack Stinging Shitbugs—again, there needed to be a serious conversation about renaming things—who, Riji had delighted in informing him, injected unpleasant toxins when they stung.

"No, thanks," he muttered.

"Vetch, check in," Belos called.

"I assume you all saw the flare. It also dumped out a whole lot of pissed-off . . . Uh, do you know what hornets are?" Fergus asked.

"I remember," Belos said. "There's a lot of things I don't miss about Earth. Kaybe, where's our friend now?"

"Still up on the ramming arm but standing up now, looking toward Vetch's position," Kaybe said.

"Unless he climbs down, he's got the high ground," Fergus said. "I'm not sure how you can sneak up on him without—"

"We got this," Belos said. "Get down here quick if you don't want to miss the fun."

"On my way," he said, and left the bugs to their directionless, impotent rage.

———

Fergus had gotten line of sight on *Rattler* just in time to see Trinket lob a rock out of the trees. It hit the scraggly, emaciated, hirsute man in the tattered remains of an Alliance officer jacket, standing on the top of the wreck, in the back. The man reacted faster than Fergus would have expected, half-turning and leaping down from the ramming arm, hitting the ground running and dodging like a jackrabbit in full panic.

Trinket threw another rock, well to one side of him, but it spooked the man into veering away from where it hit, right into the fist of Kaybe Shale.

The man landed on his back and immediately began scrambling away, pulling a knife from his boot and holding it toward Kaybe, until a sudden shadow over him made him glance up and back, and Bas Belos put his boot down on the man's neck. "Drop it," Belos said.

The man complied and went limp, but his eyes darted around as if he was already calculating his chances and means of escape.

"You must be Earlan," Belos said. The man tried to nod but couldn't move his head. "Your fellow Islanders asked me not to kill you. I told them I'd take their request under advisement."

"Did . . ." Earlan squeaked out. His voice was hoarse, despite the pitch, and not from Belos's boot. "Did you kill them?"

"No," Belos said. "Why would I?"

"You're the enemy," Earlan said.

Trinket joined them, set down a handful of rocks, and pulled out her own knife. She patted Earlan down thoroughly for weapons and removed what little he had in his pockets. Once she was satisfied he was no danger, she sat just out of his reach and grinned at him in a way that made the man squirm and go pale.

"I suppose we are enemies," Belos said. "Not with the others, unless they make it so, but *you*. You were the intelligence officer. You planned the trap that drove my sister here to her death. Didn't you?"

"Yes," Earlan said, defiance returning. "It was my *job*. I didn't know about the jump. I got almost everyone killed."

"Is that why you ran away from your camp? All those deaths on your conscience?"

"No. I ran away because of Thacker. *Fire Island*'s first mate."

"Ah," Fergus said. "The sixth survivor who drowned in a lake."

"He had help with that," Earlan said, glowering.

"Why? Why was that the one death that broke you?"

"Because he was my commanding officer and a friend, and I'm the one who held him under," he said. "I don't want to talk about it, certainly not with you rabble. Just get it over with and kill me quick, okay?"

Belos held out a hand, and Trinket put her knife into it. He knelt beside Earlan. "You had a mole, in Ijikijolo, who fed my sister the lies to get her to fly into your trap. Who was it? If you tell even one lie, you won't get a chance for a second."

"We had a plant named Lestov who worked the fueling depot. He had an unwitting dupe better positioned on the station that he'd launder the tips through to cover his tracks. We didn't know who he would send our way, mostly low-level opportunists and drug runners, but we weren't going to turn down the chance to finally bring down one of the famous Belos twins," Earlan said. "I saw your ship come down, the other night. The fact that you're here means I eventually got you, too."

"My reasons for keeping you alive are only the slightest margin more compelling than how much I want you dead," Belos said. He stood up again and handed the knife, handle-first, back to Trinket. "I may have more questions. Do not make me reevaluate my priorities, for you will find I'm vindictive, unforgiving, and not above making overly dramatic gestures of my displeasure."

Belos strode away from where the man lay, looking bemused to still be alive, and regarded *Rattler*. "Have you disturbed anything inside?" he asked, without turning back.

"Never could," Earlan said. "Ship wouldn't let us."

"It's mindsystem is still alive?" Belos asked.

"Must be. I've tried talking to it, though no answer. Zaps you hard if you touch the airlocks, though," Earlan said.

Belos stopped close enough to reach out and touch the ship, if he wished to, though he didn't. He took out his earpiece, changed the settings, then spoke to it. "Fang?" he asked. "It's me."

There was a long, long pause, then they heard the tiny, faint, scratchy voice of the ship's computer, identical to the one aboard *Sidewinder*. "I waited," it said.

"Yes. Thank you," Belos answered. "May I come in?"

The airlock door ground open about halfway and then jammed. Belos looked back at the group. "Kaybe?" he asked.

"I'm coming," Kaybe said. He touched Trinket's shoulder on his way past. "If this man moves, twitches, sneezes, breathes too loud, or even just looks at you funny, you have my permission to slice his throat or any other damned part of him you want. We'll be back."

The two of them disappeared into *Rattler*.

"Don't know you two," Earlan said, after a while, eyeing Trinket and Fergus. "Been pirates for long?"

"Shut it," Trinket said.

"I mean, clearly you're just some hired muscle, not important enough to merit a dossier of your own. Belos got you in over your heads, though, and I bet he didn't even ask. Where's the profit now?"

"I said shut it," Trinket repeated, and kicked him.

Earlan let his head fall to one side, and he studied Fergus for a while. "You're more than a grunt. What do you do?"

"He's our wizard," Trinket said, and laughed. "He can turn you into a rat, but me? I can turn you into a tongueless corpse if you don't stop talking. You ain't getting into our heads that easy."

"Can't blame me for trying," Earlan said.

"Sure I can," she answered.

The man was silent for a stretch at that. He looked exhausted, malnourished, and Fergus noted he smelled bad for someone who had just been thoroughly rained on. An illness or a lingering infection? It was hard to know.

Fergus had just decided it wouldn't hurt to ask if the man needed medical care when Kaybe emerged from *Rattler*, and then Belos after him. The captain's expression was one of disbelief and bleak, bottomless despair, and he abandoned any further concern about Earlan and hurried over.

"It's empty," Belos said. "No bodies. Nothing. She's not here. None of them are here."

Chapter 13

◆

"Lifepods?" Fergus asked.

"All there," Kaybe said.

"Shuttle?"

"Also present. It looks remarkably undamaged," Kaybe said. "If they'd had to abandon ship for some reason, why not take it?"

"Could the Alliance have got to *Rattler* before the aliens did? Taken them prisoner?"

"No way," Earlan said from where he was still lying on the ground, Trinket toying with her knife nearby.

"Shut up, you," Trinket warned.

"No, let him talk," Belos said. "Why no way?"

"Because I saw *Rattler* cripple both *Stiletto* and *Silver Mist* with my own eyes," Earlan said.

"And? Tell me the whole story," Belos said.

"Fine, okay. We were the last out of jump and arrived just as *Rattler* was moving in for the kill on *Mist*. I was on the bridge. We had the element of surprise and got a couple of good shots in. Hit her engines, left her drifting," Earlan said. "The captain and first mate were arguing about whether to board and secure *Rattler*'s crew before they could get their engines back online, or finish her off so we could help our people without worrying any more about your sister, when the aliens appeared."

"Then what happened?" Belos asked.

"The aliens hit us first, because we were closest still to the jump-conduit terminus, then went after the others. *Rattler* blew all her cannonballs at the lead alien, and when they turned for her, we ran for our lives. *Rattler* crashed about twelve, maybe fourteen hours after us."

"Then they're on this planet," Belos said. "They survived after all."

"No. We got here as fast as we could, Thacker and Cole and I. We were thinking we could capture the crew and use *Rattler* to get home again, but there was no sign anyone had exited the ship, nothing. And the ship's mindsystem has kept us out ever since."

"You can't know that no one got out," Belos said.

"I used to do fugitive tracking. Not just chasing pirates in space, but planetside too. I was the best. I *do* know," Earlan said. "And even if I didn't, look at that wreck. You know no one walked away from that."

"Could the aliens have taken them?" Trinket asked.

"You see any signs up in that graveyard that they wanted prisoners?" Belos snapped. "There has to be an explanation. They have to have gone *somewhere*."

Fergus got a strange, itchy feeling on the back of his neck, and he didn't like the other possibility that leapt to mind. Belos must have caught the expression in his face. "Vetch? You have any ideas?"

"Fang should have logs," Fergus said, avoiding having to lie or, even worse, tell the truth. "That could have some answers."

"The ship has very limited power left. Just enough for Fang to be guarding its perimeter and not much else. We'd need a power source."

"The detonator that Earlan used to set his trap would have had its own small power cell," Fergus said. "We could chain more of them up, get a short boost that way."

"That within your skills?" Kaybe asked.

"Yeah," Fergus said. "If Earlan can tell us where the rest of his traps are. I mean, you must have set some around the ship, too, right? Stands to reason."

"Five," Earlan said. "I can show you, if you let me."

"Let him up, Trinks," Kaybe said.

Earlan sat up, brushed dirt off his pants and out of his beard, and then got up wearily to his feet. "First one's over here," he said, and pointed. "I buried them."

"Only five? That's not very good coverage," Fergus said.

Earlan shrugged. "Might have been six. I'm not sure. I didn't really count."

At least I'm not the only liar here, Fergus thought; he could clearly sense eight. "Okay then. Dig 'em up."

"You want a knife?" Trinket asked. "I have spares."

"No, I'm not worried about Earlan," Fergus said. "He should be worried about me. I don't like a man who tries to drop an entire bag of angry bees in my face."

"Missed, though," Earlan said, "more's the pity."

He led Fergus to the first hidden charge; the man had done an impressive job repositioning the leaf litter so that it looked undisturbed, not that it mattered in the slightest with the shriek of electricity underneath. "There?" Fergus asked, pointing at a spot of ground not quite where he could feel the signal. "You sure?"

The man smiled, smug. He knelt, brushed the leaf litter away from the correct spot, and then carefully pried up the small charge and disabled it before handing it and its payload over. Fergus could feel it was off now, so he took it casually, carelessly.

The payload was another flare, but Fergus was pretty sure, from the way the canister was rigged, that there was also shrapnel inside. "Huh," he said. "This one rattles."

Earlan said nothing, but the smugness went up a notch.

Two traps later, Earlan handed him a still-live one. It was easy to short the sensor attached to the charge just from contact with his palm, and he added it to his growing handful as if nothing was out of the ordinary. Earlan hesitated for only a few seconds, puzzled disappointment crossing his face before he got his disinterested mask back up.

He tried it again with the next one, and the one after, and Fergus could tell he was becoming flustered. "Next one's over there," Earlan said, pointing at an empty spot of forest a fair ways ahead of them, in a straight line directly over and beyond the next actual trap location. "You go on ahead; I've got something in my boot."

"Sure," Fergus said. He walked ahead, and when he put his foot down on top of the hidden trap and felt it set, waiting for his foot to lift again to detonate, he shorted that out too and kept walking.

Belos and Kaybe were deep in conversation, but both of them had eyes locked on Fergus and Earlan.

When he reached the spot Earlan had pointed at, he turned around to see Earlan glaring at him. "What? What was in your boot?" he asked.

"My . . . Oh. Just a pebble," Earlan said. "I already shook it out."

"Great! So, last one, you think, right about here? The others were all spaced really evenly, though," Fergus said. He bent down and picked up a small rock. "See, from your pattern, I'd've thought it would be about *there*."

He tossed the rock at where the trap actually was, and Earlan threw himself to one side, face-down on the ground, and put his arms over his head to protect it.

The rock hit with a dull *thump*, rolled about a meter, and stopped.

Earlan lifted his hands and openly stared, as Trinket began to guffaw behind them.

"Hey, friend, did you trip?" Fergus asked, innocently. "Do you need a hand up?"

"Fuck you. You're messing with me. You must have got here ahead of me and watched me plant those," Earlan snarled.

"Didn't you just tell us that you were Earth's greatest tracker, though?" Fergus asked. "If so, wouldn't you know it if I'd been here? Or maybe you've lost your touch and you should stop underestimating all of us and thinking we'll fall for your lies. Or that we'll put up with them indefinitely."

Earlan said nothing.

"No apology?" Fergus asked. "That was six. Two more, right? And I bet they are nice and evenly spaced like all the others."

The man didn't try any other tricks, which was just fine with Fergus.

After he'd disconnected the energy cells, he handed off the rest of the parts to Trinket, who added them to the pile of stuff she'd dug out of Earlan's pockets. "These need to be wired in manually," he said to Belos. "Do you need instructions?"

"No. Kaybe will back up Trinks; you come inside with me this time. A new set of eyes on things can't hurt," Belos said.

Fergus followed Belos in.

The interior of *Rattler* was almost, but not quite, identical to *Sidewinder*. Little details varied; conduits here and there off slightly, touch panels in different places. Also dust and very old dried blood.

Belos saw him pause. "Enough for someone to be dead, not enough for someone to have become a fine red mist," he said, and gestured around. "No body."

On the bridge, Fergus crawled under the console and sneezed several times from the stirred-up dust as he connected up the chained energy cells. "That should do it," he said.

Belos sat in the captain's chair. "Fang," he said. "What's your status?"

"Forty percent online, which will conserve the added power for another twenty days," Fang said. "I can go to seventy percent, but that will reduce my operational window to eight."

"Proceed, please," Belos said. "Tell me what happened to your crew."

"We were left with no escape aside from the Ghostdrift and jumped, but we were followed. On arrival, despite extensive damage from the transit, we engaged two Alliance ships, the warship *Stiletto* and the small cruiser *Silver Mist*. We were able to gain on both, when a third cruiser appeared, the *Fire Island*. I am sorry to say it took me by surprise and hit my engines," the ship's computer said.

"It's okay," Belos said. "Then what?"

"Nine alien ships appeared in our local space. They attacked *Fire Island*, and then one split off and headed toward us. We fired upon the alien ship, but it had only a very limited effect. As the Alliance attempted to retreat, the aliens followed them. We drifted into the ship graveyard, and Captain Belos ordered me to shut down everything on the ship. We played dead."

"Then?"

"The aliens left."

"Left . . . chasing the Alliance ships?"

"No. *Silver Mist* had catastrophically decompressed, and *Stiletto*, which was losing its own internal atmosphere, crashed into this planet with sufficient force to render any remaining crew no longer viable," Fang said. "*Fire Island* crashed a short while later, but it was a more-managed collision. We anticipated the possibility of survivors but prioritized the survival of our own remaining crew."

"Who was still alive?"

"Captain Belos, Needles, Aisu, and Blinks," Fang answered, "though Aisu's personal health status was not favorable to long-term survival."

"Then what?" Belos prompted.

"I crashed," Fang answered.

"With everyone still on board? Did they survive the landing?"

"No one was onboard," Fang said.

"You said they were, and they were alive, while you were playing dead in the ship graveyard," Belos said. "Where did they go?"

"They were on board. Then no one was on board," Fang said. "My life-support systems were failing, so I went to the planet to wait for them to return to me. I have been waiting a long time."

"They left the ship while you were still in space?" Belos asked. "Why did they leave?"

"They did not leave," Fang said. "They were on board. Then they were not on board. There is no memory of time between."

Belos got out of the chair. "This makes no sense! Fang's logs are scrambled."

"How much time elapsed between those two memories?" Fergus asked.

"I have a gap of thirty-nine minutes and forty-four seconds," Fang said.

"Do you have any visual data or sound?"

"I have data with timestamps that indicate they were recorded during that time gap, but they are not assigned to any corresponding cognitive-processing records or contextual metadata," Fang said.

"Can you play them for us?" Fergus asked.

"Retrieval and processing will exhaust the remainder of the extra power you provided," Fang said.

"Do it. We'll bring you more power," Belos said.

The screen flickered on, showing only a dim horizontal line. It took several seconds to realize they were looking at space and the distant band of the other galactic arm.

"Zoom in here," Belos said, and indicated a portion of the line. The line became a thick band across the screen, and the flickering resolved into three black triangles, growing in size as they approached, until the darkness eclipsed the screen and there was nothing to see.

Sound was badly muffled; voices arguing, maybe? It was hard to tell, but eventually those were eclipsed too, by a sound like crickets and water falling.

Belos was watching Fergus. "You recognize that," he said. It was not a question. "I can see it in your face. What was that? Who was that? Dammit, don't *dare* lie to me."

"Those are Asiig ships," Fergus said. "They came after the other aliens left. They must have taken your sister and crew."

"So, they are dead, after all that," Belos said. "They were stolen from *Rattler*, right when they were defenseless and no threat to anybody. The Asiig leave no one alive."

"I don't know if—" Fergus started to say.

"No more words," Belos interrupted. "I need to be alone. Get out."

"But—"

"Get out or I will break your neck with my bare hands," Belos said.

Fergus left.

———

When Fergus emerged from the wreck, Kaybe took one look at his face and got up from where he'd been sitting, and met him near the open airlock door. "That bad?" Kaybe asked.

"Probably," Fergus said, "but he's only hearing it as an absolute, at least from me."

"I'll go," Kaybe said. He put his hand briefly on Fergus's shoulder. "Thanks, Vetch. If he said anything bad—"

"I'm not a stranger to grief," Fergus said. "There was no harm done."

Kaybe nodded and went inside. Fergus took his spot where he'd been sitting on a rock not far from Trinket and Earlan.

"Found the bodies after all, huh?" Earlan said. "Guess they got off easy."

Trinket sat up straighter. "You skulked around the Barrens long enough you must know there's a code, an understandin' of honor even as we do what we do to live in an honorless, heartless universe. Our Mr. Vetch here, though, is odd. He don't like to kill, says he won't unless he has to. When he come aboard, I thought he was just bein' all full of himself fer the sake of trying to make us feel lesser, put himself up, but that wasn't it. He has his own code, but he holds to it just as tight as we do ours, and he makes it work."

"So?" Earlan asked.

"So, he's the one with mercy in him, not none of the rest of us. Can't you feel the anger, too, mighty deep, that's built up behind that code of his? Bad to be the one standing in front of that dam, tryin' to kick holes in it, when it finally lets go."

Earlan made a small, skeptical sound, and glanced at Fergus.

"Whoosh," Fergus said, raising his hands up high like he was a wave about to crash. "Got a whole ocean of fuck-it-all back there waiting for me to crack." He'd been riffing off Trinket's analogy, but as he said it, he realized it was less of a joke than he was entirely comfortable with, and a lot of that anger was very much the fault of—and fairly directed at—the Alliance.

Earlan, though, was a bitter, sickly old man, and Fergus felt mostly just pity for him. The man must've seen that in his eyes, because he scowled and turned his face away.

When Belos and Kaybe finally emerged, nearly an hour later, the captain had regained his composure. "The shuttle looks good, though we'll have to work to get it out," he said. "*Rattler* itself is a loss, but I want to get Fendi over here, get his opinion on what can be salvaged to repair *Sidewinder*. I don't know what to do about Fang, but we need to get her some power to keep her going until we figure that out. I'm not willing to leave her to slowly degrade further."

Fergus nodded, understanding. It was hard not to think of the more-sophisticated mindsystems as people, even when repeatedly told they weren't and couldn't be; it was even harder when you knew that wasn't true.

"Once we have the means to escape, we need a plan. I see no reason for us to linger on this world longer than necessary," Belos continued. He strode over to Earlan. "If I put you in the care of your fellow Islanders, I expect you to remain there," he told the man. "If you can't do that, or I find you working against me, with or without their knowledge, I will kill you. There will be no further warnings. Understood?"

"Got it," Earlan said.

"Great. If you have any other belongings nearby, point them out. Trinket and Vetch will gather them for you. Now get moving. It's a long hike, and you're taking lead."

———

They left Earlan with Safani and Cole. Fergus made a point to voice his concerns about the man's health loud enough for Earlan to hear, and his expectation that the man would submit to their care. Kaybe then passed on Belos's warnings about him staying put, with a similarly loud concern that failure to do so might prove detrimental to that same health. Belos himself had headed straight back to *Sidewinder* with Trinket, once they'd reached the path fork near the lake that could take them to either camp.

Kaybe invited Riji back to *Sidewinder* to discuss engineering plans, and she accepted. After she loaded Fergus down with several heavy bags of tools, they followed.

"Earlan didn't look that bad last time we saw him," Riji told Fergus, guiltily, as they walked. "Not that he would have let us help him, even if he had."

"He told us about Thacker," Fergus said.

"Oh." Riji was quiet a while, then added, "Don't judge him on that. He and Thacker were close."

"Then what happened?"

"This planet happened," she said. "Thacker outranked us, which was fine when we were just trying to figure out how to survive, but once it was clear no rescue was coming, and we were on our own . . ." She trailed off.

"He handled it poorly?" Fergus guessed.

"Thacker *loved* it, particularly the idea that he was now an absolute authority," she said. "He had . . . ideas about what sorts of things he was entitled to. If Earlan hadn't taken him out, one of the rest of us would've, and he knew it. Earlan gave us that, not having it on our hands. Hey, so, see any interesting wildlife while you were up over the mountains?"

Fergus recognized the deliberate change of subject. "You mean other than the bag full of angry face-stingers that Earlan tried to drop on my head? No," he said. "Though I thought I heard a number of very large creatures in the distance, heading away from us. Didn't see them, though. I think everything gave us a wide berth. Maybe your Stomper-Chompers?"

She laughed. "Not if they were running away from you. I don't know. Earlan might tell you, when he stops being pissed about being caught and then stuck in camp."

"I'd almost rather find them myself, so then I can give them a reasonable name. Not to hurt anyone's feelings, but you people are terrible at that," Fergus said.

"Most of those names came from Safani," Riji said. "She needed something distracting after the attack and the crash. There wasn't a thing she could have done to save anyone aboard, or Ajac's leg after the crash, but she felt responsible anyway for a long time. Medics, you know."

"Yeah," Fergus said. "But I'd been hoping it was Earlan who had named everything. He tried repeatedly to blow me up, so I was going to rename all his stuff as petty revenge. Although I was going to keep Trigger Trees."

"They got you, huh?"

"Yes. Yes they did," Fergus said. "It was a very undignified experience."

"Always is. Stupid things are always at ass height," she said. "But, really, this is not a bad planet. Humidity is only this bad for about a quarter of the year, and it doesn't get too cold here where we are. There's a lot of nature about, some clearly plants, a few clearly animals, and a lot of stuff weirdly in-between or both. I think most of it just avoids us, and I can't really blame them on that when we keep crashing things into their world."

"How much of a survey have your lot managed?"

"Almost none. We didn't have any drones or much other survey tech that made it intact through the crash. With *Fire Island*'s mindsystem dead, that left us just old-fashioned footwork, and with five of us and a lot of higher priorities, it didn't ever get much of a priority," Riji said. "Earlan's explored the most of all of us, but pretty much just back and forth between here and the wreck of *Rattler*. He was obsessed with the idea that Bas Belos was coming, and turned out he was right. Maybe it's because I was a ship's engineer, not an officer, but the mission wasn't ever anything that felt personal to me, you know? You root for your team, but you're up in the cheap seats, mostly just wanting a good, close game. It wasn't supposed to be survival for us."

"You've done very well at that, all things considered," Fergus said.

"I suppose so. Could be a lot worse. I mean, I want to get back to civilization, be around people and music and, oh, *stars,* do I miss Italian food, but I think I'd miss this place, now and then," she said. "Anyway, I'm not leaving here unless we have a good shot at not dying, and I don't see how that's possible. This life's not bad; you'll all get used to it before long."

"You have no idea how stubborn some of us can be," Fergus said.

"Yeah, well, I haven't been working on trying to repair *Fire Island* all these years out of boredom."

"No?"

"Well, a little."

"Boredom is a fantastic motivator, in my experience," Fergus said. They reached the edge of the waveforest along the lakeshore, with *Sidewinder* not far ahead. Fendi was outside, staring up at the engines, and waved when he saw them.

They walked along the edges of the shore to the clearing. "The others are inside," Fendi said. "Captain wants everyone in for a meeting in twenty."

"How's Rabbit?"

"Same," Fendi said. "Not any better."

"Not any worse, either?"

"No. Just gotta hope we catch a break," the big engineer said.

"Uh, speaking of catching things," Riji said, "your cat just ran off into the forest with something in his mouth."

"Shit," Fergus said. "Which way?"

She pointed.

"I'll be back," Fergus yelled, and ran off into the waveforest after the cat.

"Twenty minutes!" Fendi called after him.

The forest grew dense, and he caught small glimpses of black fur as he weaved between frond stalks, trying not to trip, afraid to slow down. "If you make me get lost . . .!" he called off after him, but the cat had no intention of being deprived of its prize. He was reminded of reading about remote islands, on Earth, where one cat, brought with humans, wiped out entire species, and wondered what that karmic debt would feel like on a planetary scale.

Fergus ran up and over a small hill, jumped a stream that must feed the lake below, nearly tripped when he hit slippery mud on the far side but caught himself on a sturdy wavetree and got his balance again. He stopped for a few seconds to catch his breath and try to spot his cat again, and, sure enough, spotted that lone black blob cresting the next hill. "Mister Feefs!" he shouted. "Stop! Please?"

The cat did not obey.

He reached the same hilltop the cat had gone over, stumbled down out of the wavetrees into the beginnings of a meadow, and stopped in his tracks.

A man stood there, with his not-quite-human face and wearing an old-fashioned Victorian-era gentleman's suit, bent down and tickling the top of the cat's head. On the far side of the meadow, a herd of six-legged animals, easily the size of elephants but shaggy and blue, looked up from grazing to watch him warily.

"Mr. Ferguson," the man said.

"You," Fergus said. He couldn't help himself but glance up toward the sky, looking for those triangle ships he knew were never, ever, very far away. The man was an agent of the Asiig and had never been, in Fergus's experience, an omen of good things.

"Me," the agent said.

"You took Bel Belos and her crew off *Rattler*," Fergus said. "What did you do to them?"

"*Kitty kitty*," the agent said, then straightened up. "This world is interesting, don't you agree?"

"I mean . . . I guess?" Fergus answered. "It's in an interesting place, anyway."

"Oh, you noticed that? How observant of you!" the agent said. "An interesting and strange place, possibly even mysterious and unlikely, out here all by its lonesome self; surely, that's what you mean?"

"Yes, all that," Fergus said. "And, in case you haven't noticed yet, there's also a bunch of interestingly homicidal aliens on your doorstep."

"The Havna," the agent said.

"So, you know them," Fergus said. "They work for you too?"

"I feel like you have unexplored anger issues that come out whenever we talk," the agent said. "We know *of* them."

"You could stop them," Fergus said.

"Could we? Possibly, possibly not," the agent said. "But without understanding why they do what they do, how could we step in? The consequences would be unpredictable and, unlike the small nudges we give here and there, potentially unmanageable. We aren't *sloppy*, Mr. Ferguson."

"You could ask them."

"Oh? How?"

"You know their name. You must have some way of communicating."

"To be precise, we know the *Bomo'ri* name for them. As far as we are aware, the Bomo'ri have not been able to communicate with them either, though there is certainly plenty of circumstantial evidence of their failure."

"And *Rattler*? So, what did happen to her crew?"

The agent reached down and gently pried whatever small, still-wriggling creature Mister Feefs had caught out of his mouth, then held his hand flat until the creature shook itself and ran off. The cat jumped up to pursue, but the agent *tsk*ed, and the cat sat back down, glaring resentfully toward Fergus as if he'd been the one to stop him.

"Don't be distracted by irrelevant matters. There is too much here to learn," the agent said. "I can't keep holding your hand and spoon-feeding you clues forever, you know. Take some responsibility for once!"

"Really?" Fergus exclaimed. "You think you *help*?!"

"No need for thanks," the agent said. He smiled, though all the muscles in his face didn't quite move as they should, in some way Fergus couldn't specifically put his finger on. The agent snapped his fingers.

Somewhere behind him, there was a brief, intense burst of signal. Fergus startled at that, and Mister Feefs raced up his bare leg to cling, claws out, to his shoulder.

"There," the agent said. "Some help. A bit too much, if you ask me, but nobody ever does. Oh, and here, have this."

The agent reached under the side of his jacket and drew out a heavy, thick book with an ornate red cover and blackened corners, as if it had been pulled hastily from a fire. He held it out, and Fergus, not at all confident he wanted it, reached to take it anyway.

The moment his fingertips touched the book, Fergus's eyelids felt impossibly heavy, and he fought in vain against closing them. His legs gave out and he fell, unable to do anything about it, and barely noticed the scratchy plants that broke his fall.

He awoke to his cat sitting on his chest, meowing at him. The sleepiness was gone, but in its place was a pounding headache. The herd of blue animals had moved closer, almost surrounding him, and were staring at him with long, thin faces and double pairs of compound eyes.

Holding the cat, he got slowly and dizzily to his feet, trying not to startle the animals, but they backed away immediately. One stood its ground, watching him as the others turned and fled, whistling and humming at each other until only the solitary guard remained. Then it too turned and ran.

Both agent and book were nowhere to be seen.

He tried to feel where the agent had gone, or how, but there was nothing, just the faded remnants of that signal burst, like a map pin stuck directly into his brain at the epicenter of pain.

Eventually, he realized he could hear someone bellowing his name. Or at least, his current alias.

"Come on, cat. Back we go," he said, squinting up at the suddenly too-bright sun as if it were personally to blame for his throbbing head. "We're late for a meeting."

Chapter 14

◄—◆—►

Most of *Sidewinder*'s crew was already sitting at the table when Fergus came in, after securing Mister Feefs back in his cabin. Fendi and Riji were still off looking at the ship's damaged undercarriage while waiting for Cole to arrive, so he took the opportunity to start a pot of coffee. He wasn't optimistic it would help with his headache, but maybe it would make him less grumpy about it, Asiig agents, and books that were given then immediately taken back again before he could even peek inside.

Actually, he thought, *I'm not optimistic about that, either.* If he wasn't stuck on a planet with a two-digit population and no bars, he'd be sorely tempted to start an anonymous bar fight just to work his frustration out.

He stood there with his eyes closed, listening to the coffee brew, and trying to remember the last bar fight he'd actually been in. Ijik-ijolo didn't count, since the fight was before going to the bar, and he'd been remarkably well behaved during his years on Coralla. Fights in sandwich shops didn't count, either, which meant—

"Do I smell *coffee?*" Cole exclaimed, walking into the conference room. "I will give you anything you want, including the deed to my one-fifth share of ownership in this planet, for a single cup."

Fergus opened his eyes, got an extra mug out of the cabinet, and, after filling it, handed it to Cole. The man took it as if being handed some kind of life-saving serum, then glanced up and nearly spilled it. "Stars, Vetch, you sick?" Cole asked.

"No?" Fergus said. "I have a headache."

Riji and Fendi came in, and Fendi reached out one large hand and tilted Fergus's head toward him. "Your eyes are completely bloodshot," he said. "You eat something you shouldn't'a?"

"Shoulda stuck to me healthy groats an' not nommin' the local weeds ahstead," Len said from the table.

"The amount of rum you put in your groats is hardly healthy," Kaybe pointed out.

"Rum kills all the germees," Len said. "Never seen me sick a day."

"That's because even germs are terrified of you," Kaybe replied.

Len grinned. "Sactly," he said.

"Safani can take a look when she comes over to check on Rabbit," Cole said.

"I'm fine," Fergus said. "I've survived worse."

"What if it's something contagious?"

"Then you can bury my body in a ten-meter-deep lead-lined pit," Fergus said. "Until then, leave me alone."

"Oooh, someone's cranky," Marche said.

"Yes. It's me," Fergus said.

"People." Belos spoke sharply, cutting across whatever reply Marche might have been about to make. "We have business."

Everyone took seats at the table with a minimum of noise.

"First, what's the status of *Rattler*'s shuttle?" Belos asked.

"It's pretty close to functional," Fendi said. "Power cells are completely depleted, so I can't run a systems check, but the mechanics look good. Getting it out is the problem. *Rattler*'s shuttle-bay doors took heavy damage during fighting, and then when she hit the planet, enough of the hull warped and bent around them that they won't budge. We have to cut the doors into pieces to get the shuttle clear."

"Will that cost us material we need to repair *Sidewinder*?"

Belos asked. "What are our prospects of fixing both *Sidewinder* and *Fire Island*?"

"I've done a lot of work on *Fire Island* already, but without the right tools and only a handful of us who could salvage material from other wrecks, it's been slow going," Riji said.

"Given what she had to work with, she's done amazing," Fendi said. "With more of us working on it, it could be made spaceworthy. The problem is its mindsystem was fried by the alien EMP pulses, and that's not something we can fix. The whole core logic system would have to be replaced, and while I could fab a physical template, we don't have an initial code imprint."

"Could we copy Eyes or Fang?" Kaybe asked.

"Not really, because the cognition-seeding process is heavily hardware-dependent, and *Fire Island* is a totally different ship," Fendi said. "It'd be like trying to heal your brain-dead mouse by booting it up with a spare goldfish mind—the firmware instructions are just gonna be all wrong, and under duress, lots of critical things will be dangerously unstable."

"What about the lifepods? Could their systems be used to rebuild the *Island*'s mindsystem?" Marche asked.

"Not really. They're not smart, just scenario-optimized within a narrow set of desired behaviors," Riji said. "We could use them to repair some of the peripherals, but without a mind to drive them, that won't help us much."

"So, *Fire Island* is dead," Belos said.

"Not necessarily. I've been working to modify what I could so that we could run most of the systems manually, but it would take more than just the five of us," Riji said.

"There's nine of us now," Cole said quietly. "Not counting your crew, Captain Belos."

Four survivors out of the seven lifepods, Fergus thought. *No wonder Todd's people were uncooperative.*

"I'll clarify. It'll take more than five *competent* and *cooperative* people to fly it," Riji said. "*Sidewinder* has the tools, and the mechanical and operational expertise we need. And so far, no one here is trying to order us around like we're a bunch of new recruits they dug up like potatoes fresh from the stupid farm."

Cole darted a glance at the rest of the people at the table, but no one had an opinion to offer on that. "You remember what it was like, right after we crashed. None of us were at our best," he said. "They'll settle in and come around."

"Yeah, and how long do we wait for that?" Riji asked.

"Can we argue about this later?"

"Fine," Riji said. She leaned forward in her chair and spoke to Belos. "To finish answering your question, we could make the *Island* fly again, if all of us crewed it, and with a lot of practice. It'd require constant attention with some of the more-complex systems, but it could get us off this planet."

"*Silver Mist* was the same build of cruiser. If we could get off the planet and reach it, assuming we don't attract attention, could we take and transplant its mindsystem?" Belos asked.

"You thinking we take the shuttle up?" Fendi asked.

"It's a possibility," Belos said.

"Odds are *Silver Mist*'s mindsystem is just as dead as *Fire Island*'s, since they got hit with the same kind of weapon," Fendi said. "Eyes and Fang only survived because I designed each o' them with a tertiary, physically encoded persistent buffer just in the event a catastrophic electromagnetic pulse hit took out the main and the normal, protected backup. And even I thought I was being overly paranoid."

"The entire front end of *Silver Mist* was missing," Fergus said. "No buffer was going to help that."

"None of that is the real challenge, though," Marche said. "There's still the aliens. They may not care if we go poking around in their graveyard—and I wouldn't bet a single half-cred on that—but they sure as hell aren't letting us near the jump point back out."

"One problem at a time," Belos said. He turned on the holo table, and it lit up with landscape data taken by drone. "If we were to try to maximize our options with both *Fire Island* and *Sidewinder*, we're going to need materials. Show me where the other wrecks are."

"As near as we can tell, this whole planet is littered with them," Riji said. "It's like this star is the only candle burning for hundreds of light-years, so you get more than your share of dead moths. The nearer they are, the more parts I've pulled off 'em already, although it's been limited to stuff we could pry off and carry or drag back."

"Show us the ones you've explored?" Belos asked.

Riji and Cole took turns pointing to different parts of the map, many places well outside the known area rendered, and lighting them up with small holographic *X*s.

"Anything over here?" Fergus asked, and indicated an area at the periphery of the data, nowhere near any *X*s. It was, he guessed, roughly where the agent's blast of signal had originated. He could still hear it, a loud, annoying, needle-prick awareness, and he suspected it wouldn't shut up until he physically went there.

"We haven't been over that way," Cole said. "Why?"

"I don't know. I thought I glimpsed something when we were coming down," Fergus lied. "It all happened fast, so I might not even have the right area."

"It's well out of range of our drones," Kaybe said. "Not worth hiking out that far unless you were more certain you saw something useful, or if we can't find something we need among the nearer wrecks."

"Agreed," Belos said, before Fergus could speak up in defense of the idea. "Fendi, if you can work with Riji to put together a full list of everything that needs fixing on both *Fire Island* and *Sidewinder*, we can assign teams to go survey the wrecks and produce a comprehensive inventory of what's available and where. Then we can work on extricating the shuttle."

"Why not focus our efforts on *Sidewinder*?" Cole asked. "It's the more-fixable ship, and it's larger than *Fire Island*."

"Two working ships gives us more options," Belos said.

"Like, the option of you using us as a distraction with the aliens so you get away and we all die?" Cole asked.

"That isn't it," Belos snapped.

"Then what? What's your logic?"

"I have an idea for dealing with the aliens, but I don't know if it will work," Belos said. "If it goes wrong, we'll need that second ship."

"What's the idea?" Marche asked, crossing her arms in front of her chest. She glanced over at Fergus. "This another of your brilliant schemes, Vetch?"

She's mad she wasn't consulted, Fergus thought. The idea that Belos had left both of them out of his thinking was a little worrisome. "Not mine this time," he said.

Kaybe spoke up. "Or mine, but I'm just as eager to hear it."

Uh-oh, Fergus thought. Not Kaybe either?

"Later," Belos said. "First, we need those assessments and a timetable. And we need to find out if the survivors of *Paradigm* want to be involved in escaping this world or get left behind when we go. Because one way or another, however long it takes, I am *leaving*."

———

Fergus borrowed one of the drones before setting out on a hike with Riji and Yolo toward the wreck of the *Stiletto*; it wasn't exactly in the direction he wanted to explore, but it was closer, and he hoped he'd get some time to himself after they finished a comprehensive scan of the wreck, before they dismantled portions of *Stiletto*'s stabilizer systems and prepped them to be hauled back to the Islander camp. There was a well-worn trail, thanks to the Islanders' previous forays for smaller materials, and Fergus found his thoughts drifting unerringly back to the meeting.

I am leaving, Belos had said. Not *we* but *I.* It could have easily just been a meaningless slip of the tongue—despite his short time in the company of the captain, he found it impossible to believe Belos would leave his crew behind while he himself escaped—but it didn't ring arbitrary. What it meant, Fergus had no idea, but with Belos's anger and grief, it felt ominous.

He kind of wished he'd been teamed up with Marche, to get her take on it, but she was off with Fendi, Cole, and Trinket heading to *Rattler.*

Belos, Kaybe, Safani, and Ajac were going to speak with the podders, see if they could at least crack the door open of mutual cooperation. Fergus would also have loved to be on that team, just to hear how that conversation went, but was glad to not be face-to-face with *Paradigm*'s Captain Todd, who had fresher reasons to dislike him than the others of Belos's crew.

You did lock him out of his own ship's systems, he thought. *You can't really blame the guy if he's holding a grudge.*

At least his headache was mostly gone. The agent's signal had lost its edge of intensity and, with it, some distinction, but it remained resolutely stuck in his thoughts.

On their way across a wide meadow, they startled another herd of the six-legged blue bison-things, which immediately melted into the far edge of the forest. "What did you name those?" he asked Riji, almost not wanting to know.

"We didn't," she said. "First time I've seen 'em. Heard them plenty, though. You wanna?"

"Want to what?"

"Name them," she said.

"Oh," he said. "Yes. Let me think about it."

"Don't think too hard, or it won't fit the established naming vibe," she said.

"Is that vibe 'pulled out of our asses'?" he asked.

"Yes," she answered. "Mostly Safani's. Earlan's probably named a bunch of things too, because he's been the one wandering off exploring while the rest of us work, but if so, he hasn't told us. So, why'd you bring the drone?"

"I was thinking I might get a chance to look around, expand our maps," he said.

"You after that thing you thought you saw on your way in?" she asked.

"Kind of," he said.

"We're still not going to be close enough for you to reach it," she said. "What do you think you saw, then, that you're this interested?"

"It's hard to say," Fergus hedged.

"Can you describe it? Even a little?"

"Not really," he said.

She gave a short laugh. "There are a lot of nearer and more describable wrecks still to check out, before we have to go hunting that far out. One thing we're not short of on this planet is broken shit."

"You ever think how weird it is that this planet is here, though?" Fergus asked. "I mean, middle of the Gap, nothing else at all nearby, but here's this one happy little planet with its happy little star, as if everything is perfectly normal."

"And two happy little moons," Riji said. "I mean, I'm not a planetary geophysicist, so I can't weigh in on just how odd or not odd it is, but I'm grateful it exists, because there weren't any other survivable outcomes for us other than crashing here."

"Yeah," Fergus said. "I just don't like not understanding things. Woadebeests."

"What?"

"The herd animals. Woadebeests. It's a rip-off of *wildebeest*, and *woad* because—"

"Because they're blue?" she said. "Safani would probably suggest something like Scampering Trampering Woadebeests, but shorter works for me."

"Speaking of things that could work for us, I wonder if they could be tamed, like oxen, and used to drag stuff back for us," Fergus said. "Now, that would be useful."

"I mean, sure, give it twenty, thirty years, a couple of generations of selective breeding, maybe," Riji said. "As much as your captain seems to think escape is possible, I know for sure that even if it is, it's not going to be quick. And we still don't understand the slightest thing about our murderous alien gatekeepers."

"Yeah. I'm not giving up on the idea of getting out of here, but I don't see how yet," Fergus said.

"We're all going to die here," Yolo said, from where he was bringing up the rear a fair ways behind them. It was the first time he'd spoken since they'd set out, and Fergus had almost, but not quite, forgotten he was there. "We never should've gone through the Ghostdrift, and the aliens are here to make sure we never get out alive."

"Maybe," Fergus said, "but I've gotten out of some pretty inescapable traps. Until this place kills me, I'm going to keep trying."

"You didn't get outta Aurora on your own," Yolo said.

"Aurora?" Riji asked.

"He got himself captured and he only got out 'cause we traded for him," Yolo said. "No idea what we traded, but probably worth more than what we got."

A half-dozen snarky answers leapt immediately to mind, but instead, Fergus just stopped and turned, waiting for Yolo to catch up to him. Riji sat down on a rock to watch. "Yolo, if you want to pick a fight with me, just say so, so we can get it over with," Fergus said. "None of us are happy to be here, and I've got nothing against you, but if it'll make you feel better, I'm ready."

Whatever Yolo had expected, that wasn't it. Fergus could see temptation, and disappointment, cross his face before his shoulders slumped and he slowed down. "Won't make me feel better, anyway," he said. "And Trinket'll just be madder at me."

"I won't tell," Riji said.

". . . Naw, it's okay," Yolo said, though he sounded much less certain than a moment before.

"If it helps, we're about to go tear apart an Alliance ship," Fergus said. "Once we get any parts off we need, you can destroy as much of the rest of it as you want."

Yolo nodded. "That helps a little," he said.

"I brought some explosives, in case we needed to access sections too mangled to get to as is," Riji said.

"That helps more," Yolo said.

Riji smiled. "See? This is why we're the *fun* team," she said. "We got about another hour of hiking 'til we get there, then we can set up camp, make some food, and get started."

"Then let's go," Fergus said, but Yolo was already going. At least, Fergus thought, he wasn't going to have to fight the man today. Tomorrow, who knew, but he'd worry about that then.

———

The wreck of the *Stiletto* was sobering in its magnitude. It had been a full-sized warship, and it had hit the ground with enough force and angle to shorten itself by easily a third of its length. Even so, the gaping holes in its hull were still starkly clear.

A patch of ground nearby was dotted with stone cairns. "We buried what bodies we could," Riji said, seeing him looking over that way.

"How many crew were on board?" Fergus asked.

"Fifty-eight, originally," Riji said. "Some must've gotten sucked out into space during the initial attack, and there was fire in some of the interior spaces that held. We only got eleven bodies out. Some . . . might have been parts of a couple of people, or just one that got more widely distributed, but . . ."

"You don't have to tell me, if you don't want to," Fergus said. "But if you need to, I'll listen."

"What's the worst thing you've ever seen?" she asked. "I mean, the thing that just absolutely haunts you."

He'd seen a lot of very terrible things, but one leapt immediately to mind. "I went into an old, abandoned deep space hab once," he said. "Spore ticks had got in, and the people there cut themselves off so it wouldn't spread out to any other habs. There were families. Kids."

"Ouch," she said. "I've been in training sims for dealing with spore ticks, but they're pretty sanitized, you know? And we all got very drunk afterward."

"Not a bad choice," Fergus said.

Yolo grunted. "Saw spore ticks hit a ship, once. We got in just far enough to see why they were so eager to let us catch them— dunno if they hoped we could save them, or if they thought at least they could get us killed too—but we got out as fast as we could. Blew up their ship. Mercy ain't really our thing, but that . . . Yeah. We did them a favor. Felt itchy for weeks after. Nightmares were bad, when I could sleep at all."

"A lot of the other wrecks have had bodies too," Riji said, "but not recent, mostly just bones. These here were people I *knew*. Some smarter, most of them nicer, so I asked myself a lot, why did I get to live? Maybe, I decided, just so someone who cared and would remember could bury them."

"I know this is hard to believe, but I used to be kind of an asshole," Fergus said. "Childhood trauma, yadda yadda, but I knew what I was doing. Sometimes, I think the universe keeps you around just for the challenge of trying to make you a better person than you think you are."

"Ooh, so it turned you into a Pirate Philosopher," Riji said, her voice lighter again.

"I still think you're an asshole," Yolo offered helpfully.

"Thanks," Fergus said. "I do my best."

Riji looked up at the wreck, shading her eyes. "Let me show you what we've got and what we're looking for. There's a stream on the other side; we can set up camp next to it and get the portable water filter drawing up a fresh supply, and then I can show you the sorry excuse for tea I've managed to put together from local stuff. Don't get too excited; it tastes like crap."

"Ever had Corallan beach tea?" Fergus asked.

She made a face. "You drink that, you might not hate this after all," she said. "I built a ladder up under the portside wing. Get your scanner, and let's go."

————

By midmorning on the second day, they had a list of all the salvageable parts categorized by *essential, useful, maybe useful,* and *if better options don't come along somewhere else*. If anything was in need of more than minor repair, it only got listed if it fell in the first two categories, though if they had to come back later to scrounge, they had the original scans to remind them of what they'd rejected on this pass.

From there, they broke down the essentials list into things that could be carried back in one trip, and set to work collecting them just inside the shelter of *Stiletto*. The wind was picking up, and the air smelled of incoming rain. Somewhere in the front, Fergus could feel the electric potential. "Maybe thunder and lightning," he said. "We want to camp inside, too, until it passes?"

"Rain can get pretty intense this time of year," Riji said. "Flooding's more likely than not, especially right near a stream, and if you think we might get thunder, we might also get hail. Concussion-sized."

"I vote indoors," Yolo said, and went out to take down the tents and move them into the cavity that had been *Stiletto*'s shuttle bay. Most of the floor and the deck below it had been ripped away during the crash, but they were still solidly enclosed from above and the sides, not counting the gap where the bay doors had been. Sand and dirt had settled inside, trying to reclaim its territory as best it could. Either that or the wreck was slowly sinking into the ground, not that the distinction, if any, mattered.

"If we pitch up on the floor, we'll be above any water running in," Riji said. "Also, marauding Night Nibblers."

"Up it is," Yolo said, and heaved the tents and their packs the meter and a half up onto the bay floor.

The rain hit suddenly, and hard, and smelled strangely like a mix of cut grass and burnt sugar. It didn't take long for the dirt below them to become muddy, their boot prints filling with water until all connected, and the water rose steadily upward, with no let-up outside.

"Dammit, I wanted to take an external stabilizer housing apart," Riji complained. "The rain might not stop for a while."

"What in here could we salvage?" Fergus asked. He pulled up the list they'd made of essentials, scanned down it, then over to the useful list. "There's a . . . Hmmm. A secondary wastewater bacterial agitation chamber. It's on the critical list, but is it something we really need?"

"Do you like the idea of your entire ship reeking of poop two days into travel?" Riji asked.

"As it happens, no," Fergus said.

"The whole system on *Fire Island* took enough of a knocking when we crashed to warp some pipes, pop a few seals, stuff like that," Riji said. "This chamber is one of two that you really want to be sure won't leak on you, and on the *Island*, it's pretty shaky. And since the ship extracts heat generated by the waste system to supplement other sources of heat on board, that means any kind of gas escaping is gonna go right into your air systems. Which would be less of a problem, normally, but we haven't changed out the filter medium or screens since the mid 2450s."

"I don't need further convincing," Fergus said. "The words *poop reek* were wholly sufficient unto themselves."

"As they should be," she said. She looked at him, and frowned for a sec. "You have the weirdest mix of accents."

"I've been to the weirdest mix of places," Fergus said.

"Lotta Mars in it, but not at the root of it," she said. "Definitely not Titan."

"Yours has a lot of Titan in it, though," Fergus said.

"Yeah. Grew up there, until I was about eleven, then we moved off to Lunar Seven, and then I went to Olympus Mons University before enlisting in the engineer corps," Riji said.

"Hence the interest in Marsball."

"Yeah. Ares One was kinda boring, if you weren't the sort inclined to get in trouble. And if you were, it was a poor place to exercise that inclination."

Fergus laughed. "I can personally attest to that," he said. "Symphony was good, though."

Riji made a surprised noise. "A pirate who goes to the symphony? The universe is much stranger than I ever knew."

"Hey, you almost need to be a pirate to afford those ticket prices," Fergus said. "If it restores your sense of order, I was there to pickpocket someone. Waited until the intermission, though. Would've stayed for the whole thing, but it would have been harder to get away."

"Man must've been very rich, to go after him there," Riji said.

"No. He was a thief too. I was just stealing from him the thing he stole from someone else." Fergus thought about whether he was giving more information than he should, but then, the notion that any of it could matter required much greater optimism than he could muster with the constant drumming of the rain overhead and the swirling morass of mud below that seemed to carry chill in with it.

"How much you sell it for, the thing you stole?" Yolo asked, as he finished with the last tent.

"I didn't," Fergus said. "I gave it back to the person who it was originally stolen from."

"That was stupid," Yolo said.

"I got quite a substantial reward for it."

"Oh. That's okay, then," Yolo said. "Tents are set. I don't know what to do now."

"We probably can't build a fire in here without filling the whole bay with smoke," Fergus said. "That rules out ghost stories around the campfire."

"No ghost stories," Yolo said, emphatically.

"Guess I'll just have to work on that agitation chamber," Riji said. "It's going to take me a couple of days at least to get it free, and there isn't room for more than one of us to work on it at a time. And no offense, but I don't want to risk popping the seals on this one, which means you two need to find something else to entertain yourselves."

"If you get that free, it's going to take two of us to carry it back," Fergus said. "What do we want to leave behind?"

She made a face. "None of it. Shit. That's a good point."

"I'll take a load," Yolo said. "Then I can be back in time for the second trip."

"You sure?" Fergus asked.

"I don't do sittin' bored well, unless I got people to hit to pass the time," Yolo said. He brightened up. "You want to fight?"

Fergus shook his head. "Not if I have to carry heavy stuff later, no. I know what kind of bruises you leave."

"Okay," Yolo said. "How long 'til you think the rain stops?"

"Probably the morning," Riji said. "At least it should be lighter by then."

"Okay. I'll go anyway, except if it's hail," Yolo said. "Just make a pile for me. That helps?"

"That helps a lot," Riji said. "Thanks, Yolo."

He nodded, and a small amount of the misery and guilt the man had exuded like a bad aura since his fight with Belos on the bridge lifted. "I'mma sleep, then," he said, crawled into his tent, and sealed it shut behind him.

————

When sunrise came, after a long night of listening to Yolo's snoring echoing around inside the empty bay, the rain had dwindled down to occasional, tiny drops, like being aggressively misted on. Riji set up the portable cook unit, while Fergus dug an old two-wheel cart out of the remains of a storage closet, and helped Yolo load up and secure a pile of hull plating and other assorted parts to it. "We can use the wheels to build a lighter one out of wave-tree stalks," Fergus said, "but this should work for now."

Breakfast was a grassy-flavored bread, toasted, with a thin layer of greenish jam. It was not terrible and, Fergus suspected, probably something he could get used to, and maybe even like, given a few years to forget what other foods tasted like.

Fergus refilled Yolo's water bottles and Riji packed him food, and they sent him off back toward *Sidewinder*, which was where most of those parts were needed. Once he was gone, Fergus sat on the broken edge of the floor, boots dangling over the receding floodwater below, and slowly ate his last piece of toast in the quiet.

"You look worried," Riji said, startling him.

"Do I? Yeah," Fergus said. "What happens when we run out of things to do, ideas to escape? Yolo is trying his best to be helpful, be a part of the team, but he wasn't lying when he said he likes to hit things when he's bored. And this place scares him."

"You think he's dangerous?" she asked.

"Oh, I know he is. We all are, really," Fergus said.

"Including you?"

He smiled, brushed crumbs from his hands and shorts. "Maybe me more than anyone, though I don't mean to be," he said. "Among other personal failings, I'm a magnet for attracting trouble."

"Well, the trouble waiting for me is that chamber," Riji said. "What's your plan? Oh . . . no, I can guess. You want to go check out that wreck you think you saw on your way down and have been obsessing over."

"I was thinking I would, yeah," Fergus said. "If you don't mind being left alone."

"Being left alone is my favorite ever good time," she said. "I mean that with absolute, one hundred percent sincerity."

Fergus got up, fumbled through his pack, and pulled out two small comm units, a signal booster, and a folded-up solar blanket. "I fabbed these before we left," Fergus said. "It's got a decent charge now, but once the sun comes out, see if you can get the booster up onto a wing and spread the blanket out. The signal will be stronger up there, too."

"I know how this stuff works, you know," she said.

"Sorry. I know you do," he said. "If you need help, even if it's just another set of hands again, call me?"

"Sure. And, Vetch?"

"Yeah?"

"Take a scanner, and call me if you find something worth the trip," she said. "If you find nothing at all, you owe me half of whatever non-Solo tea you have."

"Deal," he said. He took his pack, tent, water, and the drone, and set out toward that nebulous spot still burned into his brain.

———

He followed the swollen stream down until he found a spot where it widened out, becoming shallower, and waded across. The current was strong but split by sandbars, and he got to the far side without losing his footing, though it came close near the far bank, where it grew briefly deeper.

The shore was mostly meadow, and he trudged through the knee-high plants until the sun finally came out. He climbed up on a rocky outcropping, took off his boots and his socks to lay them out to dry, then put his head on his rolled-up tent, threw one arm over his eyes, and took a nap.

He awoke about three hours later to something poking his foot, and moved his arm away slowly to see several brownish, two-legged balls of fur hop away in alarm. "Sorry!" he called after them as he sat up.

One nice thing about a planet with super-long days, Fergus thought, is that you could take a nap and not feel like you wasted any time, as if both day and night came with freebie hours.

Still, he did want to try to reach the mystery spot before dark, so he reluctantly packed up his things and continued on. The meadow was easier to hike through than the waveforests, and he was making good time even including multiple stops to watch various native creatures scurry away from him. There were more woadebeests here, and something similar in size but more blue-green, with longer legs, standing in the middle of a river, that he dubbed aquayaks. When he thought of it, he captured images of each new animal with his scanner.

Meadow turned back into forest on the far side of the second river, and then gradually the land rose into gentle hills. At the top, Fergus found another rock and dried his socks again. The rock was warm, and he drank water and ate some dry crackers before he pulled on his goggles and sent the drone out, up and over the hills.

It took him several minutes of cruising around to realize that what he'd taken for another rock, near the summit of the next set of hills, was too regular and smooth to be natural. Some sort of creeping vines, with globular clusters of purplish leaves, had colonized all but its very crown, and much of the surrounding hilltop. Whatever had crashed there had done so a very long time before, to judge by how slowly the land along the crash paths of *Stiletto* and *Rattler* had recovered, and he could only get a few glimpses of it from above without risking damaging the drone in the thick forest surrounding it.

He called back the drone, put his still-damp socks back on, and headed that way. If nothing else, he was certain this was where the agent wanted him to go, even if he still had no idea why.

Fergus had to get out his knife to cut his way through the vine-choked trees the last quarter-kilometer up that hillside, and it had started to feel like an endless, futile task for no clear purpose when he caught a glimpse of smooth gray ahead.

Chopping the last of the vines away, he found himself under an overhang, against a near-vertical surface. Following it around, it was not long before he came across a door.

"Riji?" he asked, on the comms.

"Vetch," she answered sleepily. "I was napping. What's up? You find your shipwreck?"

"No," he said. "I found a building."

Chapter 15

R iji arrived first, early the next day, carrying tools to force the door. He'd set up his tent in a small clearing under the shelter of an old wavetree grove, and she'd dumped her stuff next to his before sitting down to catch her breath; he had the feeling she'd hiked straight through with little or no breaks.

"I gave Yolo my comm but left the booster up on *Rattler*," she said. "We should probably set up one at each of our sites so we can all talk to each other when we're out in the field. Damn, I can't believe I didn't think of that before now, but it's been a long time without access to a fab unit."

"Lucky for you, I made one for Yolo," Fergus said. He fished it out of his pack to hand it to her. "He took off before I remembered to give it to him, so now we're covered."

"So, where is this alleged building of yours?" she asked, as she clipped the comm to the shoulder of her battered Alliance jacket. "I didn't see anything coming in."

"A little up the hill," he said. It occurred to him that he'd only spotted it from afar because he knew he was looking for something in that exact spot, and he was taller than her. He only felt guilty about one of those advantages, though. "Drink some water first, then I'll show you."

She grumbled but drank. "We have a new water supply set up yet?" she asked belatedly, after she emptied her bottle.

"There's a stream coming down off the hills about a half a kilometer away. It tested clean, but I've been boiling it anyway," he said. He indicated the remains of his firepit, near the center of the clearing, and the single small pot balanced on a rock in the center of it.

"I brought the filtration column," she said, and nudged her pack with her foot. "We're going to need it when there's more than two of us."

"Yolo coming back?"

She laughed. "When he arrives with the news? We'll be lucky if we don't have everybody out here."

"We should get to exploring soon, then, before it becomes the popular place and we can't even get in," Fergus said. "You ready?"

"Yep," she said. "Lead on."

It wasn't very far from Fergus's camp to where he'd found wide steps cut into the rock leading up to the building entrance, though they were cracked and crumbling from vine roots and required some care. Riji followed, examining the steps briefly and muttering *huh* to herself a couple of times, until he shoved aside the curtain of covering vines that obscured the door itself.

It was tall and not scaled for humans, but it was a familiar-enough sight from the dead Bomo'ri ship he'd explored up in the orbiting graveyard. He waited for Riji to examine the door; unfortunately for his much-tried patience, whatever had once powered the door was dead enough that he hadn't had any luck opening it on his own, before she'd arrived.

"This is like those other alien wrecks," Riji said. "You said the Bomo'ri?"

"Yeah."

"This has been here a long time. Centuries, at least, judging by the surface decay and the way it's grown up around it. The Purple Wurble Vines—"

Fergus groaned.

She heaved a deep sigh. "The Vines I Wasn't the One Who Named are very slow growers. Like, maybe a dozen centimeters a year, if conditions are ideal. The wurble clusters are pretty tasty, and rich in vitamin C, so we tried cultivating them. Still don't have our first crop to harvest."

"Any wrecks you've found older than this?" Fergus asked.

"No, not even close," Riji said. "But to be fair, it's not like we've explored the whole planet. We didn't even have drones until you showed up, Ajac can't walk far, and Earlan is what we call a 'poor communicator.' Also, we crashed at night, so we didn't even get much of a look at what we were hitting until after we had. Clearly, you got a better view, if you spotted this somehow. Which I don't know how you managed it, overgrown like this."

"Didn't I mention I'm a magnet for trouble? My luck works that way. Sometimes it's a plus, sometimes it's a minus, and a lot of the time it's both. Also, I'm taller than you." He stared at the door for a bit, then said, "From their dead ships out near the jump point, I think the doors open upward?"

"That fits the one wreck I explored down here. Door was jammed halfway. Bad design if something goes wrong," Riji said.

"From what little I know of the Bomo'ri, they don't seem like the types to think their stuff *can* go wrong," Fergus said. "Maybe if we push it up, we can get enough of a crack underneath to wedge something in? I only need about four centimeters to get the drone through."

"Better yet," Riji said, and dug through the tool bag she'd hauled there from *Stiletto*. A few moments later, she emerged with a heavy-duty jack. "You get me a crack, I'll get you a gap we can both fit through."

"I think it's going to need both of us to get it moving," Fergus said; he'd tried earlier several times by himself with no luck. He put both hands flush against the door, and Riji leaned in to place her hands below his. On the count of three, they both shoved up as hard as they could.

He was about to give up when he felt the slightest bit of give. Riji must have felt it too, because she pressed harder, and just as it started to move, she kicked a small rock under the bottom edge. "I think I got it," he said. "Try the jack?"

She let go, and the door settled downward, despite his best efforts, to be stopped by the rock. "Or I don't got it," he lamented. "Is that enough of a crack to get the jack in?"

"Should be," she said. She placed the jack vertically against the door, set the stability feet, and slid its two metal prongs into the thin opening they'd made. "Max is a half-meter, setting it for that," she said, and with an angry groan, the door rose up.

Stale, musty air rushed out, and they both backed away.

"What do you think? Give it ten minutes?" she asked.

"Before we go in? At least that," he said. "I'm going to go get the drone. If there are more sealed doors inside, we're going to have to contend with more pockets of bad air. Which could be just because this is old, or because the Bomo'ri breathe a different mix. I have no idea. I wish I'd brought my exosuit, after all."

She pulled her handpad from a pocket. "Yolo should be getting back to *Sidewinder* about now," she said. "I expect as soon as he's able to brief your crew on the situation, we'll be getting a call. Someone can bring it. I've been working on a list in my head, but I should note it all down before I forget."

"Good idea," Fergus said. He searched around until he found a fairly flat stone of decent size, then hauled it, grunting with the weight, over to the door. Propping it upright inside the opening, it was only a few centimeters shy of where the door bottom was being held by the jack. He wedged smaller stones under the edges of the bigger one to hold it more securely, and Riji lowered the jack just enough to determine that the stone would hold it up. Pulling the jack out, she powered it down and put it away again.

"Now what?" she asked.

"How sturdy do you think those vines are?" he asked in turn.

"Very, in my experience, but it depends on what you want to do with them."

"Climb them?"

She stared at the vines running up and over the door over-hang, thinking, before she said, "Should be strong enough. I'd be more worried about them coming loose than breaking. Why?"

"The building must have had some sort of power source," he said. "Maybe they had a small cold-fusion reactor inside and either shut it down or took it with them, but there could be some sort of solar on the roof that's been grown over. If so, and we clear it . . ."

"Okay, that's probably worth the risk to check out," she said. "If we do find something up there, we should make ourselves a ladder, though I don't have a pot big enough to boil sap."

"We can add it to your list," Fergus said. "I have a feeling we'll need it for something, and if not, well, it wasn't us who'll have to haul it here, right?"

"Right," she said. "But what do I do while you're climbing around?"

"You wanna run the drone under the door and get a first look-see? It's in my pack with my goggles."

"Sure," she said. "I thought you'd never ask."

The vines were sturdy but slightly stretchy, which was alarm-ing until he got used to it and compensated. The surface of the vines was also oddly rough under his hands, and bumpy, but that helped with his grip; if they'd been slippery, the stretchiness might've made them almost impossible to climb.

He pulled himself over the lip of the overhang, sat, and watched as Riji tried on his goggles. "Whoa," she said, looking up at him. "These are *nice*. Can't afford stuff like this on a military engineer's salary, that's for sure. If you die, can I have them?"

"Only if I didn't die because you killed me for my goggles," Fergus said. "There's a lot of wurble clusters growing up here. Should I bring some down with me when I'm done?"

"You can just drop 'em," she said. "The outer leaves are tough as hell, and you have to smash 'em to peel 'em, anyway."

He yanked several clusters off and dropped them over the edge like bombs. When he'd run out of ones he couldn't reach without leaning too far out for safety, he got up and headed up the incline of the roof toward the center. The structure was larger than he'd guessed from below, and he thought maybe it had been built partially into the rocks of the hillside it was nestled up against, though the roof had been colonized by enough vines and full-grown wavetrees that he still couldn't get a view of the whole thing.

He found the first of what he assumed were solar panels because he nearly slipped on the slick surface as the vines crisscrossing the structure moved under his boots. Catching himself on a tree, he knelt down carefully to examine it. It was made of odd, shiny green hexes, but as he moved the vines out of the way and the sun hit it, he could feel the very faint tingle of response.

"Found solar," he shouted down. "Going to try clearing them off, then we can see if the systems will still power up after all this time."

"That'd be good, because there's another door not far inside," Riji called back up from somewhere now out of sight. "I'm limited on what I can see until we can get in and force that one open, too. I was thinking— No, hang on, someone's calling."

Fergus went back to clearing off panels, either shoving vines to the side or, when necessitated by the level and intransigence of their entanglement, cutting them apart. Many had a thin layer of a green-turquoise fuzz that he scraped up carefully and dumped in another sunny spot between panels. When Riji called up to him again, he'd only managed to clear about a dozen and was regretting not hauling his water bottle up with him.

Going down the vines back to the ground was, at least, easier.

"That was your first mate, I think. Kaybe? It rhymed with *maybe*," Riji said, and handed him the comm unit. "I gave him the rundown of some additional tools we could use, what we'd earmarked for salvage, and where it needed to go. He says he and

Cole are going to organize a team to head to the *Stiletto* and pick up what's ready. I guess they'll call from there and see if we need more people here. Oh, and he said your captain has 'concerns' about you going off on a distraction."

"Yeah, well, it's not a distraction if we find out anything useful," Fergus said. He sat for a moment, listening to the sounds of an entire alien ecology around them and the breeze rustling through the fronds of the wavetrees around them. If it weren't for the circumstances under which they'd arrived and their dubious chances of ever leaving, it would have been almost as peaceful as Coralla's beaches. Add a few good takeout food places—noodles, pizza, a good curry stand—and it would be a very bearable final destination.

With a shake of his head, he finished off his bottle of water. "And since I think we've found out the Bomo'ri had a non-accidental, once-permanent presence on this planet, possibly from before all the shooting, crashing, and dying started, I'd say it's already justified the walk over here."

"Not me you have to convince," Riji said. "But let's explore as much as we can before you get hauled off to disobedient pirate jail or worse."

"I want to set up the filtration column so we can get more fresh water, then show me what you've found so far," he said. "After that, we can break some more doors."

"Unless your solar panels get things running again," she said. "Might be charging itself up nicely."

"Just a trickle so far, I'm afraid," he said, only just barely able to sense the faint charge, somewhere deep inside the structure, and even that required concentration to pick up.

"How can you know that?" she asked.

"Guessing, I guess," he said quickly, and busied himself digging the water filter out of the pile of tools. "There's a lot of roof surface for panels, and I only got a handful cleared. Be right back."

He found a stable part of the stream bank, bolstered by rocks, where he could get the water-filtration column set up and pulling steadily. He watched it for a bit, comfortable in the shade of a large wavetree, and interrogated himself about how and why he'd become so careless yet again. Was it creeping conviction he was never leaving there, or just being rusty from years spent sitting on a beach, serving tea to tourists who had no interest in who he was, much less who else he once had been?

All those things, he decided, but something more. Once he was able to put that piece together with the others, everything made more sense. All that time on Coralla, though he'd made local friends, he'd missed his found family, and his found-found family, and never quite thought about how much he'd internalized that loss.

Nor had he ever thought, in all that time in semi-voluntary exile, that he'd never see them again: his sister Isla, Noura and Effie and the other Shipmakers of Pluto, even Maha and Qai.

If you can't deal with never seeing them again, make sure you will, he told himself.

When it had drawn enough to refill his water bottle, he did, then left it to refill and climbed back up to where Riji was idly holding the drone, her mind clearly somewhere else.

"Ah," she said, when she heard him. "You know, Vetch, there's something bugging me—"

"I had—have—this friend, named Effie," he interrupted, heading off whatever uncomfortable topic she was probably headed for. "She's an engineer, like you, and you remind me of her. I haven't seen her, or really almost any of my real friends, in a long time, though."

"Lover?" Riji asked, her expression indicating she would not be pleased to be told that was how she'd reminded him of her.

"Oh, stars, no," Fergus said. "Just a good friend. The kind that's like the family you never had, you know?"

"Another pirate?"

"No. She builds spaceships," he said. "She's nice. I mean, not nice exactly—I don't think I know too many *nice* people—but kind. Smart. I used to act like quite an asshole, once upon a time, but I think she always saw through that. You two would like each other, I think."

"Well, building spaceships is cool," Riji said. "More fun than trying to patch them back together out of garbage and plant life, I'd expect. You're a weird guy, Vetch, and you say and do odd things that I just can't figure out, and the sad part about that is that if we ever do escape here, we won't be friends. You and I are different sides of a pretty sharp moral line."

"The line is probably not exactly where or what you think it is, but you're still not wrong," he said, regretfully. "But, until then, no one's watching; wanna commit some aggravated piracy on this unattended building with me? There may be loot."

She laughed. "I suspect the former owners aren't going to object, after all this time."

"The Bomo'ri? I wouldn't bet on it. We know almost nothing about them, but the one thing we do know is that they can hold a grudge like no one else," Fergus said. He dragged another rock over to the doorway and wedged it up under the other side, just as extra insurance, then got down on his hands and knees and crawled through the gap into the interior.

On the far side, he stood up and dusted off his shorts, peering around in the dark. There wasn't much he could see as he waited for his eyes to adjust after the bright sunlight outside. "You coming?" he called.

"Waiting to hear if you get jumped and eaten," Riji called back. "Make a lot of noise if you do."

"Now you totally remind me of her," Fergus grumbled. He was starting to be able to make out some details in the room, including the inner door Riji had already found via drone. The ceilings were tall, as they had been in the Bomo'ri ships, but at least there were no bodies. There was a thin strip running the circumference of the room, roughly about the height of his shoulders, that was starting, very faintly, to glow. It was far from being a useful source of light, but it was comforting to know that something was still working after all this time.

Hell, if the building had climate controls that could take down some of the humidity, he might just claim it as his own and move in.

"Hey, Riji, can you pass me the jack? I want to try opening the inner door," Fergus called out. "Also, can I have my goggles back? I can't see in the dark."

The jack slid under the door, and half a minute later, the drone itself entered, spun around, then rose, emitting a bright light. What little adjustment his eyes had managed was gone, literally, in a flash, and he groaned and shaded his eyes. "The goggles would have been better," he said.

"Yeah but then we couldn't use the drone anymore," Riji said, "and I want to see too *before* I risk getting trapped in there."

"Could you just try to not shine it right in my eyes, though?" he asked, as he set the jack up against the interior door, braced the toe of his boot against it so he could press upward with both hands, and just managed to get enough of a crack to push the jack base forward into place. This door rose more easily, and was thinner than the outer door, so he was unprepared for the full-on blast of foul air that seemed to reach out to grab him by the throat. "Danger!" he managed to croak as he fell to his knees, and his lungs fought to expel whatever he'd sucked into them. His peripheral vision dwindled away, and he hit the ground, hard.

———

He woke up lying curled on his side on a pile of leaf litter in the shade of a particularly large wavetree. His throat burned, as if he'd tried to inhale grain alcohol or worse. The sun had moved a fair distance, casting reddish-purple hues on the upper reaches of the hillside beyond the Bomo'ri building, and Riji had settled in next to a small fire, and was weaving together fronds with deft, precise movements.

She looked up as he started to cough, pulled a second pot out of the fire, and poured something into a battered old Alliance Engineering Corps Five-Year Service Award mug that she set on the ground within his reach. "Tea," she said. "Solo blend, so don't get your hopes up. Uh, and let it cool first."

"Thanks," he managed to croak. "Should've expected dead air."

"Wasn't, though," she said. "Just not our mix. Got some good readouts with the drone after I pulled you out of there and made sure you were going to breathe again. More hydrogen, less oxygen, and one hell of a methane chaser. Something seems to be generating it fresh inside the core of the building, so in hindsight, it looks like turning the power back on was a bad idea."

The tea was not the worst he'd had, though he had to admit his standards in the moment were probably low. There was a hint of something sweet and citrusy to offset the mulchiness of the brew, and he spotted a few peeled-off, purple bits of one of the vine clusters at the bottom of the mug. It did make his throat feel better, though there was still a low wheeze deep in his chest every time he tried to take a deeper breath that he didn't like the sound of at all.

"There should be some respirators in the wreck of *Stiletto* we can dig out," she said. "I don't want to make the hike in the dark, though, and I don't think you should go for at least a few days, until we're sure you're breathing okay."

That was sensible, and he said so, but she must have seen the look of disappointment on his face. "If you're okay when the sun comes up, I'll go on my own," she said.

"If you're sure—" he started to say.

She dismissed the half-formed objection with a wave of her

hand. "Do you know the population on this planet has *tripled* since I got here? I could use a little time away from the hustle and bustle of the crowds."

He laughed, though it came out half-wheeze, and he took another sip of tea to help soothe his throat.

"I still have half a loaf of bread and some jam," she said, "but I'm going to have to scrounge for something to supplement it, especially for midnightsies."

"Midnightsies?" he asked.

"When you get up in the middle of the night, kill a few hours, have a small snack . . . Your crew isn't doing that?" she asked. "Don't tell me you're sleeping all the way through a fourteen-hour night?"

"You don't?"

"No. And by winter, such as it is, it'll be closer to eighteen," she said. "We get up, socialize a bit with whoever else is up and around, whatever except no work. Then we go back to sleep a few hours later."

"I just assumed you eventually got used to it," Fergus said.

"Nope," she said. "I've been stationed places with a twenty-one-hour day, and once twenty-six, and I got used to those, but once you get above twenty-eight? Body is just not having any of it, no matter how hard any of us try," she said. "Though Ajac sleeps off and on in six-to-eight-hour chunks, so maybe he's got it down to some sort of sensible, biologically non-traumatizing pattern, and stars know what the hell Earlan does when he's not in camp. Now stop talking and work on breathing instead, okay? I'll be back."

She headed off into the woods with a knife and her canvas bag, and for a moment he thought about following, picking up some of the Islanders' no-doubt hard-learned foraging knowledge, but as he tried to rise to his feet, he started coughing again. As much as he abhorred the idea of rest, slowing down someone else while being useless himself was even worse.

He sipped his tea and thought about the beach and whatever patience, whatever practice of just existing in the moment, he had learned there and so quickly forgotten.

———

Morning came, and he was pleased to find he was breathing better. Also, he had slept much more soundly for the second half of the long night for having granted himself permission to be up and about and intentionally unproductive for a few hours, gently puttering around, re-stoking the fire, chatting about Marsball with Riji, instead of lying there tossing and turning, agitated and berating himself for being unable to drift immediately back off. Midnightsies were a habit he was absolutely going to cultivate, going forward.

Riji insisted on listening to him breathe in and out, her ear against his back, before she declared him unlikely to croak in her absence, and headed off back to the *Stiletto* to get respirators and meet up with the team coming out with Yolo to collect their treasure trove of parts.

When the boredom got to him—not long, he judged, after Riji was far enough away to not hear him overdoing things—he twisted up some more stalks and soaked them in the simmering glue, intertwining horizontal pieces between two long vertical lengths to make a ladder. He laid the whole thing out in a sunny spot on a flat rock a short distance away and marveled at just how rapidly it turned into something almost resembling steel.

While waiting on that to fully cure, he sought about for moveable rocks that were sturdy enough to hold the doors of the Bomo'ri building up, and, after the third time he had to sit and catch his breath, decided instead to cut more stalks and weave them into a loose ball. By midday, they were hard enough for him to stand atop without even the slightest give, and he used the jack to lift the door the extra ten centimeters or so to get them underneath. When he removed the jack, the door settled onto them without even a creak of protest. If they did give, the rocks in the corners would still stop the door from closing too far.

The grass balls also had the advantage of letting air pass through them; as he had gotten them placed, he could smell whiffs of methane being expelled through the door, and that meant there had to be quite a buildup of it collecting in the upper reaches of the high-ceilinged outer room. He wondered if Riji had brought any explosives with her here from the *Stiletto*, and if they'd be sufficient to make an impromptu chimney-hole in the roof to let the gas out.

He smiled at the thought of the fireball that the methane would produce, but it would probably toast much of the interior, and as much as he wanted to explore inside safely, it wouldn't net him any good information if he blew it all up first.

Instead, he ate the last bit of leftover bread, then tested out his ladder by climbing up onto the roof again. Then he sat again for a bit, wheezing and unhappy about it, and thinking again of the brief, short-sighted but no doubt intense satisfaction of blowing it all up.

He'd hauled up his goggles and drone, and after getting his breath and balance back, he pulled his goggles down and sent the drone out, up high, and eventually spotted the tiny figure of Riji moving in and out of the waveforest at the very far edges of the drone's range, already more than halfway back to the *Stiletto* wreck. Setting the drone to auto-return, he pushed the goggles up to the top of his head, then set to clearing off more power panels until the drone settled back down into its launch spot on the roof nearby.

More than a little irked at himself, he went back down the ladder and to his tent, to lie down and rest.

Three hours later, the comm unit crackled into life. "Back at

Stiletto," Riji said. "We'll be heading your way in a few hours, after I show the others what else here we want to try to bring."

"Did you find a respirator?" he asked.

"Several," she said. "Already got them packed for the trip. Anything else we need?"

"Not that I can think of," he said.

"You're not overdoing it, right?" she asked.

"No," he said.

There was a muffled conversation on Riji's end, then he heard her declare, very forcibly, "He inhaled *methane*; no way he was hiking back here today, and probably not tomorrow, either." There was a pause, then she added, "Fine, you tell him. I'm not in charge of any of you."

When she spoke to him directly again, several minutes later, she sounded deeply peeved. "Looks like the whole party is heading back with me," she said. "None of them are in a good mood, just to warn you."

"Thanks," he said. "Who's the party?"

"Your captain, Yolo, Marche, and Kaybe," she said. "I'm feeling a lot outnumbered right now."

"Belos came out?" Fergus was surprised. "Why?"

"Dunno. You can ask him yourself, if you want, but I'm staying out of Captain Cranky's way, with his scary face tattoo and stupid tight pants— Uh-oh, they're coming back; gotta go."

Fergus sighed, dropped the comm back into his pocket, then went back up on the roof to fetch his drone. At least he could get something done while waiting.

The roof was warm but, being above much of the tree canopy, had a steady, cooling breeze blowing across it, and the fresh air felt nice in his still-battered lungs. Pulling his goggles back on, he sent the drone down and in the main building entrance, running a scan of the entire room, before he ducked it under the low opening of the interior door.

Lights were definitely, slowly coming on. As he swept through the much-larger space, over oddly shaped furniture and into a dining area, and from there into small alcoves that, from their layout, likely only fit two or three Bomo'ri at a time around tall, flat-topped columns that could have been tables or almost anything else, he dumped all the data down to his handpad for later.

There were few signs of any sort of rushed evacuation, though who knew how that would look? There were more doors, still closed, deeper in past what he thought of as public areas, and he very much wanted to go in in person, touch things, find buttons to push or levers to pull or otherwise open the space up to where he might find actual information.

If he wasn't still feeling tightness in his chest, it would have been tempting to poke his actual head in again. That and if there had been anyone left around who could pull his sorry ass out again when it went wrong.

He focused momentarily on the time readout in the peripheral vision of his goggles. One way or another, he wouldn't be alone for much longer. Extracting the drone from the building, he flew it out and over the trail again, and found Riji and the others stomping along about half an hour out, and as she'd hinted, no one looked happy.

Well, he thought, *probably not much I could do about that except make it worse.*

Though that wasn't entirely true, and there was a definite advantage in trying. He left his drone parked on the roof and climbed slowly down his ladder, dropping more of the wurble clusters as he went. Once down, he collected them up in his shirt and sat near the now-dead fire, splitting them open with his knife and rinsing the soft, sweet, dark red chunks in the pot of water that had cooled to barely above air temperature. It was too bad there wasn't more bread, but that was not a problem for him to solve; he had never, in his life, spent much time cooking. He wondered if his cousin Gavin missed him yet, and if Iain—the cook at Gavin's pub in Scotland—was still burning half of every batch of chips.

Even burnt, he'd take 'em right now. Of course, if they weren't burnt, his sister would have certainly gotten to them first. Was she still in Scotland, tormenting Gav, or off somewhere, doing something brilliant and very astrophysics-y? He hoped wherever she was, she didn't spend too much of her time thinking about him; the idea that she might only made him feel all the worse for being where—and, if he had to admit it, who—he was.

He had a decent bowl of prepped cluster chunks when Riji came out of the waveforest into their camp clearing. Kaybe and Belos were behind her, then Marche and Cole.

"Up there," Riji said, pointing, and Fergus fell in behind them as they climbed up over the boulders and cracked steps to the base of the Bomo'ri tower.

"Well, that does look like a building," Cole said, standing back and appraising the structure. "And not one of ours."

"But does it do us any good?" Belos asked.

"Knowledge is always good," Fergus replied.

"And what do you know that's new, other than that you can't go inside without nearly dying?" Belos said. "I gave you a task, and I don't see where anything you've found here justifies your disobedience."

"My—" Fergus started. "You and I want the same thing, Bas, unless that's changed. Whatever happened to trusting your crew?"

"Uh, let's go back down to camp," Riji said. "We got fresh water set up, and I saw Vetch cut us up some fresh fruit."

Marche looked reluctant to leave, but Kaybe touched her elbow gently. "Let them talk. No one's going to kill anyone, right?" he said, and stared meaningfully back at Belos and Fergus.

Belos gave a curt shake of his head. "Not today," he said.

Kaybe turned to Fergus, almost as if an afterthought. "Not unless I have to defend myself," Fergus replied.

Yolo let out a deep sigh of disappointment. "Would be a hell of a fight, though," he said.

Marche kicked him in the ass, not hard enough to hurt but enough to get his attention. "Down, Yolo. None of us need a fight today."

When they were gone, Belos studied Fergus up and down. "You really think you'd have a chance against me?" he asked.

"I do," Fergus said. "I'd say maybe seventy–thirty."

"Seventy me?"

"No," Fergus said.

Belos uttered a short bark of a laugh, though it didn't have any humor in it at all. "I'll be sure to start a betting pool," he said. "I told you what I wanted from you. I want our ships able to fly us out of here. Did you think I wouldn't mind you going off on pointless side adventures instead?"

"Do you think we're going to get very far from this planet at all without knowing more about what's been happening here, why all this?" Fergus waved his hands around them. "Do you think this is *coincidence*?"

"I don't care," Belos said.

"Do you want us all to die because we were too damned impatient to do even basic diligence first?"

"I have a plan!" Belos bellowed.

"Yeah? What is it?" Fergus shouted back. "Fill me in, then!"

"No."

"I am as good as I am at what I do—and you know I'm the *best* at it—because I pay attention to everything, until I know what's important and what's not," Fergus said. "I want off this planet too but so I can go home, not so I can become just another lost corpse in space that doesn't even have enough stars to make a respectable grave. I will do what I can to try to get everyone away from here, alive. If you want to die, that's on you."

There was something, for just a moment, in Belos's expression that said Fergus had hit a lot closer to home than he should have. "Didn't think you of all people would walk away from a challenge before it was over," he said, more gently.

"It *is* over," Belos said. "She's dead."

"You knew that was likely, from the very beginning, but you know it with no more certainty now than then, unless you've found a body you haven't told me about. The only thing that's changed is we're closer to having answers, which is what you wanted," Fergus said. "Let me do my thing, Bas. Trust me."

"What if I don't?" Belos countered.

"Then maybe you shouldn't have had me kidnapped for you in the first place. But you did, and here I am, and I'm trying to help. Fucking *work* with me," Fergus said.

He turned his back on Belos and headed down the steps toward camp, and, for the first time in a very long time, could feel the bees of his electrical gift tingling against his skin, contained but ready. In that extra sense, he could tell Belos hadn't moved except to turn and watch him go. Something else caught his attention, and he glanced up to see his drone, still perched on the edge of the roofline where he'd left it, with its tiny green signal light on.

He reached the camp just in time to see Riji drop the goggles back among his stuff.

Chapter 16

Cole, Kaybe, and Yolo joined Fergus and Riji for midnight-sies, three of them sitting around the fire drinking tea—Riji had also found a few intact mugs in the wreck of *Stiletto* and brought them along with the respirators and some additional rations—and Yolo complaining loud enough to be clearly heard that no one had prioritized fabbing up a portable still.

No one commented that they had big-enough problems already, but the exchange of looks between the rest of them was audible enough anyway.

Despite that, the atmosphere was almost relaxed. Yolo seemed less unhappy than he had been, despite the lack of alcohol, and Cole and Kaybe had a friendly banter back and forth that did not feel at all forced. Riji was quiet, though she looked like she had something on her mind that she was torn by, which Fergus expected she did. Finally, something must have tipped, because she set down her mug and cleared her throat. "Tomorrow, when we leave here—" she started to say.

"No work talk," Cole interrupted, smiling, but caught the look on Riji's expression in the firelight and held up his hands in surrender. "We're leaving early enough; I suppose it doesn't hurt to talk about a *little* bit."

The current plan was that Marche would stay with Fergus, either until they exhausted any potential sources of useful information or until Fergus felt up for the hike, whichever came first. Before stomping off to his tent to sleep, Belos had made it clear his patience would be limited in either case, but Fergus wasn't going to argue; that he was willing to grant Fergus some time was, from the captain in his current mind frame, a monumental concession.

Plus, neither Fergus nor Marche were likely to be much help at freeing *Rattler*'s shuttle, which was the next big project.

". . . When we leave," Riji started again, "if you aren't certain you want to stay, Vetch, we could take it slow back to the camp and Safani could check your lungs out. We can always come back later—the building isn't going anywhere."

"If I get worse again, we'll call," Fergus said. Fendi had sent along more comm units and repeaters for both the *Stiletto* wreck and this site. When the sun came out, he was going to set it up on the roof with its own solar panel, and as soon as it picked up enough charge, they'd be online again. He'd also sent one back to Ajac for the Islander camp, but so far they hadn't asked, and the *Sidewinder* crew hadn't offered, one for the *Paradigm* survivors.

Right now, they were all doing a very good job of avoiding each other, but when that ended, Fergus did not expect it to end peacefully. *Another reason to spend more time here*, he thought.

Riji was visibly dissatisfied with his answer but had picked up her mug again and was swirling around whatever was left in the bottom with an intense but unfocused series of shakes.

"It'll be fine, I promise," he said, but her scowl only deepened.

"If there is any tech we can use here, I'm sure we'll all be involved in assessing and utilizing it," Cole said.

"That's . . ." Riji started to say, then finished off her tea. "That's exactly it, obviously. Long walk tomorrow, so I'm going to get a head start on night part two."

She left. The rest of them sat there without talking for a while, then one by one, both Yolo and Cole also headed toward their tents. Kaybe stayed until they both could hear Yolo's snores echoing through the clearing.

"I don't know what you and Bas argued about, but I can probably guess," Kaybe said.

"Probably," Fergus said.

Kaybe nodded. "I'm worried," he said.

"Me too," Fergus said.

"I've never seen him quite like this, and I need you—I'm asking you—to give him some room to get his head back in the game," Kaybe said. "We need to get back to working as a team."

"You think that's going to happen?" Fergus said. "Why do you think he's so keen on getting *two* working ships?"

Kaybe glanced up sharply. "I've known Bas most of both our lives, and he would never abandon us to save himself. If you ever fucking *dare* suggest that again in my hearing, or where it gets back to me, you won't live to draw another breath after those words leave your lips."

"That's not what I'm saying at all," Fergus said. "I think he's been putting off grieving for his sister for a very long time and has now lost hope. He blames himself for all of us being here, for Rabbit being right on the edge with no end in sight, all in the name of his obsession with closure. My worry is that he plans on doing something heroically suicidal, thinly justified in the name of revenge, hoping it buys us a chance to escape and himself a very final end."

Kaybe kicked at the edge of the fire with his boots. "What I want, more than anything," he said, "is to be able to believe that everything you just said is bullshit and misunderstanding."

"Can you?" Fergus asked.

"I don't know," Kaybe said. He got up, stretched with his hands against the small of his back, and stared up a while at the two moons, one just visible behind the silhouette of the building. "Learn what you can here. If it takes an extra few days, do it. I can smooth over small delays, and if it means we have the beginnings of an actual plan by the time we have the means of getting off this planet's surface, then it won't matter if you're right or wrong. Oh, and Vetch?"

"Yes?"

"Fill Marche in. And for fuck's sake, *listen* to her when she tries to give you advice. You keep getting in Bas's face, you're gonna need more than one of us invested in keeping you alive."

———

Marche felt it was best to test the respirators one at a time before they both put themselves in potential harm's way; she volunteered to go first, until Fergus pointed out that if something was going to go wrong, it made a lot more sense to have one person who was physically uncompromised, which wasn't him.

She parked herself in a shady spot outside and synced the drone to her own goggles. "How much did you get explored before you inhaled too much methane?" she asked.

"Outer room, mostly. It doesn't have much in it, probably functioned as a lobby or an airlock of sorts with the Bomo'ri-specific atmosphere past the second door," he said. "I scanned further in with the drone, but it's hard to know what you're looking at sometimes, especially if you can't touch things."

"Well, now's your chance," she said. "I suggest you stay within easy escape distance until you're sure the respirator is working properly."

"Don't worry; I have no desire to experience that again," Fergus said. He put his own goggles on and over to infrared, and set them to send a recording to his handpad, then stood at the door and took several deep breaths—wheezing and all—until he felt sufficiently fortified. When he was ready, he ducked under the door and in.

The hum of the drone tagging along behind him was strangely comforting.

Lights had grown a little stronger, and he saw little that he hadn't already spotted, except for a slightly darker rectangle on the smooth wall beside the inner door. He could feel electricity behind it, so he reached out one hand, but before his fingers touched it, the rectangle lit up with a 3-D hologram of a looping, intertwined script. On a sudden whim, he poked his index finger into the hologram itself, then twisted and crooked his finger in the light.

The door, which had only been kept open by the rocks he'd pushed underneath, groaned and shuddered and slowly rose.

"How'd you do that?" Marche asked through his comm earpiece.

"Dunno, just stuck my finger in," Fergus said.

"How's the air?"

"About twenty-five C, forty-four percent humidity, and a stinkload of methane," he said.

"You don't have anything on you that could make a spark, I hope?" she asked.

Fergus laughed. "Sparks? Never!"

"Just asking," she said. "How's your respirator holding up?"

He checked the display readout via his goggles. "It thinks it's good," he said. "So far, I'm breathing okay. I'm going in."

"Right behind you. Safely via drone, anyway," Marche said. "So, your cat—can it make more?"

"What?" Fergus asked, sufficiently unprepared for that turn in the conversation that he almost tripped over the lip of a stepped dais inside the room. "You mean, like kittens?"

"Oh, that's it. I knew *cub* wasn't right," Marche said.

"Well, I mean, no?" Fergus said. "For starters, you'd need another cat—a girl one—and then—"

"I get biology, jerk," she said. "I'm just wondering if it can be cloned."

"I didn't think you liked my cat," Fergus said. He wandered the perimeter of the room, watching his footing this time, and then found another panel beside the next door. It lit up, and he repeated his earlier motion, and the door rose more smoothly than the last.

He had a tiny pinprick of a headache, up behind his left eye, but his respirator's safety indicator stayed green, so he went through that door too.

"I don't," Marche said. "Safani, though . . . Never mind."

As he'd half-expected, the new space he entered was much more of a functional space. Instruments lined the outer walls, and a large circular desk-like stand dominated the center of the room. He ducked under the top through a gap between machinery and then stood up in the center of the circle. The floor beneath him lit up with a warm blue glow, and moments later, he was surrounded by shifting holographic script and symbols that moved into focus as he turned around in place to face them, then faded and fuzzed out slightly when his attention went elsewhere.

He saw the command structure for the air systems go by, and stuck four fingers in, twisting and turning as if the letters were a bunch of interlocking dials, and smiled in satisfaction as it switched internal atmosphere production from Home mode to Local. Already he could see the methane percentage in his respirator display start to fall.

"What did you just do?" Marche asked him, as the drone did a tight circle above him, near the ceiling.

"Switched over the air handling so we can breathe in here," he said.

"How?" she demanded.

"I just—" He pointed toward the glyph stack. "Oh."

If he thought about it, it was just meaningless patterns and jumbled strings, but when he let his attention lapse for just a moment, it all made sense. And it made his head hurt. *That absolute bastard,* he thought. *It must have been that damned book.*

"Oh?" Marche asked. "Just *oh*? 'Oh, I can read an alien language for a vastly superior species that *notoriously* hates humans and avoids us like we're a virulent plague on the galaxy, no big deal, carry on'?"

"It's a surprise to me, too. Do you think any explanation I could give would be believable, much less satisfactory?" Fergus said.

"Try me," Marche said.

"There was this book—"

"*Beginner Bomo'ri for Dunces?*"

"Maybe. I didn't actually see the title," Fergus said. "It probably wasn't even actually a book. As soon as I touched it, I passed out, woke up and it was gone."

"Poof, like magic?"

"Well, sufficiently advanced technology, anyway. Probably it was carrying a payload of nanobots designed to imprint memory via neural schema manipulation," he said.

"We don't have tech like that, not that I've heard anywhere," Marche said. "I mean, there are labs experimenting with identity cloning—there's quite a black market for Elvises, for example—but it's a whole wipe, nothing nuanced, nothing left of the original, and it's not exactly stable. Assuming I believe you at all, where did you encounter this book?"

He laughed. "It's just going to get harder, the strain on credibility," he said. "Air is good in here now, though, if you want to come in. I think I found a map."

In fact, he was sure he had, and when he moved his hands through the script in the right sequence, a 3-D holo-map of Solo and its two moons blinked into existence overhead and began to slowly rotate. There were two primary continents, both crossing the equator but with the bulk of their landmass to the south, though that was probably his own arbitrary determination. The biggest merged into a vast icecap at the bottom pole, while the northern cap was much smaller and at the end of a chain of medium to small islands. The second-largest continent was almost shaped like an upside-down U, with a vast bay almost bisecting it, and one of its limbs breaking up into islands as it headed toward the pole. On the other, fatter limb of the U, right along the equator, was a red mark that Fergus knew, without knowing how, was a *You Are Here* symbol.

Marche came into the room, still wearing her respirator. At her look of wary distrust, he took his off and set it on one of the console desks. She raised one eyebrow speculatively but kept hers on.

"So, we're here," Fergus said, and pointed out the red mark. At his gesture, text appeared in the air beside it. "Apparently, this is Transport Anchor Station 20."

"What does that mean?" she asked.

He shrugged. "Dunno, but it suggests there are at least nineteen others around somewhere." He poked for a while through the glyph swarm around him, spinning the virtual display slowly around himself as he looked, until he found an item menu for the holo-map, and adjusted it.

There were, it turned out, thirty-six such Transport Anchor Stations, equidistant from each other along the equator and circling the whole planet. Eight of them were in open ocean. A thirty-seventh light lit up, on the other main continent, identified as *Main Research Headquarters*. "That was their HQ," he said, pointing it out to Marche. "They were researching something here."

"What?"

"No idea. I don't know any more about the Bomo'ri than you do," he said. She glared at him. "Okay, except their language, and only when I look at it, and it's giving me a headache like someone shot an arrow into my forehead."

"Have you ever had an arrow shot into your head?" Marche asked.

"No, but I got shot in the leg with a harpoon gun once," Fergus said.

"Ouch," she said. "Okay, so, I grant you probably do know what that would feel like, but you're still exaggerating."

"I mean, yes? But it still hurts," Fergus said. He closed his eyes for a moment, and then immediately the sharp, throbbing pain began to lessen.

"I've never been shot by a projectile," she said. "I did have to regrow almost an entire leg once, though."

"Oh, damn," Fergus said. "I had to regrow an ear, and the itching was awful. I can't even imagine a leg."

"I drank a *lot*," Marche said. "Not sure it helped, but it kept me from killing my crew at the time, whose abject stupidity and inability to follow a basic plan lost me the leg to start with. Then they had the nerve to deny me my share of the haul because I was, to quote, 'not a fully contributing member of the crew for the entire duration of the mission.' Soon as I could walk, I left and found *Sidewinder.*"

He shook his head. "And you didn't kill them for that? Even I would have been tempted."

"No, but I did leave them each minus a leg, as an exercise in team empathy-building," she said. She heaved a deep sigh. "I don't know what I'm doing."

Fergus opened his eyes. "In this room? Me neither."

"No, about Safani. She's a damned Alliance medic, and I'm a thieving, maiming, and murdering space pirate, and I *like* who I am. But I also like her. She's *cute.*"

"I had a conversation with Riji about how it would be impossible for us to be friends away from here, because of who we are," Fergus said. "But for now, we are here. Who we are on this planet doesn't need to be who we were before, or who we might be after, just as long as everyone knows that's how it is. Could be here for all our lives, after all."

"I suppose," she said.

"Besides, if you were really committed to the life of high-space piracy, you'd have opted for a peg leg instead of a regrow," he said. "Might be hope for you yet."

"Hmmm," Marche said, a skeptical sound. She had wandered over to one of the other doors out of the main room. "How do you open it?"

"Do this," he said, and showed her the hook, crook, and twist gesture.

She copied his gesture, and the door slid upward. "Come look for me if I'm not back in ten," she said, and went through.

Fergus checked through the holo-map menu again, looking to see if there were other objects he could get it to display, and saw that he could widen the field. He did, and the planet and its two moons shrank down, and a yellow ball coalesced that was Solo's star. A legend popped up, declaring the star *Object 114*.

Orbital lines filled in, and then more appeared, except thinner and made of dots instead of being solid. "Huh," he said, and read through the new info that had come up with them. A few gestures, and the dotted-lines of other planets along those orbital lines appeared, where there were no planets now.

If the map was correct, this system had once had seven planets, including a gas giant that would have made Jupiter feel inadequate. There were also planets indicated where now there was only ice and rock debris in the outer orbits. "What the hell?" he muttered to himself.

"Everything okay?" Marche asked over the comms.

"I think there used to be more planets around this star," Fergus said.

"How does that happen?" Marche said. "You can't just disappear planets, can you?"

"I can't," Fergus said. "But the Bomo'ri? Who knows what they can do. Or why. You find anything?"

"A kitchen, I think," she said. "Or it's a bathroom. Or I suppose both is possible."

"Let's hope not," Fergus said. He used a twist of his hand to open the new menu items and found a listing for more stations. More dots appeared, this time on Solo's moons and in similar circumference around the outline of the missing gas giant. Then, extraordinarily, a net of dots, tens of thousands of them, evenly spaced in a halo around the entirety of the star, just far enough out to fall outside the star's corona. He tapped at the status for one of the dots, and the words for *destroyed* popped up. He sampled randomly for several minutes, but all were also gone.

The same was true of the band of objects around the gas giant: *destroyed*.

Each had a timestamp, though how that related to human time, or how it scaled, he had no idea. The gas giant's stations were destroyed first, and simultaneously. Those forming the halo around the star went next. If the rest of the notations were still accurate after all this time, the objects on Solo and its moons were still there. *Next time,* he told himself, *I should crash-land next to the HQ, if I can.*

"Hey, Vetch, you find out anything about what's below this building?" Marche asked.

"No," he said. "Why?"

"I found what seems to be an elevator down."

"What's at the bottom?"

"I haven't gone *in*," she said. "I'm a little more cautious than that."

"Okay, I'll see if I can find anything out," he said, though his head was throbbing so badly, his left eye was beginning to involuntarily twitch. "I'm going to need to take a break, though, and soon."

"I'll come back to you," Marche said. "We can always come back in after a rest and some food."

"Yeah," he said. He shut down the holo-map, and the dissipation of a large volume of Bomo'ri script helped, until he dug into the building operations menu again, looking for what was below.

When he found it, he swore involuntarily, several times.

There was no way to transfer data across alien systems, so he used his handpad camera to take photos of the schematics, until Marche appeared again through the doorway.

"You figure out what it is?" she asked.

"Yeah," he said. "It's a massive fusion reactor, and it goes all the way down through Solo's crust to the mantle."

"That's a lot of fucking power for one tiny building," she said.

"Especially as the building itself is fed by the solar panels on the roof."

"Then what's it for?"

"I don't even have the beginnings of a glimmer of a hint of a ghost of a clue," Fergus said.

"Is it . . . running right now?" she asked.

"No, and I'm perfectly fine for it to stay that way, given that the Bomo'ri seem to have been very careless with all of this system's other planets," he said. "I need water and to close my eyes for a bit. You ready to get out of here?"

"Absolutely," she said, picked up the drone, and followed him out to the mercifully data-free forest.

It was midday outside, which felt unfairly early after the toll that exploring the building had taken on him. Recalling that Riji had also talked about noonsies—the opposite of midnightsies—as a great time to catch naps, as soon as he'd drunk enough water to not feel sickly, and the headache had finally faded to negligible, he crawled into his tent and fell asleep.

When he awoke almost three hours later, the sun hadn't moved all that much from overhead, and he split some rations with Marche and sent the images he'd taken of building schematics back to *Sidewinder* and Fendi.

"I can't read any of the text," Fendi replied, after he'd downloaded them.

"I have a key, of sorts," Fergus said.

"Okay. I'll look these over and figure out what I need translated, and get back to you," Fendi said. "That's one hell of a reactor down there. And what's up under the roof?"

"Uh . . ." Fergus said. "I don't know. I hadn't noticed that."

"It's connected to the reactor below. And there's some sort of machinery below the reactor, too, not that I've ever seen anything like that," Fendi said. "When I have some solid-sounding guesses, I'll call back. Oh—and some good news."

"Yeah?" Fergus asked.

"Rabbit's waking up, we think. It looks like he finally turned the corner."

Fergus felt an unexpected amount of relief flood through him, given how short a time he'd known the man. "That's great," he said.

"What is?" Marche asked.

"Rabbit's improving," Fergus said.

Her face lit up. "That *is* great," she said.

"Yep. Got work to do; call you back," Fendi said, and disconnected.

"So," Marche said. "Now that you're rested and looking better, tell me again about this Bomo'ri language book."

Fergus groaned. "You won't believe me, and even if you somehow do, it's going to make you incredibly unhappy," he said. "And I don't need that information getting around."

"Not a lot of around to get on a planet of eighteen people," she said.

"Still more than enough," he said. "Look, Kaybe told me to talk to you, and I think he's right that there's stuff someone other than just me needs to know, but anything I tell you about me needs to stay between you and me, strictly, even if you think what I tell you is horseshit."

"Is a horse like a cat?"

"Much larger."

"Does its shit stink as much?"

"No," he said, "but don't set your expectations about the un-likeliness of my info based on that."

"Noted," she said. "So, what did Kaybe want you to tell me?"

"I think Belos is planning on taking the first working ship we manage to cobble together and go blasting off, seeking revenge for the deaths of his sister and her crew," Fergus said. "I think he'll tell himself he's clearing the way behind him for us to get away safely, but that's not going to work."

She made a face. "He hasn't been himself since we found *Rattler* and found it empty," she said. "It's plausible, though I'd have to think about it more. But if you are right, who would he be trying to get revenge on? The aliens at the gate?"

"The Asiig," he said.

"And it won't work because . . ."

"Because we are ants to them. Luckily for us, we are sometimes *interesting* ants."

"And you know this because?"

"Because that's where the book came from," Fergus said. "It also led me to this site—I lied when I said I saw it during our landing."

"No," she said. "Just no. Everything we know about the Asiig—"

"Isn't exactly correct," Fergus said.

"They gave you a book—"

"Sent it, more accurately, but yes."

"They *sent* you a book, and you've known to come here, through the Ghostdrift, to *this* planet, ever since?" she asked. "Have you just been manipulating us from the beginning?"

"No. I got the book after we got here," he said.

"What? How? And why you?"

"Because I made the mistake once of accidentally catching their attention," Fergus said. "And we're now practically on their doorstep. They notice things like that."

"Either you are the boldest liar I've ever met, utterly delusional, or I should probably be terrified," Marche said.

"As comforting as it won't be, I'll point out if I was lying, how could I read Bomo'ri? And I'm clearly reading it—nobody guesses that good."

"I hate everything about this," she said. "Everything that's happened since you came onboard has been screwed up, and it just keeps getting worse."

"Don't blame me," Fergus said.

"I do, but more, I blame the captain. He should have trusted us more, from the beginning."

Fergus stretched, finished the last bite of his rations, and drained the last of his water bottle. "Consider that maybe it wasn't a matter of trust," he said. "Maybe it was more about having an outsider, that he didn't care about, to bear the brunt of failure."

"Give me your water bottle; I need to fill mine, too, and I could use a few minutes on my own to think," she said.

He handed it over, then lay back down on the ground of the clearing, his hands behind his head, and looked at the sky framed by the forest around. The larger of the two moons was just visible, though he had no idea if it was rising or setting, or any sense at all of what this world's patterns were. He also didn't know either moon's name. The Bomo'ri map had them simply as numbers appended onto Object 114, and although he was pretty sure Safani would have names for them he'd hate, he decided he was the first one to think of it and dubbed them Tay and Tweed.

His comm earpiece buzzed, in the dried fronds on the ground next to him where it had fallen out. He slipped it back in. "Vetch here," he said.

"Fendi," Fendi said. "So, it's not my area of expertise, and it's definitely very alien, but that big-ass reactor under you could power your average planet's worth of cities, if it was on, which I'm happy to report it's not," he said. "But it looks like none of it fed your building proper—it either goes to the object that's up under your roof, which is a concave structure I can't tell you shit about other than that, or to the mechanism below the reactor, which extends down, as you said, virtually into the mantle. I can make a very uncertain guess at that piece, though, because some of the parts in it I've seen before, in our jump-engine tech."

"Which we stole from the Bomo'ri," Fergus said.

"Yeah. Now, active jump does what it does by playing with gravity, and something called gravitational lensing, and other physics stuff I don't understand and honestly never really tried to. At particular points in space that have the right local conditions, you can create a hole between one part of space and another. Once we humans figured out what made the Bomo'ri engine tick, we were also able to use the underlying concepts to make artificial-gravity systems for our ships," Fendi said. "I couldn't explain why any of it works, but whatever this device is, it's meant to do something very, very big with gravity. I don't know what, though."

"What if I told you that the whole planet is ringed with these same reactors and stations?" Fergus said.

"Then I'd say even bigger big, but still no idea," Fendi said.

"Okay. How about if I said they were also on the moons?"

"Still no idea."

"And that they used to encircle the star, and another planet in this system that doesn't exist anymore?"

"I'd say still no fucking idea at all, but I would very much like to know," Fendi said. "Don't suppose you found an operation manual?"

"Not yet," Fergus said.

"I want to come see for myself, but I want to be here when Rabbit wakes up," Fendi said.

"How's he doing?"

"Safani thinks the pod will release him from the forced coma any day now and then let him slowly wake up on his own after that. Too soon to tell how long recovery is going to take, but she seems optimistic, so I'm trying to be patient. Sorry. I know I should come out there, but—"

"You don't have to apologize," Fergus said. "Nothing here is going anywhere, and Rabbit needs you. But if I find anything else interesting, I'll send you more pics."

"Yer a solid, Vetch," Fendi said. "Call back if you figure out what it's all supposed to do."

With a *clunk*, Marche set his water bottle down on a nearby rock. "Fendi?" she asked.

"Yeah," Fergus said. He sat up and filled her in on their conversation. "The Bomo'ri probe that we stole, if I remember correctly, was being used to map jump conduits around the galaxy. Or at least that's what they told us when they demanded it back. I saw a piece of it once."

"In a museum?"

"In an Alliance high-security secret research facility. If I hadn't been there to steal something else . . ."

She whistled. "That would have brought some amazing cred, if you could move it at all. No wonder the captain is keeping you away from the podders, if that wasn't the most stealable thing in the room."

He thought it best not to comment any more on that. "So, the main building over on the big continent is called the Research Headquarters, and this one—and the others like it, around the equator—are called Transport Anchors. What if they were trying to move something really big, or really fast, through here using the planets and the star itself as part of some kind of gravity-assist accelerator?"

"Would that work?" she asked.

"No idea at all. I'm not the astrophysicist in the family," he said, with a sharp pang of guilt.

"Wouldn't that be dangerous, this kind of proximity to objects? Doesn't matter how fast you're going; you don't want to be grazing, or crashing into, a planet."

A thought struck Fergus, and he jumped to his feet, startling both Marche and himself. "What if . . ." he started, then the idea faltered.

"Keep going," she said.

"What if they were trying to *make* a jump conduit? One end was supposed to be here, hence the anchors—"

"But there's nothing at all on the other end," Marche said. "Assuming you're thinking about the conduit we came through."

"No," he said, and sighed. "There goes a good theory."

"Hmmm," she said. "It's still not bad, though."

"I had a conversation with the captain, when he first told me about the secret conduits inside the Barrens. I didn't believe there could be, because—at least as far as I knew—you need big, complex gravity wells to create the right conditions, and the Barrens is notably lacking in stars big enough to make them. And he suggested that lack was distinctly unnatural, odds-wise, and that there were a lot of remnants of things that are also normally associated with star systems. His exact words were: 'The logical conclusion is that something very bad, very beyond our comprehension, once happened' there. What if the bad thing was the Bomo'ri?"

"Are you saying maybe they accidentally blew up dozens, if not *hundreds*, of stars, and that's what created the Barrens? That's a huge leap."

"I know," he said.

"If their experiments destroyed stars on the other end, why is this one still here?"

"Maybe because it's isolated? Or maybe because whatever process they kicked off only caused destruction in one direction, and that was away from here?"

"There are rogue conduits fully inside the Barrens with nothing at either end, though," she said. "And if you accidentally blew up a fucking star—and took out enough of its planets to erase it from the map—don't you think you'd stop after one?"

"*I* would," Fergus said. "But I'm not Bomo'ri, and who knows how they think?"

"That's fucking cold, though," she said. "Evil, if I can use an overused word, and you know I have no delusions about the morality of my own actions. I mean, shit, there's *life* on this planet—who knows on how many others? And if they were willing to destroy that many stars, why stop?"

Fergus pointed up at the sky. "Lot of older Bomo'ri wrecks both up there and down here," he said. "I don't think they stopped; I think they *were* stopped."

"So, if you're right, for us to escape here, we have to get past one group of homicidally angry aliens who can run circles around a second group of aliens who used to destroy entire star systems for fun," she said.

"Yeah. Maybe we know why those other aliens are so mad, though," Fergus said. He picked up his water bottle. "I'm going to go back in and see if I can find any kind of better theory."

"I have a bad feeling you won't," she said.

"Me too," he said. "Me too."

Chapter 17

━━━◆━━━

They found nothing that contradicted Fergus's theory or suggested another, and Fergus was uncertain which of the two of them was more dissatisfied by that. He spent the remainder of the afternoon weaving and setting a longer ladder, while Marche alternately watched, wandered around the area, or sat staring off into space.

"You ever thought about how you could just, you know, start your life completely over?" Marche asked suddenly.

Fergus laughed. "You have no idea," he said. "This about Safani?"

"Like you said earlier, we're here now, and that's sort of like a new beginning for as long as it lasts, but until we've given up on trying to escape, and everyone settles in and accepts that we're here forever, it's never going to be real. And what if, in six months, she decides she's bored of me or can't let go of who I am? Or I can't let go of who I am, not with all of the rest of you around, too?"

"Are you calling your crewmates baggage?" Fergus asked, smiling as he glopped another simmering pot of goo over another section of ladder.

"Isn't everyone you ever get attached to essentially just baggage, though?" Marche asked.

Fergus let out a long, somewhat-wistful sigh. "I used to think so," he said. "What I eventually realized is that it was a way of protecting myself from the hard truth that I was afraid *I* was the baggage—or, worse, a danger—to them."

"And that was better?" she asked, skeptically.

"Oh, no, not at all," Fergus said, "but at least it was honest. We owe that to the people we care about just as much as we deserve it from them in return."

Marche sprawled out on the ground, staring up at the beginnings of sunset starting to color the sky. "You're no help at all, Vetch."

"That's probably also true," Fergus said. He stood up, poured the last of his goo in the shrubs, and rinsed out the pot with water. "This is as good as it's gonna get. Tomorrow we see if it'll reach the ceiling so we can have a look at what's up there. If I don't see you for midnightsees, I'll see you in the morning."

He left her to her ruminations, headed to his tent, and despite the lack of a purring fur-demon to keep his side warm, eventually fell asleep.

———

After an hour of trying to find some sort of hatch up into the ceiling, Fergus finally realized that the entire thing was on a pivot and could be opened by pressing up on one half to lower the other. He had been starting to think maybe the Bomo'ri had figured out how to make tech that never broke or needed servicing, and the relief to find that that was not true made up for the aggravation of constantly climbing up and down his ladder and moving it as he'd hunted.

Marche steered the drone up into the opening to shine its light around and grab scans of everything up there for Fendi. "Well, I can't tell what any of that is," she said.

"Me either," Fergus admitted. Whatever it was, it was complex, alien, and lacking any sort of handy labels on anything. "We could learn more by trying to turn it on, I suppose."

"And what do you think we could learn from *that*?" Marche asked.

"Probably only that we shouldn't have turned it on," Fergus

said. In point of fact, he didn't even know how to turn it on if he wanted to. There was no sense of anything energized up there, and without being able to feel the pathways of electricity, he could see no farther than the jumble of pipes, thick cables, and blocky, rounded shapes within his human eyesight.

He pushed up on the half of the ceiling that had swiveled down, and it swiveled shut with a faint *click*. When he reached the bottom of the ladder, he carefully tipped it down and carried it out through the fire door. "That was a letdown, after all that work to get up there. I didn't see any controls for it on the systems down here, so I thought there had to be something up there, but no."

"We can always come back with Fendi and Riji," Marche said. "They could have insights we don't."

"Yeah," Fergus said. "I suppose you're right."

"Intelligence, remember? I gotta be smart about something, this trip, because so far, I'm not feeling it."

He followed her outside and scrounged through what was left of their rations to find something to snack on, and let the sun warm him up again.

Midafternoon, Kaybe called and told them it was time to get their asses back to *Sidewinder*, and since there didn't seem to be much else to learn from what they'd been able to access in the station, they reluctantly packed up and started the hike back.

They stopped and camped inside the wreck of *Stiletto* on the way, found another cache of stuff prepped to go by Riji, and took what of it they could carry in addition to their own gear.

A fast-moving front brought in heavy rain that caught them not far from *Fire Island*, so they stopped there to shelter in the hut and catch up with Riji. Fergus showed her the same schematics he'd sent Fendi, and she also speculated about some sort of gravity field manipulators. "It's too bad we can't read any of it, to confirm anything," she said.

Marche said nothing but did side-eye Fergus so hard, he could almost feel it. "There were some contextual clues we couldn't quite capture in the images," Fergus said. "We have a theory, but it's a bit far out."

"Rain's not going to let up for at least another couple of hours, so you might as well tell me while you wait," she said.

"You explain it," Marche said. "I'm going to go check in with our crew." She hunkered down outside under one of the *Island*'s wings, the drumming of the rain drowning out any chance of eavesdropping.

"You ever peeled a potato, Vetch?" Riji asked.

"Too many," he said. "Why?"

She grabbed a sack and dumped it in between them on the floor, and handed him a knife. "These are wavetree shoots. They taste sorta like carrots, sorta like onions, but you have to remove the outer layers. It's like peeling a potato, if potatoes were made of stone. Careful; that knife is very sharp."

He resisted the immediate instinct to test the blade edge with his thumb, and instead picked up one of the shoots and made an experimental slice. "Damn, you weren't kidding," he said.

"It's worth the effort, and I'm not just saying that because starving sucks," she said. "So, what's this theory?"

He explained it as he whittled away at the pile of shoots, and as he spoke, she got slower and slower until she just stared at him, knife dangling, forgotten, from one hand. When he finished, she shook, as if waking from a spell, and gave a short half-laugh. "That it?" she said.

"Yeah. Oh, except I also named our two moons," Fergus said.

"Safani already—"

"I named them," he interrupted. "Tay and Tweed, after two rivers back on Earth."

She picked up another shoot. "I like it, way more than—" she started to say, then smiled. "I don't know why none of us thought to name them, but clearly, we must not have."

"That's what I thought," he said.

"Exploding whole star systems, huh?" she asked.

"That's my guess," Fergus said.

"And if true, and the Bomo'ri can do that, and the gate aliens can kick their asses . . . we don't stand a chance," she said. "Which is unfortunate, because your team almost has *Rattler*'s shuttle extricated, and once that's out and free, we can start moving bigger parts in."

"One thing that doesn't add up for me," Fergus said, "is that all the wrecks here and up on the edge of the system are either ours—human, I mean—or Bomo'ri. We know the Asiig like to cruise through—"

"We do?"

"I saw their ships on *Rattler*'s logs before she crashed," Fergus said.

"Oooh, that's why no bodies," Riji said. She dragged over a large pot of water, and Fergus helped her put the peeled shoots in. "Also explains why your captain's been more of a demanding pain in the ass—no offense intended—since your expedition out there. Quite the gut punch if that's the way *Rattler*'s people went."

"Yeah," Fergus said. "The thing is, there aren't any dead Asiig ships up there or down here. Or any other kinds of aliens, which surely some have to have happened by. If the gate aliens are mad at the Bomo'ri for blowing stars up, it makes sense they'd go after them and leave everyone else alone. But why not humans?"

"The Asiig are locals, relatively speaking," Riji said. "Maybe the bad aliens only go after anyone who comes through that gate."

"The Bomo'ri are also locals."

"But if they were off fucking around in the Barrens, they had to get there and back, and that means jumping. That's the only thing we know for certain about Bomo'ri technology be—"

"*Shit*," Fergus swore. "Yes. Why didn't I see that?"

"What?"

"Bomo'ri jump engines. We *stole their tech*. If all you have is the energy signature of your enemy, our ships look exactly like theirs. And if they're avenging their entire star system, they aren't going to stop and poke around in the wreckage to look for survivors."

"So, there's no way out," Riji said, just as Marche walked back in.

"We got our passive jump tech from the Veirakans, and voluntarily," Fergus said. "So, if we're right, that likely wouldn't attract the aliens, and we wouldn't need to go through that particular gate. If we found another active jump point somewhere else—"

"We're in the middle of the Gap," Riji said. "It would take us decades—and not just two or three—to reach somewhere we could jump back home. I don't know about your ship, but *Fire Island* doesn't have that kind of long-haul cryo facilities."

"Nor *Sidewinder*," Marche said. "What are we talking about?"

"The possibility that what the gate aliens might be using to identify their enemies is jump-engine signature," Fergus said. "It would explain why human ships are targeted too, but we haven't seen any other kind of wrecks."

"As a guess at the end of a long line of guesses based on other guesses, it's possible," Marche said. "Don't make a face at me; you know that's what it is, and whether or not I think you're right doesn't change that."

"No, I suppose not," Fergus said.

"The captain wants us back as soon as the rain stops," Marche said. "Fendi wants to stay with Rabbit, so you've been volunteered for the expedition out to *Rattler* to bring the shuttle back."

"Fendi thinks it'll fly?"

"He does. But there should be someone along with some engineering skills," Marche said.

"I could go," Riji volunteered. She whacked the side of her pot with her big metal spoon. "When my roots are done."

Marche smiled. "You're less expendable," she said.

"I'm sure that's it," Riji said. "Any compelling reasons why I should pretend I'm not going to fill the rest of my team in on your speculation about the Bomo'ri and our gate aliens?"

"No, go for it," Fergus said. "The worst—or, more probably, the best—they can do is poke all kinds of holes in it so we are forced to look for other answers."

Marche nudged him with her elbow. "Rain's slacking. Get your stuff together."

———

The twisted bay doors at the back of *Rattler* had been fully removed and lay discarded nearby. Both *Sidewinder* and *Rattler* themselves had been very well equipped to perform salvage operations, and not always on abandoned or cooperating vessels, though Fergus didn't want to think too closely on that. What ripped the doors off things in space worked just as well dirtside, it seemed.

There was still debris in the bay itself, where the ceiling had partially collapsed. Fendi had left it to return to *Sidewinder* when he'd gotten word that Rabbit might be coming out of his coma, and Fergus could not fault the man's priorities. The four of them on this trip—Fergus, Yolo, and Trinket, and Belos himself—took turns moving the smaller pieces, and together got the last few big chunks out of the way.

Belos had been cold but cordial in what conversations they'd had on the hike over, but those conversations had been very short and to the point on logistics and questions about what Fergus and Marche had found out from the Bomo'ri station. If the captain had opinions on Fergus's theories, he kept them to himself. The only one he seemed relaxed with was Trinket.

Now that they were working, Belos was focused entirely on the immediate task at hand. "We should have enough overhead clearance to get the shuttle out now," Belos was saying. "Fendi thinks it's flightworthy but couldn't get at the underside, and of course Fang is too deteriorated to run system diagnostics, so I want to keep it low to the ground until we're sure the systems are in fact all operational. Fendi is an excellent engineer but not a pilot."

They'd cleared the trees from behind *Rattler*, but the land sloped away sharply to one side. "There's a level clearing about half a klick on the other side of those wavetrees," Fergus said, pointing. "We can set it down there. It's far enough for a quick test flight but close enough for an emergency landing if things start going wrong."

"That will work," Belos said. "Len and Kaybe are clearing some space near *Sidewinder* for a landing field, and Cole also has a decent-sized open area near their camp. Once we're sure the shuttle is solid, we can start hauling bigger parts and material from here and other Alliance wrecks, farther away than the Islanders have been able to reach on their own. With luck, we should have a month of work, maybe two, ahead of us to have both *Sidewinder* and *Fire Island* ready to fly again."

"But then what?" Trinket asked. "Vetch said—"

"We can worry about that when the time comes," Belos said. "I won't settle for anything less than a safe way to get all our people off this planet and away from here. And Cole's people, as well; we couldn't do this without them."

"What about the podders?" Yolo asked. He was lying on *Rattler*'s hull above the bay doors, holding a last, bent metal bar in one hand that he'd just broken free from where it had been dangling inside the opening.

Belos made a face. "Captain Todd has not reached a place of being able to set practicality ahead of personal anger," he said. "That may change when we have the ability to escape for real, rather than just as a theoretical exercise, and he's faced with going along or being left behind."

He turned to Fergus. "You appreciate, Mr. Vetch, that I have gone to some lengths to keep you separated from them. You really got under their skin back at the Stank Palace."

"I sometimes have that effect on people," Fergus said.

"I've noticed," Belos said, dryly. "Nevertheless, you are part of my crew, not theirs, so they are not entitled to your time or owed any apologies. We have all suffered losses here and are contending with our own griefs, none of which need have happened if they had not been pursuing us both, all these years."

The captain rubbed his hands together, as if ridding himself of troublesome dust. "Time to see if she'll fly," he said. "Everyone keep clear until I'm out and landed."

Belos stepped up into the bay, and a few minutes later, Fergus heard and felt the shuttle power up. He and Trinket stepped back to the edges of the cleared area as Yolo clambered to his feet and moved away from the edge.

Rattler's shuttle backed out smoothly, barely a half-meter above the bay floor, with impressive precision, especially knowing that, with Fang's dock guidance systems down, Belos was piloting it manually.

The shuttle cleared the wreck, to great cheers from Yolo. "I see the clearing," Belos said over their comms. "Turning for it now."

As the shuttle began to bank, there was a piercing metallic squeal, and a support strut on one of the portside maneuvering jets snapped, and the jet angled down. "Got a problem," Belos said, as the shuttle turned and began to turn over, nosediving in slow motion toward the ground.

Yolo leapt from the top of *Rattler* to land heavily on the tilting roof of the airborne shuttle, scrabbling for a hold as he was tipped toward the ground. His feet found the short wing, and he threw himself around it and yanked the jet back up by hand.

The shuttle righted, and Belos landed it immediately among the wavetrees, the overheating engines setting several to smoldering.

Trinket grabbed a fire extinguisher from their stuff and ran toward the shuttle, while Fergus got there just in time to grab Yolo as he slipped off the wing, and they both landed heavily but safely on the ground. The whine of the engines was picking up in pitch. "They won't shut down," Belos told them. "Stand back, in case they blow."

"Fuck that," Trinket said, and sprayed down the trees in danger of bursting into flame. Yolo was scrambling back, looking around for anything that could help, as Fergus got to his feet, ran over to the side of the shuttle, found the right spot, placed both hands against the hull, and fed electricity in.

"What are you—" Yolo started to yell, and the shuttle engines spluttered and shut down.

"What just happened?" Trinket asked, holding the empty extinguisher. She had flecks of foam in her hair, and on her left eyebrow.

Fergus stepped away. "Captain, you okay in there?"

"Yes, everything shut down. Some sort of temporary systems short," Belos said. "What happened out there?"

"Vetch did something," Yolo said. "He touched it."

"I just wanted to see if the hull was heating up," Fergus said.

"It shut down the moment you touched it," Yolo said.

Fergus snorted. "Lucky for me it did," he said. "It was bad instinct on my part, more panic than anything about losing the shuttle. I could have burned my hands."

Belos emerged from the shuttle. "It's all shut down," he said, walking directly toward Yolo and Fergus. Yolo stiffened but stood his ground, and the captain got right in his face and wrapped him in a hug. "Welcome back, Yolo. Glad to see you're back to your usual, fearless self. I've missed you."

Trinket wrapped both her arms around the two of them. "You done good, Yolo. Sorry I let myself stay mad at you so long."

Yolo, for his part, looked almost stricken, and when he caught

Fergus's eye, he blushed. "Shit. You're embarrassin' me. It was nothin'," he said, then raised his chin in Fergus's direction. "You try to hug me too, Vetch, an' we're fightin'."

Fergus held up his hands in mock surrender. "No need to go *that* far," he said. "Good save, though."

"Yeah. Thanks," Yolo said. Belos had already stepped back, but Yolo had to insert his arms under Trinket's and forcibly pry her off; her expression was one of absolute amusement at his discomfort.

"Vetch, you want to take a look at the shuttle before we try to get Riji or Fendi out here?" Belos asked.

"Yeah," Fergus said. "If nothing else, I can try to figure out what else is broken so someone brings us the right parts."

"Do it," Belos said. "Since we're not flying out of here today, Yolo, please set up camp. Trinks, find a spot for the water-filtration unit. I'm going to go look at that port jet." He ditched his shirt, grabbed hold of the side rungs on the side of the shuttle, and nimbly climbed up on top.

Fergus entered the shuttle. Its internal systems had rebooted, but there were breaks in the signal running from the bridge toward the rear engines, some a complete loss, some just a drop of intensity of signal. Going back out, he rummaged through their tools and pulled out several he thought he might need.

"Vetch!" Belos called down from the roof of the shuttle. "Throw me up a number three hex socket, would you?"

Fergus found it and tossed it up to the captain. Belos moved as if he'd shed some terrible weight, at ease and—maybe—even happy for the first time since they jumped into the Ghostdrift.

Was it that they were at least a step closer to escape? Fergus thought it more likely that it was the combination of Rabbit improving and the rift with Yolo having been finally closed. Either way, it made Fergus's shoulders feel somehow lighter, too. *We might get through this after all,* he thought.

Belos threw down the two halves of the broken strut. "Hairline fracture," he called down. "Couldn't have spotted it until it snapped. Someone ping Fendi and see if we can get a whole one off *Sidewinder*'s shuttle, or if not, ask if a replacement can be fabbed."

"On it," Yolo said.

Fergus went back inside the shuttle. Most of the wiring and signal conduit ran along the upper bulkheads to either side, which should have provided redundancy, but that was mostly predicated upon the idea that combat damage would likely come from a single direction. Getting shot, then bellyflopping onto a planet, with any expectations beyond trying to keep any occupants alive, was a catastrophe scenario the original engineers could be forgiven for not being able to buffer against.

He found and fixed several connections that had come loose, replaced two sections of wire, and then worked his way back to where he could feel the signal dim but not cut out.

That relay was the one that should have caught that the engines were malfunctioning and sent an automatic cut-off signal, but Fergus didn't think it was getting enough electricity to process that incoming alert. The dead wires on the other side had lost the emergency shutdown signal from the helm. He took a pic of the relay with his handpad, then sent it to Fendi, with his theory on why it failed.

"Right, one of those," Fendi said. "I should have a spare. You know enough to replace and test?"

"Not really," Fergus said. "I'm just guessing here, as it is."

"Okay, let me see if Riji can come your way with parts," Fendi said. "Try to get me a full list soon?"

"Will do," Fergus said. "How's Rabbit?"

"He opened his eyes," Fendi said, "and tried to give me the middle finger."

"That sounds good."

"Yup," Fendi said. "Call me back when you have more."

Fergus switched over to the other side of the shuttle, fixed more connections, and found one panel full of tiny, purple, fuzzy ball-things that, when he disturbed them, exploded outward and clung to his hair and new beard growth. When he tried to pull them out, he discovered they had sharp spines concealed in the fluff and, from the immediate tingling in his fingertips, were possibly slightly poisonous.

He went back outside and stood there until Trinket turned around, saw him, and doubled over laughing. "Maybe help?" he asked, plaintively.

"It suits you, though," Belos said, from up on the shuttle roof. "Violet Vetch."

"Fuck you all," Fergus said, and headed off to find enough water to see if the things could swim.

———

Riji arrived the next day with more tools and parts, including a replacement strut. "I was already going to head out to *Stiletto* to grab some more parts," she explained. "It'll just have to wait until I'm done here."

"If you can get the shuttle in the air, we'll go to *Stiletto* with you and pick up whatever you want," Belos said. "Anything that'll fit."

"Now, *that's* a deal," she said. "Lots of stuff I can't carry back on my own."

Fergus followed her into the shuttle and watched as she replaced and tested the relay. "The rest looks good," she said. "Surprised none of the connectors let loose."

"Eleven did," Fergus said. "Those I can deal with. This was outside my competence."

She nodded. "At least you know where that line is. Not everyone does."

"Ain't that the truth," he said. "There were a bunch of nasty purple thing—"

"Smu—"

"No, don't tell me the name," Fergus said. "Unless it's not annoying."

"It's annoying," she said.

"Then I'm just going to call them burrbugs," he said. "They were inside the paneling. Do they do damage?"

"Not really. They like tight little spaces," she said. "They don't like noise, so once the shuttle is moving again, they'll abandon it."

Belos came in. "The strut's fixed. How are you doing in here?"

"Done," Riji said.

"Excellent. I want to make a test flight solo, and if everything is running smoothly, we'll head to *Stiletto* and then back to your camp," Belos said.

"Sounds good," she said.

Fergus followed her out, and they stood beside Yolo and Trinket as Belos started the shuttle up again and this time lifted off smoothly, then did a few circles overhead.

Fergus glanced at Riji, and saw her wiping away a tear.

"I didn't think it would be a thing," she said. "All these years, working trying to get *Fire Island* repaired, I don't think I ever believed we'd actually get off the surface. Until now."

Belos set the shuttle down again in the same spot where it had taken off. "Get your things, people. We're in business again."

———

They landed near the wreck of *Stiletto* and spent most of the remainder of the day filling the back of the shuttle. Riji kept muttering, mostly happily, to herself, trying to prioritize what to take from a long list of things she'd long ago ruled out being able to scavenge. "We can always make another trip," Fergus told her, and she nodded at that but continued to manically run back and forth throughout the ship, worried she was missing something too good not to take immediately.

Fergus broke out rations for everyone, then took his share and sat on a rock, watching the frenetic activity of the *Island*'s engineer as Yolo and Trinket tried to keep up with her.

Belos sat down not far away. "You think our passive-jump engines won't attract the aliens?" he asked.

"It's a theory," Fergus said. "Hard to test without risk."

"If it was just you, would you risk it?"

"Yes," he said, "but I'm maybe not as adept at self-preservation as I should be."

"You're alive, aren't you? Can't be that bad."

Fergus laughed. "You have no idea. I think the universe just doesn't want to give me up when it still has some kicking to inflict."

It was Belos's turn to laugh. "I get that," he said. "When we get back to *Sidewinder*, I want to have an all-hands meeting to see what we can do with that, especially once *Fire Island* and *Sidewinder* are spaceworthy again. If we can get both ships positioned near the gate, then create a distraction, we can possibly jump out in the chaos."

"Maybe," Fergus said. "I'd be concerned they'd follow us back through the Ghostdrift and then find a whole part of the galaxy full of ships they think are the enemy."

"Hmmm," Belos said. "That could be disastrous."

"Yeah."

Belos picked up a can of soup, twisted the cap to start it heating, then looked around at the shuttle, *Stiletto*, and the others still working. "This isn't a bad world, though. Miraculous that it was here. It saved us."

"The Bomo'ri research headquarters is on the other continent and should have a lot more information about what they did and why. That might give us clues about the aliens and other ways around them," Fergus said. "With the shuttle, we could get there easily."

"If we have to," Belos said. "One step forward at a time."

"Hey!" Trinket yelled from near the shuttle. She and Riji were trying to wrestle an entire console section into the back. "We need more hands!"

Fergus went to help, and left Belos with his soup and his thoughts.

———

They set the shuttle down near *Fire Island* to offload Riji's scavenged parts. They'd only been on the ground a few minutes when Cole came running out of the woods from their camp, whooping and shouting in joy.

Safani was close behind him, and eventually, Ajac shuffled out of the woods with his cane. Both wore wide grins. "We heard you coming in," Cole said. "I never thought the sound of an engine was beautiful before, but man, it's like fucking *music*."

"Couldn't have done it without your people," Belos said. "We're all getting off this planet, together, as a team."

He and Cole clasped hands.

"Well, well," a new voice said, and they all turned to see four people still wearing tattered Alliance uniforms emerge from the woods. Fergus recognized Cardenas, Lester, and the man with the concussion from the throne room, who he was pretty sure was named Rosso. The two bars on the collar of the last made it clear that was *Paradigm*'s Captain Todd. Behind the four of them, Earlan slunk out of the forest.

"Todd," Cole said, warning in his voice. "This is not the time or place—"

"Imagine finding the Alliance's most wanted man, just standing around in plain sight like he has nothing to fear," Todd said.

"You flatter me," Belos said, crossing his arms over his chest and looking amused.

"Not you," Todd said. "*Him.*" And he pointed at Fergus.

Every single person in the clearing turned to look at Fergus in surprise. "I'm sure you must be mistaken," Fergus said.

"I don't believe so," Todd said.

"He's part of my crew, and under my protection," Belos said.

Cardenas took a half-step forward toward Fergus. "Maybe you're not as smart as you think you are," she said to him.

"Oh?" Fergus asked.

She smiled. "Gojira. Rodan. Mothra. Ghidorah—"

"Cardenas," Todd warned.

"—Gamera," she added.

"*Cardenas*," Todd snapped, and she shrugged and stepped back, looking smug.

Todd turned back toward Belos. "I'm willing to negotiate, but I'm not backing off. You have something to gain but a lot more to lose."

"Whoever you think he is, it does not matter. If you try to mess with him or any of my people, you will discover I have no use for, or loyalty to, any of the four of you," Belos said. "If you wish to continue breathing, you will let the past drop. *Now.*"

Yolo came out of the back of the shuttle, carrying a heavy crate of parts, and stared around at the people in the clearing, taking in the hostility and that at least three people had their hands at their sides, where weapons would be. "What the fuck is going on?" he asked.

Earlan stepped out from behind Todd, frowning as he stared at Yolo. Then he broke out into a wide grin. "Lestov's pet idiot from Ijikijolo!" he declared. "How wonderful. Did you already know he's the one who set up *Rattler* for us, or do I get to be the first to break that news?"

Yolo dropped the crate, grabbed a bar, and tried to rush the man, but Fergus and Trinket both tackled him before he got off the bottom of the ramp.

He didn't know what he hated more in that moment: Earlan's raspy, delighted laughter or the single sob that came from Yolo beneath them on the ground.

Chapter 18

—◆—

"For now, he's staying at *Fire Island* to help Riji move heavy things," Marche said. "He swears he didn't know."

"And you believe that?" Kaybe asked. They were sitting at the conference table, missing only Belos, Rabbit, and Trinket; the latter was refusing to leave her cabin.

"Yes and no," Marche said. "I think he legitimately didn't know it was bad info or that Lestov was an Alliance plant. When it was just drug runners and low-profile scum not coming back from his tips, I think he just didn't notice or care. There are plenty of other reasons in the Barrens ships don't make it back. But after *Rattler* vanished? He's not the brightest, but he has to have suspected."

"I remember Lestov," Kaybe said. "He wasn't someone I would have had conversations with, other than about fueling, you know? And if I had, I wouldn't have taken anything he said at face value, because I just didn't know or trust him. But Yolo? He was a bouncer at Ratte's, and most everyone liked him, and none of us would've thought him sharp enough to be playing an angle."

"I got someit sharp for him," Len muttered.

"He's absolutely shattered as it is," Marche said.

"You on his side?" Len asked.

"No, I am not on his fucking *side*," Marche snarled. "He asked me to listen to his story, and I said I would. I'm just telling you what he told me."

"He joined our crew, knowing he got the captain's sister and her whole crew killed," Kaybe said. "How could he have possibly thought that was all right?"

"It wasn't until he was already on the crew that he put two and two together, from things the rest of you said, and began to suspect what might have happened. By then, it was already too late."

"Not any less late now," Len said. "Coulda said any time, faced his consequences truth-first, but someaw else told us. That counts bad."

"Someone stuffed Lestov into a sewage processor a few years later. I checked the logs, and *Sidewinder* was back at the station at the time. It would take someone very strong to pop one of those hatches."

"And?" Len said. "Not enough. Can't get no honor back, not then, not now."

"Secrets destroy crews," Marche added softly.

"Speaking of secrets, what the hell did you do to the Alliance, Vetch?" Kaybe asked.

"Destroyed an entire top-secret military operation of theirs, then broke into one of their highest-security research installations and stole something they were apparently very keen on keeping," Fergus said. "There may have been some public humiliation involved, both times. They didn't seem to like that."

"No," Kaybe said. He put his hands palms-down on the table and took several deep breaths. "For now, we all need to focus on what's important, which is finding a way off this planet without getting ourselves killed. This Yolo thing doesn't change our priorities, and we can't let it become a distraction."

"I can make it a short—"

"No, Len," Kaybe said. "Not yet. Not unless the captain gives the order. We need every set of hands we got, and if you kill Yolo, then we make ourselves a bigger problem with Trinks, and she doesn't deserve that. Let Yolo make himself useful to the Islanders for now. I'm going over to meet with Cole later and make sure we're all still committed to working together."

"And Earlan?" Marche asked.

"He's moved to the podder camp," Kaybe said. "As long as he stays out of our way, we need to let him be, too."

Len let out a strangled, choking sigh, and banged his head on the table. Then he got out of his chair, nearly knocking it over. "Gonna go chat-chat with the captain," he announced. "You all do your gottas."

The room was quiet for some time after he'd left. Fendi, who'd stayed silent through the entire conversation, got up next, although much less abruptly. "Going to go check on Rabbit," he said.

"I'll come with," Marche said, and left with him.

Kaybe got up, made coffee, and set a mug in front of Fergus. "This is terrible fucking timing," he said.

"Yeah," Fergus agreed. He slid the mug closer. "Thanks."

Kaybe took a jar out of the cold store and with a spoon added heaps of what Fergus took to be mashed-up purple fruit clusters into his coffee. He caught Fergus's eye. "Running low on sugar," he said, by way of explanation. "This isn't half bad, though. Bas says he thinks you can figure out how to get us out of here."

"Maybe," Fergus said. "I'm still thinking."

"Well, you're probably smarter than the rest of us, except possibly Marche," Kaybe said. "We all know different stuff though, so it's not a comparison. And of course the captain, but lately it feels like he's giving up, and I don't like that. This Yolo thing . . . he's handling it *bad*."

"I don't know how anyone could handle it better," Fergus said. "If it was my friends, my sister? I don't think I could get over that."

"Me neither," Kaybe said. He slid the jar of jam over. "Try it?"

"Sure," Fergus said, though he usually drank his coffee black. He put in a spoonful, stirred it around until it dissolved, then tasted it. It was less sweet than he'd feared, adding just a slight undertone of flavor. "Not bad. Not bad at all," he said.

"As I've said, Bel Belos was also like a sister to me," Kaybe said. "I'd have gone for Yolo myself, and fuck the consequences, except I'm more worried for Bas than I am angry at Yolo. Whole lotta both feels, though. And unless we leave the *Paradigm* survivors here—which I'm fine with, but the Islanders might feel an obligation—soon as we get away, Todd's gonna make a move on you. Too many crazy-moving pieces, and I still can't see the board. Feeling like we can't win any way we play it."

"Yeah," Fergus said. "The things we know aren't looking good. It's the things we don't know yet that could save us."

"Bas told me that, if there's a way out, you'll be the one to find it," Kaybe said. "He's feeling like his judgment is compromised, but he seems still confident in that. Or, at least, wants us to believe he's confident; I've never seen him doubt himself like this before. And I don't mind saying I don't like it one bit."

"No," Fergus said.

"So, this Bomo'ri headquarters thing you want to check out? Might have more info on our homicidal gate-aliens out there? I need to check with the others what we got remaining for big salvage, but if tomorrow looks clear, you and Marche can make a trip. Maybe take Trinks with you, if she'll come out of her cabin, and scout out other wrecks on the way, too," Kaybe said. "That work?"

"Yeah," Fergus said.

"Okay," Kaybe said. He stood up, drained the last of his coffee, and took his cup and spoon over to the sink. "I hate being in charge. Sooner we can figure out how to fix all this shit and go back to some kind of normal, the better."

After he'd gone, Fergus put the jam away, washed both their mugs, then went out to see what he could help with in the meantime.

Fendi was sitting along the lakeshore under the woven canopy shade that Fergus had been working on, in between other tasks. In a chair beside him, wrapped in a blanket, was Rabbit.

Rabbit was pale and painfully thin, but his eyes found Fergus and he gave a lopsided grin. "Nice paradise ya found us, Vetch," he said. "Jess need coconut drinks an' a beach party."

"Fendi could fab me a ukulele, and I could sing for you," Fergus said, and sat down on the ground under the canopy beside the two old friends.

"How's yer singing pipes? Sweet?" Rabbit asked.

Fergus laughed. "No. Like knowing you're about to be strangled with your own ukulele strings."

Rabbit snorted. "Then pass," he said. He closed his eyes for a moment, grimacing in pain. "Healin' sucks."

"Beats dying," Fendi said.

"Not sure this time," Rabbit said. He opened his eyes again. "Grateful to yer efforts, Vetch. I weren't ready to go, much as I'm crabbin', but seems like is'all gone belly up bad an' nothing I can do to fix any of it."

"Fixing yourself is the best you can do for all of us," Fendi said. "Gonna need you soon enough. Put you back to work, you lazy old cudder."

"Anything I can get you two?" Fergus asked.

"Naw," Rabbit said. "Fendi keeps threatenin' to fab me a cane. Maybe shoulda taken him up on it, tah hit him in the head with."

"You'd have to chase me, and right now you can't even stand for more than a minute or two," Fendi said. "Fucking rocks could outrun you."

"See?" Rabbit said. "Needs hitting, he does. Fendi, okes, make me a cane? Solid as solid."

Fendi shook his head. "The captain's in Engineering, using the fab unit. Now you're gonna have to wait."

"What's he making?" Fergus asked.

"No idea. He kicked me out," Fendi said, unconcerned. "Figure he's the captain and it's his ship, so he's entitled, and being busy for a while might do him some good."

"Vetch, can ya get a man some water?" Rabbit asked.

"Sure," Fergus said, and stood up.

". . . and can ya put in a coconut with a fancy umbrella and some rum?" Rabbit added.

"No alcohol," Fendi said. "Too dehydrating."

"That's why I asked for it in water," Rabbit said. "Little frozen cubes o' it, though, mind."

Fergus went back into *Sidewinder*'s kitchenette and made a tall cup of water with ice. One benefit of being stranded on this planet was that there was a source of freshwater immediately to hand, so the ice didn't have that subtle funk of water that had been cycled through the ship's reclamation systems.

He brought it back out to Rabbit and caught the blur of something running past him in the other direction. "Haha, Vetch, what happened to your cat?" Fendi called out, pointing. "He's all covered in purple balls!"

Somewhere inside the ship he heard a yowl of indignation.

"Shit," he said, and set the water down hastily before chasing his cat back into the ship.

Mister Feefs had proven himself quite adept at hiding, but this time, Fergus could easily follow the cat by the unhappy cries he was making. "Don't lick them, you idiot!" he yelled, even though he knew it was futile.

He found the cat in Rabbit's workshop under a bench, trying and failing to bite the burrbugs off his front legs. "Let me help, you dope," he said, grabbed a rag off the bench top, and got down on his hands and knees and crawled underneath beside the cat. Using the rag to protect his hands, he pulled the burrs off one by one and dropped them in a pile, until he realized several were now trying to somehow half-roll, half-crawl away. "Hang on," he told the cat, and got up from under the bench to look for a can or box he could put the burrs in. There were several shelves of clear-walled cannisters along the back wall, tucked into slots to keep them in place; it worked well enough that only a half dozen or so had fallen out during the crash. Fergus picked them up and tucked them back into empty slots with a *click*, so Rabbit wouldn't have to later, before searching through the rest for an empty one.

As he stood there peering at the containers one by one, he realized he could hear the faint sound of voices coming from Engineering next door. One was definitely Belos, and after a few minutes, when the other spoke up, he recognized Len. Whatever they were doing, he couldn't make out most of the words— something about night and waiting until everyone was sleeping.

I don't like the sound of that, he thought.

Mister Feefs yowled to get his attention, and he bent down and swept up the scattering burrbugs with the rag and shook them out into the jar, then crawled back underneath and got the remaining lot off the cat, who, in true cat gratitude fashion, immediately took off out of the room again.

He couldn't hear anything further next door over the steady hum of the fab unit, now chugging away.

Fergus snapped the jar lid on, considered for just a moment the hilarity of adding it back among the other parts containers in the shelves for some future surprise, then sighed and took it outside, his mind whirling with too many, too nebulous concerns.

———

Fergus had complained of a nonexistent dizziness not quite bad enough to bother trying to summon Safani to look at as an excuse to take a long midafternoon nap under the canopy, cat curled up happily on his stomach. Since that meant he could keep an eye on

Rabbit—also dozing, looking better than that morning—freeing up Fendi to go see Riji and compare checklists, no one gave him a hard time about it.

Fire Island was starting to look good; other than its dead mindsystem and its destroyed landing gear, the latter of which every wreck on the planet had in common, it might actually fly again. It would still need to be heavily operated by hand, but Cole was sure the *Paradigm* survivors, when it came to their one and only opportunity to get home, would cooperate.

Kaybe, Marche, and Trinket were off in the shuttle, grabbing more large parts from *Rattler*, and when those were put in place, *Sidewinder* was going to be close to operational too.

Of course, they still had no solution to how to get past the gate aliens.

When he wasn't dozing or exchanging brief chatter with Rabbit, he also listened to the rest of goings-on in and around the ship. Thus, he overheard Len telling Belos that the door code on Engineering had been temporarily changed, though not what to. Not that it would keep Fergus out, but Belos was spending most of his time in there, so opportunities to go snoop were few and dangerously brief.

When darkness finally fell and the fire died down, everyone headed off to bed. Fendi carried Rabbit into the ship, and the weapons master was so exhausted, he barely managed to complain about the indignity of it before giving in.

Belos came out when it was only Fergus left around the faint glow of the embers. "You should get sleep," Belos said. "Going to be another busy day tomorrow."

"Yeah, you're right," Fergus said, and got stiffly to his feet. "Goodnight, Captain."

"Goodnight, Vetch," Belos said, and stood there watching until Fergus had disappeared into the ship.

Fergus turned the lights off in his cabin and lay down in his bunk, still fully dressed except for his boots, and listened to the ship, feeling out and untangling the electrical signals of ship, machine, and people. There was also something much closer, under his bunk up against the far corner of the wall, that hadn't been there before. Lying on his stomach, he leaned down over the edge of the bunk and reached under, dragging back the box his hands found there in the dark.

When he thought he recognized it, he turned on the light on his handpad to be sure. It was the puzzle box that the palla was stored in, and from the faint tingle within, it was still there.

Why give it to me now? he wondered. The obvious answer was that Belos didn't expect to be around—or alive—to give it to him later, and he was unwilling to break his word.

He could feel someone coming up the corridor, stopping briefly at each cabin, making virtually no noise. Hastily, he tucked the box back under the bunk, where no doubt he was not meant to discover it for several days, and pulled his blanket up to his ears, calming his breathing, until he knew he could pass for asleep.

If he had been sleeping, he never would have heard the very faint *sssssh* of his door opening and, if his cat had not stirred briefly beside him, would not have been any the wiser when Len entered and stood over him for a half minute, listening to him breathe, before departing again.

Shit, he thought. He had never in his life encountered someone who could move that silently, and it chilled him to think how fast that could have been the end, if Len had intended him harm. Or had realized he was faking being asleep.

Unsure what else to do, he unlocked his handpad and left a message on it, on his bed. If he made it back, no one need be the wiser, but if not . . . some things needed to be said.

When Len had left the floor, he tiptoed carefully down the corridor and found the door to the downtube was now locked. He went forward instead, climbed up to one of the emergency escape hatches, and opened it as slowly and silently as he could. Pulling himself up to lie on the top of *Sidewinder*'s hull, he carefully closed and sealed the hatch behind him.

He stayed atop the ship for a long while, listening and waiting. Eventually, Len came out of the cargo doors, rolling something heavy and spherical, close to a meter in diameter. It had to be one of *Sidewinder*'s so-called "cannonballs."

What are you going to do with that, now? he wondered.

Len rolled out three more, then one by one pushed them up into the back of the shuttle.

He came out with Belos. "I'll get the loader, next up," he said. "Then we can test the fittin' and new seal."

"Good," Belos said. "I'll go get the bomb."

Fergus almost swore out loud at that. Though he managed to choke it down, he was grateful that there were enough night noises to cover the small sound of dismay he'd made instead.

The two of them spent about an hour retrofitting a firing chamber for the cannonballs into the back of the shuttle and then putting in a seal around it so they could open the back cargo doors and fire them out without decompressing the entire ship. Then Len maneuvered a bulky, oblong object that Fergus guessed had to be the bomb up toward the nose of the shuttle and carefully clamped it in place on the underside.

Belos came out. "Looks good," he said. "Systems all check out. You sure we're not going to have company, as soon as I fire the engines up?"

"Yep. Locked 'em in. If they can't unlock theyselves in the morn, sad excuses for pirates one an' all," Len said. "Not our problem no more."

"You sure you want to go?" Belos asked.

Len snorted. "Stupid ta ask," he said. "Always with ya; you know that. Kaybe gonna be hurt, though."

"Can't be helped. Kaybe needs to be here to get the crew

through and out, and I want him to live. He's the last of the three of us that started all this, all those years ago," Belos said. "He'll understand, eventually. It's asking too much to expect him to forgive me, though."

"You do what you gotta," Len said.

"You do," Belos agreed. "I'm going to fire the engines up, run the last set of system tests. Check the payload and seal to make sure nothing vibrates loose, then we'll be away."

"Gotcher," Len said. Belos went back into the shuttle, and moments later the engines started up, loud in the night as all the creepers and critters fell silent around them.

Len checked the new seal one more time, then went back to where he'd attached the bomb to the nose of the shuttle. He did his best to shake it, tightened some more clamps, tried again, and then stood back in satisfaction. Fergus considered it a definite win that the man did not hear him slide down off the far side of the hull and sneak up toward him.

At the last second, Len whirled around, a knife appearing in each hand where seconds before there had been none. "Vetch," he said.

"Hey, Len," Fergus said.

"You should be sleepin'," Len said.

"Yeah, probably. Insomnia, you know. Thought I'd wander out and get some fresh air."

"Through a locked door?"

"Was it locked?" Fergus said. "I didn't notice."

Len frowned. "What ya gonna do, now? You can't stop th' captain."

"I don't want to stop him," Fergus said. "I want to know what he's doing."

"No business fer you. Turn around now an' go, while ya can."

"Can I wish you luck?" Fergus asked, and stuck out a hand as if to shake. Len didn't take it. "No? Oh, well."

Len shifted his stance, just slightly, and Fergus knew that meant he needed to yield or fight, right now. Yielding had never been in his nature, so instead he summoned up his internal electrical bees, letting them run down his arms but not yet escape his skin, and the moment Len moved to strike—fast, so fast, and right for his throat—he let it go, and a bright arc of electricity leapt from one of his hands and crossed between them. Len's attack turned into a stumble, and dammit if the man didn't look *incredibly* pissed off about it.

Soon as Len hit the dirt, Fergus slapped his other hand on him and put him out. He picked up Len's earpiece from the dirt and let himself into the shuttle through the new seal.

"We good to go?" Belos asked, over the comm.

"Good," he said, as gruffly and Len-like as he could, and then grabbed for a wallbar as the shuttle took off, vertical until it cleared the waveforest, then accelerating on a trajectory for orbit.

"Come on up and see the sights one last time, Len," Belos said. "Moons are beautiful. Not sure I'll miss this place, but I feel like I could have, if the circumstances were different."

Fergus entered the bridge and threw himself down in the co-pilot seat.

Belos glanced over, and froze, for just a second. "You didn't kill him?" he asked.

"No. Left him sleeping," Fergus said.

Belos burst out laughing, deep and loud, and for a long while. "You are such an unpredictable asshole, Vetch," he said, at last. "I should have guessed that was why Len was taking so long outside, though I never thought anyone could get the jump on him. You just bought yourself a one-way ticket to your own death, you know. We aren't coming back from this."

Fergus put his feet up on the dash, aware he was barefoot once again, just as he had been when he left Coralla, and the symmetry felt like destiny at its pettiest.

"We'll see," he said. "So, what's the plan?"

Belos pointed as the atmosphere thinned and was left behind, leaving only the distant band of stars on the far side of the Gap, ahead.

"Revenge," he said. "The only justice left."

Chapter 19

◆—◆—◆

Belos took the shuttle into passive jump, on course directly toward the Asiig space, then got up to stretch, and tried to conceal several jaw-popping yawns. Unlike Fergus, he'd worked through the day and most of the night, and had likely counted on being able to swap off shifts sleeping with Len.

As if he'd been thinking along the same lines, he scowled at Fergus. "I have to think about how to handle this," he said. "By *this* I mean *you*. We've got one cryopod in the back, and we were going to trade off for the year or so it'll take us to cross the gap into Asiig space, but at least I could trust Len not to turn us around the moment I'm unconscious."

"I won't," Fergus said. "I could give you my word on that, but I can see where we might have some trust complications right now."

"That's one way of putting it," Belos said.

"If it's any consolation, I doubt we'll need to worry about it more than a day or two," Fergus said.

"Is that a threat?" Belos asked.

"Oh, hell, no," Fergus said. "I just mean we're not going to get far."

"You don't think we can reach the Asiig?"

"Captain, I am one hundred percent certain that the Asiig are going to come to *us*. They watch all the time, and they already knew we were on that planet," Fergus said.

"How do you know that?"

"Because I ran into one of their agents in the forest," Fergus said.

"What?! Why didn't you tell me this?!"

"Would you have believed me?"

"No," Belos said.

"So, that's why," Fergus said.

"What's your game?" Belos asked.

"I don't really have one. Survive, mostly. After that, get home safely, with as many of you as possible," Fergus said. "That, Captain, includes you."

"If you think we're heading right into an Asiig trap—"

"Not a *trap*," Fergus said. "Well, maybe not a trap. The Asiig are complicated, inscrutable, and terrifyingly dangerous, but they have reasons behind what they do, even if it's not something we can fathom."

"That's not their reputation," Belos said.

"Nor do you fit yours, Captain. The elements are there, but the truth is much larger than them alone. The Asiig are like that."

"You talk as if you've met them."

"I have."

"It is well known that they don't let anyone live."

"It is not something those of us who have like to talk about," Fergus said. "It is also true that none of our lives are ever the same, and not least because they never leave you alone for very long afterward."

Belos yawned again. "I think you're mostly full of shit, but I'm going to have to sleep soon," he said. "If you got past Len, it's probably not much good tying you up, and I doubt either of us thought to pack rope. I could kill you, but you may be useful. Your word: you won't change course or otherwise alter our path?"

"My word," Fergus said.

"Don't touch a damned thing. Just keep an eye out for alerts or signs of trouble," Belos said, and with a long, lingering, suspicious look, pulled down one of the fold-down bunks, tethered himself in, and curled up to sleep.

Fergus slouched down in his chair and stared out at the weird distortions that were movement in tiny hyperspace hops, like blinking in and out of the universe. He hoped someone would remember to feed his cat until he got back; when he'd left his cabin, he didn't think he wouldn't be back later that night.

If I get back, he corrected himself. One thing he knew was that the Asiig couldn't—or, more importantly, wouldn't even if they could—solve the gate-alien problem, but if anyone could get the Bomo'ri to talk to Fergus, it would be them. And then, who knew?

The stars across the Gap seemed very, very far away and cold.

———

As it turned out, Fergus's guess wasn't far off; four days out—standard days, not Solo days, and though he'd never adjusted to the latter, he'd still managed to lose a decent sense of the former—he started feeling odd tingles, all over his body, as if something was trying to reach out to him via the strange, alien organ the Asiig had stuck in his gut so long ago.

"We should drop out of jump," he told Belos.

"Why?" he asked

"I think they've arrived," he said.

Belos shook his head but set the engines to transition them back into normal space. "I only hope I don't die so fast I never get an explanation of how you know all these things," he said.

The shuttle dropped into normal space, and they were alone in the vast emptiness, Solo's star now so far behind him it couldn't be picked out against the dim field of stars that was their home arm of the galaxy. "There's no one here," Belos said. "Scans don't pick anything up within a thousand kilometers. I'm going back into jump—"

"Wait," Fergus said.

"How long are we supposed to—" Belos started to say, when all of a sudden, a massive black triangle ship was directly in front of them, nose to nose. Belos physically jumped in his seat. "Fucking hell," he swore.

Two more popped into existence to either side of them, flanking them. Belos unclipped his safety tether and went into the back of the shuttle.

"What are you doing?" Fergus called back.

"What I came here to do," Belos said. "Getting their attention."

"I'm pretty sure we have it already," Fergus said. "Don't launch—"

There was a loud *thumph*, and the shuttle shook as one of *Sidewinder*'s cannonballs shot out the back of the shuttle, spun around them, and then, just as it was bearing down on the left side Asiig ship, abruptly stopped. It spun in place for a while, generating its shield-penetrating magnetic chaos, then all its lights went out and it floated dead in space.

Belos had already come back to the bridge, and gritted his teeth. "Not good enough?" he called out. "Then see how you like this—"

He was reaching for the helm, even as Fergus was reaching out to stop him, when a familiar voice spoke from behind them. "We'd rather you didn't."

Belos spun around, threw a knife that the agent easily ducked, and pulled his energy pistol out in that moment of distraction and fired. The agent just blinked at him. Belos fired again, to no effect.

"Please?" the agent said, and indicated Belos should lower the gun. "We came to talk."

"You killed my twin sister and her crew," Belos said. "What talk can fix that?"

"I've never killed anyone," the agent said, then paused. "No, that's a lie. I've killed thousands of people, but I've never killed anyone that the universe wasn't better off without. Did your sister deserve to die?"

"No," Belos said. "She did not."

"Is that your objective assessment?" the agent asked, then *tsk*ed. "I think you can admit both she and you fall into a bit of a moral *gray area*. Dark, *dark* gray."

"Who are you to judge?" Belos asked.

"Oh, I don't," the agent said. "I just do what I'm told. Go here, do that, go there, do this other thing. Isn't that right, Mr. Ferguson?"

Belos darted a quick glance at Fergus, but Fergus couldn't read anything from his expression. "So, you're a lackey," he said. "Where are your masters?"

"Oh, would you prefer to speak to management?" the agent asked, smiling. "So be it."

The agent snapped his fingers, and then they were somewhere else, standing on a square of light in pitch dark, surrounded by the sounds of crickets. Fergus had the growing sense that it wasn't actual instantaneous transportation but some sort of trick messing with short-term memory to make it seem that way, but damn, did it *feel* instant.

The agent caught his eye, winked, and put one finger to his lips.

"Where the fuck are we?" Belos asked, turning around in the square, then taking a step toward the agent, who moved backward out of the light and vanished.

The alien that entered the light next had filled Fergus's nightmares for a long time. It had thick, armored plates along its horizontal upper body, out of which six thin, multi-jointed legs and a whip-like tail emerged. Suspended beneath the plate-covered body was a secondary structure with compound eyes, like a three-meter-tall spider in an armadillo shell, and all of it as black as the darkness around them.

It spoke, a chittering sound that echoed in the room, and was answered by several more, which also stepped into the light, until they were surrounded.

The square of light began to divide into two, sliding apart from each other, with Fergus and Belos standing on separate ones. "Wait!" Fergus exclaimed, reaching out toward Belos, but the moment their squares were fully separated, he was no longer visible.

"Separate audiences," the agent said.

"Please, don't kill him," Fergus said. He remembered all too well the screams of Borr Graf, when they'd been picked up drifting in space, before they turned the man into meatcubes. Graf had deserved that, or worse, but Belos . . .

"Oh?" the agent said, who had stayed with Fergus. The Asiig were gone. "Why not?"

"He came all this way just to find out what happened to his sister. To avenge her, though he never stood a chance, because he swore he would," Fergus said. "That kind of dedication has to count for something."

"Why?"

Fergus let his hands fall to his sides. It felt helpless to argue with this man, who wasn't human, about humanity. "Because it's too easy not to care at all," he said.

"Like you?" the agent asked.

"No? I care," Fergus said. "I care too much."

"But for a long time, you pretended you didn't," the agent said. "Why?"

"Because I didn't want to get hurt, and I didn't want to hurt anyone else," Fergus said. "But I did anyway."

"You mean, in part, your friend Dru," the agent said.

"Yes," Fergus said. "Is she well?"

There was the sound of slow crickets from the dark around them. "She is well," the agent answered, after the Asiig finished. "Quite well. You bring us the most interesting people."

"Is she still among you?" Fergus asked.

"For now," the agent said. "The question is: what brought you here?"

"As I said, Belos is looking—"

"That's what brings *him* here," the agent interrupted. "Did I ask a more ambiguous question than I thought?"

Was it Fergus's imagination, or was his own square getting ever so slowly smaller? His anxiety spiked. "There are shipwrecks, both human and Bomo'ri, on a planet around the lone star in the middle of the Gap," he said. "I want to help the survivors stranded on the planet get home."

"And yourself," the agent said.

"Yes," Fergus said. "Though I don't really have a home to go to, not that's safe for everyone around me."

"Who else are you helping?"

His square *was* getting smaller. "What do you mean?" he said.

"Belos came here seeking justice. Is he alone in believing himself wronged?"

"No," Fergus said. "Or at least I don't think so. The aliens guarding the gate, that you told me were called the Havna . . ."

"Ah, yes! Them again. A lot of trouble they make out there. If one had a sense of humor, one could find the one-sided mess they've made of the Bomo'ri's much-bragged-about elite warships entertaining." There were more cricket-sounds, and the agent added, "I have been reminded I don't have a sense of humor. So, a tragedy it must be—a waste, to be sure."

"We think the Bomo'ri were destroying star systems on our side of the Gap, in an area we now call the Barrens, as part of some kind of research," Fergus said. "Did they destroy the Havna's planet?"

"We don't know," the agent said. "How interesting a conjecture. What do you think they were researching?"

"A guess? That they were trying to somehow artificially create jump conduits between the Barrens and the star system in the Gap but couldn't get it quite right, and then the Havna attacks made them abandon their research," Fergus said.

The crickets talked for a long time, back and forth, while Fergus's square had shrunk down to almost the tips of his toes. The urge to step back and away was almost overpowering, but he had no confidence any light remained behind him, and he didn't dare look.

The agent rolled his eyes. "They can go on and on," he said to Fergus. He turned behind him. "Isn't that a spoiler, though? He hasn't figured that out yet. Fine, fine, I'll explain."

When he turned back, he held his hands out, about shoulder width apart, palms facing each other, and an image of the lone star system appeared between them, Solo with its two moons tiny specks rotating the miniature sun. "You are correct that the Bo-mo'ri wished to learn how to create jump conduits, which are pinholes in the fabric of space," he said. "What do you know about how those endpoints form?"

"Gravity," Fergus said. "Big and complicated gravity fields."

"One can think of gravity, in ridiculously simplistic terms you might understand, as something heavy sitting upon a soft surface, like a blanket. It creates a dent, which attracts other things to it because the dent makes things want to roll toward it," the agent said. "Space, though, has some memory. If you have a heavy object and you move it, the dent remains for a while. If you explode the heavy object, though, that energy release causes space to react and snap back to its natural state as if that mass was never there."

"That's why blowing up star systems didn't work," Fergus said. "You'd think they'd have figured it out faster, before they'd destroyed nearly every system in the area of the Barrens."

"Oh, I think they figured that out eventually," the agent said. "Think about it."

"I don't know," Fergus said. "How could I?"

"The system in the Gap," the agent said, "was not always in the Gap."

Fergus blinked at him as it all started to add up. "They moved it, thinking that it would leave a track in the fabric of space along its path, creating their jump conduit," he said.

"Yes," the agent said.

"But it didn't fully work," Fergus said. "The conduit is unstable and ends shy of the system itself."

"Think on the ball—representing the mass of the entire solar systems you are trying to move—rolling across a soft surface analogy," the agent said. "What would make the dent lessen?"

"Losing mass—the six other planets," Fergus said, and almost slapped his forehead. "Why destroy those on the way, then?"

The agent laughed. "The Bomo'ri, for all they would have everyone think otherwise, are not infallible," he said, "nor immune, as you humans so delightfully put it, to having everything *shit the bed.*"

"I don't know if that's comforting or not," Fergus said.

"I cannot say, either," the agent said. "This is the longest conversation we've ever had without you cursing at me, though. I feel like we are growing, you and I. But I must ask: what do you want from us?"

"Whatever the Bomo'ri did to the Havna, they need to fix it or pay for it," Fergus said. "They can't just leave the Havna killing human ships who stumble into the Ghostdrift because they can't tell us apart."

"Again, how does this involve us?"

"Do you think if I went to the Bomo'ri on my own and said, 'Hey, fix your mess,' they'd listen to me?" Fergus said.

The agent laughed. "No. They don't see the value in humanity that we do, with your highly customizable physiology and insatiable need to do irrational, beautifully creative things. So much more interesting than playing with boring old wormholes. Ah—" The agent pointed down, and the square of light beneath Fergus's feet was now almost gone.

"Time's up," the agent said, and when the light winked out, so did everything else.

———

He woke up sitting in the shuttle's copilot chair. Belos was at the helm, his head bobbing as he slowly returned to consciousness himself. ". . . What happened?" Belos asked, a few seconds later.

"Apparently, they decided to let you live," Fergus said. "Congratulations on having been found *interesting*."

"I feel weird," Belos said. He stood up, steadied himself with one hand on the back of the chair, then whirled around to look out the front window. "They're gone."

"Yeah," Fergus said. "I'd hoped—"

"What is on your *feet*?!" Belos exclaimed.

Fergus glanced down and discovered he was now wearing a pair of bright pink bunny slippers. "Couldn't leave me with boots, could they?" he complained. He had a thought, and in a panic reached down and pulled a slipper off. "Thank the stars they come off. Just slippers."

"What else could they have been?" Belos asked.

"They could have replaced my feet," Fergus said.

"Would they—"

"Maybe," Fergus said.

"Do I look—"

"Normal? Yes. Don't count on it, though," Fergus said. He touched the console and checked the time. "We were out for about thirty hours."

"Now what do we do?" Belos asked.

"I don't know. I didn't expect them to just ditch us and leave," Fergus said. "I suppose I should be grateful they gave me one thing I asked."

"What was that?"

"For them not to kill you," Fergus said. "Do yourself a favor, and don't get yourself med-scanned in a public Dr. Diagnosis booth."

"That sounds like the voice of experience," Belos said. He still looked shaken and pale.

"Yeah. The Asiig like to give little gifts to people they let go," Fergus said. "Mind you, the gift is more for their own entertainment than any desire to make you happy."

"This is not the first time you've spoken to them."

Fergus had to think. "If you don't count the agent, I think this is the third time."

"And they gave you a so-called gift?" Belos asked.

It was not an unexpected question, and out there in the middle of nowhere, after what they'd both just gone through, it felt pointless to keep his secret. He had no doubt that soon enough Belos would find himself with a new one, too. "Yeah," he said. "Remember how I said I could hear electricity?"

"Oh, right," Belos said. "That's not too bad."

Fergus held his arms out to the side and let electricity suddenly leap and crawl over his skin, arms and chest and head, feeling his new beard growth do its best to stand on end from his chin.

"Now I know how you got past Len," Belos said.

"In his defense, it wasn't really a fair fight," Fergus said.

Belos chuckled. "On the contrary, it may be the first fair fight he's ever been in. At least I understand some things now, possibly including why you are so very wanted by the Alliance."

"I would say they don't have any of the details, but in a general sense, yes," Fergus said. "They only had a very partial biosignature on me and one alias, but I'm guessing *Paradigm* ruined that for me before they jumped behind us and got stuck in the same trap. I just don't know what we do next. I thought there was at least a chance the Asiig would help, but no."

"I'm not so sure they're done with us," Belos said, and waved a hand toward the front viewer. Another black triangle ship was approaching, at almost reasonable speeds instead of the instant in-your-face of their usual arrivals. In less than a minute, it stopped, nose to nose, where the previous ship had been. It was smaller than the earlier ones.

Fergus spun around in his seat to see if the agent was back on board, but the shuttle remained empty. "I guess we wait?" he said.

The underside of the triangle ship opened, and the ship edged forward, enveloping the shuttle like a big fish swallowing a minnow, and the door slid shut behind them.

When nothing happened, Fergus got up and slipped in a comm earpiece. Then he opened the seal into the back of the shuttle, stepped through, and sealed it behind him again. "What are you doing?" Belos asked.

"Going out to say thanks for the slippers," Fergus said. "Oh, by the way, your cannonball is back."

"I'll come with you," Belos said.

"Wait until I get outside and don't asphyxiate," Fergus replied, as he opened the outer shuttle cargo doors and walked out. It was the usual inconveniently dark space he'd come to associate with the Asiig, and he wondered if their eyesight was limited in brighter light, or if there was plenty of light around in a spectrum he couldn't see. If he had thought to bring his goggles from his cabin when sneaking out after Len, he could check, but it was too late now.

An agent was standing there, and it took a second for Fergus to realize it wasn't his usual tormentor but someone taller, lankier, just as not-quite-right-looking. "Hello," Fergus said.

"Hello, Mr. Ferguson," the new agent said. "It was decided there was cause to assist you in conversing with the Bomo'ri, and you have been assigned a liaison ship. When your pirate friend decides to come out and join you, I'll take you up to the bridge to meet the captain."

"I'm coming out," Belos said over the earpiece, and moments

later hopped down out of the back of the shuttle to stand beside Fergus.

Fergus could tell, just by a glance, that Belos had taken the opportunity to arm himself first, and hoped that the captain would have the sense to use his weapons judiciously, and only as last necessity.

Walking through the Asiig ship was a surreal experience, and if they hadn't had their guide to follow, it would have felt like trying to navigate a creepily dark fun house while in the grip of significant hallucinogens. The path lit up ahead of their feet as they walked, and sometimes there were walls nearby, sometimes a feeling of nothingness even under his feet, and here and there were the cricket sounds of Asiig on board, never quite seen as more than a peripheral sense of movement.

At some point, Fergus's ears popped, and he realized the floor was rising, carrying them upward even as they walked, and at last it stopped, and the agent stepped aside to reveal a tall doorway, its frame lit in yellow. "The bridge," the guide said, and held out a hand to indicate they should go through.

Fergus had expected a door, but instead, it was as if he walked through an immaterial black curtain, no sensation of any matter except one moment he was in the dark, and with the next step he was on the bridge, blinking from the sudden, bright light.

A human form stood before them, arms folded, waiting, and he opened his mouth to speak when Belos entered and nearly ran into him. "Sorry," Belos said, rubbing at his eyes. "I can't see a damned thing yet."

"It's—" Fergus started to say, but the triangle ship's captain spoke first.

"Welcome aboard, Bas," Bel Belos said. "Good to see you again."

Chapter 20

"Have a seat," Bel said, and pointed toward a pair of chairs where Fergus had not noticed them before. Bas sat, his expression still of a man too stunned to know if he was more happy or more confused. Fergus took the chair beside him.

She waved toward her bridge crew, who turned around in their own seats and saluted Belos.

"Blinks?" Bas asked. "Needles? You both are alive too?"

"And Aisu, but they had other things they wished to do," Bel said. She looked remarkably like Bas with her jet-black hair, down past the small of her back in a tight braid, though flecks of gray showed here and there in the light. "Mind you, we very nearly were not."

"I found the wreck of *Rattler*," Bas said. "There were no bodies. Fang showed me—"

"Fang made it?" Bel interrupted, a smile spreading across her face.

"Not entirely," Bas said. "The mindsystem is there, but there's so much damage to the ship and Fang's power supply. It was all we could do to have a basic conversation. When I saw those shipwrecks up in orbit and scattered across the planet, I assumed the worst. After all these years of looking, to think that's what happened . . . it was more than I could bear. Why didn't you let me know you were alive? Why didn't you come back?"

"I'm not who I was, Bas. And it was too dangerous."

"You've survived worse—"

"Too dangerous for *you*," she clarified. "I have . . . new responsibilities. A new life. Here."

"Among monsters?" Belos asked.

Around them, there was chirping, and Fergus realized there were Asiig on the bridge as well, in the darker corners.

She laughed. "When were we ever not among monsters, Bas? How long since either of us could claim not to be monsters ourselves?"

He was quiet, stewing on that.

"So, ah, you're taking us to the Bomo'ri?" Fergus asked.

"Not much of a one for long family reunions, I see," she said.

"If you'd met my family, you'd understand why," he said.

"Even your cousin? And your sister?" she asked.

It was his turn to be surprised and dismayed. "When . . . How?"

"I was filled in when I learned that my brother had actually found his way through the Ghostdrift and then somehow survived the Havna. As you might imagine, you are a significant portion of the explanation. I would rather he not have found you at all and been left back in the Barrens none the wiser but vastly safer, but here we are."

Bel turned toward the man Bas had identified as Blinks, *Rattler*'s old first mate. "Take us toward Bomostar," she said, and like that, the stars visible behind her jumped to become lines, racing toward them, but smooth, no sense of physical transition. She regarded Fergus and her twin again.

"Have you ever heard the ancient saying that life is the universe's way of understanding itself?" she asked. "If you think about it, the more we living beings understand each other, the more we also understand the universe. The Asiig wish for that perfect understanding. Knowing that life is infinite, and infinitely diverse, they know perfection is impossible, but that the pursuit of it is nonetheless the worthiest work."

"So, they fuck around with humans, thinking it's noble?" Fergus asked.

"No, they fuck around with humans because humans are so incredibly fuck-around-able," Bel said. "We are tenacious, illogical, brilliantly inventive—"

"—easily manipulated—" Fergus interjected.

She sighed in exasperation. "—and frustrating," she said, "by which right now I specifically mean *you*."

"I don't like being a pawn," he said.

"Only you see yourself as that," she said. "I would like to talk to my brother, if you don't mind being shown to your room."

"I—" Fergus started to say, as one of the Asiig emerged from its shadows, and then he was standing in a small room with a bed, table, and a small sink, all alone.

"I object," he announced to the room. He threw the bunny slippers across the room against the door, washed his face and hands, and then, because he was exhausted, lay down on the bed. It was unfairly warm and irritatingly comfortable, but he found some measure of pleasing dissatisfaction in that it lacked the company of his cat. "So there, not perfect at all," he muttered, before allowing his eyes to close.

Then he lay there for several more hours, wondering if the Asiig had done something to him *again*, and taking every tiny exhausted muscle twitch as a sure sign of impending doom.

———

When he did wake up, some unknown number of hours later, he was relieved to discover he had not turned into a giant bug. Nor was anything else amiss, as far as he could tell, except for being extremely hungry and still somewhat annoyed at everything.

There were no locks on the doors, nor really a door at the door, just that weird curtain of discrete darkness that let him pass out as easily as he had entered.

On the bridge, Bas was still talking to his sister and, from his haggard look, had been up the entire time. The stubborn set of his jaw, and tightly folded arms, suggested there had been disagreement, and Bel's identical body language gave Fergus the clear impression that neither felt victorious.

Their ship was now surrounded by stars; they'd crossed the Gap. One star in particular was bright and, surely not coincidentally, directly ahead.

"Bomostar," Bel confirmed. One of the Asiig in the room came forward out of the deeper shadows on the periphery of the bridge, and spoke for a bit with Bel, who replied back in the same chirps and clicks as it had, sounds Fergus was fairly sure an unmodified human could not make.

He had thought it likely that Bas was the only original-form human aboard, and was even more certain now. He also expected Bas was the only one aboard who didn't know that, but there was no way he was going to be the one to break that news.

Blinks—a short, round, dark-skinned man with the same Lekos Brotherhood tattoos that Bas had—tilted his head toward where Bel and the Asiig were talking. "Bomostar has replied to our request for a diplomatic rendezvous, with the statement that they are unaware of any matter worth discussing between us."

"Tell them we would like to discuss the Havna," Bel said.

"Yes, Captain," Blinks said. A few minutes later, he spoke again. "They wish to express deep unhappiness with us for bringing up what they consider a topic not of our business, but will dispatch an envoy. We are asked to wait here."

The Asiig spoke briefly, and Bel shook her head. "I got this," she said. "Blinks, please inform them we do not wish to inconvenience them unduly, and that if their envoy is unable to make it here within six hours, we will be glad to do them the courtesy of coming to them."

All the Asiig on the bridge whistled, a low, mournful sound, and Fergus wondered if it was their laughter. Being surrounded was disconcerting, even with Bel and her remaining crew there, relaxed and unconcerned. Other than size, there seemed to be little way of telling the Asiig apart, and it was hard to scrutinize them for minor differences in the low light without some primal fear grabbing hold of his heart and twisting.

"So, uh," he asked. "Do the Asiig have names?"

"Of course," Bel said. She pointed around the room, including toward a few dark corners where he hadn't realized there were more, and with each made a series of clicking, whistling, chirping sounds that were meaningless to him, and which he had little hope of being able to remember, much less imitate.

What he did get from it was that there were eight Asiig on the bridge, lurking mostly out of sight. How much of his life had changed at the hands—long claw-pincers—of these aliens? It could be argued that good had come of it, on a larger scale, but personally? He was a wanted man on Mars and Earth and throughout Alliance space. He still flinched at the right pitch of rattle, remembering being chewed down to the bone by Devourers in a multidimensional tunnel, trying to keep them from reaching and devastating this side of the galaxy. He was far away from friends and family, unable to see them without fear of being hunted, and when a hunter finally caught up with him, there he was once again in the company of the Asiig, doing the big work that needed doing, but put there once again through machinations and manipulations without anyone asking what he needed, what he wanted.

"I want to go home," he found himself saying out loud, surprising himself, and breaking the silence on the bridge as they waited for the Bomo'ri. "When this is over, I mean. I want to find a way to go home."

One of the Asiig spoke, and Bel translated. "They ask: have you found home yet?"

That stung.

"Home is people," Fergus said. "It's the people who get you, who love you for who you are, who put up with you when you're an arse but set boundaries and call you out when they need to, who miss you, who do their best to pick you up when you fall if they can't catch you, and who you would do the same or more for, just because of who they are to you. Home is the people who give you the chance to be your best self. And I have been away, or hiding, or running away too long."

"See? He gets it," Bas said.

Bel growled under her breath. "Maybe your home and my home are no longer the same, Bas. I'm not arguing this with you again, and I am not going back to my old life in the Barrens, no matter how much you try to insist. The Bomo'ri will let us stew until the very last possible minute. You should go get some rest."

"I don't need—" Bas started to say, and this time, Fergus got to see the party trick from the outside. Bas's face went slack, and his eyes glazed over, and one of the other Asiig stalked up behind him, looming over him, and gently prodded him forward and off the bridge.

Bel's eyes met his. "You understand," she said.

"Sometimes, yeah," he answered.

"You have more questions?" she asked.

"I have *endless* questions."

"Well, you have five and a half hours, or until the Bomo'ri get here, whichever happens first," she said. "I suggest you use most of that time to come up with a plan if they aren't cooperative, because they are *never* cooperative."

"That's my impression, yeah," he said. "Here's what I was thinking: how do you feel about *bluffing*?"

———

Just as Bel had predicted, the Bomo'ri waited until their six hours were nearly up before appearing ahead of them, another giant

rounded-brick of a ship like the wrecks they'd seen in the graveyard near the Ghostdrift terminus. The Bomo'ri ship sat directly
in front of them for several hours, responding to queries with only
"Wait."

Fergus had wondered if his imposed knowledge of the Bomo'ri language was limited to reading, but it turned out he could
understand by listening as well, though it gave him one hell of a
headache to do so. Speaking it, however, much like the Asiig language, was far outside his physiological abilities.

At last, the Bomo'ri envoy appeared on their ship's main screen.
"What do you want?" it asked.

The Asiig beside Bel answered in stilted, almost whistled Bomo'ri. "We wish to discuss the matter of the Havna."

The Bomo'ri considered only a brief moment. "It is not the
business of your people," it said. "We require no further conversation on the matter."

Fergus stepped forward. "We do," he said, and the Asiig translated his words to Bomo'ri for him.

"We do not speak to vermin," the envoy answered.

"Inform the envoy that it will discuss the matter with us or we
will bring dozens of ships of 'vermin' to Bomo'ri space," Fergus
said, and the Asiig did so.

"We will destroy all your ships," the envoy replied. "It will be
no effort on our part."

"Before we come, we will pass through where the Havna wait,
and because our engines are the same as yours, they will follow us
here," Fergus said. "Do the Bomo'ri not fear the Havna knowing
the location of Bomostar, after the Bomo'ri destroyed their home
star and planet with their experiments?"

After the Asiig translated Fergus's threat, the screen went blank.
Nearly an hour later, the envoy reappeared. "We may discuss the
matter," it said. "We will receive you."

Bel and the Asiig spoke briefly, then she crooked her finger at

Fergus. "You're coming, obviously," she said. "Blinks, you have the bridge. If my brother wakes up, tell him we went out to pick up some green chili."

"How are we—" Fergus started to say, when a doorway just appeared on the side of the bridge, like the other curtain-of-darkness leading to the back. Their Asiig went first, then Fergus followed Bel through.

On the other side was space. They were walking through a tunnel of some sort, though what it was made of, Fergus could not tell, as none of his normal senses saw or heard or smelled or felt anything, though his electricity sense assured him *something* was there.

For a moment, he was beside the Asiig, close enough to touch, and to see hairline fractures in its plating. It reminded him, startlingly, of the network of fine lines that crisscrossed his entire body. Was this Asiig old, or were they battle scars? How long did the Asiig live? Was their ability to heal themselves less than their extraordinary ability to heal humans, or did the Asiig keep it out of pride or as a humble reminder? For all that they had put Fergus back together from the bloodied, nearly flayed mess he'd been after the Devourers, they had left him with those lines, and they had made sure the scar on his leg remained.

As lightly as he could, he touched the Asiig. It was hot, which he had not expected, and the armor plating had a faint texture to it, invisible to the eye. There was something surreal, terrifying and empowering at the same time, about touching your nightmares.

Fergus pulled his hand away quickly, hoping the touch had gone unnoticed or at least had not offended.

The tunnel connected directly to the side of the Bomo'ri vessel, and they walked through the far curtain to find themselves in a large room with three Bomo'ri waiting. As Fergus stepped in, just ahead of Bel, one of the Bomo'ri hissed and grabbed him by the neck, lifting him off his feet with one of its arms, its many thin fingers clamped around his throat. "Vermin!" it hissed.

The Asiig moved faster than Fergus could have imagined, given their normally ponderous gait, and one long arm shot out, the pincer-claws forming a point, and jabbed it into the Bomo'ri's chest. The Bomo'ri dropped Fergus with a howl of indignation.

The Asiig removed its claw, and there was a dark, bluish mark on the Bomo'ri's skin where it had hit. It rumbled and chirped, and Bel translated into Bomo'ri for it: "You will not disrespect our companions."

"Your pets," another Bomo'ri sneered.

"Nonetheless," the Asiig replied.

"We have come to discuss the Havna," Bel said.

"And what of them concerns you?" the envoy asked.

"You destroyed their home planet, and their star system, trying to create artificial jump conduits," Fergus said. "They attacked you in retaliation. You abandoned your research outpost in the Gap, and have let the Havna lurk there for a hundred years, homeless and adrift, attacking human ships mistaking them for yours, and you have done nothing."

Bel translated again.

"The mistaken identity is your fault for stealing our jump technology," the Bomo'ri envoy said.

"You shot your probe right through our home system," Fergus said. "There is a noble precedent among my people known as *finders keepers.*"

All three Bomo'ri hissed when Bel repeated the words.

"I wish to step on this vermin and crush it," the one who had picked up Fergus said.

"It is understandable but inadvisable," the third said. Bel translated neither of those comments for him, but she looked ready to step on some people herself.

"It is unfortunate our research team did not destroy the Gap system Object 114 when the experiment failed, after we knew we were the target of unprecedented hostilities in that area," the envoy said. "It had been our expectation the Havna would give up, or die out, and we could return to our work."

Fergus thought about the wave forests, the herds of woadebeest, and all the other strange little critters and plants that lived there, and his electrical bees stirred at his anger. "You," he pronounced, "are the biggest shitheads in the whole galaxy."

Bel translated with some obvious glee, which involved gesturing toward her own butt and miming poop, and all three Bomo'ri pushed closer to Fergus only to find the Asiig suddenly blocking their way. "You will provide the Havna with justice so they will be at peace," the Asiig said. "You will leave the system you relocated into the Gap alone."

"Why should we?" the envoy asked. "Now that we know of the vermin's plan to lead the Havna here, we can intercept them safely away from Bomostar."

"You haven't had much luck fighting them so far," Bel said.

"We do not need to destroy the Havna, only those guiding them," the envoy said. "The sacrifice on our side will be minimal."

"Would you fight us?" the Asiig asked.

The envoy's color changed. "We have no argument with your people, nor you with us," it said.

"You disrupt the great work of the universe with your precipitate acts of destruction against living worlds," the Asiig said. "That is an affront to us."

"Your people are constantly interfering with other worlds, in your arrogance. How is that different?"

"We do not annihilate. We *garden*," the Asiig said. "Take care that you have not become like weeds."

"The destruction was not an intentional outcome of the process," the third Bomo'ri said.

"How many times did you try it?" Fergus asked. "How many worlds, how many stars, destroyed while you tried to figure it out?"

"We did not destroy the Havna planet," the envoy said. "It survived the move intact, though its many moons did not. We were more successful with the planet now in the Gap by using locally positioned rather than remote mechanisms, but we could not continue our research after being attacked."

Fergus stared. "The Havna planet still exists? Where is it?"

"It is within our territory," the envoy said. "When we were attacked, we sealed it and put it in a quarantine zone until we could resume our studies and examine the effects on the world more closely."

"Well, put it the fuck *back*," Fergus said. "Were there survivors? Are there still Havna living on that world?"

"Some. We do not know if they remain, as it is not of concern or interest to us," the envoy said. "We believe the attackers near our experimental conduit were on one or more of their world's moons and have been living and hiding among their fragmented remains, possibly within the halo of the Drift. We do not know this with absolute confidence, but it seems their technology is more advanced than ours in certain, uneven ways."

"Can you put it back safely?" Fergus asked. "Reverse whatever you did, use the better techniques you used for Solo?"

"We could," the envoy admitted, "but also, we cannot."

"Why not?" Bel asked.

"The experimental conduit partially collapsed and would need to be re-formed," the envoy said. "It is not something that can be accomplished in a hurry, or amid chaos, and the Havna are in the way. They would attack us."

"So, talk to them, tell them what you are doing," Fergus said. "I'm sure they'd be willing to set aside their anger if it meant a restoration of their world."

"We do not speak their language," the third Bomo'ri said.

"All this time, and you've never talked to the Havna still living on the planet you stole?" Fergus asked.

"We have no interest in other peoples," the envoy said.

Fergus felt himself bristling and knew that there were now tiny sparks crawling up and down his arms, and didn't care. "You—" he started to say, struggling to find words for how outrageous he found their casual callousness.

The Bomo'ri, if they noticed the electricity building around him, did not seem concerned. "If you wish us to do as you ask, you must talk to the Havna and convince them not to do us harm. As none of you speak their language either, I believe the discussion on this matter has reached an inevitable end. You may return to your vessel and territory."

"If we talk to them, you will return their planet?" Fergus asked.

"You cannot talk to them. It does not matter."

"If we do, though, you will return their planet."

The Bomo'ri stomped all four of its feet in irritation. "Yes, yes. Do the impossible, and we will do the inconvenient. Until then, leave and do not bother us!"

The Asiig said something to Bel, and she put a hand on Fergus's shoulder. "Time to go," she said to him.

"But—"

"We'll talk when we're back aboard our ship," she said, and steered him toward the curtain to the tunnel. Just before she pushed him gently through, she turned back toward the Bomo'ri. "This is not over," she told them. "We will be back."

The walk back through the tunnel felt like defeat. No one spoke. Fergus tried to remember the feel of sand beneath his bare feet, salty wind across his skin, and mentally walked through the steps, one at a time, of preparing and serving Corallan tea. When he was done, he felt calmer, if no happier, and his gift had gone back to sleep, coiled somewhere in his gut, waiting.

They stepped back out onto the bridge of the Asiig ship and found Bas waiting. He was scowling, pacing, and clearly irritated, but as soon as he opened his mouth to say something, Bel shot him a look, and he shut his mouth again, hard.

"Now what?" Fergus asked.

"Now we figure out how to talk to the Havna," she said. "You weren't going to give up, were you?"

"No," Fergus said, with more conviction than he felt.

"Good. We need ideas," she said. "Get thinking, already. We need you on this."

"Me?" Fergus gestured around the bridge. "The intelligence and knowledge of anyone else in the room—"

"I'm a potato," Blinks said from the helm. "Don't look my way in your pawning of responsibilities."

"I am more of a smell pebble, intellectually," Needles said. "Solid but tiny. No growth potential. Move along."

Their Asiig said something and Bel laughed. "Don't tell me the Asiig are claiming to be pebbles now, too," Fergus said.

"No, they were agreeing that Blinks is a potato," Bel said.

"Hey," Blinks complained.

"I have no idea what's going on or what you're talking about," Bas added. "Fill me in or leave me out. I have never felt as useless and unwanted in my life as here, now."

"It's a feeling you get used to," Fergus said. "And yet, in the moment, everyone still expects you to somehow pull magic out of your arse and save the day."

"All I'm *saying*," Bel said, "is that you're the professional problem-solver here. If you can't figure this out, how can we?"

"What about them?" Fergus asked, pointing at the Asiig.

"We garden. It is the flowers themselves that must bloom," their Asiig answered.

Fergus groaned and put his face in his hands, rubbing at his eyes, as he thought furiously. "Fine," he said at last. "I'm going to need some things. And when it fails spectacularly and I die in a horrible, excruciating, messy way, it'll all be on your heads."

"That's the spirit," Bel said, and punched him on the shoulder in encouragement.

Chapter 21

◀◆▶

*T*he universe really is incredibly vast, Fergus thought. It made you feel infinitesimally small when contemplated from within the thin protective shell of a ship, which any being of any awareness and intelligence whatsoever would consider the absolute bare minimum for venturing out into it. Sure, the Asiig had once dropped him out into space in a giant transparent baggie, but he'd been unconscious for the experience and had no say in the planning or execution of it. Now there he was, trying to recreate the experience.

Well, you finally did, he told himself. *You've gone to the most extreme lengths your childhood trauma will take you, trying to run away and be free:* floating around in a transparent bubble in the big empty between two spiral galactic arms, wearing only shorts, his Marsball Marauders T-shirt, and a pair of bunny slippers. He thought about his da, who rowed out onto the loch with his broken leg in a cast and deliberately tipped himself overboard, and whether more than two decades of running around the universe, trying to forget he couldn't save him, forgive himself for not knowing how to swim—not being allowed to know how to swim—wasn't at the root of everything he did even now, every risk he took, every extreme he embraced like it was life or death.

"You okay out there?" Bel asked, over his earpiece.

"Yeah," he said. "Just floatin' along in my bubble, like one does."

She laughed. "Like one does," she echoed. "The interior surface of the bubble has embedded oxygen that'll release as needed and respirate out carbon dioxide to keep a decent balance, but it'll only last about eight hours, depending on your activity level. Either way, that's an hour longer than the thermal provisioning will last, so keep that in mind. Depending on what the Havna do, we may not be able to easily retrieve you."

"I understand," Fergus said.

"Right. Transferring remote control of the shuttle to you," she said. "We're ready when you are."

Rattler's shuttle was parked on the outskirts of the ship graveyard, about a quarter-kilometer behind him, with no one on board. A very large screen had been assembled hastily and was attached to the shuttle's roof, dwarfing it and reminding Fergus of pirate sails. It was a shame that a Jolly Roger would send the wrong message, or he'd have felt compelled to suggest it.

Three kilometers ahead of Fergus, in the direction of the unstable jump point, was a cylindrical object they had had to bully out of the Bomo'ri; he suspected they only went along with the request because they were certain Fergus and his team were going to fail and die, and it was a small price to pay to be rid of them.

They were probably not wrong. If nothing else, he hoped the Bomo'ri and any watching Asiig got a good laugh at his gloriously ignominious end.

He had a remote for the cylinder probe in his hand, and all he had to do was push a button to unleash chaos. There wasn't any reason to wait except nerves. "Okay. Here goes nothing," he said, and pressed the button.

Ahead of him, the Bomo'ri jump engine in the cylinder powered up, and even from there he could feel its rising energy. It slowly started moving, drawn toward the conduit, and began putting on speed rapidly.

This time, because he was looking for it, he felt the other conduit, the one left behind by the passage of the Havna's world, come alive. It was so close to Solo's that it could so easily have been mistaken for the same one. Before the Bomo'ri probe could reach its exit point, four Havna ships appeared and sped toward it.

"They're here," Fergus said. "I'm turning on the screen."

Behind him, a brilliant rectangle of white light appeared, and he could see it reflected in the surface of his surrounding bubble. He didn't dare take his eyes off the Havna ships, who had already destroyed the probe and were now circling, looking for other enemies.

"All right, now," Fergus muttered. "Notice us. Come for a closer look."

One of the maple-seed ships drifted nearer, close enough to the remains of the probe that he now had a sense of scale. They were smaller than he'd thought—for all their firepower, they were only about half again the size of their shuttle. Fergus had already let go of the remote for the probe, its job done, and with his free hand he snagged the small drawing tablet that also shared his meager space. His drawing skills were mediocre, but he did his best to draw an outline of the Havna ship, knowing it would display behind him across the full visible light spectrum and into the fringes of infrared and ultraviolet. Hopefully, *that* would finally draw their attention, in a more curious, less immediately lethal way.

The Havna ship had come to a stop facing the screen. He expected they were scanning the hell out of his shuttle and the ship graveyard, looking for the responsible party; his bubble should be nearly invisible, and wherever the Asiig ship was waiting, he couldn't see or feel it anywhere nearby; he knew that didn't mean much, except that he probably didn't have to worry about it.

Worry about yourself, ye daft bugger, he told himself.

He swiped his hand across his tablet, erasing the image, then drew a passable likeness of a Bomo'ri ship. Another of the Havna ships pulled closer as the third began weaving in and out of the junkyard and the fourth took up a guard position near the two jump points.

"Okay," Fergus said. "Time to throw some logic at you." He wiped the screen, then drew a large dot on the left side, and another on the right, and put an equal sign between them. He waited until the count of ten, added a second dot to the right, then put a slash through the equal sign.

He let that sit a little longer, then added a second dot to balance it out, and removed the slash. "Got it?" he asked. "Hope so. Time to level up!"

Clearing the dots, he drew the Bomo'ri ship again to one side and on the other side of the equal sign did his best to draw an actual Bomo'ri. Had the Havna seen them in person? It was impossible to know, but grim as it was, he thought they must have at least seen the bodies flung free of their ships at the moment of their destruction. Even if not, he had to hope that a species capable of surviving within the fringes of the Drift could infer his meaning.

"They're bombarding the entire graveyard with sensor noise," Bel informed him. "You've definitely got their interest. Is that why you're out there in the middle of nowhere in a bubble, to keep them from finding you?"

"Not exactly," he said. "I don't want them to find me until they've decided they want to *talk* to me. Now we find out if we've reached that point."

He erased the Bomo'ri, drew a genuinely terrible outline of a human, and put the slash back through the equal sign. Then he drew a circle around the man. *Me in my bubble, not one of the bad guys,* he thought.

The second of the two ships near the screen had turned and was slowly circling outward now, seeking. When it finally came close enough that it should be able to detect his bubble, it stopped and hung in space a short distance away.

Fergus waved, then drew himself waving on the screen. *Don't let that be an obscene gesture,* he hoped.

The other two ships converged around him. "Yes!" he called out. "Here I am, right here. No danger at all. I don't even have a ship, right? Don't you wanna know what I want?"

After a solid twenty minutes of doing nothing he could see, the answer seemed to be no. One by one the ships moved away, heading back toward their jump point.

"Shit," Bas said through his earpiece. "They didn't bite."

Fergus sighed. "I got one more trick," he said. "If that doesn't work, I'm out of ideas."

"What is it?" Bel asked.

Instead of answering, Fergus closed his eyes, letting the tablet float free from his hands, and dug way down into his awareness of his own body, and the Asiig gift that was, for better or worse, a part of who he was. He tried to remember the feel of the energies that the Bomo'ri probe had put out. When he thought he had the music of it resonating in his gut, in his bones, like his body was an instrument of electricity, he put everything he had into it and let loose the best imitation of it he could make, tuning it to improve the mimicry and feeling the bubble around him humming and vibrating around him.

Terrifyingly, he could feel the faint stirrings of the jump points, in the distance.

"What the fuck, Vetch?" Bas said, somewhere dimly in the periphery of his attention. "You're glowing."

"It's working. They're turning around again," Bel said. "Can't help you if they decide to kill you, though."

"Worth the gamble," he managed. He cracked open one eye, trying to hold his output where it was, and saw the nose of the Havna ship heading right toward him.

His energy finally flagged, spent, and his dearest wish, as his bubble tumbled into the dark, opening maw of the Havna ship, was that someone there would be kind enough to give him a glass of water.

The interior space where his bubble came to rest—bumping a few walls, then drifting to the center—was cavernously large and awash in blue-green light. There were six beings waiting, all of them tall and wisp-thin, mottled white and silver that was cast a slightly turquoise hue in the light. Their main forms were indistinct underneath tendrils and vine-like appendages that dangled and moved around them. Thicker appendages curled and uncurled, propelling them through the room, and their heads were narrow and long, bristling with whiskers below and behind, and dominated by large, glossy, cobalt-blue eyes.

When he was a kid, he'd stolen change from his da and taken the train into Glasgow to go to the aquarium, and there had been these extraordinary seahorses, their whole bodies evolved to blend in with seaweed; these were like those, if one also gave them some octopus legs. There could have been something creepy about them if they were not so incredibly graceful in their movements and strangely beautiful.

They clustered around his bubble, cautiously at first and then with obvious curiosity. They brushed against it, poked it, and then rolled him over and back again, startled by his flailing to keep himself upright.

One produced a long needle and stuck it through the surface of his bubble, drawing out a small sample of air before retreating. They spoke amongst themselves, a gentle, rushing burbling sound, and every now and then, one would speak toward him, making gestures he assumed were meant to be reassuring, though it was impossible to know.

It jumped into his mind that the name Havna was a Bomo'ri word, meaning *interruption*, and he resolved to find a name they called themselves as soon as he figured out how to ask.

Fergus held up his tablet and tapped at the little person outline in the bubble. "Human," he said, then pointed at himself. "Human."

The alien in front of him crossed two of its tendrils in front of itself, then stretched them out toward the others in the room. "Janaandera," it said, or something like it; its voice was hard to put into human-language sounds.

"Janaandera," Fergus repeated, and the alien tipped its head to one side, then the other, as if to say, *close enough.*

To either side of himself he drew a triangle and one of the alien's ships. "Asiig, Human, Janaandera," he said, then enclosed them in a circle. "Friends. Good."

On the other side of the screen, outside the circle, he drew a Bomo'ri ship. "*Not* friends," he said, and put a line through the ship. "Bad."

The enormity and complexity of what he needed to tell them was suddenly overwhelming, and he sat down in his bubble. He wasn't good at explaining things normally, to other humans who spoke the same language, much less when limited to having to draw. The Sunshielders of Cernee, with their vast pictorial histories covering their walls, would probably enjoy seeing him at such a loss now.

Maybe that's the key, though, he thought. *Don't explain. Tell the story.*

The Janaandera who he'd just spoken with sat down, copying him, and doing it like feathers tumbling gently to the floor. The other three were talking softly to each other in the back of the room and occasionally gesturing in his direction; they might have been arguing, but Fergus couldn't tell.

He set the tablet down on the floor of the bubble, where both he and the alien could see it, and cleared it. Taking a deep breath, he gathered his thoughts and drew what might have passed for the arms of their galaxy. In the space between them, he made a dot, and pointed to the Janaandera and himself, and the ship. "We're here," he said, though he didn't expect they'd understand.

The alien leaned slightly forward. "Shasha jedesh toh," it said.

"Sure, that," Fergus said. He zoomed in to roughly where the Barrens was, and drew a star, and a circle next to it. "Janaandera," he said. Then he drew a Bomo'ri ship next to it, and tapped it. "Bomo'ri."

The three aliens at the back of the room became louder, their words sharper and more dissonant, until the alien sitting near Fergus turned and made a single loud snapping sound. They grew quieter again, though their bodies were rippling in what Fergus was reasonably sure was agitation.

The sitting alien got up, suddenly, and left the room. It returned a short while later with a large bundle, which it unrolled on the floor in front of the bubble. Using the end of one of its tendrils, it touched the screen, which lit up where it had touched and made a passable imitation of Fergus's drawing. It pointed at the Bomo'ri ship it had drawn, then at the planet and star, and, when it was sure Fergus was following it, wiped the star and planet off the drawing with a curt gesture. It then tapped its screen near where they were, making a number of small dots. "Janaandera unshun," it said.

Fergus drew another star and planet, not far from where he'd drawn the Janaandera one in his map of the Barrens. "Solo," he said, and pointed to it. Then he drew a Bomo'ri ship near it. Then he gestured over his shoulder in the direction he thought the star and planet now were. "Solo."

The alien fluttered for a moment.

Fergus drew the star and planet in the Gap, and then drew an arrow from the one in the Barrens. "Solo," he said again, and traced the arrow from the old to the new, setting the screen to animate moving the circle along the path from the first point to the second. "Solo, moved."

Then he drew yet another star and planet, out in the other galactic arm, and an arrow from the Janaandera planet he'd drawn in the Barrens. "Janaandera moved," he said. He picked up the defunct probe remote and moved it to the far side of the bubble. "Moved."

The alien stood up quickly, speaking to the others, and there was great agitation in the room. It turned back to him. "Ishinik danad," it said, and then they all left the room, leaving Fergus alone.

"Ishinik danad," he repeated. Did it mean *Wait here; we are leaving you to die* or *We're off to fetch you a sandwich*? There was no way of knowing. His burst of electricity earlier had taken a lot out of him, and absent water or food, he lay down across the bottom of the bubble, folded his arms under his head, and closed his eyes to listen to the Janaanderan ship and wait for whatever came next.

When his alien returned, it drew one of its own ships, then Fergus in his bubble, outside of it. With a gesture, it set the drawing to moving slowly across the surface of the scroll. "Moov," it said, then nudged its ship forward. "Moov."

Fergus picked up his remote and held it in one hand, the tablet in the other. He swung the remote outward. "Move," he said, and then chased it with the tablet. "Follow."

"Follow," the alien said, then drew another circle ahead of the animated drawings. "Janaandera."

———

They ejected his bubble and then waited beside it in their ship. Now that he was back in space, his comms were working again, and he called to Bel and the others to come get him.

The Asiig ship arrived, as they almost always did, as a sudden appearance, less movement than transition. Nose-to-nose with the Janaandera ship, they pulled Fergus in and broke him out of his bubble. He arrived back on the bridge, after a small stop by a bathroom and a source of drinking water, to see one of the strange tunnels connecting them to the Janaandera ship.

"They are talking," Bel told him.

"I didn't think anyone knew their language," Fergus said.

"They didn't. They are learning it now," Bel said. "It might take an hour or two, so make yourself comfortable."

"You can pass the time by telling us what happened out there," Bas said. "It's like everyone in the whole fucking galaxy has been keeping secrets from me, and I'm starting to feel like the butt of a joke."

"One does not encounter the Asiig and leave unchanged," Bel said. "If you leave at all. That's the secret."

"Vetch—MacInnis, Ferguson, I have no idea which is your right name, if any—showed me his electricity trick," Bas said. "The Asiig did that to you?"

"Yes," Fergus said.

"You asked them to?"

Fergus laughed so hard, he nearly doubled over. "Oh, no, not *at all*," he said, when he caught his breath. "I don't think you get to ask. They just *do*, and you figure out how to live with it."

"You'll see," Bel said.

Bas turned his head sharply, eyes wide. "What?"

"There are the Asiig. Then there are people like the agents, who were probably human seven or eight generations ago," Bel said. "My theory is that the first encounter between the Asiig and humans was an old, lost colony ship, one of those deep-sleep jobs before we had active jump, where three-quarters of them ended up crashing into a planet or sun or malfunctioning and turning into a flying morgue. Their descendants are the Vanin."

One of the Asiig off in the shadows chirped something, and

Bel shrugged. "Okay, the ship was the *Toledo Vanguard*. They've never told me that before. Anyway, then there are the people who fall into their hands—"

The Asiig chirped again, and Bel rolled her eyes. "It's a *metaphor*," she said. "That was Mr. Ferguson here, what, six or so years ago?"

"About that, yeah," he said. "I'd just been stabbed in the gut by an asshole named Borr Graf, and because I didn't want to die without taking him with me, I flushed us both out an airlock into space. The Asiig picked us up. I guess they decided they liked me more than him, because I was the only one who left alive."

"As I'd told you, I met Borr Graf once," Bas said. "If your goal was to improve the universe, removing him from it was an easy call. Though I guess I should be lucky they decided not to kill me, too."

This time, several of the Asiig spoke up, like crickets calling back and forth across the bridge, and mid-conversation, Bel turned in surprise to Fergus. "It seems it was less luck and more someone advocating for you," she said. "I'm grateful you did, Mr. Ferguson."

"Oh, just call me Fergus," he said.

"They really were going to kill me?" Bas asked.

"They were thinking about it. They took a closer look after Fergus's plea on your behalf when they realized you were my brother," she said. "They say they can still kill you, if you'd like."

"No," he said. "I'm good as is, thanks."

"'As is' is a funny turn of phrase," Bel said. "What we're trying to tell you—"

She broke off as the Asiig entered the bridge from the tunnel, followed by one of the Janaandera. The Asiig spoke, and Bel snapped around. "Helm, set course back to Bomostar," she said. "Time to go get the Bomo'ri to live up to their promise."

"Yes, Captain," Blinks said, and a half-second later, the stars shifted out around them.

Fergus turned back from watching them to find the scarred Asiig had moved right up next to him and was reaching out one of its front arms. It spoke, and Bel helpfully translated. "You require revision," she said. "Bas, brother, do me a favor?"

"Yes?" Bas asked.

"Catch him," she said, as the Asiig touched his forehead, and it was like being hit by a hammer from the inside of his brain, and all went dark.

They walked the tunnel onto the bridge of the Bomo'ri envoy ship, Fergus with Bas and Bel, flanked by the old Asiig—Fergus was starting to think of it as theirs—on one side and the Janaanderan on the other.

The envoy had five other Bomo'ri behind them and did not look pleased to see any of them. "Why are you back again?" it asked. "We will not give you more help or give the vermin another probe."

"I have a really terrible headache right now, because someone thought it would be a great idea to burn two alien languages into my brain without warning or permission, and I am not interested in your disrespect," Fergus said, speaking Bomo'ri directly, though it made his throat ache and he was sure his accent was atrocious. "This is Anenadi of the people of Janaandera, and we have come to collect on your promise of returning their planet."

The envoy stomped all its feet. "The Havna! You brought a killer here?!"

Fergus translated that for Anenadi himself; the Asiig had made clear that they were along to assist and observe, and protect, but not lead. Fergus was fine with that, in his current mood.

"You committed the mass murder of my people and the theft of our entire star system," Anenadi said, and Fergus translated for the envoy. "Now that we know where you live, what is to stop us coming for revenge?"

"We have your surviving people," the envoy said. "We are sure you would not wish harm on them."

"Return them safely, with our planet and star," Anenadi said. "This is not a negotiable demand."

"We cannot," the envoy said.

"What? Why not?" Fergus asked.

"It was our conclusion after moving Object 113—the Havna star and world—that we required transponders on a planet's surface to move it safely, as we then achieved with the world you call Solo," the envoy said. "We reclaimed our stellar signal array for reuse, but we no longer have any terrestrial units."

"Take the ones still on Solo," Fergus said. "You know, the other planet with a thriving ecosystem you didn't care about."

"Ecosystems arise and decline, with or without us," the envoy said. "But the Havna—Janaanderan—world is of greater circumference than your 'Solo.' We would not have enough."

"How many are you short?"

"One," the envoy said.

"Can't you *make* one?" Bel asked.

"To generate the signal in the correct frequency, we would need to locate the original specifications for the project, which may have been lost when we attempted to evacuate the planet and were assaulted."

"The research headquarters on Solo," Fergus said. "Whatever information you need should be there."

"You are demanding great effort of us," the envoy said. "It is a presumption on our time and goodwill."

"Goodwill?" Fergus almost choked on the words. He closed his eyes for a moment, took several deep breaths, then opened them again and spoke more calmly than he felt. "It is a small effort compared to that of war," he said. "Send one of your technical people with us, and we will get the info you need while you figure out how to make another transponder."

"The company of vermin is an affront, yet you wish us to volunteer to be in your presence?"

"You must have someone competent to do this task that you don't like," Fergus said. "Order them to go."

The Bomo'ri was silent for nearly half a minute before it gently stomped one of its front legs on the floor. "I have such a crewmember. They are intemperate in speaking of their enthusiasms and annoy me without cease. I will summon them and they will go with you. Is that satisfactory?"

"That is," Fergus said.

They landed via *Rattler*'s shuttle on Solo's other continent, in a clearing near the Bomo'ri research headquarters. Bas and Bel watched, talking between themselves, as Fergus and the Bomo'ri assigned to them entered the station. It was not dissimilar to the one they'd explored near the wreck of *Stiletto*, but larger, and for all that the Bomo'ri had been taciturn and morose on the trip over, as soon as systems started powering up, it became positively giddy at explaining it all, producing a nonstop stream of only somewhat-intelligible technical details for several hours straight as it worked at the consoles. It even described, at excruciating length, how the waste-displacement system worked, which was pretty much a high-tech means of dumping it out the building, through a biofilter, and into a local swamp.

Fergus's head was pounding so badly, even his eyes hurt. "Do you have the signal information we need?" he finally interrupted to ask.

"I obtained that immediately upon entry. I did not wish to waste the remainder of my opportunity to explore while here," it said.

"So . . . we can go?" Fergus asked.

The alien huffed unhappily. "If we must." It slid open a large bank of systems and pulled out a rectangular box. "We will need the coordinator."

"And the transponders themselves?" Fergus asked. "How do we collect those?"

The Bomo'ri walked outside, and Fergus followed. "See?" it said, and gestured back at the headquarters as it also fiddled with the controls on the box it had just taken. With a horrendous groan and the snapping of vines, the top of the building opened, and the dense mass of machinery he'd also seen in the ceiling of the other station rose from within. "The transponder," the Bomo'ri explained.

After a few more tweaks on the box, the transponder began to rise, picking up speed, until it vanished up into the high clouds and was gone.

"Okay," Fergus said. "That's one."

"That is all," the Bomo'ri huffed. "They are all in orbit now, to be collected and set. I would now like to be returned to my own kind, who, while much less dutiful and patient at listening to important and fascinating information, do not smell as bad as you."

———

"All transponders from Object 114 are accounted for and active," the envoy informed them, when they returned to where the Bomo'ri ship and Bel's Asiig triangle were still connected. "The number is still inadequate for the task, and we cannot take responsibility for any additional damage to the world that may occur upon moving."

"The transponder just emits a signal?" Fergus asked. "You can't just fab one or something?"

"We can, but it is not just a physical broadcast. The signal it emits must be tuned constantly, in keeping with all the others, and that mechanism would require time to manufacture."

"How strong is this signal? For how long?"

The Bomo'ri said something Fergus didn't know the words for. The Asiig spoke, and Bel translated for him. "About fourteen megajoules," she said. "For approximately forty minutes."

"I can't do that," he said.

"'Do that'?" Bas asked. "What the hell are you thinking?"

"If we can make the right-frequency signal and keep it tuned, can it be amplified?" Bel asked the Bomo'ri.

"Yes," the envoy admitted, grudgingly. "The tuned signal would still need to be sustained for the forty minutes but could be reduced to as much as one kilojoule."

"Over the forty minutes?"

"Per second," the envoy said. Was it smiling? How could you tell if a Bomo'ri was being smug, Fergus wondered?

Fergus turned toward the Asiig. "Could I do that?" he asked.

The Asiig spoke, and Bel translated. "It may kill you," she said. "Even if not, there is a good chance it could also burn out your ability. Is that risk acceptable to you?"

"To get the Janaandera their planet back? Unless someone has a better idea, then yes," Fergus said. "Uh, I'm going to need a lot of water."

The Asiig spoke. "Also salts and electrolytes," Bel translated.

"Then that's it. We're doing this," Fergus said. "Take me to the Janaandera home world."

"I will need to contact my people and have them be out of the way when the Bomo'ri reopen the path home," Anenadi said. "If this fails, and our planet is damaged further or destroyed, we will be coming here in force. We were a peaceful people when the Bomo'ri descended on us, but we are not forgiving."

"This is your doing and thus your fault," the envoy said to the Asiig.

Before the Asiig could answer, Fergus did. "No. This was your fault, and forcing you to fix it will be *my* doing," he said. "If I survive this, you can take it up with me then."

Their Asiig said something too low for Fergus to hear, and the Bomo'ri stomped all its feet again but also stepped back several times. Bel did not translate but crossed her arms over her chest and smiled very, very sweetly. *I think they've just been threatened on my behalf,* Fergus thought, and it felt good.

The envoy turned to the others behind it. "Give the orders to gather the transponders and set them onto the quarantined world. They should not be harassed. We will deliver this vermin directly, after we summon the science vessels required back into service."

"We're coming along to observe," Bel said.

"I will also join, to meet the survivors of my people and prepare them for what is coming," Anenadi said. "It has been over two hundred of your years, and much has been lost already."

"Fine. Then after this is complete, we will be done with you all," the Bomo'ri said.

"Yes," Anenadi said, "though if we ever see any of your ships on our side of the Gap, we will take it as a deliberate act of war."

"If we see you near Solo, or see signs of you resuming your research at the expense of star systems anywhere," their Asiig added, "we will regard that as requiring our direct and unsubtle intervention."

"As will I," Bas said. "I may be vermin to you, but we have eyes everywhere."

"Awesome," Fergus said. "Now that we've got this all worked out, let's go move a planet."

———

The surface of the quarantined Janaanderan world was a mix of beautiful and broken. The rocky outcropping near where he walked was striated reds and oranges, with a thick vein of something purple and gleaming running between one set of layers. Amethyst, he wondered, but he didn't know enough to say one way or the other.

There were plants, of a sort, like tall blue grass with feathery tops, and things fluttered and flew up into the air around him as he waded through to the spot he'd been told to go to.

The sun was strong but not blinding, a little more yellow than Earth's, the planet's gravity about sixty percent of Earth's, the air cool but breathable with the help of a small, unobtrusive nose filter he'd already mostly forgotten he was wearing.

If he was going to die doing this, this was a good place.

The ground also had terrible cracks in it, and he took care to watch his step. The scorching of fires still marked parts of the cliff and the edges of the faults, and Anenadi had told him those were not there before the Bomo'ri came. The Janaandera lived long lives, and Anenadi had grown up in these fields, near these mountains, before leaving the surface for one of their moon settlements as a young person. They'd been there when the Bomo'ri arrived and their four moons had been sucked into the nascent conduit with their world, only to fragment and then become trapped at the edge of the Drift, where their once-flourishing and self-sustaining moon colonies struggled to survive. The Janaandera who survived among the shattered bodies of their moons had feared the Bomo'ri would hunt them down and complete their extinction, never imagining such an attack would or could have been see by the perpetrators as *impersonal*—and they remained vigilant for any signs of the engine signature of their enemy at the gate of their mostly collapsed conduit. When detected, they acted swiftly and decisively, to make sure no word of their existence could be carried back and invite a final assault.

Anenadi had expressed, when they arrived, that it almost hurt more to know their destruction hadn't been an act of intentional hostility but that they were just not regarded as worth acknowl-edging at all in the course of an experiment gone awry. "For most of my life, I have wanted nothing more than to kill them all," they told Fergus. "I should feel differently now, knowing we will be at least somewhat restored, but I do not."

Then they'd been hailed by an elder of a nearby village, and Anenadi had gone down to speak with them, leaving Fergus to his own path.

He found what he was certain was the spot, and checked the coordinates against the small handheld Bel had given him, before moving another few meters to his left. He set down the large transmitter dish, currently folded up like a big beach umbrella, heaved his pack off beside it, then set down cross-legged on the warm, smooth rock. "I'm in place," he said.

"The Bomo'ri are just setting down the last few transponders taken from Solo," Bel said, from somewhere up in orbit. "Another half hour or so before they're ready. You set up yet?"

"Working on it," he lied.

"Okay, then. I'll check back in when I know more," she said.

He grabbed the handle of his pack and dragged it closer, pull-ing out a bottle of water and taking a long drink, grimacing at the salty tang of it. Then he stood up and popped open the dish, flip-ping the shiny parabola upside-down, and untangled the wires that dangled out from underneath it.

Sitting again, he took his last few personal things out of his pack, last of which was a small pebble he'd been carrying as a personal charm of sorts since he'd first run away from home at fifteen. He set it down in front of himself, then realized there was a remarkably similar pebble, except reddish, not far away. Reach-ing out, he scooted it closer to his own. "If this is going to work, and I'm going to survive it," he told the pebbles, "I'll definitely need double the usual luck."

Inside the pack was a medium-sized box, turned off, that was the signal amplifier. He plugged the parabola into it, made sure the connections were good, then drank some more water.

He closed his eyes, letting the intermittent breeze chill him and then the sun warm him up again, until his earpiece crackled to life again. "They say they're ready. They're going to turn on the two emitters nearest to you. If you can't pick up and replicate the signal, we'll have to wait until they can take one of these units apart and replicate it," Bel said. "We can do that anyway. You don't have to do this."

"The longer we put it off, the more chances the Bomo'ri change their minds. And if they get time with the transponders when we're not watching, you know they'll go try this again eventually, somewhere they think we won't catch them," he said.

"True," Bel said.

"I want to see this done and then know that the Asiig are going to oversee the complete destruction of the transponders afterward," Fergus said. "And also, no doubt foolishly, I need to know if *I* can do this."

"Gotcha," she said. "Okay, the Bomo'ri are starting their power-up of the stellar array, and then they're going to bring the planetary transponders online. That includes you."

There was so little there that made signal, even the village in the distance quiet, that it wasn't too long before he noticed he could feel his skin prickling, just faintly, reacting to something. "I feel it," he said. "Turning my amp unit on."

As soon as he switched it on, he had to fight to tune out its electromagnetic white noise to find the other signals again. Once he did, though, it only took him a few tries to absorb it, feel it out, sing it back. He sat the amp in his lap and wrapped his arms around it, letting his energy feed into it. "How's this?" he asked.

"The Bomo'ri say it'll do," Bel said. "You ready to go to full?"

"Yes," he said.

"Okay. On the count of three. And, Fergus?"

"Yeah?"

"Thanks for bringing my pain-in-the-ass brother safely through," she said. "Three, two, one. Go."

There was an immediate blast of noise and heat through his whole body, and he could now feel all the stations, feel the entire circumference of the bloody whole *planet*.

He could tell Bel was talking to him again, but he had no attention to spare for her or anything other than the great circle he was a part of. Energy rose around each of the transponders, enveloping the whole planet, and he recognized the cadences of the Bomo'ri jump signature, but it was stronger, deeper, like it vibrated through the very atoms he was made of, that he sat upon, that he breathed in—was he still remembering to breathe? He wasn't sure.

Well, duh, he thought. *We're punching a hole in space with a* star.

The planet began to move. Or, more, everything shifted around the planet and its star, the fabric of existence giving way, and he felt frozen and boiling and torn apart and flattened down to the width of a single proton all at once, and it was terrifying and elating and it seemed to be both an instant and to go on forever, and he was so, *so* thirsty—

They were back in space. Had it failed? Had he dreamt the entire thing? Someone was yelling in his ear, so he took the earpiece out and left it on the ground, pushed the amp out of his lap, and lay down on his back, looking up at the sky, marveling at the momentous beauty of *stillness*.

Someone picked him up, a sensation rather like being wrapped in and lifted by scarves. He tried to focus on their face, only to find big blue eyes. "Friend," Anenadi said, in Fergus's language, and he knew, in that moment, he had done the impossible.

And lived.

Chapter 22

———◆———

"Will you please stop *giggling*?" Bel said, for the dozenth time.

"Sorry," Fergus said, but it came out all raspy, like a frog croak, and that set him to low giggling again. He was lying in the back of *Rattler*'s shuttle, its giant screen-sail gone. Bel was keeping an eye on him—apparently, he'd gone into shock a couple of times and scared them with a bout of uncontrollable shaking where he'd been babbling nonsense—while Bas brought them down through the atmosphere of Solo.

"They've been busy while we were gone," Bas said. Bel got up to go forward, and Fergus tried to follow, and merely ended up falling on his face on the floor beside the bunk.

Bel groaned, came back, and helped him up. "Should've strapped me in," he mumbled.

"Sorry, I mistook you for someone with at least an ounce of common sense," she retorted, and that set him giggling again until she pinched him, hard.

He stayed quiet as she hauled him up to the bridge and dumped him into a seat. "Buckle yourself in," she said, and sat beside her brother.

They circled over *Sidewinder*. The last exterior bits that had needed replacing were fixed, and although it was a patchwork of hull colors and welds and visible repairs, it looked ready to fly. In the bright morning sun, parts of it even shone.

"Oh, that's a sight for sore eyes," Bel said. "Never thought I'd see that old shape again. About *Rattler* . . ."

"It's bad," Bas said. "We can go later. There's still a little bit of Fang running, waiting for you all this time, but she's too broken to extricate and fix. Maybe you should be the one to shut her down."

"Yeah," she said, and sat there pensively as they finished their flyover and headed toward the clearing beside *Fire Island*.

By the time they came in to land, everyone was there waiting, including the Alliance personnel from *Paradigm*. "I knew they'd be coming for us, and I don't trust them to keep to any arrangement we could make," Bas said. "Figured we'd meet them head on, with allies as witnesses. You in particular, Fer—Mr. Vetch."

"I have a plan," Fergus said. "Or at least the beginnings of one. It requires me being able to stand up without passing out first."

"You're sounding a little stronger," Bel said. "How's your, ah, other talent recovering?"

"It's gone," Fergus said. "It's like there's a ball of emptiness deep down inside, where the center of it used to be. It's a strange feeling."

"It could come back," she said.

"It won't," Fergus said. "Somehow, I know. It's gone. I spent so long trying to figure out how to get rid of it or turn it off for good, and now . . . For all the trouble it brought me, I think I'll miss it. On the bright side, I can now speak and read fluent Bomo'ri and Janaanderan."

"Uh, those are a forced restructuring of your neural mappings," Bel said. "Eventually, they'll snap back to where they started, and you'll lose that knowledge."

"Well, shit," Fergus said. "There goes my plan of taunting the Bomo'ri with insults from the Gap for the rest of my life."

Bel chuckled. "I can see if we can get you an extension, for such a noble cause."

There was a gentle bump as Bas set the shuttle down and powered the engines off. Bel leaned forward. "Is that Len? And Kaybe? And is that . . . No, I don't know who those two are," she said.

"Marche and Trinket," Bas said. "Intelligence and breaking things. Which is which is probably obvious."

"And there's Yolo," she said, darkly. She unbuckled her safety tether. "This one's mine."

Bas glanced at Fergus, who got out of his chair and, stumbling and supporting himself on chair backs and walls, followed after her. "This I gotta see," he said.

"Me, too," Bas said, and followed, giving Fergus a hand out the door and down as Bel strode across the clearing directly at Yolo.

"Miss . . . Captain Belos?" Yolo stammered, just as Bel reached him and punched him sharp and hard in the face.

Yolo stumbled backward under the blow and went down. Bel kicked him in the stomach. "That's for my crew who died," she said. Then she stepped back and looked around at the gathered shocked and confused faces, and rubbed her hands together, as if washing them of something. "I'm done. You're forgiven, Yolo, but only because you were too stupid to know you were being played. Don't ever screw up like that on me or anyone I love again, though."

"Yes, ma'am," Yolo replied weakly from his fetal position on the ground.

Riji stepped up to check on Yolo, who waved her away, then took in Fergus leaning on Bas. "Vetch? You hurt? Safani is still back at the camp, but we can go get her—"

"No, it's okay," Fergus said. "I'll be all right."

"Coming through! Coming through!" Kaybe shouted, and pushed his way through the crowd to wrap Bel in a long, tight hug.

Len was right behind him and stopped to regard Fergus. "Ye got th' drop on me, fast-like," he said.

"Sorry," Fergus said.

"Didn't think me or Bas was comin' back livin', much less

bringing ghosts back, too," Len said. "Seems he needed you ah-stead a me."

Bas nodded. "It turns out I did, this time."

"Don't make no habit a it. Hurt my feels a little. And you!" He jabbed one finger toward Fergus.

"Uh, I'm still sorry?" Fergus said.

"Naw, you was quick. Makes an *impression.* Good ter have a man that fast on yer own team, yanno me?"

"Thanks, Len," Fergus said.

And then Len hugged him. It was a quick, loose, awkward contact, and the man was so skinny, it was like being embraced by a coatrack, but it was still the least likely thing that Fergus could have imagined. "Thanks fer bringin' both me captains back," Len said. "Sneak up at me 'gain an' I cut you, though."

"I would expect no less," Fergus said.

"We were going to come try to rescue you," Marche spoke up. Safani had joined her and had one arm around her waist.

"How?" Bas asked.

Riji gestured over his head, a wrench still in her hand. "We put all our effort on *Sidewinder,* because *Fire Island* is still dead without a mindsystem. We're only a day or so away from being able to fly. She's a fucking tank of a ship, and she'll hold."

"Would have been easier if someone hadn't stolen our shuttle, so we could get more parts, though," Fendi said. His voice was critical, but it didn't match the big grin on his face, nor the one of Rabbit, pale and shaking but standing beside him, leaning heavily on a cane. "Might've asked, first. Sir."

"You rebuilt *Sidewinder* in nine days?" Bas exclaimed. "How lazy were you all being before now, then? Did the podders help?"

Cole coughed. "Our *Paradigm* friends were less than enthusias-tic about our plan to chase off after you," he said. "Fortunately for us, there's a whole set of Alliance rules about dealing with

independent colonies, which because of how long we've been isolated, we qualify as. They have to defer to local authority on terrestrial matters."

"I can speak for myself and my crew," Captain Todd spoke up,
walking into camp with his three people at his side. "I need—I
would *like* whatever new information you got during your trip,
and if you've found a way to avoid or overcome the gate aliens."

"We met, had tea, did some arts and crafts together, and came
to an understanding," Fergus said. He let out one inadvertent
half-giggle before Bas elbowed him sharply in the ribs.

"Mr. Vetch got hit in the head and is not himself," Bel said,
only the latter half of which was true. "Probably he should go
back into the shuttle and *lie down*."

"As Mr. Vetch alluded to, we have secured safe passage home,"
Bas said. He surveyed the gathered people. "If *Sidewinder* is ready
to fly, we will take all of you as are willing to go and who agree
to our conditions."

"Conditions? Of course there would be," Todd said.

"Those conditions are that you will be unarmed while aboard
Sidewinder, and we will all agree to a strict and complete pause on
any hostilities until we are safely back in the Barrens and able to
go our separate ways," Bas said. "If we encounter difficulties before such a time, you will all follow my orders as captain of my
ship, or face the same penalties as any member of my own crew
would face for disloyalty."

"I'm an Alliance officer," Todd said. "I'm not going to swear
any loyalty to an outlaw, no matter how temporarily."

"The winters aren't so bad here," Riji spoke up. "You just
gotta make sure you keep your hut sealed at night, and check your
boots carefully before putting your feet in them in the morning,
or you're gonna get chewed on something awful."

"I want to go home," Lester spoke up.

"I'm still your captain," Todd snapped.

"There aren't enough of us to operate *Fire Island*, even if we get the last of it fixed, and none of us are engineers," Lester said. "We go home this way, or we stay here until we die."

"You don't know that other help won't come," Todd said.

"You don't know that it will," Lester retorted. "You see a lot of successful trips to this planet? 'Cause I see a hell of a lot of wrecks."

"That's *Bas Belos*," Todd said. "We can't just sign on with him. We're better than that."

"Fuck your pride. *Captain*," Lester said.

Cardenas pushed both Lester and Todd aside and stood in front of Belos. "If we agree to your conditions, we have a few of our own. You won't put us in a situation of having to violate our oaths to the Alliance, or commit or be made complicit in any criminal acts. You will take us directly to a place where we can be released safely and can contact our own people to come retrieve us."

"That is acceptable," Belos said.

"Then that works for me," Cardenas said.

"And me," Rosso, the fourth *Paradigm* survivor, added.

"And me," Lester said. "You have a duty to us, too, Captain. And to yourself—you have family, back on Earth. They deserve to have you back alive too."

Todd stood there fuming, clenching and unclenching his fists, until Cardenas put a hand on his shoulder. "Come on, Captain. This isn't the end, unless you want it to be."

Paradigm's captain's shoulders slumped, and he heaved a deep, angry sigh. "Fine," he said, then glared at Belos. "If you double-cross us, any one of us, I will spend the rest of my life seeing that you are hunted down. No mercy."

"Same," Belos said evenly.

"Then, against all better judgment and everything my life has stood for, I agree," Todd said.

"Excellent," Bas said. "I need to talk to my crew and check on

Sidewinder, then we can all meet here this afternoon, and I'll get everyone up to speed on our situation at the jump gate. Fendi, once I get Mr. Vetch back to the ship, you can have the shuttle for whatever you still need it for."

"Right," Fendi said. "Coming with you. Riji?"

"I'll be along in a bit," she said.

Fergus stumbled back into the shuttle with the others for the short ride back to *Sidewinder*, his cabin, and a cat who was probably very, very annoyed with him.

————

Fergus woke up midafternoon, a cat curled up under his chin. As soon as he got up to wash up, he discovered he was horribly weak and easily exhausted, so he hung out in the sunshine with Rabbit near the lakeshore as the others headed over to the Islander camp for Bas's big meeting. Rabbit was disappointed Fergus had little information about the armaments of either the Bomo'ri or the Janaandera, but was grateful they'd not lost any more cannonballs or, secondarily, their lives and the shuttle on their excursion.

Two hours after the others had left, Riji arrived. "They're still meeting," she said. "Right now, they're talking food logistics, what we'd want to bring with us from here, stuff like that. Important but dull. Can we talk?"

Rabbit got up. "I don't need no hint. I'mma leave you two all 'lone," he said. He shuffled off back toward the ship with his cane, and only glanced back once to waggle his eyebrows and wink at Fergus.

"I heard Todd and Earlan talking, before the meeting," she said. "They're going to make a grab for you right as your captain drops them off, threaten to kill you if Belos tries to get you back."

Fergus laughed. "They think they can pull that off?"

"They think they have a good shot at it, and if they have to abort, they're going to come back for you all," Riji said. "Not only is it whatever you're already wanted by the Alliance for, but they want to know how you got the gate aliens to stand down. Bas said it was you who gets all the credit for saving us, but won't say how, and you could see Todd's little brain starting to smoke from all the thinking he was doing about mining that knowledge. What *are* you wanted for, anyway?"

He smiled. "Would you believe I took down an entire rogue Alliance operation hiding under the ice of Enceladus that was trying to build a superweapon using kidnapped scientists and engineers?"

"Maybe?" she said. "Some of those R&D guys are scary."

"And then I broke into one of their secure research facilities on Earth and stole an alien artifact?"

"That's harder to swallow. Those facilities are some of the most tightly secured places there are, even tighter than Captain Todd's ass, and he's so uptight, if he sat on the ground, he'd probably suck up a rock."

"I had to short out several city blocks of Baltimore to get in," Fergus said.

"Just that?"

"Well, I also had to dress up like an electrician," he said.

She laughed. "Forget I asked, okay? I'm just saying, Todd and Earlan aren't planning on forgetting you. I figured you deserved to know."

"Thanks," he said. "What are you going to do when you get back? You'll all be heroes."

Riji's face fell, and Fergus sat up straighter. "What is it?" he asked. "I can keep secrets."

"No shit," she said. She was quiet for a long while. "I regret nothing, but I made some choices that were a lot clearer when I thought none of us were ever getting away from here."

"Is this about Thacker?" Fergus guessed. "Your first mate, that Earlan drowned? Or did he?"

"Yes, but it's more complicated than that," Riji said. "I told you Thacker had ideas. He tried his bullshit with me once, and I left him with bruises and no ambiguity about what would happen if he tried anything with me again."

"He did anyway?"

"Not with me," she said.

"Ah," Fergus said.

"I'd beat him half to death when Earlan heard the noise and came running. Drunk as shit, too. Got mad at me and Safani, as if it was our fault," Riji said. "I told him it had to be finished, and he said as next ranking officer, he'd do it. Watched him drag Thacker off to the lake and hold him under. I got no problem with that, but when Earlan sobered up, he couldn't handle the guilt, and never has. I heard him tell Todd."

"And Todd blames you?"

"No. Todd was pretty clear Thacker got what was coming to him," she said. "But it's still going to be a thing, because Todd is a by-the-regs kinda guy, and I just . . . I want to go back to civilization and eat a whole fucking chocolate cake all by myself, but I also want things to stay simple, you know?"

"Yeah," Fergus said, "though when I look back at times where I thought things were simple, I'm not sure they ever were."

Riji nodded, then stood up abruptly. "Sorry. I didn't mean to come dump my problems on you," she said. "I just wanted to make sure you were warned."

"And so I have been," he said.

"Right. I should go pack, and Safani wants me to help her collect a bunch of bio samples to take back for our science division." she said. "Looks like we're flying outta here tomorrow morning. After that, who knows what comes next?"

"Only the future," Fergus answered.

"All preflight checks are good," Kaybe said, coming down to the open back of the cargo ramp where Bas was standing with Marche, Len, Cole, and Fergus. "Soon as we're done loading up, we're clear to go. Just missing Todd and Lester."

"Here comes Todd now," Cole said, and pointed to where the two Paradigmers were emerging from the woods along the path, dragging along the data recorders from their pods. Yolo walked along behind them, carrying the rest of their meager belongings.

"You could have lent them the shuttle, you know," Marche said.

"I know," Bas said.

Bel came out to watch, standing aside as Todd and his team dumped their stuff up on *Sidewinder*'s ramp. "Where do we stow this?" Todd asked.

"There's nets along the side wall," Bel said, pointing. "Tuck it in, and ask Trinket to show you where you're bunking. Going to have to double and triple people up, I'm afraid."

"We'll live," Lester said. "Who we waiting on?"

"Just you," Bas said. Lester disappeared up the ramp with their things, while Yolo stood at the bottom uncertainly, sporting a massive black eye. He might have also been missing a tooth, Fergus thought. Bas finally shook his head in frustration. "You too, Yolo. Get your ass in."

Bas tapped the comms on speaker. "Final head count. Everyone please check in."

One by one, everyone who wasn't still standing in the cargo bay checked in to say they were safely aboard. Cole heaved a sigh of relief. "We're actually going home," he said. "I never thought I'd see it."

"Go fire the engines up, Kaybe," Bas said.

"Yes, Captain!" Kaybe said, saluted with dramatic gusto, and headed off to the bridge.

Bas pointed. "Is that a crate left under your canopy, Mr. Vetch?" he said. "Is that something we need?"

"It's not one of ours," Cole said.

"I'll check," Fergus said. He jumped down off the ramp, went to where the small crate was just visible sticking out from behind the woven shelter he'd made what seemed a lifetime ago. He popped the locks and opened the lid. "It's empty!" he called back.

"Just so," Bas said. He drew his energy pistol out of his waistband. "Thank you for your service, Mr. Vetch."

Bas fired, and Fergus tumbled over the still-open crate, red blooming across his shirt.

He was still lying there on the ground, blinking up at the impossibly bright sun, as Bas pushed Cole and Todd away from the door and into the ship, sealed the cargo bay, and *Sidewinder* lifted off into the sky.

Chapter 23

After the sound of *Sidewinder*'s engines had faded off into the distance, out of sight and long gone, Mister Feefs came and sat on his chest and yowled in his face until Fergus sat up. "Ugh," he said, peeling off his T-shirt. With his luck, the squashed-up wurble-berry paste now spread everywhere would stain.

It was going to be a while before he had the opportunity to buy himself a replacement.

"C'mon, cat. Just you and me now," he said, and hiked back toward *Fire Island* with Mister Feefs at his heels.

In the waveforest just outside the camp he found the real, not-empty crate Bas had left him. It had several months of supplies and every imaginable tool Fendi could spare or fab. Sitting atop it all was a smaller box, open now, with the palla inside.

He lifted that out and sat in the shade, Feefs curling up in his lap, as he turned the orb around in his hands, running his fingers lightly over the inscribed *eta*. "You got me into a lot of trouble," he told it. "I'm guessing whoever created you all and sent you out had more optimism about what would happen to you than maybe they should have. Two for two in trouble so far."

The orb didn't answer, but he didn't expect it to. It had taken Tau, on Enceladus, quite some time to trust him enough to talk to him, and who knew how many bad hands this one had been through before it got to Bas and became the perfect bribe?

He was about to set it back in its box when he spotted something in the bottom, and he pulled that out, too. It was a data chit wrapped in a piece of vellum.

> *This is all that was left of Fang's mindsystem. I don't know if it'll be of use to you, but I couldn't bear just to shut her down cold. See you around the galaxy.*
> *-Bel*

It would help. *Fire Island* couldn't fly without a mindsystem or a much-bigger crew than one man and a cat, but between Fang and Eta—assuming the latter decided to wake up and talk to Fergus, and was willing to be part of a ship—it would have one again.

Fergus wondered when Bel would make her exit from *Sidewinder* and go back to the Asiig, or if she had done so already. He wasn't sure if he'd rather she just upped and vanished from a sealed ship in the middle of space, or gave Todd and company the full Asiig jump-scare experience. She'd made it clear that she liked working for the Asiig, and not just because they'd saved her life and that of some of her crew. They'd pulled survivors out of other wrecks, dead ships, and lost escape pods elsewhere in the Gap and kept conflicts on the human side from spilling too far out into other parts of the galaxy. Also, she really liked the power of being able to appear as if out of nowhere in front of petty scavengers and absolutely terrify the piss out of then.

He also wondered if the Asiig were going to follow Bas around now, tormenting him for a bit, and decided he felt pretty conflicted about that, too.

Inside *Fire Island*, he discovered to his surprise that Fendi had left him his fab unit, and Kaybe had left him the last of his coffee. He pulled that out, taking a deep whiff of the rich aroma, and then sealed it up again.

He was in a mood for his Corallan tea today.

Rabbit had left him a gun, and Len a knife that had clearly seen much use, probably all of it something he didn't want to know more about. There was also a food container that, when Fergus pulled it open, turned out to be filled with rummy groats. If that didn't give him motivation to get off this planet soon, nothing else would.

"No chocolate cake, huh?" a voice said behind him, and he whirled around to find Riji standing there.

"What are you doing here?" he asked, incredulous. "You should be long gone, on your way home by now. *Sidewinder* didn't come back?!"

"Naw, I jumped ship before it took off. Figured you'd need help," she said.

"You should have thought I was *dead*," he said.

"Yeah, saw that. Very convincing. Do you know how many wurble-berry stains I've had to soak out of my clothes? I know that color," she said. "And anyway, I saw Fendi sneaking around and Marche shooing your cat off into the forest, and knew something was up, so I ditched out when no one was looking. Not hard to say 'here' even when you're somewhere else. So, what's the plan?"

"What if I don't have a plan?" Fergus asked.

"Then I'm going to be incredibly disappointed and angry with you," she said.

He laughed. "The plan was to replace *Fire Island*'s mindsystem, and then go visit friends who can finish repairs and make her no longer identifiable as an Alliance cruiser," he said. "Then I was going to go visit my sister and my cousin, eat a lot of badly burnt chips and a curry or two, and then go out into the galaxy and find something useful to do." He held up the palla. "For starters, I'm going to try to find the rest of these and make sure they're not in bad hands."

Did a blue light just, for a split second, blink on the palla's exterior when he said that? It was gone before he could be sure.

"What is that thing?" Riji asked.

"Ooooh, now, that's a long story," he said.

"We have time," she said. "*Fire Island* is almost ready to fly, but she's not there yet."

"With the Alliance believing I'm dead, I got time," he said. "What about you?"

"I told Safani I didn't want to go back and deal with the BS and inquiries and paperwork and all that," she said. "I got used to my time being my own, doing what I do best unhindered. If they even let me back onto a ship's crew, I'll still be answering to some assvalve in a uniform who doesn't know a tenth of what I do, and I don't have the patience to deal with that anymore. I guess this means I've quit the Alliance."

"Congratulations," he said. "It seems I've also quit being a pirate. It never did quite suit me." Even as he said that, he knew he would miss the *Sidewinder* crew, and when the chance came to get back to Ijikijolo, he would definitely take the captain up on his offer of a drink. Maybe not even watered down, just once. He supposed he'd eventually need to find Maha and Qai and tell them they didn't need to track down and murder Bas for kidnapping him, after all.

"No more pirate, no more Alliance, means we can be friends after all," Riji said. "You do owe me a chocolate cake, though."

"That's fair," he said. "Tea?"

"Sure," she said.

He dug his tea stuff out of the rest of the crate, gathered up some dried fronds and kindling, and added it to the firepit. Riji was busy poking through the tools from the crate, so he leaned over the pit and held the spark that leapt up across his fingertips against the fronds until they ignited. It had been so easy to tell people his gift was gone instead of sleeping, to make himself human again in their memories, to make his secret his own again.

When he handed her a cup, she tasted it and made a face. "It's bitter," she said.

"It's a metaphor for life," he explained. "Do you know what I've learned from it?"

"No," she said.

Fergus took a handful of wurble berries left over from his fake-blood pack and dropped several into his cup before holding out the rest to her in the palm of his hand. "That it's only bitter if you let it stay that way," he said.

He held up his cup, and she clinked hers against his. "To friendship and the next adventure," he said. "Wherever it finds us."

Acknowledgments

There has been a bit of a longer gap between this book and the previous one, which was mostly out of my control, as so many things in publishing (and life) tend to be. I trust the world hasn't let you get bored in the interim? No? What, you'd rather it had been a little *more* boring?

When I wrote the acknowledgments for the previous book, *The Scavenger Door,* we were just nearing the one-year mark into the COVID pandemic. Everything felt fraught, and frequently surreal, but also there was an obvious path of how we got there (nature! mutation of germs!) and how we would or could get out together (vaccines! responsible social behavior!). Optimistically, I'd expected that by the time I was writing this, Things Would Be Better. Instead, everything wrong right now feels so big, so out of reach of anything any of us could do to change.

It's late November right now in New England, so it's cold and dark and nothing is green or flowering anymore, and in the moment it's a little soul-crushing. At the same time, I know that it will eventually become spring, and all the daffodils and tulips and other random bulbs I've spent ridiculous hours burying all over the fringes of my yard will pop up through the old, dead leaves and whatever snow is hanging around trying to be an obstacle, and they will *shine* with color and life, even if they have to bore a hole straight through inches of matted, compressed, nasty-moldy leaves to do it.

Am I trying to imply we should just be happily optimistic for the future? Obviously it's not—is *never*—that simple.

For one, you gotta get down in the dirt and plant all those effing bulbs in the first place. For another, you have to make it through the dark long enough to see them bloom.

I don't know that it's unreasonable, at this point in history, to feel hopeless, to be convinced that the only people with power right now are those that want to burn everything down, but I still firmly believe it's not over until we all give up and decide it's over. Even when we've lost sight of the future, we have to *act* like we still have it, for the sakes of our children who deserve a better world than we've made for them so far, because they shouldn't have to fight for that world alone. And I mean not just our own kids (if you have 'em) but all the kids out there. The ones sprawled on the couch in my living room stuffed full of Thanksgiving dinner fighting over who has to empty the dishwasher next. The ones not very far away from any of us who didn't get enough to eat, and maybe never do. The ones not very far away who already believe they have no future, even though haven't even gotten out of middle school yet. The ones who are scared, hungry, tired, made to feel ashamed for being who they are, and maybe angry that this is the world that's been given to them. And yeah, the ones with rockets and bombs falling on them.

A better world for only some is no better world at all.

So what does this have to do with writing a novel? I mean, not much? But also everything. Stories matter, even silly ones, because we need to be able to imagine a world with heroes in order to *be* a world with heroes. And we need heroes more than ever, right now, to stand up, shout, fight for the future when they can, how they can. None of us can do this alone, but also, acts don't have to be big to make a difference. A thousand-foot-tall daffodil would be an incredible thing, but a thousand normal-sized ones that make one stranger smile is also a victory. Small things add up.

Truth matters. Love matters. Art matters. Hope is one of the few things we can wish into existence.

I started writing largely on a whim, not expecting it to be more than a brief exercise, and certainly not expecting to have any success at it. I am still rather bemused by the whole thing, at the same time that I am keenly aware that it has fundamentally altered the course of my life, and (other than contributing massively to sleep-deprivation) all for the better. I have met so many people, from so many places, that I never would have otherwise. I have now had the extraordinary privilege of making two trips to China, most recently this fall for the World Science Fiction Convention, and met other authors and artists and fans from all over the world, and if I could presume to reduce such an ineffable and life-altering set of experiences and interactions to one pithy statement, it is this: that all of us who yearn for a better, more just, more sustainable world are a family that geography and culture and language cannot divide, and it is our shared stories—art, music, words—that build bridges between us, over which we trade the greatest riches of human civilization, which is friendship. Together we can be an immovable bulwark against those who traffic in division and despair.

Writing Fergus has been a pleasure, and even as this series comes to a close, I dare to hope that these books have brought at least a few of you out there some escape, some entertainment, maybe even some joy as well. I hope, if you've been struggling with the dark, it's helped carry you a little further through.

And on the subject of carrying (a segue, huzzah!) getting a novel out into the world requires a lot of coordinated heavy lifting, and I continue to have a great team without whom this book could not exist. I want to acknowledge first and foremost my agent, Joshua Bilmes, and his crew at JABberwocky Literary Agency, as well as my editor, Katie Hoffman, and the team at DAW/Astra. Cover art is once again by Kekai Kotaki, who is fantastic at bringing my vision to life. My copy editor, Richard Shealy, likewise has done a great job making me look a lot smarter than I am. I also continue to have the best first readers ever: Jonathan Turner, Robin Holly, and Laurie Vadeboncoeur, but I'd be remiss in not just shouting out my appreciation to all my friends who still put up with me even though I keep disappearing for long stretches of time into my hermit cave while trying to get a few good words down.

Thank you, especially, my readers, for also being part of this wild journey. I don't know what comes next, but whatever it is, I'll look forward to seeing you here, at the back of a book, once again. (-:

Peace,

—Suzanne